Annie Jordan:

A NOVEL OF SEATTLE

Annie Jordan:

A NOVEL OF SEATTLE

Mary Brinker Post

GARDEN CITY, NEW YORK

Doubleday & Company, Inc.

1948

The lines from "And the Band Played On" are reprinted by permission of the Herman Darewski Music Publishing Company, London.

PRINTED IN THE UNITED STATES

AT

THE COUNTRY LIFE PRESS, GARDEN CITY, N. Y.

FIRST EDITION

*For Harry, whose book
this is, too*

Annie Jordan:

A NOVEL OF SEATTLE

Chapter I

Eighteen eighty-nine was the year of the Johns-town flood, the year that Washington Territory became a state of the Union, but to Seattle-ites it was the year of the Big Fire.

At first no one knew how the fire started. Some said one thing, some another, the way people will because they like to give out information, they like to be in on the know. Jim Petley said it started in a waterfront brothel when a big Swede fisher-man chased one of the girls and knocked over a piano lamp. But Jim was a newspaper reporter and liked a good story. Actually, it started in a paintshop, but that came out later when they had the investigation.

Once started, there didn't seem to be any stopping it. It swept through Front Street on a high wind, and the jerry-built frame buildings went like tinder. They said you could see the red glow for miles around, that ships coming into the bay from British Columbia saw the red banners like a flag of warning against the black sky. Like as not the Siwashes out on Alki Point, seeing the white man's town burning, took it as a sign from heaven and danced for glee.

It burned out the entire business district. It burned the docks. It burned the freight cars standing in the yards, twisted the rails as if they'd been tinfoil. There's nothing like a big fire, once it gets out of control, for wanton, magnificent destruction. Even when you knew it was burning up everything you owned in the world, the town you'd built with your own sweat and capital, you couldn't help but admire its power, its sweep.

Nearly everybody in town lost something in the fire. Will

Carlton lost his sawmill and three freight cars of new saws that had come in from Pittsburgh that afternoon and hadn't been unloaded yet. He fought the insurance company for twenty years to recover that loss, spent three times what the saws were worth, and had the satisfaction, the year he died, of getting full restitution.

Mrs. Cecil Brookes lost the dry-goods store she'd let her husband sink her inheritance into, and what was worse, she lost her husband too. He dashed into the back office to save his records and strongbox and the roof fell in on him.

Kitty Jordan just got herself and her two girls out of her rooming house on the waterfront before the whole side of the house caved in.

The men and boys worked all night putting the fire out and keeping it from spreading to the residence district.

Everyone else, the women and girls and the little boys too small to help, huddled on the First Hill and watched the place go up in smoke and flame. There were little groups all over, knots of silent or sobbing women, and gradually they moved together for comfort, for consolation, out of common misery.

The women stood together, crying and murmuring, frantic for their men and their property. The children ran from group to group, calling to each other, pointing to the flames that would shoot up in a sudden burst whenever the fire bit off another piece of the town.

Children wandered away from their mothers, made new friends or enemies, spoke to children of people their mothers wouldn't have let them associate with. They darted about, bright-eyed, shining-faced, hopping with excitement, or else they stood and stared in wonder and awe at the great, elemental, unleashed force that was too tremendous for them to comprehend.

Kitty Jordan sat on the little iron trunk, all she'd been able to save from the rooming house, not worth saving at that, full of old worthless truck like photos and mementos, letters, canceled bills, a bit of her wedding veil, stuff that she was ashamed of having kept. She was dead beat and her clothes were smelly with smoke and streaked with soot. She pushed her graying hair out of her eyes and looked around for the two girls.

Crazy, scatterbrained young ones, they'd high-tailed it off

somewhere to run with the rest of the kids. What did it matter to them that the town was burning, themselves burned out of house, home, livelihood? To them it was just a lark, a chance to see people they'd never see on the waterfront, kick up their heels on the First Hill. Annie was off running with a bunch of other wild Indians, whooping and cavorting, but she'd be all right. For not quite seven, she was independent as a hog on ice. After tonight's lark she'd have to be whacked just to keep her from getting too big for her britches. The one she ought to keep her eye on was Mae, thirteen and pretty and quiet and shy.

It's the shy kind you got to watch. They're the ones get into trouble and don't know how to get out, thought Kit with a wry smile, remembering the dark-eyed boy who'd helped her carry the little trunk up the hill and who'd stared at Mae when he thought her ma wasn't looking. Well, the devil with the young ones. I got enough troubles without tryin' to find them in this crowd. And Kit took out the pint flask that she always kept handy in case of emergencies and had had presence of mind enough to grab from her bureau, and took a long, hot, comforting pull at it.

Annie Jordan was having the time of her life. Her long, red, uncombed mane flying, she ran and hollered and pushed the little boys who chased her and tried to pull her hair. She led the little girls in a wild game of tag, darting in and out of groups of grownups, making the proper, tight-lipped mamas cluck in disapproval and ask whose young one she was and why didn't her mother keep track of her.

The most fun to Annie was playing with these children she didn't know, daring the nice little boys in knickers and bow ties to chase her, making the pinafored girls with their neat corkscrew curls run so fast that their hair ribbons came loose. None of them had ever seen her before, she being from the waterfront, while they were First Hill children. But the minute she appeared in their midst with her unkempt, flaming hair, her mischievous grin, and her fearlessness of grownups, they'd taken to her, followed where she led.

One by one, though, the nice little boys and the wide-eyed little girls were scooped up by frowning mothers and taken in tow and presently she found herself alone. She knew where her ma was, but she didn't want to go back and sit with her, maybe get cuffed for running off. Annie stood a minute and watched the fire. The smoke rolled up into the sky in great black clouds. It was exciting to watch. Then she caught a glimpse of her sister Mae, walking with a dark-haired boy, and grinned. It might be fun to go and tease Mae for walking with a fella, but there wasn't enough excitement in that. Mae would only blush and look scared, maybe go and tell Ma. It wasn't any fun teasing anyone who wouldn't fight back.

She wandered about, kicking at stones, and then she heard someone crying, "Papa! Oh, Papa!" She turned and looked behind her and there stood a pretty little girl her own age with soft, fluffy, gold hair, her eyes tightly shut, shrieking with terror.

"What's the matter, little girl?" asked Annie curiously, and the child opened her eyes suddenly and stopped crying. Her eyes were very blue and frightened and she stared at Annie so blankly that she looked like the wax Christmas dolls Annie'd seen in Brookes's Dry Goods Store window. She couldn't seem to say a word, but the tears kept on popping out of her round blue eyes.

Annie hated to see anyone cry. She never cried herself; even when Ma whacked her she just yelled tearlessly in anger and rebellion. She put her arm around the little girl and wiped away the tears with a corner of her own dress. The other child stiffened and wrinkled up her nose. "You smell funny," she said suddenly with a fastidious frown, and pushed her away.

Annie's cheeks felt hot. "Do I?" She sniffed at her arm and her dress. They smelled of fried meat, sweat, and smoke. The other girl had smelled like soap and starch when she'd put her arm around her. Lots of people on the waterfront smelled like Annie, some of them worse. She'd never thought about it before. Now she felt ashamed and angry. She tossed her wild head and gave the other child a defiant glare.

"I don't care. Anyhow, I'm not a crybaby. I'm not scared of the fire."

"I'm not a crybaby. I'm not scared," cried the blond girl, but she looked as if she would burst into tears again just the same.

Annie laughed. "I'm not either. I think it's fun. An' I was almost burned to death, too. So was my ma and my sister, Mae. They had to carry us out."

The other girl looked at her in awe. "Did your house burn
down?"

"Uh-huh. Right to the ground. An' old Mr. Sorenson was
dead drunk in the back bedroom and when they carried him out
he didn't even wake up." Annie giggled and the other child
giggled, too, though she didn't even know what Annie was
talking about.

"Where will you go? What'll you do?"

"I don't know. Maybe we'll sleep in the woods tonight. I
hope so." Annie was all at once overcome with the excitement,
the fun of it all. She grabbed the little girl's hand. "C'mon.
Let's run!"

The other child laughed suddenly, caught up in Annie's excitement, and they went tearing madly along the hill, shrieking
with delight. When they had run until they were out of breath
they stopped, still holding hands, and looked at the people
around them. A weeping woman was being led down the other
side of the hill toward one of the big houses by a man who supported her with one arm, while a young girl, sniffling, trotted
beside her.

"That's Mrs. Brookes," whispered Annie importantly. "Her
store burned up and so did her husband."

The other child gasped and stared. Suddenly she screamed,
"Papa! My papa's down in the fire too. Maybe he'll be burned
up," and began to cry noisily.

Before Annie could say a word there was the rustle of skirts,
a scent of lavender, and a pretty woman in a fur jacket was
bending over the crying child, murmuring, "Emily! Thank God
I've found you. What are you doing out here alone?"

"Papa!" sobbed Emily, clutching the woman. "He'll burn up.
Oh, Mama!"

"Shh!" said her mother. "Don't cry. Papa is all right."

Annie stood staring at the pretty woman with her tiny waist
and huge sleeves, the silver combs in her hair, watching her
kiss and pet her daughter, kneeling to dry her eyes and brush
back her hair with a tender hand. How wonderful it must be to
have a mother like that, pretty and kind, who showed her concern for you with kisses instead of whacks and angry words.
It must be that people who lived on the First Hill were a different race altogether. Annie's mother was no worse than the

mothers of the other waterfront children, better in many ways. She didn't get drunk like Sally Kelly's ma and she never whacked her without a good reason. But Annie couldn't ever remember that she'd kissed her or brushed the hair gently off her forehead.

While she was standing there a heavy hand grabbed her by the shoulder. "Annie, you come back here and stop skedaddling all over the place," cried Ma hoarsely. Annie tried to wriggle out from under her mother's hand but she held her fast. Ma glanced at Emily's mother and nodded briefly. "It's all your life's worth to keep track of the little imps, ain't it, Miz Carlton?"

Emily's mother returned the nod, but her voice was cool and distant. "Indeed it is, Mrs. Jordan. I've been looking all over for my little girl." She stood up, took Emily's hand, as if to go.

"My, this is a terrible thing, ain't it?" went on Annie's mother garrulously, not seeming to notice that Mrs. Carlton was avoiding her gaze. "I lost ever'thing I own. Ever'thing."

"It's awful. I'm so sorry to hear of your loss. But I'm sure everyone will pitch in and help. If you need anything, send word and I'll fix up a bundle for you."

Kit Jordan's face hardened and her head went up. "Thanks, but I don't need help from nobody." Gaunt, smoke-streaked, her gray hair in wisps about her hatchet face, she eyed the smaller woman coldly, grabbed Annie's hand, and, pulling her after her, stalked away.

"Well, well," murmured Mrs. Carlton after her stiff back, "some people seem mighty touchy." She looked down suddenly at Emily. "That little girl didn't say anything she shouldn't to you, did she, Emily? I mean—not anything naughty."

Emily nodded her head. "Yes, she did, Mama. She said I was a crybaby. And I'm not, am I?"

"Ma," said Annie Jordan, skipping beside her mother, "who was that little girl?"

"Will Carlton's kid. He runs the saw works." Kit laughed sharply. "He's cleaned out as slick as a whistle, too. Mill's burned to the ground. Maybe his wife won't be runnin' around makin' up bundles for other folks so fast when she finds that out."

"She's pretty. Kin I play with her?"

Mrs. Jordan snorted, laughed. "Not likely."

"Why not? She's nice."

"Ask me no questions and I'll tell you no lies," snapped her mother. "First Hill kids don't play with waterfront rats. Run along and find Mae. I'm tuckered out. I got to find us a place to sleep tonight."

Her sister Mae, tall and too slender for her thirteen years, came toward them with a tall young boy. "Ma," she said eagerly in a pleased, shy voice. "Rolfe Linden's mother's invited us to sleep at their house tonight. Is it all right? I said we would."

Mrs. Jordan looked at her older daughter's pale young face and at the dark-haired, nice-looking boy at her side. "I dunno, Mae. We ain't goin' to impose on folks just because we've had hard luck."

"It's all right, Mrs. Jordan," said the boy quickly. "My mother told me to ask you. We've plenty of room."

Annie pouted, disappointed. "Ma, Ma, I wanta sleep in the woods tonight."

"You tell your ma thanks. We'd be pleased to stay at your house," answered Mrs. Jordan with dignity.

"Mother's gone on ahead to make up some extra beds and fix you something hot to eat. But I'll show you the way," said the boy proudly. He took Mae's hand and they started off together, laughing and talking. Mrs. Jordan followed slowly, watching them, a curious smile on her haggard face.

Annie kicked stones, scowling. "I wanta sleep in the woods," she insisted stubbornly.

"You hush up, Annie, and mind your manners when we get to the Lindens'. Mr. Linden's an alderman and he owns the bank, too. That's a nice-lookin' boy they got." Mrs. Jordan laughed. "I allus wanted to see the inside of their house. Took a fire to get me there."

Rolfe Linden's mother was tall and thin, with such white, fine skin you could see through it. You could see the little bluish veins in her clear, high forehead and the sharp, delicate bones of her high-bridged nose. She wore glasses on her nose and they were attached to a thin gold chain that was pinned to the bosom of her dark green serge dress. The sleeves of the dress were like balloons at her shoulders and came down tight on her arms and wrists. She looked something like the school teacher, but finer and prouder. She spoke very graciously to Ma and Mae and she smiled at Annie and said, "My, what beautiful hair."

Mr. Linden had thick gray hair and sharp blue eyes that pierced right through you when he looked at you. There was a smudge of dirt along his big hawklike nose and he'd torn one of his trouser legs. It looked funny to see such a dignified man in such a state.

He came into the house while the Jordans were having hot chicken broth out of thin white china cups with two handles in the kitchen. Mrs. Linden wanted them to sit in the dining room and let the maid serve them, but Annie's mother gave her sharp laugh and said no, they were all covered with soot and grime from the fire and they wouldn't want to dirty up those fine needlepoint chairs.

Annie thought Mrs. Linden looked relieved, though her cheeks got pink and she swept on into the kitchen ahead of them and served them the soup herself. Mae got awfully red and looked ashamed at her mother for refusing to eat in the dining room like a lady. She sat at the table with her eyes on her plate and didn't look up even when Mrs. Linden asked if she wanted more. But Annie had two cups of soup and a glass of cold milk and three cookies. She liked drinking out of the thin white cups that felt so smooth and dainty against her lips.

When Mr. Linden came in, banging the front door, his wife hurried out to meet him. Annie heard his deep, rumbling voice and his wife's low, ladylike one in the next room. She heard him say, "Well, it's your funeral," and then Mrs. Linden said something in a low voice and he laughed and said, "And you'd do your Christian duty if it killed you, wouldn't you?"

Annie's mother heard, too, and she looked funny and started to get up, but suddenly Mae said in a tight little voice, "Ma, please don't. *Please.*" Mrs. Jordan looked at Mae hard and then her eyes slid around to the Linden boy, who didn't seem to have heard because he was staring so at Mae, and she laughed harshly and sat down again and finished her soup.

When they'd eaten, Annie's mother herded them all back

again into the front room where Mr. and Mrs. Linden were still talking. They looked solemn and worried and Mrs. Jordan said to the alderman, "I'm right sorry about the bank, Mr. Linden. Guess you've got your hands full being alderman at a time like this."

"I have indeed, Mrs. Jordan," he answered gravely, just as if she were Emily Carlton's mother or one of the other ladies from the First Hill, instead of the proprietor of a waterfront rooming house that had burned to the ground. "And I'm sorry about your loss too. What do you plan to do now that your house is gone?"

"I aim to build another, Mr. Linden. A bigger house with improvements," said Annie's mother without turning a hair.

Mr. Linden gave her a look out of those sharp blue eyes and then he laughed. "That's the spirit, Mrs. Jordan. You hear that, Susan? That's the Seattle spirit. We're going to build another, only bigger and with improvements." Then he looked serious again. "If you need any financial help to get started again, Mrs. Jordan, come down to my office next week and I'll see what can be done about a loan."

"Your office, Ned?" cried his wife. "But I thought it was burned."

"Sure it was, Susan. But I'll be doing business on the same site next week, in a tent!"

And he was, along with the other businessmen who'd been burned out. A tent city rose first out of the ruins, as soon as the debris and wreckage had been carted away. Business went on as briskly as ever to the sound of hammers and the shouts of workmen. And when they built again, they built bigger and better.

Just the week before the fire the town had taken up a big collection for the relief of the Johnstown flood victims. After the fire there was a town meeting and some timid soul wanted to know if they'd send the money to Johnstown or use it for their own relief. "Keep the money? Hell no!" roared Will Carlton. "They're worse off than we are by a long shot. They're stuck back there in Pennsylvania and we're in the Pacific Northwest, thank God. Send 'em all the money. We'll make out okay." And they did.

Annie's mother put up a big, rambling rooming house with gingerbread along the eaves and a red and gold and green stained-glass window in the front hall, two washrooms instead of one, and an inside toilet with a long hand flush on a chain.

Things were different after the fire. It wasn't only that the new buildings were bigger. The whole town seemed to expand, to look around and say, Let's make a new start. Let's do things in a bigger way. Let's move on farther up the hills. All right, our town burned to the ground and we rolled up our sleeves and made a better one. See, nothing can stop us. We've got the best damn harbor on the Pacific coast, enough lumber to build a hundred cities, to supply the whole danged country with good Douglas fir and spruce and hemlock. We've got fish and water power and rich earth and rain and open winters. We can grow anything anyone wants to eat. Hell, we've got a metropolis on our hands if we'll work for it. What are we waiting for? Let's go.

Of course there were some to whom the fire brought hard times. There was Mrs. Cecil Brookes, the minister's daughter from Boston, whose husband and dry-goods store went up in smoke. She didn't rebuild. She sold the property where Brookes's Department Store had been to Mr. Linden at the bank and bought a house on the First Hill and took in boarders to support herself and her daughter, Marguerite. It was a comedown for her, but she took it with dignity and managed to make it seem very genteel for a widow woman of good Boston ancestry to run a select boardinghouse.

After a while people stopped talking about the fire and in a few years there was the gold in Alaska to talk about. But for a long time Emily Carlton had nightmares and would waken, screaming, in the night, calling for her papa. She forgot all about the little girl with the red hair who'd dried her tears with her skirt and had run hand in hand with her while the town burned.

But Annie Jordan didn't forget her. Whenever Annie thought of the fire she remembered the pretty little blond child her mother said she couldn't play with. She remembered, too, the feel of the thin white china cups and the nice, sweet-smelling sheets on the bed she slept in.

Her sister Mae never talked about it, but she remembered too.

She remembered her mother making them eat in the kitchen instead of the lovely plush-curtained dining room. And she remembered the tall, nice-looking boy with the dark eyes and the shy smile who'd taken her hand and walked down the hill with her that night.

Chapter II

What Annie liked to do when she could slip away from her mother's sharp eye and demanding voice was to loiter around the docks and see the boats riding at anchor, with the green, oily water washing smoothly against their stained and battered hulls. There were the small, sturdy fishing smacks, reeking of their cargo, the island steamers with their black- and red-banded funnels, the bilge water gushing from their sides. Once in a while a big black freighter came in from Portland or San Francisco and the little girl would sit on a pile, watching with fascinated eyes as the burly longshoremen unloaded her.

Sometimes the sailors called to her and waved and she waved back and wished she could go aboard. Most of all she wanted to go with them when the boats got up steam, weighed anchor, and steamed slowly out of Elliott Bay, their prows cutting a foamy path through the dark water.

She loved the rattle of the anchor chains, the cheerful, blasphemous voices of the sailors, the triumphant blast of the whistle as the boat slowly backed away from the slip. She would stand and wave until the boat was only a tiny black dot in the vast, shimmering expanse of the bay and its plume of smoke a thin, frayed banner trailing behind.

Then she would throw crusts, saved from her mother's kitchen, to the swarming, circling gulls that wheeled boldly above her. They glared at her with red, angry eyes and their hooked yellow beaks opened to laugh their strange, raucous laughter and she could see the curious black tongues. They swooped upon the bread she threw into the water, squabbling and shrieking and beating their strong gray and white wings, lighting upon the water and bobbing gently up and down on the long oily green swells, like little boats themselves.

When they rose with long red legs dangling and wheeled up into the air, they were so beautiful and proud and graceful, her heart ached to see them. The curve of their wings made her think of music, of the organ in the Catholic church where she used to go with Pop when he was alive. But when they lighted on the docks and waddled awkwardly along, they looked pompous and smug, switching their sleek, fat bodies as they walked, and she laughed at them.

When all her bread was gone they would fly over her head, scolding her, demanding more until the cook from one of the boats dumped garbage overboard into the bay and then they would begin to scream greedily and fly away, to swoop upon the bobbing vegetables and refuse. She knew they were greedy and cruel, that they were hated by the fishermen because they picked the eyes out of the salmon that swam too close to the surface, but she loved them. She would have liked to be a gull, with two strong wings beating up into the blue, free and independent and wild.

After she had fed the gulls she would peer into the dusty, smoke-grimed windows of the ship's chandler shops, staring at the coiled, tarry ropes, the swinging ship lanterns, the heavy anchors, the kegs, the oilskins, the boathooks, the strong brown fishing nets draped from the ceiling. She liked the burly, red-faced, bearded men who swaggered with rolling gait through the doors. They smelled of the sea, of strong tobacco, of rum, of tar and oilskins. Their faces looked as if they'd been chiseled roughly from red rock and their eyes were the hazy blue-gray of distant horizons. They called her "Red" and "Carrot Top" and sometimes they gave her strange gifts—a gold earring, a piece of petrified wood, once a tiny, delicate blue starfish that she could hold in her palm.

On her way home there was still another place of wonders that she could never pass without going in. It was the Old Curiosity Shop on Colman Dock, and the bright-eyed old man in the black skullcap and shiny alpaca jacket who ran it didn't mind how long she stayed, gazing into the glass-topped showcases where all the wonders of the far-flung world were kept.

Over the door was the huge white jawbone of a whale, and in one of the cases was the Lord's Prayer etched on the head of a pin. There were tiny sea horses, fantastic, legendary little creatures out of a dream. There were grinning masks cut by the Alaskan Indians from driftwood. There were spears and dried heads from the South Sea Islands. Baskets and blankets of the Siwashes, totems from Alaska. Exquisite ivories from the Orient. Gongs and temple bells, daggers and headdresses. There were Indian war bonnets, ceremonial masks of the medicine men, tomahawks, wonderful beaded moccasins, feather capes of chieftains.

Annie never tired of looking at them, but she never wanted to possess them. It was enough that they were here for her to see and to wonder about. The shop was dim and dusty and smelled of moth balls, and nobody, not even its owner, knew how much treasure trove it held. It was often full of visitors to Seattle, buying curios and souvenirs, laughing and exclaiming over the curiosities. Annie liked to listen to them, to smell the perfume and sachet of the ladies who swished their long skirts so elegantly. They were part of the great world, too, and Annie was hungry for the world and its wonders.

She wanted to see and smell and know it all. She wanted to know all its people, the proud ones with their fine clothes and tinkling, cultured laughter, the ones like Emily Carlton and Rolfe Linden, who lived in great houses and drank soup out of thin white china cups, the girls from the Variety Theater with their painted mouths and bright clothes and bangles, the red-faced, swaggering sailors, the rough longshoremen who drank beer at her mother's saloon, the strange, yellow-faced Chinamen in pajamas who ran the laundries and the fan-tan houses in Chinatown on Yesler Way.

She was never unhappy, because there was so much to see and hear and dream about. Her mother was often harsh with her and she had to work hard in the rooming house and saloon, but so long as she was allowed to run wild after her chores were done she didn't mind. She even liked going to school, because that was another part of the world that she must find out about. The teacher, Miss Gray, was a different kind of being, a stiff, aloof, sometimes cold, sometimes impatient person, who wore dark brown serge dresses and a high white collar, glasses on a chain and her hair piled on top of her head. But she had a thin, aristocratic face and fine white skin, a delicate way of turning her head, small hands and a precise, dry way of speaking, and Annie knew that she belonged with the people who lived on the First Hill. She even boarded at Mrs. Brookes's select boardinghouse. Annie never thought much about whether she liked her or not, but she was impressed with her, and Annie's small white face would go pink with pleasure if Miss Gray threw her a tiny crust of praise for a lesson well done.

"Where in tarnation have you been?" her mother would yell at her when she came skipping into the rooming house. "I been lookin' all over creation for you. There's a pile of glasses to be washed and Mae's sick in bed with a cold."

"Oh, I been down to the docks to see the boats," Annie would say cheerfully, tossing her red mane.

"Waterfront rat. That's what ye are!" Her mother would sometimes smack her across the side of the head, or else burst out laughing, depending on how she was feeling, or whether she'd had a drink or two with one of her customers. "Get, now, and wash up them glasses. It's nearly five o'clock an' the boys'll be dropping in for their beer soon."

Off Annie would skip to the kitchen to wash the piles of dirty glasses smelling of beer and whisky. Like as not she'd sing as she swished the soapy water in the dishpan, and as she dried glasses she'd dance a bit, too, capering around the kitchen with her red hair flying.

Soon the lamps would be lighted and the saloon would begin to fill up with men from the docks and there'd be the cheerful sound of men's loud voices and harsh laughter, the clatter of glasses and later the tinkle of the piano when some of the Variety girls came in after the first show. Annie loved the Variety girls, they were so gay, always laughing, always brightly dressed with their pretty bare arms covered with bracelets. There was Milly, plump and blue-eyed, with dazzling yellow hair and tiny feet she was inordinately vain of. She spent all her extra money on fancy shoes, wonderful pointed white kid ones that buttoned clear up to her calf, or red ones with three-inch heels. She sent clear to Chicago for her shoes.

Lorna was the dark one and Annie liked her the least. She

had a bad temper and she was jealous of the other girls, always being hurt by some imagined slight. She'd been in love with a gambler who'd left her for a redhead and she took an instant dislike to Annie. Sometimes she drank too much, sitting by herself in a corner and insulting the men who wanted to talk to her. Once she threw the tiny jeweled knife she kept in her bodice at Maizie and it stuck in the wall, quivering, the light flashing from the bits of bright stone in its hilt. But Maizie only laughed and bought her another drink.

Maizie was Annie's favorite. She was the beautiful one, tall and slim, with a queenly way. Her eyes were large, a clear, dark gray, and she had a cloud of soft brown hair that framed her slender face. She used to take Annie up to her room and tell her about when she was a little girl and lived on a farm back East. Sometimes her eyes filled with tears and she would catch Annie to her and kiss her and send her home with a trinket. The nicest thing she ever gave her was a lovely gold silk scarf all covered with shiny black sequins. Annie liked to drape it over her head and shoulders and dance in front of the long mirror in her mother's room. She kept the scarf for a long time, even after she was a grown girl. Maizie was the only person besides Pop who gave Annie any affection. Her mother was too busy and too harsh; if there had ever been any affection in her heart for her children, the constant struggle and her own desire to get ahead had long since hardened over it. Mae was nice enough to Annie, but she lived in a dream of her own and there was no room for Annie there.

One night when Annie slipped into the saloon from the kitchen, Milly was at the piano playing "The Band Played On," Annie's favorite tune.

"Hello, Annie," called Milly gaily. "How about dancing for us?"

So Annie, flattered by the attention, began to twirl on her toes, trying to imitate the girls at the theater. Maizie and Milly laughed and encouraged her, and the men began to applaud and to toss her coins. Her mother was in the kitchen and Mae had gone to bed early with a headache. Andy, the wrestler, who had bought Milly her last pair of satin shoes, picked up the little girl and put her on one of the tables. "Now we can all see you, Annie," he cried, clapping his hands to the music.

Milly played tune after tune, "After the Ball," "A Bird in a Gilded Cage," "Take Me out to the Ball Game," all the fine new pieces that Annie had heard when she sneaked into the Variety Theater. And Annie danced and danced, till her hair came loose from its ribbon and tumbled about her shoulders and her face was hot and flushed and her heart was pounding.

Then her mother came in and pulled her down from the table, smacking her across the bottom with an angry hand.

"What d'ye mean, makin' a show of yourself like that?" she cried furiously. "Get along to bed."

But the men and the Variety girls pleaded to let her stay and the men slapped coins down on the table and stamped their feet, shouting drunkenly, "We want Annie! We want Annie!"

Mrs. Jordan looked around at them all, still frowning and angry. Then she began to scoop up the coins the men had tossed to Annie and when she saw how many there were she laughed harshly. "It seems my little girl is very popular. No more for tonight, though. But come again tomorrow, boys, and mebbe I'll let Annie dance for you."

So after that her mother encouraged her to dance for the customers. She even bought her a fluffy blue dress to put on and a pair of white kid dancing slippers with ribbons that tied around her ankles. She didn't make her wash glasses in the kitchen any more and often Annie would look up and catch her mother looking at her with a curious, thoughtful expression on her sharp, weathered face.

Ned, the scrubby little son of an overworked washerwoman, who worked for Mrs. Jordan as errand boy and odd-jobs man, fell sick one day and Annie had to carry the buckets of beer to the regular customers who sent out for orders.

"See that they pay cash, now," warned her mother sharply. "And bring every cent home. No stopping at the candy store for jawbreakers."

"I don't like jawbreakers anyhow," said Annie snippily. Since she'd begun to dance on the tables she was developing an artistic temperament and was no longer afraid of her mother. Mrs. Jordan wasn't so quick to slap her now that she'd become an asset to her business.

"Don't be saucy, young'un," she snapped, and laid a hand on Annie's arm. The little girl shrugged it off and stood eying her mother defiantly. The woman began to smile crookedly. "Smart as paint these days, ain'tcha? Well, if you get any tips you can spend a dime for caramels if you like."

Annie laughed and skipped off, a bucket of beer in each hand. One bucket was for Jim Petley at the *Argus* office and the other was for Lorna at Considine's. She walked along the wooden sidewalks, gazing up into the faces of passers-by, peering into store windows, standing to watch a team of big-buttocked work horses toiling up Jackson Street with a load of lumber. Building was going on steadily; not a boom, for money was tight since the panic in the East, but still new houses kept going up, made of the white boards cut from Douglas firs, the queen of Northwestern trees, sound as a bell, the only lumber that the continual fogs and dampness couldn't rot.

Annie wondered where the lumber was going and if she hadn't been on an errand for her mother she'd have followed the sweating team, driven so relentlessly up the steep hill by their cursing driver. She loved to watch builders at work, to prowl through half-finished houses and smell the fresh, pungent fragrance of the new wood, the damp, clean smell of mortar and bricks and cement. She liked to stand in the unplastered empty shells of rooms and wonder about the people who would live there, what they looked like, how they talked, what sort of furniture they'd put in the rooms.

It was midafternoon and the air was strong and salty with the smell of the sound and the tide flats. Annie breathed it deeply, savoring it with relish. As long as she lived no other smell would make her blood tingle and her spirits rise so much as that rank, wild odor. The sun was bright and hot on her face and a brisk offshore breeze made the waters of the bay, glimpsed between buildings, ruffle from shimmering sunlight to dark, choppy blue.

The bustle of the streets made her dance along faster and when lumberjacks from the woods, swaggering in blue jeans and checked red-and-green shirts, or longshoremen from the docks recognized her from having seen her dance at the saloon and called to her, she shouted back in her clear child's voice, feeling that the world was good and she had hosts of friends.

At Considine's Variety Theater she went up the side stairs to the dressing rooms backstage until she came to Lorna's room.

She was going to run in to see Maizie as soon as she had
delivered the beer to Lorna, so she stood impatiently on one
foot and then on the other, after she'd rapped at Lorna's door.
There was no answer, so at last she opened the door and went
in.

It was a dingy, dark little room with a litter of costumes
and soiled undergarments tossed over the chairs and hanging
from hangers on the wall. A purple feather fan lay on the
dressing table and from a corner glinted a short sequin-covered
skirt. There was a queer smell in the room, grease paint,
powder, and sweat and with no windows open it made Annie
feel choked.

"Lorna," said Annie timidly, not quite sure that she should
have come in. There was no answer and she tiptoed over to
the dressing table to look at the fascinating pots of cold cream
and rouge, the tubes of grease paint, the bottles of perfume.
Timidly she put down the two buckets of beer and fingered
the bracelets and beads spilled out from an open box. She stuck
her finger in the pot of rouge and traced a smeary mouth on
her lips, grimacing at herself in the cloudy mirror. She tried on
a bracelet, turning it this way and that, to watch it sparkle on
her skinny, freckled arm. She picked up the feather fan, spread
it out with a flip of her wrist as she'd seen Lorna do, and waved
it languorously, twirling before the mirror.

Suddenly the room seemed very still and hot and close. She
turned slowly with a beating heart, feeling that someone was
watching her. But the room was quite empty and the only
sound was a fly buzzing against the windowpane. Then she saw
the cot, half hidden by a shabby wooden screen. Something
pushed her across the room. Something made her pull aside the
screen.

Lorna was lying on top of the bedclothes on the cot and at
first Annie thought she was asleep. Her long dark hair was
tumbled on the soiled pillow and her Japanese kimono was
disheveled and awry, exposing her white thighs and the full
curve of her bosom. And then Annie saw the knife. The
sunlight coming from under the half-drawn blind sparkled on
its little jeweled hilt and the blade was plunged deep into
Lorna's naked breast.

For a long, terrible moment Annie could not move and no

sound would come from her dry throat. Then her eyes met the open, staring eyes of the woman on the cot and they seemed to be glaring malevolently at her. "Lorna!" Her voice didn't sound like her own at all. It sounded like a tiny, thin mouse squeak and it frightened her almost as much as the dead woman's glaring eyes and the dark red stains beginning to ooze through the cheap silk kimono. She turned and ran out of the room.

"Maizie!" she cried, still in that thin, high squeak, and she pounded on her friend's door with her fists.

There was no sound for a moment until Annie began to cry noisily, then there was a creak, quick footsteps, and the door opened a crack.

"Maizie!" sobbed Annie. Maizie stepped out into the hall, closing the door behind her, tying the sash to her kimono as she did so. Her brown hair fell to her shoulders and her cheeks were flushed. She was breathing rapidly and her breasts fell and rose under the gaudy flowered wrapper.

"What's the matter, kiddy?" she asked in a quick, soft voice, twisting her hair into a low knot on her neck.

But all Annie could do at first was weep and Maizie knelt, put her arms around her, and held her against her soft, full breast. Annie smelled whisky on her breath. For some reason that made her stop crying. She pushed herself away from the woman's embrace and stared at her. "Lorna's dead," she said flatly, realizing for the first time, as she said it, that it was true.

"What?" cried Maizie, standing up suddenly.

"I saw her. There's a knife sticking out of her," whispered Annie. "Her own knife. The one she threw at you that night at Ma's place."

"Dear Jesus!" breathed Maizie, crossing herself quickly. Then she ran down the hall to Lorna's room and Annie followed her to the door. She wasn't crying now, but she didn't want to go back into that dark, close room.

Maizie bent over the still figure on the untidy cot and Annie heard her gasp. Then she came quickly out into the hall, her face white, her eyes dark with horror. "This is no place for you, kiddy. Go on home," she said harshly, and she gave her a little shove toward the stairs.

"I left the beer in there," cried Annie, suddenly remembering it. "But I don't wanna go back and get it."

"I'll get it for you. Then you take it and get out of here, honey. You shouldn't have had to see—that in there." Maizie disappeared again into Lorna's room and came back with the two buckets of beer.

"One of 'em was for Lorna," said Annie uncertainly. "But now——" She looked up at Maizie with awe in her round, freckled face. "Gee, Maizie, now she'll never drink any more beer—or dance at Considine's or come to Ma's place—or anything."

"No," replied Maizie quietly, "she'll never do anything like that again, Annie. It's all over for Lorna—the good and the bad. Maybe she's lucky, at that." She sighed deeply and stared over Annie's head. For a moment they stood there in the hall in silence and then Maizie whispered, "God rest her soul, anyhow." She looked at Annie, holding the buckets of beer. "Give me the one for Lorna. I can use it even if she can't." She felt in the pocket of her wrapper and handed Annie a quarter. "Here's two bits. Keep the change, kiddy. And now you'd better get out of here before the police come." Annie handed her the beer and she opened her door and went into her room. Annie heard the rumble of a man's voice as she shut the door behind her.

It was still sunny outside on the street and, looking up, Annie saw the deep, bright blue sky as calm and serene as if a woman were not lying with a knife in her breast backstage in the dingy little dressing room at Considine's. People went by, brisk and busy and unconcerned, the horsecars rattled over the cobblestones, a steamer whistled out on the bay, and a gang of boys, yelling and shouting, tore past, chasing a dog with a can tied to its miserable tail.

Annie took a deep breath of the fresh, salty air and was glad she was outside and not still in Lorna's room. She was glad she was alive and not dead. She tried to think how it would feel to be dead. Did it hurt? It must have hurt when the knife went in. But now, Maizie said, it was all over for Lorna, the good and the bad. So now that she was dead, it couldn't hurt any more. But to have it all over—everything—all the wonderful, exciting world, not to smell the tide flats any more or feel the wind and sun, that must hurt lots more than the sharpest knife.

"I don't want ever to be dead," whispered Annie tensely, and suddenly tears popped out of her eyes. She hadn't liked Lorna and Lorna hadn't liked her, but she was sorry for her because she was dead. All at once she was sorry for all the people who were dead, with everything all over for them. She walked slowly down Occidental Avenue, sniffling, the tears stinging her cheeks, with a dark ache of sorrow in her heart.

Her eyes were still red when she went into the *Argus* office and put the bucket of beer on Jim Petley's desk. Jim was sitting bent over a long galley, correcting proof, and he didn't look up until she said, "Ma says I was to get cash for the beer, Mr. Petley." Then he pushed back the green eyeshade he wore on his forehead and looked at her as if he'd never seen her before.

"Oh, it's you, Annie," he said, and grinned. "The sweetheart of the Nugget Saloon, herself."

In spite of how sad she was feeling, Annie grinned back at him. There was something about the way the reporter said things that she liked; it was a kind of joking, but it wasn't like the coarse, broad jokes the men made in the saloon, it was joking that you didn't quite get right at first.

"Oh, go on, Mr. Petley," she giggled, the way she'd heard the Variety girls do when the men joked with them.

"What's the latest news down the skid road?" he asked, winking at her.

Suddenly she remembered Lorna. Her face grew solemn and she blurted out, "Lorna's dead. I saw her. She has a knife in her chest."

Jim Petley stopped grinning and looked puzzled but alert. "What's that again? Who's dead?"

"Lorna—from the Variety Theater. I brought her beer to her dressing room and she was lying on the cot with the knife in her and her eyes were wide open."

The reporter grabbed her arm and held it hard, staring at her intently. "Let me get this straight. You brought the beer up to her room and you found her on the cot with a knife in her heart. Whose knife was it? Who killed her? Are the police there now?" He bombarded her with questions so fast that she could only stare back at him. "Well, why don't you answer? Or did you make this all up?" he cried, frowning at her.

She flushed and shook her head. "I didn't make it up, Mr. Petley. It's true. I saw her. It was her own little knife, but I don't know who stuck it in her. If you don't believe me you go down to Considine's and see for yourself."

He got up from his desk so fast he barked his shins and swore. Then he grabbed his hat and coat, tossed the eyeshade on his desk, crammed his hat on his head, and started out the door, struggling into his coat. Annie ran after him down the street, pulling at his sleeve.

"Ma said you was to pay for the beer." He fumbled in his pants pocket for some coins and handed her a dime. Then he laughed and said, "Here's a tip, just in case you've given me a right steer on this story," and he reached in again and brought out a quarter.

Now she had plenty of money for caramels or stick candy or even chocolate drops if she wanted, but suddenly her taste for candy was gone. She peered into the window of Harrison's candy store at the round glass jars of jawbreakers, gumdrops, green and red and orange and yellow, but she kept seeing Lorna lying there on the cot. Her stomach began to feel queer and she turned quickly away from the window and walked back toward Considine's Variety Theater.

There was a crowd gathered in front of the theater when she got there and the police wagon, with its two big black horses, was drawn up to the curb. Suddenly the crowd fell back before a big red-faced policeman who cleared the way for a bedraggled and protesting little group of girls from the theater, herded along the street to the wagon by two more policemen. Some of the girls were in street clothes, but some were still in their cheap, gaudy wrappers. Most of them were sullenly silent, not raising their eyes to the curious gaze of the onlookers, but one or two, like Milly, cursed the officers shrilly. Maizie held her head high, but she jerked her arm away from the policeman who tried to hurry her, and her face was chalky.

Annie saw Jim Petley standing at the curb scribbling in his notebook. Then when all the girls had been pushed into the police wagon he swung up behind just as the horses started up, and hung on for dear life while the wagon clattered over the pavement and the crowd laughed and jeered.

Some of the boys from the waterfront ran after the police wagon and Annie ran after them. It wasn't far to the police station and the jail with its barred windows was right beside it. A policeman standing outside tried to shoo them away, but Annie and some of the older boys hung around, peering at the windows. The boys pretended to know all about the murder and boasted about having seen the corpse taken out by the undertaker. Annie was bursting to tell them that she was the one who'd found Lorna first, but something made her keep still. Maybe it was what Maizie had said about the police or the sight of the barred windows of the jail or the queer feeling in her stomach when she thought about it.

She was still outside the station when Jim Petley came out, frowning and stuffing his notebook into his pocket. She ran up to him. "Mr. Petley, who did it? Who killed Lorna?"

"You still here, kiddy?" The reporter grinned at her, rumpled her hair. "None of the girls know anything about it, or at any rate they won't talk. My bet is, they'll never find out who did it. The girls stick together when they're in a jam, and most of them hated Lorna. If it was a man, you can bet he's blown town by now, or else is hiding in Chinatown. And nobody can find him if he's there."

"Why did they take Maizie? She didn't do it," cried Annie.

"They just took the whole lot of them and tossed them into the jug. They'll keep 'em there a few days, till Considine raises a big enough fuss, and then they'll have to let 'em go. Anyhow, I got a good story out of it and I'm much obliged to you, kiddy. Tell you what I'll do. The Yesler trial is coming up next month. If you want, I'll get you into the courtroom on my press card."

When she got home, her mother scolded her for taking so long, boxed her ears for forgetting to bring the empty beer buckets back, and made her count out the money into her palm.

"Did you get any tips?" she demanded sharply.

"Yes, but you said I was to keep 'em to buy candy," Annie replied. Then she blurted out, unable to hold it any longer, "I got a tip from Mr. Petley for telling him about Lorna."

"What about Lorna?"

"She's dead, with a knife in her, and I saw her when I went in with the beer. I found her."

Kit Jordan grabbed her by the shoulders and shook her. "Are you telling the truth?"

Annie nodded. Ma ought to know she never lied.

"Then for God's sake, don't tell anyone else you found her, if you know what's good for you. We don't want the police around here, snoopin' and askin' questions. It'll ruin business." Kit's face was worried and she tightened her hold on Annie. "Don't tell another soul or I'll beat you within an inch of your life. They might even make you go to court and answer questions. I don't want no kid of mine mixed up with the law."

Annie promised and Kit knew she'd keep her promise, but her fear of the police, and a deep-buried maternal anxiety for the girl that she usually had no time or inclination to indulge, made her keep Annie at home for the rest of the week. She wasn't allowed to go to school, to step out on the street. At last, when Saturday came and the Variety girls had been released and a statement came out in the *Argus* that Lorna Dugan had met her death by a person or persons unknown, Kit relaxed her vigil and Annie was able to go out of the house. She'd promised her mother to stay away from Considine's and now she had no desire to go there, anyhow. She bought a bag of caramels at Harrison's with the quarter Jim Petley had given her and made straight for the waterfront docks.

The smell of the waterfront seemed doubly wonderful to her after the days of confinement in the stuffy cabbage- and onion-scented house. She sat on a pile, eating caramels, with the oily green water sloshing below her and the gulls circling overhead, looking out over the wide, rippling sound.

Far out in the bay a steamer was making a leisurely progress into the harbor. The smoke from her one funnel poured in a long black plume behind her. Annie ate caramels dreamily, wishing she were on a boat going somewhere. She wished she were grown up, as beautiful as Maizie, only more aristocratic-looking, like her teacher or the picture of Mary Queen of Scots in her history book, and dressed in a long flowing gown and a hat with an ostrich feather. And then, of course, there would be a prince, who would lay his heart and kingdom at her feet. Only I think I'd like a pirate better than a prince, she thought. A pirate with a gold ring in his ear.

There was the rattle of wheels and the clop-clop of horses' hoofs on the pavement behind her and she turned to watch a smart, shiny black carriage, drawn by a big bay horse, come up the street. As she watched, it pulled up by the curb and a tall young man in a stylish, tight-fitting checked suit and a bowler hat got out, spoke to the driver, and walked over to where she was sitting. The carriage drove off and the young man leaned on his arm on the pile next to her and stared out over the bay.

Annie stole glances at him with bright, curious eyes. He didn't belong to the waterfront, that was certain. His clothes, his manner, even his pale, slender face with its fine features spoke of gentility. He must be from the First Hill or a visitor to Seattle. Annie thought him very handsome, as handsome as a prince, and while she was staring at him he turned and looked at her.

"Hello, little girl," he said in a soft, slow voice. His eyes were the oddest color, clear, dark gray with little flecks of yellow in them, and his lashes were short and thick and black. They looked as if someone had smudged them with a sooty finger. Yes, he was handsome as a prince, but the funny lights in his eyes gave him a reckless look, too, like a pirate.

"Hello," said Annie, tossing her head. She rather resented being called little girl by a stranger, now that she was going on thirteen and tall for her age. Tall and skinny as a bean pole, Ma said.

"So this is Elliott Bay," remarked the young man, looking out over the water again. "The finest harbor on the Pacific coast, they say."

"You don't live here, huh?" observed Annie, swinging her legs.

"From now on, I expect to. My father lives here."

"What's your father's name?" asked Annie.

He grinned at her inquisitiveness. "Judge Deming."

"Oh. What's your name?"

He laughed. "Hugh Deming. What's yours?"

"Annie Jordan. My ma runs the Nugget Saloon." She said it with as much aplomb as he had in mentioning his father. "Where did you live before?"

"Virginia. I was at school when Father decided to pioneer in the West." He laughed again. "Now he insists that I go to school here at this frontier University of Washington with the backwoodsmen. I suppose instead of Greek they teach Siwash."

"I know some Siwash," said Annie.

"Say something in it, then," he challenged.

"*Tillicoom*," she answered, and giggled.

"What does that mean?" He was looking at her with interest and she tossed her head and murmured, "It means 'friend.' "

"*Tillicoom*—friend. That's rather nice, Annie. Sort of symbolic, don't you know, that my first word in Siwash should be 'friend' and taught to me by such a pretty young lady."

Annie blushed and popped another caramel into her mouth, at a loss to reply to such gallantry. Hugh Deming was smiling at her and she felt the need to respond, to make some sort of gesture. So she hopped down from the pile and offered him the bag of candy.

"Caramels," she said in a voice muffled by the one in her mouth. "They're good."

"Thank you very much," said Hugh, and took one. There was a long, mournful whistle and Annie looked up to see the steamer coming into the slip, her prow parting the green water neatly, her engines churning it into foam behind.

"What boat is that, Annie, and where does she come from?" asked the young man.

"She's the *North Pacific* from Olympia. She stops here on the way up to Victoria. Cap'n Blaine's a friend of mine and someday he's going to take me for a trip," said Annie proudly.

"It ought to be a good trip. Father says the sound is very scenic. Maybe I'll take it myself before I start school again." He was watching the steamer with an absorbed, intent expression. "I like boats and the water. Maybe I ought to be a sailor instead of a lawyer."

"If I was a man I'd be a sailor," cried Annie. The steamer was sliding in between the sides of the slip now and a deck hand in dungarees and a black jersey ran out onto the bow with the landing rope in his hands.

"Watch out, Annie!" he yelled, and she skipped away from the pile where she'd been sitting. The sailor threw the rope neatly over the pile, then leaped lightly onto the dock and made it fast.

"Hello, Pete," said Annie.

Pete grinned at her and pinched her cheek. "How's my sweetheart?" he laughed, winking at Hugh.

Annie switched away from him. "I'm not anyone's sweetheart," she cried.

Pete laughed. "Not now, mebbe. But it won't be long, the way you're growin'. Run tell your ma the *North Pacific's* in and the cap'n's thirsty. Tell her she better break out a case of that Jamaica."

"You go tell her yourself," said Annie snippily, but she started toward home.

Just then the carriage Hugh Deming had ridden in came clattering up the street again and he called to her, "Wait a minute, Annie, and I'll give you a lift."

She felt very important and grown up as Hugh held out his hand and helped her into the carriage, but as they drove past Pete, the deck hand, she leaned out the side and stuck her tongue out at him. Hugh laughed at her and said, "Why'd you do that? Don't you like him?"

"He's too fresh," she answered. "He thinks he's smart."

"I guess you haven't got red hair for nothing," he said.

"Ma says it's the meanness coming out in me. She says the Devil gave me red hair to show I belonged to him."

"Don't you believe it," said Hugh. "It's a gift of the gods. The most fascinating woman in history had red hair. She was a queen and her name was Cleopatra."

"Will I be fascinating when I grow up?"

"With that hair and those violet eyes, I shouldn't be a bit surprised," laughed Hugh.

Her mother was standing at the door, shading her eyes with her hand and looking up and down the street for her when she got out of the carriage in front of the Nugget. "Thank you very much, Mr. Deming," said Annie politely, and Hugh waved to her as he drove away.

"I've been looking all over for you, you young devil," cried her mother angrily, grabbing her by the arm. "Where do ye think ye've been? And what's all this, drivin' home with a swell?"

"He's a friend of mine," said Annie calmly. She knew she was in for a licking, but she didn't care. She'd made a new friend, a grown man who treated her like a person instead of a child. She'd been driven home in a fine carriage by a real gentleman who looked like a prince and a pirate and who'd told her she'd be as fascinating as a queen when she grew up. Nothing her mother could do would take away the flavor, the fine edge of her experience.

Chapter III

"You ought to be in school, young'un," whispered Jim Petley, grinning down at Annie where she sat beside him in the front seats of the courtroom, designated for "the press."

"This is lots more fun than school!" Annie whispered back, her eyes bright and dark, darting for just a moment from the judge, solemn and austere in his black robes, the lawyer who was cross-examining the witness and failing to shake her story that Mr. Yesler and his wife were on the best of terms at all times, to Jim's thin, freckled face. It was the second week of the trial and Annie had managed to skip school almost every afternoon on the pretext that her mother was ill and needed her at the rooming house, to see and hear the sordid drama of a woman on trial for conspiring with the two doctors who attended her husband in his last illness to destroy his will. It was Seattle's most sensational trial, what with old Mr. Yesler so prominent in town, pioneer and one-time mayor, owner of the big old house on Third Avenue, who'd married after his first wife's death a woman nobody knew, much younger than he and to whom, after his sudden and unexplained death, he had left all his money and property.

It had been clear to Annie's direct, uncomplicated mind from the first that the quiet, pleasant-faced woman in trailing black widow's weeds, attended always by her frail old mother who, folks told, once took in washing, couldn't have done what they said she had. She just didn't look that mean. She thought the judge felt the same, too, from the nice, courteous way he spoke to her, calling her "ma'am" and snapping at the district attorney when he got too smart and made her cry with his silly questions.

"Why don't they let her go, Jim?" she whispered when Mrs. Yesler's cook got down from the witness chair and the lawyers began arguing with each other over some point of procedure. "Anybody can tell she didn't do it."

"I don't know why they brought her to trial, Annie, except that the bigwigs in town were annoyed at Yesler for marrying her in the first place and now they're sore because he left her all his money," said Jim, jotting down some notes on his yellow pad. "A young woman like that deserves all she can get for putting up with an old codger his age. All the servants testified that Mrs. Yesler waited on him hand and foot and made his last years mighty pleasant. And Dr. Van Buren and Dr. Jordan are too decent to be mixed up in anything crooked. They don't need to be, with the money they're making. The way the district attorney talks, you'd think Minnie Yesler had something to do with his death, too. The fact of the matter is that Mrs. Yesler wasn't born on the right side of the tracks, but she's always kept her place and worked hard for what she's got—some folks can't stand that in others."

The lawyers were talking to the judge now, and finally he banged on his desk with the gavel. "Judge Deming is going to adjourn court for today till the lawyers stop quibbling over technicalities," whispered Jim.

"Is that Judge Deming?" hissed Annie so loud that the bailiff looked at her.

"Sure. You've been here every day, monkey. Didn't you know the judge's name? You'll never be a good reporter at that rate." Jim grinned, stuffing his pad into his side pocket and putting his pencil behind his ear.

Annie stared at the judge with quickened interest. He was tall and angular and his nose was like a hawk's beak. He had a habit of taking off his nose glasses and pointing at people with them when he was angry. He didn't look very much like Hugh, the handsome young man who'd driven her home in his buggy, but there *was* something, now she thought about it. Yes, his *voice*—he had the same soft, low drawl that never got very loud even when he scolded the lawyers.

"I know his son," said Annie proudly. "He doesn't look much like him, but they talk the same. I like to hear them talk."

Jim laughed. "It's that old Virginia drawl, honey. It gets all the women. Where on earth did you meet Judge Deming's son? Don't tell me he's one of your ma's patrons."

Annie shook her head. "Oh, I saw him down on the docks. He likes to watch the boats too. He gave me a ride home in his carriage. He's going to the university, he said."

"So I hear. It seems the old man had quite a time getting him to leave the University of Virginia and come out here to the sticks. His brother was talking about it the other day. Seems there was a Southern belle down on the ole plantation he hadn't the heart to leave. But Hughie's doing all right for himself among the barbarians, I understand." Jim laughed his short, wry laugh and got up. "Come on, kiddy. The show's over for today. You better get home before your ma starts looking for you with a hairbrush."

Annie dawdled on the way home, watching the construction crews working on a new department store on Second Avenue. The business district was beginning to move up from the waterfront and First Avenue. All of the better shops and office buildings would soon be farther uptown.

By the time she reached the Central School it was four o'clock and the boys and girls were pouring out onto the playground. She saw Joe Baker and his gang of roughnecks chasing a smaller boy in a Lord Fauntleroy suit and a big straw hat. The boy was an awful sissy and she enjoyed the sight of the straw hat tossed into a mud puddle. But when Joe got him down and began drubbing him with his fists, a tall boy from high school grabbed Joe by the seat of the britches and lifted him off his victim. It was Rolfe Linden, the banker's son, from the First Hill.

"Pick on someone your own size," said Rolfe sternly, "and don't gang up on little kids."

Joe and his cohorts scampered off, yelling defiance and derision, and the tall boy helped up the bedraggled figure, handed him his hat, and told him to run home and ask his mother to buy him a pair of knickers and a jersey. "It's not you they're after, kid. It's those sissy clothes your mother makes you wear."

"Where've *you* been, Annie Jordan?" cried Bessie Thomas,

the girl who sat behind Annie in school. "Miss Seton was asking if you was sick."

"I been to the trial," said Annie snippily, walking along with Bessie. She saw her sister Mae standing on the schoolhouse steps, swinging her books by their strap. She seemed to be waiting for someone. "You coming home now, Mae?" called Annie.

Mae glanced at her, flushed oddly, and shook her head. "Not right now, Annie. I—I've got to stop at the library for a reference book. Tell Ma I'll be home in time to start supper."

"I bet I know who she's waitin' for," whispered Bessie, giggling. "Rolfe Linden. He's her fella."

"How do you know?" cried Annie, looking back over her shoulder at her sister's tall, slender figure on the schoolhouse steps. Mae was pretty in a pale, delicate way, with her soft brown eyes and light, wavy hair. She was eighteen and a senior, but she'd never had a fella. At least, not that *I* know, thought Annie, but then she didn't know very much about Mae, after all. Mae didn't talk much to her. She lived in a world of her own and she seemed to have little connection with the world of the waterfront, the saloon, Annie, or Mrs. Jordan.

"He walked her home from choir practice at the Methodist church a couple of times," replied Bessie knowingly. "My sister saw them."

"We stayed at his house the night of the fire after ours burned down," said Annie, remembering the plush-curtained dining room, the thin white bouillon cups, the nice-smelling sheets. She remembered, too, Rolfe Linden and Mae, hand in hand, going down the hill. He must have liked her even then, she thought.

"There he is now." Bessie nudged her. "See, he's talkin' to Mae. Now he's takin' her books. Ain't he handsome?"

Annie looked back again. Rolfe was standing beside Mae, looking down at her, saying something very earnestly. Mae was smiling at him, her face more alive than Annie had ever seen it. The boy had dark hair and eyes and a nice, shy smile.

"Pooh!" scoffed Annie, "he's not so handsome. I know a boy who's a lot handsomer."

But she managed to be hanging around in front of the rooming house when Mae came down on the other side of the street with Rolfe Linden. At the corner before they reached the saloon Mae stopped, said something to the boy, and he gave her back her books. Mae hurried on across the street, not looking back, but the boy stood watching her for a moment, his face serious, then he turned and walked away.

Mae's face was flushed and her eyes softer than ever when she came up the steps. She hardly seemed to see Annie at all and would have gone right in without speaking to her. But Annie said, "Is Rolfe Linden your fella, Mae?"

Mae stopped and gave Annie a swift, surprised look. "Of course not," she said quickly, but the color deepened in her delicate cheeks.

"Bessie Thomas said he was," insisted Annie. "She said he walked you home from choir practice."

"Well, what if he did? That doesn't make him my fella," murmured Mae in a low tone as if she were afraid someone, maybe Rolfe himself, already halfway up the block, might hear.

"He's not so handsome," said Annie provocatively.

"He is, too," cried Mae with sudden vigor. "He's wonderful-looking and, what's more, he's *very* nice." She started to go into the house, but Annie gave her a parting thrust.

"If he's so nice, why doesn't he bring you all the way home instead of leaving you on the corner?"

Mae turned, her hand on the door knob, and her face went white. For a moment Annie thought she was going to hit her. But she only said in an odd, proud voice, "He would if I'd let him. But I don't want him to. It's bad enough to have to live over a saloon without having a nice boy like Rolfe Linden see it."

"But, Mae, doesn't he *know* you live here?" Annie was sorry she'd brought it up at all, Mae looked so miserable.

"Yes—I suppose he does." Mae's voice had a note of quiet despair in it that pierced Annie's heart. For the first time her sister seemed to have come out of her dream, to be a part of the life around her, to feel pain and bewilderment. Annie suddenly knew that Mae was helpless, that she couldn't fight back at life, the waterfront, the world, as she herself could. Mae's only safety lay in her dream, whatever it was—and Annie was beginning to see that Rolfe Linden was part of it. She scrambled to her feet and threw her arms impulsively around her sister.

"Oh, Mae, don't feel bad. It doesn't matter. He'll like you

just the same, don't you see?" she cried, tears stinging her throat. For a moment Mae returned the pressure of Annie's arms and they stood there, half weeping together over the bitterness of their fate, but Mae's tears fell softly, with resignation and despair, while Annie's grief was fierce, violent, the salt of anger. They were almost the same height, Annie was shooting up so fast, but Mae seemed much taller because of her willowy slenderness, while Annie's adolescent body had a sturdiness, a promise of depth in bosom and breadth in shoulder.

The door opened suddenly and the girls jumped apart, embarrassed at their sudden unwonted outburst of affection. One of the roomers came out, glancing curiously at them. "Your ma's been lookin' for you, Annie," he said. His small watery eyes slid over Annie's face and budding figure, then Mae's. He seemed to be sizing them up. Then he grinned, put out a calloused hand, and pinched Annie's cheek. "By golly, you're gettin' to be a big girl, ain'tcha?" he chuckled.

Annie shook off his hand, made a face at him, and ducked under his arm into the hall, slamming the door behind her. Mae had already slipped inside and was running up the stairs.

"Annie! You—Annie!" bawled her mother from the kitchen. "Come out here. I got somethin' to say to you."

Annie swung the kitchen door open and her mother looked up from the kitchen table where she was adding up her accounts. "You weren't at school today, young lady. You played hooky."

"Who told you?"

"Never mind that. Where were you? What kind of mischief you been into? If you were over to the Variety Theater, hangin' around them no-good girls again——"

"I wasn't. I went to the trial with Jim Petley. I've been nearly every day," said Annie proudly. She never lied and her mother knew it. She'd rather take a licking any day than wriggle out of something by lying.

"If you got so much time to go to trials and such, maybe you better quit school and work for me all day," said her mother sarcastically.

"I won't go again, Ma. But you can't make me quit school."

"Oh, I can't, can't I?"

Annie met her mother's sharp gaze steadily. "No. It's the law. I got to go to school or they'll put you in jail."

"We'll see about that." Her mother frowned, but Annie knew she was only bluffing. The law was one thing she'd never tamper with. "You go change your duds and make up the beds in the back room. I got two new roomers comin' tonight."

That night Annie lay awake, thinking about Rolfe Linden and Mae. It was just too bad Mae lived in a waterfront rooming house with no nice parlor to entertain her fella in. But he must like her a lot to walk home with her even if he did leave her on the corner. And he *was* good-looking, not in the same way that Judge Deming's son was, but in a different, shy, dark way. His face had lighted up wonderfully when he smiled at Mae. Annie sighed, wondering if ever a nice boy like Rolfe would smile at her that way. She glanced over at Mae's bed. Was she asleep or was she awake thinking about Rolfe too?

"Mae . . ."

A sigh, the mound under the covers stirred. "What?" Mae's voice sounded choked, as if she'd been crying.

"Rolfe Linden's nice, I think," whispered Annie, and then when Mae didn't answer, "And he's awfully handsome. I didn't mean it when I said he wasn't."

"It doesn't matter." Mae turned toward the wall and Annie was certain now that she was crying. She must like him an *awful lot,* thought Annie, and she felt very sad. She wished there was something she could say to Mae to make her feel better, to let her know she understood. She wished she could tell her that someday they'd both leave the waterfront, live in a fine house, drink soup out of their own thin white china cups. But Mae would think she was crazy. It was the first time Annie had ever wanted to reach her sister, to get to know her as a person, and she knew almost without trying that there was no use. Mae was shut up in her secret life, Annie in hers. There was no bridge between the two. Annie felt bad about it, lying wakeful in the dark, but she didn't know it would always be that way with everyone she wanted to reach out to. She thought it was just because she and Mae were different and she was sorry about it.

Rolfe Linden walked Mae home from school every night and

he took her home from choir practice too. Annie went once to the Methodist church to hear Mae sing in the choir. Mae had a sweet, high young voice and Annie was proud when she sang her solo, "O for the Wings of a Dove." The wings of a dove, thought Annie, thinking yes, Mae was a dove, gentle, soft, with gray wings. But I'd rather have the wings of a gull, strong white wings, crimson in the sunset, wings to carry me up into the clear blue air and over the sea.

Annie didn't go to the Methodist church again because it didn't seem like church. No altar, no cross, no candles, no incense, no images, no priest in vestments, no kneeling to pray. Just a dull, thin-faced man with a straggly beard, in a shiny black suit preaching on and on and people sitting straight-backed and sober-faced to hear him, or bending their heads stiffly for the long, lugubrious prayers. Only Mae's voice singing about the dove seemed like church. Annie thought God would hardly bother much about a service so drab, so lacking in beauty and intensity. She didn't listen to the sermon, but she sat where she could see Rolfe Linden's profile and she stared at it all during the service. There was something about his face that stabbed her heart. It looked so very young and shy and *good*. The way his dark hair grew down his neck was nice too. When the service was over and the people were leaving church he saw her and smiled at her and her heart stumbled. She wondered if he knew she was Mae's sister, or if he'd smiled at her for *herself*.

Now Mae was more lost in her dream than ever, except that there seemed to be an edge of pain, a sorrowful cloud in the dream that made her sigh and the corners of her mouth turn down appealingly.

"What in tarnation are *you* mooning about, Mae Jordan?" her mother scolded one morning as they sat in the kitchen at breakfast. She got up and brought the big blue granite coffee-pot to the table and poured the dark, bitter liquid into three thick white cups. Annie hated those cups; the thick edges were hard to drink from, the china was heavy as stone. How good coffee would taste from thin china!

Mae glanced at her mother unseeingly, her brown eyes wide and clear.

"Drink your coffee and finish your wheat cakes and get along to school."

"I've had all I want, Ma," murmured Mae, wiping her lips with her handkerchief. Kitty Jordan never bothered with such truck as napkins.

"If it's that Linden boy you're lookin' so soft about, my girl, you might as well forget him. First thing you know his ma'll find out he's been walkin' out with a Jordan and that'll be the end of it," said Mrs. Jordan with her sharp, bitter laugh.

Mae's slender face flushed painfully and she didn't know where to look. Annie thought she was like a dove now for sure, a poor little dove caught by the hawk, fluttering helplessly. Hot anger at her mother swelled big in her heart.

"That was a mean thing to say, Ma!" she cried, her blue eyes snapping. "You got no right to say things like that to Mae."

"Oh, I haven't, hey? I'll teach you what right I got to talk to my kids." Mrs. Jordan fetched her a sharp box on the side of the head and Annie jerked away, biting her lips to keep from crying out.

"I don't care!" she yelled, pushing her chair away from the table with a clatter. "Mae's got a right to like him if she wants to. And *he* likes her too. And I bet his ma can't make him stop, either."

She ran out of the room, her wild red mane flying, the color hot and high on her cheeks. Ma was a mean old thing. She seemed to like to make people feel bad. She ought to let Mae alone; Mae couldn't fight back, never even sassed her like Annie. It was cruel to spoil Mae's dream—to say things about Rolfe. Rolfe wasn't the kind of boy who'd stop liking a girl because his folks told him to. Rolfe was—well, *special*. There was his smile, the quiet nice way he had, his deep slow voice—Rolfe was *good*. Annie didn't understand what she meant by that or how she knew it, but it was the only word she had to express the thing about Rolfe that had stabbed her heart when she saw him in church that time. As she marched indignantly off to school she wasn't sure which made her maddest, her mother's picking on Mae or saying mean things about Rolfe.

That night after they were in bed Mae whispered, "Annie?"
"Uh-huh."
"Thanks for sticking up for me to Ma this morning."

"That's all right, Mae. I knew you wouldn't. She was awful mean."

"Uh-huh—but I guess she's right, Annie."

"No such thing."

"I got no business thinking about Rolfe Linden." She was talking in a low, dreamy voice, more to herself than to Annie. "He ought not to be walking home with me either."

"Oh hell, Mae, don't be a sissy. You're as good as he is—it don't matter about Ma or the saloon. You got a right to like anybody you please."

"Annie, don't swear." Mae sighed. "You see—that's what living down here does to you. Girls your age on the First Hill don't say 'hell.' "

"I didn't mean to," said Annie quickly, chagrined. "It just slipped out."

"Annie, do you know what I'd like to be?"

"What, Mae?" This was exciting, having Mae talk to her like this, letting her in on what she thought and dreamed about. Annie held her breath, hoping it would go on. It was thrilling, finding out what people were really like.

"I'd like to teach in a mission school or in the Philippines."

"Honest?" Annie was disappointed. What a thing to want! Gee, Mae was sweet and you wanted to be good to her, but she *was* spineless. What kind of a dream was that—being a teacher, and a missionary, at that?

"Yes. There was a missionary from China who spoke at the Methodist church last Sunday. She's a teacher and she says they need people for the field. Think how wonderful that would be —to go to heathen lands and teach them about Jesus!"

Annie felt uncomfortable. She couldn't have spoken that name so easily. The nuns at the parochial school where they went before Pop died had called Him Our Lord. That was better, more respectful somehow. To Annie, He wasn't someone you could talk about to other people so glibly. He was the burning red heart of the sanctuary lamp, He was the golden glitter of the altar, He was the mysterious, sweet, choking cloud of incense rising from the thurible. He was the compassionate Love that you prayed to when you were scared or had been bad or ill used. He was the hand upraised in the sign of the Cross.

"But what about Rolfe?" she asked after the long silence.

"Rolfe?" Mae sighed. "I would give him up, of course." Her voice sounded noble and exalted, but Annie snorted.

"Well, *I* wouldn't, by heck. I'd take him sooner than a lot of heathen, any day," she cried.

Mae went about looking exalted and pale for several days after she'd heard the missionary and she walked home from choir practice alone that week. Annie guessed she must have started giving up Rolfe already and she felt uneasy. For Mae, Rolfe was the way out of the waterfront, Annie had decided, and she had already made up a beautiful romantic story about Rolfe taking her sister away to live in a fine house on the First Hill where she could come to visit them.

Then one day Mae came home from school with her cheeks flushed and her eyes bright. "Annie!" she breathed in the new confidential tone she used to her since their talks in bed. "Rolfe's asked me to the school dance!"

"I thought you'd given him up for the heathen," said Annie dryly.

"He says he won't let me," smiled Mae dreamily. "Anyway, I can't be a missionary *yet*, not till I finish high school and go to normal."

"Are you going to the dance?" A little core of—not exactly envy, but longing, budded in Annie's heart. How thrilling it would be to be eighteen and going to a dance with Rolfe Linden.

"I can't. I haven't anything to wear." Mae sighed and her face settled into its usual sweet resignation.

"Oh, you ninny!" cried Annie. "Make Ma buy you a dress."

Mae shook her head. "She won't, I'm sure. She'd just laugh at me for wanting to go with Rolfe."

Annie ran to her dresser drawer, took out a shiny red purse that one of the Variety girls had given her. It was fat with coins. "Here," she said, spilling its contents on Mae's bed. "There's over five dollars there. I saved it from the money the men gave me for dancing at the saloon. You take it and buy a dress. A pink one with ruffles. I saw one in the window of the Boston Dry Goods Store."

Mae stared at the coins, shook her head. "Oh, I couldn't take that money, Annie." Annie knew what she meant. She hated it that Annie danced for the men. She'd even spoken to her mother about it. She thought Annie was getting too old and that it wasn't proper.

"All right, don't," Annie snapped crossly. She'd been saving it to buy a tartan cape she wanted and it was a snub to have Mae refuse her generous impulse.

Mae got up and began to take off her clothes and Annie scooped up the coins and stuffed them back into the purse. But she knew Mae was sorry she'd refused the money and that she didn't know how to get around to saying she'd take it. So the next day after school Annie marched down to the Boston Dry Goods Store and bought the pink dress herself. She spread it out on Mae's bed so that she'd see it first thing when she came in. But she stayed downstairs, helping her mother, till Mae had had a chance to see it.

When Mae came down after changing her school dress for a gingham pinafore her face was pink and her eyes shining, but she didn't say a word to Annie, who carefully avoided her covert glances. After supper Mae insisted upon doing the dishes, though her mother told Annie to do them and let Mae study for her exams. It was curious the way Kitty Jordan did with the two girls—sparing Mae as much of the work as she could and yet never missing an opportunity to poke fun at her or deflate her. With Annie she seemed to know that nothing she could say would touch her, so she piled the work on her until Annie would suddenly rebel and walk out, leaving it for her to do. So when Mae did the dishes Mrs. Jordan made Annie empty the garbage pails, which she did with a great clatter.

Once they were through and upstairs in their room with the door shut, Mae turned to Annie impulsively and threw her arms around her.

"Oh, Annie! I saw the dress!"

"Do you like it?"

"It's simply gorgeous! Oh, Annie!" She went to the bed and stood looking down at it, touching the soft pink folds reverently. "But you shouldn't have done it—you spent all your money on it, didn't you?"

"It was my money. And you've *got* to go to the dance!" cried Annie fiercely. Since she wasn't going, then Mae had to— she'd at least get a thrill out of her sister's happiness. "Try it on."

Miraculously the dress fitted, was most becoming, brought

out all the lights in Mae's hair, the glow to her cheeks. Annie loved pink and it was a color she couldn't wear with her flaming hair.

The night of the dance Annie was upstairs helping Mae get ready when her mother opened the door and came in. Just as Mae had predicted, she'd laughed at the idea of her going with a Linden, and had told Annie she was a fool to spend all her money on a dress Mae'd never get much wear out of. She stood at the door now, with her hands on her hips, looking at Mae.

"Ma," cried Annie eagerly, "don't she look grand?"

"Yes. She does," said Mrs. Jordan surprisingly. And she sighed, and for once Annie saw the hard, weather-beaten face soften a trifle. "She looks like a lady."

"Oh, Ma," breathed Mae shyly, her eyes bright and glowing.

Mrs. Jordan turned in sudden fury on Annie, as if betrayed by her eagerness into expressing too much sentiment. "Annie, get into your dancing dress and shoes. The men want you to dance for them."

"But, Ma—I'm helping Mae dress," protested Annie. She wanted to see her sister leave in all her glory. More than that, she wanted to see Rolfe Linden when he came for her. This night, at last, Mae had said he could come to the rooming house to call for her.

"I'll look after the grand duchess here," snapped her mother. "You go down and dance for the customers."

Annie scowled. "Can't I wait till Mae goes?"

"Why're you so interested in your sister all of a sudden?" asked Mrs. Jordan dryly.

"Someone's got to be here to let Rolfe in," said Mae, giving Annie a pleading glance.

"I'll let your young man in myself." Mrs. Jordan laughed, jerked her head toward the door. "Get your duds changed, Annie, and do like I told you. There's a friend of mine downstairs wants to see you."

Annie knew there was no use arguing with her mother where her business was concerned, but she took her time about changing her clothes. Still Rolfe hadn't come by the time she was ready to go down.

"Quit your dawdling now and get," snapped her mother, and Annie gave Mae a hopeless look, murmured, "Have a good time at the dance, Mae," and went downstairs, through the side door that connected the rooming house with the saloon.

Maizie was at the piano playing a sentimental song and some men were grouped about her, their arms across each others' shoulders, trying to sing it. Maizie didn't look well. The proud, queenly look that Annie had admired was gone and she was very thin. Her shoulder blades in the low-cut, sequin-covered evening gown were sharp and bony. Her face was haggard and would have been pale except for the spots of rouge on her cheekbones, but she laughed and sang with the men and when she turned to call to Annie her eyes were very bright and glittering. Annie hadn't seen very much of her for a long time, since she wasn't allowed to go to her room after Lorna was murdered. They never had found out who killed her, but all of the Variety girls had been under suspicion for months, dragged down to the police station every now and then for questioning. It was after that that Maizie had begun to lose her looks and her quiet serenity.

"Here's Annie, boys!" she cried, and swung into "The Band Played On." The men all turned to look at Annie and clap and shout at her to get up on the table and dance. A big man with a beard whom she'd never seen before helped her onto the table. For a moment she stood there, looking pleadingly at Maizie. For the first time she felt self-conscious and awkward. She didn't want to dance for the half-drunk, raucous men. She felt foolish in her gauzy short dress and beribboned dancing slippers. She wished she were dressed in a long pink frock, going to a nice high school dance with Rolfe Linden.

But the men kept shouting and clapping their hands and Maizie kept thumping at the piano, and she began to dance. The music went faster and faster, the men whistled and stamped, and she whirled round and round, her hair coming loose and tumbling about her shoulders.

Suddenly there was someone standing by the table, reaching up his hand. Above the noise she heard a voice say, "Annie! Annie, stop it. Get down from that table." Rolfe Linden was standing there, all dressed up in his best dark serge suit, with his hair neatly plastered down and his face white and shocked.

Annie stopped dancing and looked at him. His dark, deep-set eyes blazed into hers. He looked as if someone had slapped him. She stared at him for a moment, while the men shouted for her to go on and then she leaned down, took his hand, and he pulled her down beside him. He didn't say a word and neither did she, but he took her hand and led her through the suddenly silent crowd of men and through the side door to the hall of the rooming house. Then he caught her roughly by the shoulders and gave her another long, blazing look.

"Don't ever do that again, Annie," he said sternly.

"I didn't want to do it tonight," she whispered, "but Ma made me."

"Don't ever do it again," he repeated.

She shook her head and suddenly burst into tears. He put his arm around her and she laid her bright head on his breast and sobbed. It was the first time she had cried since she was a very little girl. It was wonderful and terrible to be crying in Rolfe Linden's arms.

"Someday I'm going to marry your sister, Annie," he whispered tensely, "and I'll take her away from this place and I'll take you too. I'll give you a good home." He patted her shoulder and she dried her eyes and took deep gulps of breath, unable to say a word. And then Mae was coming down the stairs, shy and lovely in the pink dress with a shawl about her shoulders, and Annie ran past her and up the stairs to their room and slammed the door.

She tore off the fluffy dancing dress, ripping it, and when she saw that it was ripped she tore it into pieces. Then she threw herself on her bed and began to weep again. When she could cry no more she lay face down on the bed, hearing the piano tinkling downstairs and saying over and over, "Rolfe Linden is good, good, good. Even if he does marry Mae, I'll love him. I'll love him till I die."

When her mother came up to storm at her, she was in bed and she turned her face to the window and pretended to be asleep. There were tearstains on her face and her mother stood looking at her and the torn dress a long time, then she took the lamp and went away.

Chapter IV

Annie was sitting on a pile, feeding the gulls, when the *Portland* steamed into the harbor. It was early in the summer of 1897, and in a few weeks she'd be fifteen. She hadn't any business being there, because Mae was sick in bed with a bad cough and the rooming house was full. She'd catch it when she got home. Her mother would give her a clip across the head and yell at her and she'd have to get supper and take a tray up to Mae. But she didn't care. She did what she wanted to, knowing perfectly well that punishment was inevitable, but willing to take it and grit her teeth. It was the only way she knew how to live. She *had* to do the things she liked to do and the fact that she'd suffer for it made no difference. She lived in the moment completely. She gave herself up to its savor and enjoyment and ignored the retribution that was to follow.

The gulls circled over her head, screaming, and she broke up bits of bread and tossed them into the oily green water. The sun had been out off and on all day and the air was mild. Now it had started to drizzle, but she didn't mind that. She lifted her face and let it fall on her eyes and lips, smiling at its coolness.

Because of the rain and the mist that covered the bay, she didn't see the steamer until it suddenly parted the gray veil and came plowing through, the white foam curling about its dirty prow. But she had heard it whistling inquiringly all the way in, the long, deep-throated blast that asked its way, that warned the fishing boats to scurry, that proudly announced its coming. She'd listened to it with parted lips and that lift of the heart that a boat whistle always gave her.

Now the harbormaster and some stevedores came out of the waiting room at the end of the dock. The harbormaster wore a shiny blue serge uniform and a visored cap and he had a sheaf of papers in his hand and a big silver watch that opened when he pressed the back and glanced at it. He nodded at one of the stevedores, a husky in a black jersey and brown corduroy pants. "She's just twenty minutes late. Not bad with the mist all up the sound today."

"What's she bringing in this time?" the stevedore asked, yawning broadly and snapping a match with a scarred thumb to light his pipe.

"Mostly passengers, I guess. Maybe some furs and walrus ivory and a little gold."

The steamer was ringing its bell now, clang, clang, clang, and edging up to the pier. The decks were crowded with passengers and Annie stared at their dark, bearded faces in fascination. They were all of them men, except for one or two pale-looking women in fedora hats and feather boas, who looked like the wives of government officials or schoolteachers.

"Hello!" shouted the harbormaster. "What's new in Alaska?"

From a dozen throats came the shout, "Gold!"

A man ran to the side and leaned over the rail, waving a small leather bag. "I've made my stake! Got ten thousand dollars in dust right here."

"Christ!" cried the stevedore. "Must be a new strike up there."

The man with the bag of gold dust laughed and spat over the side into the dark water. "You're damn tootin' there's been a new strike, bud. They're diggin' it out and pannin' it out by the bucketfuls. Nuggets as big as walnuts. It's the biggest strike since '49. We're all gonna be rich."

"By God!" cried the stevedore. "I should grow bunions workin' for two bucks a day. If it's a sure 'nuff strike I'm headin' north on the next boat. Me and the missus could use a bagful o' them nuggets."

As soon as the gangplank was down the men began to pour off the boat, shouting and laughing, jostling each other, tossing their luggage onto the pier. By the time the passengers were off there was a crowd gathered, miraculously growing by twos and threes until Annie had to push her way through. The onlookers buttonholed the travelers, pumping them about the gold strike, and the travelers each had a tale to tell. Gold in the Yukon, gold in the mountains—Dawson City, White Horse River, Chilkoot Pass. The words rang in Annie's ears. She went from group to group, listening eagerly.

In the crowd she saw Jim Petley, his thin face alive with excitement, grabbing men by the lapels, asking questions, scribbling in his notebook. Annie edged up to him to listen.

"How much gold did she bring in? Where's the strike located? Who made the first strike? Is it really big?" Jim fired questions right and left.

The miners were almost incoherent in their eagerness to tell the tale. One man held up a bag of gold dust and when Jim asked him how much it was worth he threw it up in the air and caught it again, laughing crazily. "Ten thousand dollars, the gov'ment assayer at Dawson said," he cried, "and there's more where that came from, son. Soon as I buy me some new boots and supplies I'm goin' back to get my share."

"When's the next boat for Alaska?" one of the bystanders asked excitedly.

"The *Portland's* makin' the return trip next week," said the miner with the ten-thousand-dollar bag of dust. "An' Big Joe Slattery's gonna be on her, too, by God!"

Jim Petley scribbled madly, went from man to man, and Annie tagged along after him. Finally when he slipped his notebook into his pocket and started through the crowd, she tugged at his sleeve. "Jim," she cried, her eyes shining, "is it a scoop?"

He looked down at her and laughed. "Is it a scoop, kiddy! It's the biggest scoop in years and the *Argus* will be the first to tell it. Why, sweetheart, when this news goes out over the wires the whole country will be gold-crazy. This is the biggest strike since '49. And Seattle's got it in her lap. Seattle's the gateway to Alaska. They'll come pouring in here from all over. We'll have the boom of our life. If this doesn't put us on the map, I don't know what will!" He laughed again. "Run home and tell your ma to get ready for the deluge. She's in for her own private gold rush, you tell her."

He hurried away, his face set with intensity, and Annie, caught up in the excitement, ran all the way home. Oh, what a wonderful life, where something exciting was always happening under your nose! What a wonderful city, where boats came in laden with treasure and tales of marvels!

She burst into the kitchen where her mother was yelling at the poor old drab from the streets who cleaned the pots and helped with the meals. "The *Portland's* in," Annie shrieked, the excitement that had been mounting in her all the way home exploding the moment she opened her mouth. "There's been a gold strike in the Yukon. I saw a man with a little bit of a bag of gold dust worth ten thousand dollars. I heard a man say his brother was shot in the back and robbed of his nuggets."

"Gold?" cried her mother, forgetting the tirade she'd been about to loose on her for staying away when she was needed. "On the Alaska boat?" She laughed and her eyes glinted. "You'll have to help in the saloon tonight, Annie. I know miners—soon as they hit town with a poke of gold they can't rest till it's spent. They'll have worked up a powerful thirst grubbing for nuggets and they'll be heading for Kit Jordan's saloon to satisfy it."

Her mother was right. Every night the Nugget was jammed with miners, spending their money as fast as possible, as if eager to get rid of it, so they could go back to the gold fields and risk their lives getting more. The piano tinkled, drunken voices sang, shouted, cursed all night long. Sometimes there would be the sound of broken glass, of chairs being overturned, women screaming. Annie, upstairs in bed, listened to it and felt both repelled and exhilarated. It was coarse, brutal, terrible, but it was lusty, it was life. Mae lay listening, too, and coughing, coughing, coughing.

Their mother had less time for them than ever. Now and then she'd run up to see how Mae felt, would give her a dose of bitter medicine that made her choke and did nothing for her cough. She had two bartenders now and all she did was to move through the saloon, seeing that the waiters refilled glasses and that drinks were paid for on the spot and that troublemakers were quickly ejected.

Annie stayed out of the saloon, refusing to dance when her mother suggested it. She worked in the kitchen washing glasses and cutting bologna and cheese for the free lunch, but one night her mother took away her apron, gave her a little push, and said, "If you won't dance, go out and sing a song. They're yelling for entertainment. Maizie's there. She'll play for you."

Annie held back, gave her mother a sharp, penetrating look. "Not unless you promise to give me half of everything the men throw me."

Kit Jordan met her daughter's steady, relentless gaze and laughed harshly. "Half it is, my girl. Maybe someday you'll be as good a businesswoman as your mother."

Annie dried her hands on the roller towel, tucked back loose strands of her flying hair, pushed up the sleeves of her white blouse so that her round, milky arms showed, and went boldly out into the noisy saloon. There wasn't an empty space at the bar and all the little round tables were crowded. Maizie, in a red satin dress that was so low you could see her breasts, was at the piano, with men clustered so thick around her that Annie could hardly see her. But she tapped one of the miners on the shoulder, a thickset, heavy-faced fellow with a scrubby beard, and with a laugh and a low bow he made room for her.

Annie caught Maizie's eye. Maizie smiled at her, but her eyes sharpened and hardened at the sight of the fifteen-year-old girl with the soft, sweet curves, white skin, full red lips, and hair like a flame. Once she'd been a funny little kid who made the Variety queen feel sad and sentimental over her lost innocence, but now she was turning into a beauty—and in every pretty woman Maizie saw a threat to her frail hold on security.

"Play 'A Bird in a Gilded Cage,' Maizie," said Annie.

"Where you been for so long, honey?" drawled Maizie in a honeyed voice. "You ain't been to the theater in ages."

"Ma won't let me," said Annie. She hated to look at Maizie now. She used to be so beautiful, like a queen, and gentle and sweet. But now she was scrawny and the rouge made her eyes glitter and her voice had a brittle quality to it.

"Well, maybe you're too old, at that." Maizie laughed and it was a bitter sound. "You're growing up, honey. Maybe your ma's afraid you'll get ideas, huh?"

Still laughing, she brought her hands down on the keys and began to play the chorus over once. The miners around the piano clapped enthusiastically and when Maizie had finished the first chorus Annie began to sing.

Her voice wasn't sweet and birdlike as Mae's was, but she

kept on key and it had a low, husky, warm tone that seemed oddly mature for her soft young face and just budding body.

The noise in the saloon quieted down and by the time she'd finished the first verse the men were all looking at her, listening. She glanced disdainfully at them. Since Rolfe had pulled her down from the table and made her promise never to dance there again she had no pleasure in making a show of herself. The man who'd made way for her, the heavy-set miner with the scrubby red beard, stared at her with a strange, hungry expression on his face. She glanced quickly away from him and looked out over the heads of her audience.

After she'd finished the song there was a storm of applause and coins flew through the air. When there was a ring of them around her, she coolly stooped down, picked them up, and put them in her pocket. The heavy-set man retrieved a five-dollar gold piece and gave it to her, and as she reached for it his thick fingers tried to close over hers. But she jerked her hand away, without looking at him, rubbed the gold piece on her blouse, and stowed it away.

Her mother followed her upstairs after she'd given the men two more songs and had walked out, deaf to their shouts, claps, and stampings. She was tired and the smoke and smell of liquor had given her a headache. She wanted to go to bed and dream of Rolfe Linden, of whom she saw a lot, now that he and Mae were both graduated from high school, and Rolfe took Mae out in spite of his parents' disapproval. He and Mae were both twenty-one now and nobody could stop them from going together. Sometimes he stopped her on the street when she passed the bank where he worked for his father, running out when he saw her to talk about Mae. He was Mae's, all right, but he was Annie's in her heart.

"You did just fine," said her mother warmly, and held out her hand.

Annie shrugged. "I hated it. I won't do it again." She counted out half the money in her pocket and put it in her mother's palm. All but the gold piece. She'd be darned if the old miser was going to get that.

Her mother put the money in the little coin purse she kept tucked into the belt of her skirt and fastened securely by a pin. While Annie undressed and brushed her heavy, shining hair, her mother stood watching her with a speculative gaze. After Annie'd braided her hair she pulled off her dress and petticoat and stood in ferris waist and long muslin drawers. She felt her mother's eyes upon her and glanced up to meet her sharp, knowing gaze.

Slow color swept up the girl's throat and cheeks and she glanced away quickly. She'd never blushed before in her life but there was something in her mother's face that made her aware of her ripening bosom, her bare arms and throat.

"You're getting to be a big girl, Annie," said Mrs. Jordan with an odd smile. "You're more developed right now than Mae'll ever be."

The color burned in Annie's face and she grabbed her flannel nightgown and went into the closet to put it on, away from her mother's smile and whatever it was that lay back of the smile.

"No need to be ashamed, girl. You're going to have a fine figger, just like mine was at your age." Kit Jordan laughed. "You'll have the men crazy for you, too. Shouldn't wonder if they were already. Maybe you got a fella right now."

From the depths of the nightgown she was struggling into, Annie snorted. "Fat chance. I wouldn't look at any of the ones *I* can get."

"Oh, so you think you're too good for 'em, is that it?"

"Maybe." What business is it of yours, old woman? Do you think I'd tell *you* if I did have a fella? I wouldn't even tell you about the time I let Joe Baker kiss me in the vacant lot because I wanted to find out what it was like! I wouldn't even tell you about the time I had to kick one of your dirty old roomers in the shin because he got me in the back hall and put his hands on me. I'd rather die than let you know that I love Rolfe Linden, that I dream about him every night, and if Mae wasn't my sister, I'd make him notice me. I could, I know I could. I could take him away from Mae, but I won't, because she'd just sit by and let me and that would be like kicking a dog that follows you.

"A friend of mine heard you sing tonight," said her mother when Annie came out in her nightgown with her two thick red braids down her back. Her full breasts made her nightgown go up in the front and she hated it. "He wants to meet you."

"Who is he?" Annie's voice was cold. She would not look at her mother.

"Fred Carew. He came in on the *Portland* with a poke of dust. He's going back to the Yukon when she sails again. I knew him years ago out in Montana."

"Then he must be an old man," said Annie scornfully.

"Not so old," replied her mother in a low, odd voice. "He's about forty."

"Forty!" cried Annie, and laughed. "You better introduce him to Maizie or Mrs. Bellows in the kitchen. What does a man that old want to meet *me* for?"

"He likes your singing. He thinks you're pretty." Her mother's tone was wheedling. "He's rich, Annie. If he took it into his head, he might be very nice to you."

"Well, I don't want him to be nice to me. And I don't want to meet him," cried Annie disgustedly. She opened the window, blew out the lamp, and leaped into bed. "Good night," she murmured, turning toward the wall.

"I've asked him to supper tomorrow," said her mother in a flat voice, "you'll meet him then," and she went out, shutting the door quietly.

Mae was still sick in bed with bronchitis when Fred Carew came to supper. Annie reluctantly changed her dress and brushed her hair, but she was careful to put it into braids, pulled back from her forehead. Her mother took one look at her and sent her back upstairs to unbraid it, tie a blue ribbon at the back. She herself was resplendent in a purple dress with jet trimmings and they ate in the dining room, with quivery-chinned Mrs. Bellows to serve them, instead of in the kitchen, with Ma serving the food straight off the stove.

When Annie, sulky and withdrawn, came down at her mother's call, Kit Jordan and her guest were sitting in the parlor. It was the ugliest room Annie had ever seen, little and dark, with hideous red curtains, a red carpet that had a sour, musty smell, stiff oak furniture, a leather settee, a round marble-topped table with a spindly pale green fern that turned brown at the ends, a decorated shell her mother had got at Coney Island, and pictures all over the walls of her mother and father when they were young, pictures that had been saved from the fire in the old iron trunk.

She knew they were her mother and father because she'd been told they were, but the stiff, awkward-looking man in the pictures, holding a bowler hat, with his hair parted in the middle and plastered down over his forehead, staring straight ahead with round, startled eyes was a stranger. He wasn't Pop, whose cinnamon-colored hair was always tousled, whose blue eyes had such a merry twinkle.

The buxom, soft-mouthed woman with the fringe of dark curls and the tiny waist was certainly not the gaunt, hatchet-faced, gray-haired Ma of the heavy hand and the harsh voice that Annie had always known.

Now Ma sat on the settee, dressed up, with company manners, and chatted pleasantly with a thickset, squat man with a scrubby reddish beard who looked up and grinned at Annie as she came reluctantly into the room. She frowned when she saw him. He was the man who'd picked up the gold piece for her and tried to grab her hand.

"Annie," said her mother in the nicest voice she'd ever used to her, "meet Fred Carew. Fred, this is my girl, Annie."

Carew got to his feet and held out his hand to Annie, but she only glanced at him scornfully, mumbled, "Hello," and pretended not to see his hand.

Her mother gave her a sharp look. "Shake hands with Mr. Carew, Annie," she commanded.

Annie darted an angry glance at her, shrugged, and put out her hand just long enough for him to touch it, then pulled it quickly away. A shudder went through her at the feel of his hard, dry, calloused fingers and he seemed to sense it, for he flushed darkly.

"Not very sociable, is she, Kit?" he said with a dry laugh.

Her mother smiled a tight smile at him. "Oh, she's sorta shy with strangers, Fred." She was furious, Annie knew.

"Go get the whisky bottle out of the sideboard, Annie, and two glasses. You'll have a little drink before supper, eh, Fred?" She gave the man an arch look and he grinned.

"Don't mind if I do, Kit," he laughed.

Annie stalked out of the room, her legs stiff with anger. What was her mother up to? Why had she got all dressed up? Why was she being so arch and coy with this bearded, ugly miner? Did she think she could catch him for a husband? The thought of having Fred Carew for a stepfather made Annie sick. I'll run away if she marries him, Annie said to herself, unlocking the liquor cupboard in the sideboard and taking out the special bottle of Old Crow that her mother kept for herself. Horrid old man, with his dirty red beard and his little pig's eyes. I won't have him ordering me around or pawing me. Ugh! Ma can't really like him, but she said he'd struck it rich in the Yukon. So it's his money she's after. Ma'd do anything for money.

She put the whisky bottle and the two glasses on a tray. No, not *anything*—Ma wouldn't kill a man for his money or steal or do anything she could be put in jail for. But I'd rather steal a man's money than marry him to get it. She marched into the parlor with her lips set in disapproval. She'd made up her mind that the only way she could spoil her mother's plans was to be as disagreeable as possible to Fred Carew. He'd not want to take on a widow with a red-haired, bad-tempered brat, that was certain. Ma wasn't that attractive, though she'd fixed herself up. She looked nicer than Annie'd ever seen her.

Mrs. Jordan and her guest tossed off several ponies of Old Crow before Mrs. Bellows tottered to the door and said, "Supper's on, Miz Jordan." Annie had sat in stony silence, staring out the window, and refused to be drawn into the conversation, though Fred Carew asked her if she didn't want to hear about his experiences in the Yukon. She'd have listened eagerly if it had been anyone else. But she wouldn't give her mother that satisfaction.

Her mother's stony face was relaxed and flushed from the whisky when they rose to go in to supper. Fred Carew had just told a smutty story and, laughing at his own joke, he put an arm around her waist and gave her a squeeze. Then he turned, saw Annie standing by the window, waiting for them to go past her, and he slipped his other arm about her before she could dart out of his reach. She stiffened like a rod, but he pulled her roughly against him and gave her a quick, whisky-scented kiss that landed on her chin as she turned her face away. He laughed, squeezed her unyielding waist, and said, "You've got a mighty pretty gal here, Kit, but she needs softening up. Maybe if I bring her a gold nugget when I come back from Alaska next trip she'll be nicer to me, eh?"

As soon as supper was over Annie escaped upstairs, flung off her clothes, and got into bed. Mae was awake, her face hot with fever, but she insisted that she felt better. "I'm going to get up tomorrow," she said. "I'm tired of lying here in bed."

"Mae, I think Ma's got a notion to get married again," said Annie, leaning on her arm and staring over at her sister's bed where the moonlight lay in a pool on her white, pinched face.

"Honest? But who'd marry Ma?" cried Mae with a laugh. "She's so old and ugly now. Though once she was pretty, I guess. You can tell from her pictures."

"It's that Fred Carew she had to supper tonight," Annie snorted. "You should of seen her. She's all dressed up in that purple silk and she's got on the jet earrings and curled her hair. And oh, the silly way she looks at him and smiles."

"Is he nice, Annie?"

"He's awful! Got a moth-eaten reddish beard and watery little pig's eyes and he's short and squatty. Oh—he's just horrid. He tried to kiss me!"

"Annie! He didn't!" Mae gasped.

"Yes, he did, and Ma was mad because I jerked my head away." Annie scowled in the darkness. "If she thinks I'm going to stay around here and have that old fool for a step-pa, she's crazy."

"But what will you do?" Mae propped herself up on an elbow to stare at her sister, hunched up on her bed in the moonlight.

"I'll run away," announced Annie flatly.

Mae began to cough hard. Her thin shoulders shook and Annie got out of her bed and knelt beside her. When the paroxysm was over, she caught Annie's hand and squeezed it. "Don't leave me, Annie," she whispered. "I wouldn't know what to do without you."

Tears stung Annie's throat and she squeezed Mae's hand back. "All right. I won't leave you, Mae. But we'll go away together then. We won't stay here if Ma marries Fred Carew." Though Mae was six years older in years, Annie knew she depended on her.

In the morning while they were having breakfast Kit was more brusque than ever with Annie.

"You acted mighty snippy last night to Fred Carew, young lady."

"I didn't like him."

"You made no bones about it, either. I was ashamed of you."

I was ashamed of *you*, thought Annie, dressing up and acting like a silly schoolgirl over that old goat. But she said nothing, only lifted her chin and stared out the window.

"Remember this, my girl. I'm your ma and you're under age and as long as ye're under my roof ye'll do as I say and be nice to my friends."

Annie met her mother's gaze defiantly. There was a hard glitter in Kit's eyes and she gave Annie a long, searching look that made a faint, odd drum of fear beat inside her. What did Ma have up her sleeve? What was she trying to get across to her?

"Fred's going back to the Yukon on the *Portland* next week, but he'll be down this way again in the spring. He said to tell you he'd bring you a present. He said he hoped you'd treat him nicer next time."

The girl's deep eyes widened and darkened as her mother's steely gray gaze held them. For a long hostile moment they looked at each other, each trying to probe the other's thoughts. Then Annie suddenly pushed back her chair and flung out of the kitchen, an undefined suspicion making her heart cold. I ought to get away, run off somewhere. She's planning something, but I don't know what it is. If it weren't for Mae, I'd get out, get a job. But I can't leave Mae, not till Rolfe can marry her. Oh, Rolfe, if it was only me you loved and wanted to marry. I'd marry you today and live in a shanty with you!

The night before the *Portland* sailed for Alaska again, Rolfe Linden came to see Mae. She hadn't seen him since she'd been taken sick. Annie had a sneaking notion he'd come around and Ma had sent him away without telling Mae he'd been there. That'd be like Ma. In a way she was proud that one of her girls had attracted a First Hill boy, but she had another kind of pride too. "No stuck-up alderman's son's gonna come hanging around here," she'd say. Annie had the impulse to tell him herself about Mae's illness, but something had prevented her, some base hope that if he didn't see her for a while he might forget her.

But it was Mrs. Bellows who let him in this time. Ma was in the saloon, keeping an eagle eye on the cash register, and Annie was upstairs with Mae, rubbing her chest with camphor.

The old drab wheezed up the stairs and knocked on their bed-room door.

"There's a young gentleman downstairs to see Miss Mae," she gasped, holding a hand over the stich in her side.

"What's his name?" breathed Annie.

"Linden. Mr. Rolfe Linden."

"Go and see him, Annie," murmured Mae from her bed.

"Show Mr. Linden into the parlor," said Annie quickly. She ran to the mirror, patted her hair, bit her full lips to make them redder, wished she'd had on her prettiest dress, remembered that Rolfe was Mae's beau, and went slowly downstairs, her heart pounding heavily in her breast.

He was standing with his hat in his hand beside the marble-topped table with the potted fern. His face was flushed and eager and when he saw Annie he smiled. but some of the glow went out of his face.

"Hello," she said shyly.

"Hello, Annie," Rolfe said.

"Mae's sick, Rolfe." She went toward him, hardly knowing what she was doing, only knowing he was here, in the same room, and they were alone.

"I'm sorry, I'm sorry she's sick. Is she—very sick?" He looked worried and Annie didn't want him to look that way.

She laughed. "Oh no—just a bad cold. She'll be all right in a day or two. Could I—take her a message?"

Rolfe stared at her in a funny way, as if it were the first time he'd ever seen her. She had her hair up, the two thick braids in a coronet around her head, and the excitement of seeing him made her eyes very large and bright.

"Well, I'm going away tomorrow, Annie. I just—wanted to say good-by." He kept staring at her in that funny way. His face was pale and his eyes seemed very dark and solemn.

"Going away?" It was a cry, a lament, it came from her heart. "Oh, Rolfe . . ." She put out her hands and without thinking he moved toward her and took them. At the touch of his hands she trembled.

"Yes, Annie. To Alaska, the Yukon." Her hands gripped his tightly, her great violet eyes widened as they gazed into his. "Mr. Carlton grubstaked me. I'm going to look for gold." He pulled her toward him, not knowing why, knowing only that she stood gazing at him as if she could never stop and that her hands were strong and warm. "I want to strike it rich, Annie, so I can come back and marry Mae."

Her hands bit into his now and she swayed slightly. He had never seen hair so alive, nor skin so white, nor eyes so vital and alive.

"Oh, Rolfe!" she cried, bursting into tears, and suddenly she was in his arms and he was holding her warm, trembling body close to his. She pressed herself against him, she clasped him to her, she lifted her tear-stained face for his kiss. And as their lips met in the strange, unexpected, unplanned kiss, the door to the parlor opened and Mae, in her dressing gown, stood looking at them.

Annie sensed her presence before Rolfe did. Suddenly she went cold all over, tore herself from his arms, turned and looked at her sister's pale, thin, anguished face. Without a word she ran from the room, slamming the door behind her.

Mae never said a word about seeing Annie and Rolfe kissing and finally Annie decided it hadn't bothered her. When she found out Rolfe was going away, she probably thought he was just being nice and kissing her little sister good-by. Maybe that's all there'd been to it, too, Annie thought—for him. Maybe he hadn't meant another thing. But to Annie it was like having a dream come to life. It was the first time she'd ever kissed anyone out of love and longing, and her cheeks burned, her heart beat fast every time she thought about it.

No, the kiss hadn't upset Mae, but his going away had. She cried all that night, between coughing spells. "Why does he have to go? I don't want a lot of money. I'm willing for him to wait until he can win his folks over. He's got a job in the bank, he's been saving his money. In a few years he'll have enough for us to marry on," she sobbed to Annie, who lay in her own bed, her eyes dark with pride in Rolfe for what he was doing, for his wanting to be part of the great adventure.

"If I was a man, I'd go!" she cried. "Oh, Mae, don't you see? This is his big chance. He doesn't want to wait years for you. He doesn't want to have to grub away in the bank and save money and fuss with his folks. He wants to find gold in the Yukon and bring it back and lay it all at your feet!"

But Mae would not be comforted. It was not she who went

to the dock to see him off to the gold fields, but Annie. Even if she'd wanted to, Mae was too ill to go. And Annie—well, even if Rolfe Linden hadn't been sailing, nothing could have kept her away from the docks that misty summer morning.

The *Portland*, loaded to the gunwales with supplies for the North—boxes, bales, trunks, dog teams, and sleds—and crowded with men bound for the fabulous Golconda that was to make them all rich and from which half of them would not return, was scheduled to sail at seven in the morning, but it was nearly noon before she finally weighed anchor.

Men fought for places aboard, sailors shouted and cursed the gold-crazed landlubbers who got in their way, the crowds gathered black around the dock to see them off. Women wept because their men were leaving them or shouted encouragement and last-minute advice. The Variety girls were there, mingling their bright dresses and bright, painted faces with the soberly dressed wives and mothers. Little boys with wide eyes scrambled all over the piles of luggage waiting to be loaded. The dogs, a conglomeration of breeds, barked, whined, growled, snapped at each other and the crowd. There were several fights and two dogs had to be taken off the boat, mangled and bleeding. The noise and excitement were deafening and the poor captain sat in his cabin, fortifying himself with bourbon and wondering if he'd ever get his boatload out of the harbor.

Annie, lost in the crowd, buffeted and elbowed, strained her eyes to see Rolfe, but she never did. She watched all the tender, tearful farewells, the lusty, drunken ones, but though she stayed till the warning whistle blew, the gangplank was taken up, and the overloaded, historic steamship churned slowly out of the slip, she caught no glimpse of him.

Gradually the crowd thinned to a few stragglers who stayed to talk in groups, but Annie still stood on the pier, staring out into the harbor at the dwindling shape of the boat as it steamed into the sound, toward the straits, to the northward, its banner of smoke trailing proudly behind. At last, when all that remained was a thin black smudge that the breeze lifted and dispersed, she turned and went slowly homeward, wondering if she would ever see Rolfe again.

Chapter V

It was Annie who was with Mae when she died. Annie who knelt, weeping, by the bed and lifted the frail young body in her strong arms and held it against her breast, her tears dropping on Mae's face. Annie who ran all the way to the priest's house and brought Father Donegan. Annie who cried as if her heart would break after the priest had made the sign of the Cross over the quiet figure and folded the delicate hands and murmured the Latin prayers for the commendation of her soul.

Kit Jordan was in the saloon and though Annie sent Mrs. Bellows wheezing to fetch her, she arrived too late. Mae was gone. Annie was on her knees on one side of the bed, sobbing hard, dry sobs, and the priest stood looking sadly and pityingly down at the still, remote face, already sharpened by death. Mrs. Jordan stood at the door, her face like a block of granite hewed out by a hatchet. Not a tear was in her eyes, but she couldn't speak. She could only stare at the bed and her mouth set harder than ever and she hit her fist sharply against the door jamb.

"She's gone," she said at last in a flat voice.

"Yes," said the priest quietly. "She's gone. But I know you'll be glad that she was given the last rites of the Church before she died, Mrs. Jordan."

Kit Jordan gave him a scornful glance. "Who sent for you?" she demanded harshly.

"Your other daughter, Annie." The priest's voice was quiet, calm, but his eyes met hers steadily.

"You better go now. And don't come hanging around for a fee, neither."

Father Donegan gave her an ironic smile and then, completely disregarding her belligerent frown, went round the bed and put his hand on Annie's shoulder.

"My child," he said softly, "don't grieve so. She's better off where she is now."

Annie lifted her tear-stained face and gave him an agonized look. "She was so good, Father," she choked.

"You're a good girl, Annie," he went on quietly. "Because of you, her soul is safe. She made her confession and received the absolution of the Church. She made a good death."

Annie dropped her head on the counterpane again and sobbed even more wildly. Father Donegan said another prayer, patted Annie's shaking shoulder, and walked past Mrs. Jordan, who stared at him stonily, and went out of the room.

Kit Jordan walked slowly toward her eldest daughter's bed, her dry eyes glittering, her lips set in a straight, thin line, but her hands kept clenching and unclenching, as if, impotently, she girded herself against an enemy who had already triumphed over her. When she stood above the still, slight figure, with the hands crossed piously by the priest, she looked down at Mae's quiet face, and her mouth twisted crookedly. Still she did not shed a tear, but one of her gnarled hands went out and hesitantly touched the soft hair that tumbled over the pillow. It was the first caress that she had given either of her children since they were babies, and as if ashamed of her own emotion, she drew her hand back quickly before Annie should raise her head and see.

"No good blubbering," she said harshly to Annie. "She's gone, poor girl, and like the priest said, maybe she's better off. This world's not such a wonderful place that any of us should be sorry to leave it. I'd not be, God knows." She sighed deeply and Annie looked up at her wonderingly. If her mother had wept or reached out to her, Annie would have forgiven all the years of harshness and coldness. She would have flung herself, weeping, on Kit Jordan's breast. But her mother gave no sign, only stared over the girl's head as if facing all the bitter, graceless years that suddenly crowded into the silent room.

"Ma," whispered Annie, wanting to comfort and be comforted, wanting to merge her grief for Mae with her mother's, wanting a hand stretched out to her across the awful finality of death, wanting reassurance, hope, warmth. "Oh, Ma . . ." The tears gushed out, hot, blinding, but Mrs. Jordan made no move toward her.

"You'd best sleep with Mrs. Bellows tonight," was all she said, and with her face set like a flint, she pulled the counterpane over Mae's face and went out of the room.

"No," whispered Annie tensely, her lips white, "I won't sleep with Mrs. Bellows. I'll sleep here, in my own bed, beside Mae, just as I've always done. I won't leave her here alone all night. Oh, Mae dear, sweet Mae." She clasped her hands together. "Why did you die? Why did you have to go and die?"

The still figure under the white counterpane was frightening and strange. It wasn't Mae. It was the figure of death. Annie pulled off the counterpane swiftly and there was her sister's pale, sharp face with the eyes closed, the sweetness on her mouth.

"She looks like she's sleeping," whispered Annie, and a strange, impossible hope sprang up in her heart. Perhaps she *is* sleeping. Perhaps she isn't dead, after all. How often had she come to bed and seen Mae asleep, her face just like that in the moonlight. "I'll go to sleep too," she whispered, "and when I wake up—Mae will be all right." She began to pull off her clothes, tossing them in a heap. Then she opened the window, blew out the lamp, and got into her own bed and pulled the covers up high. Once or twice she glanced over at the other bed with a queer, cold feeling in her heart, but soon, worn out by emotion, she fell into a deep sleep.

She had strange, confused dreams. Once she dreamed that there was a light by Mae's bed and her mother knelt there, straining Mae's cold body to her breast, weeping and murmuring endearments to the dead girl. But when she woke in the morning and looked toward the other bed, it was empty. Mae was gone, the bedcovers had been stripped off, and only the blue-and-white mattress was left. Annie turned away and bit her lips against the sobs that wanted to come. Now, she knew, Mae was dead and gone.

She began to cry again, sharp, bitter tears that made her breast ache and her throat sting. Why did she grieve so for

Mae? Until this last year they had never been close, they had never understood each other. Was it because of the wasted years, when they might have come to know each other, that she wept? Was it because now Annie felt alone, with no youthful ally against her mother and the world? Or was it again her terror and sorrow at the idea of death? She did not know. Only there was an emptiness in her breast now, a pain that sharpened every time she went into the room they'd shared and saw the empty bed.

The bed was soon removed. Another roomer needed it and Annie was glad to see it go. At first the thought of one of her mother's rough miners or lumberjacks sleeping in the bed that had held Mae's slender young body had seemed horrible to her. But now she wanted to try to forget. And against her will the thought of Rolfe Linden crept into her mind. Mae is gone, but I am here, thought Annie, and wept sometimes at her disloyalty. But the memory of the kiss he'd given her, that half-reluctant, half-insistent kiss, was stronger than her loyalty to her dead sister. After all, she is dead and I am alive. I am alive! She looked at herself in the stained, off-focus mirror and she knew that when Rolfe came back she could make him forget Mae. She was sixteen now, and men turned their heads to watch her go by on the street.

The sense of life was urgent within her. She breathed the salty, pungent air off the bay with deeper relish, listened to the foghorns, the boat whistles with a sharper, more poignant joy. It seemed she had never been so keenly aware of the wonder and delight of living.

Annie was in the saloon, helping to serve drinks, when she heard a man who'd just come in say, "The *Portland's* due in about half an hour." It had been over a year since Rolfe had sailed for Alaska on her and the last letter Mae had had before she died had said he'd be coming home on her return voyage in the spring.

Annie slid the glass of beer across the table to a bearded man, who grabbed it in time to keep it from falling to the floor. She didn't even wait for him to pay. She pushed her way through the crowded saloon to the door leading into the rooming house, ran up the stairs, her heart pounding in her breast, slammed the door of her room, and began to strip off her dress.

There was nothing but cold water in the pitcher, but she poured it into the heavy white bowl with the crack that ran around the center, and washed her arms and neck and face and breasts. Then she put on her best underwear that she'd been saving for a special occasion. Her heart was beating so hard as she fastened the strings of her chemise that her firm, round breast trembled. She put on her new white linen suit with the nipped-in waist, the leg-o'-mutton sleeves. In it she looked older, almost a woman. She was glad; she wanted him to see that she was no longer a child, the little sister. Her rich hair she swept up in a pompadour and on top of it she pinned a dashing little straw sailor with a bunch of red cherries on the brim. She shouldn't wear red because of the color of her hair, but she loved it—it was such a gallant, defiant color—and today she needed courage.

Suddenly her knees began to tremble and sweat filled her palms, her armpits. What would she say to Rolfe? How would he act when he saw her? Had he received her letter telling about Mae's death? Would he be glad to have her meet him at the boat or would he think it too forward of her?

A long-drawn-out whistle from the bay made her jump. With a last swift glance in the mirror at her white face and blazing violet eyes, she dashed out of the room, down the steps. Her mother called to her from the hall, "Where in tarnation are you going, all togged out like a Variety girl? The saloon is full and I need you."

"The *Portland's* in," she yelled over her shoulder as she opened the front door. "I'll be back later."

The sun was bright and sharp, the air sweet and fresh and bracing, the sky washed blue from an early morning rain. Annie, pushing through the crowded streets, thought she had never seen such a fine day, had never been aware of such deep, piercing joy. Rolfe is coming home, her heart kept saying. Rolfe, Rolfe. Now everything will begin for me. He'll look at me with his dark, deep-set eyes and his shy, kind smile and he'll see how pretty I am now. He'll smile at me the way he smiled at Mae. Maybe he won't know me at first and I'll tease him a little before I tell him who I am. And then he'll laugh and take my arm and walk home with me. Maybe he'll be so glad to see me that he'll—he'll kiss me. Oh, dear Lord, please make him kiss me!

She jostled her way through the knots of men in front of stores and saloons, and they turned to look at the tall, well-built, red-haired girl, striding along in her grown-up skirt and hat, like an overdressed, impatient goddess.

When she reached the pier there was already a crowd waiting. The steamer was in, but the gangplank was just being let down. Annie pushed her way to the front, oblivious to the stares and remarks that followed her. She found herself standing beside an elderly, stout man with piercing blue eyes and a delicate-faced, slender woman in a modish silk suit, whose pale lips trembled and eyes strained toward the crowded decks of the steamer. She recognized them as Rolfe's mother and father. Her heart beat sharply and she glanced quickly away. Oh, I hope he sees me first, she thought. If he sees them first, maybe he won't notice me. And I can't go up to him in front of them. Excitement, fear, and anxiety made her go hot and cold.

Now the gangplank was down, the men swarmed off the boat, shouting and laughing, the crowd surged forward, calling out names. Annie searched the faces of the men as they stepped off the gangplank into the waiting arms of relatives and friends. Will I know him when I see him? Or will he be changed? Maybe he's grown a beard. Oh, Rolfe, Rolfe—where are you?

"Hi, Red, lookin' for someone?" cried a young miner with a boyish grin and a knapsack on his back.

"Yes," said Annie, "but not you. Have you seen Rolfe Linden?"

"Never heard of him." The boy laughed, gave her a crooked grin. "But won't I do? I've got a bagful o' nuggets, sister, and I'm achin' to spend 'em. I could show you a good time."

She gave him a cold look and moved away. He looked at her ripening figure, her red mouth, her violet eyes, and edged closer, his hand on her arm. "Aw, listen, honey," he murmured, "don't be mean. I'll be good to you."

She whirled on him savagely. "Get out," she cried, beside herself with fury. "I'm waiting for Rolfe Linden."

The boy shrugged, laughed. "He must be quite a guy."

"He is," said Annie coldly, and the miner moved away. She

suddenly knew that Rolfe's mother and father had heard what she said and were staring at her. She didn't dare look at them; she couldn't move away. She could only stand rigidly with the hot blood rushing over her, her gaze fixed on the deck of the *Portland.*

One by one the men got off the boat and each time Annie stared hungrily, expecting it to be Rolfe. Where was he? Hadn't he come after all? Presently there were only a few stragglers left of the crowd at the pier, and Mr. and Mrs Linden and herself. All her eagerness and excitement had gone cold and heavy within her.

Mrs. Linden was murmuring something to her husband and Annie heard him say, "You wait here, my dear. I'll go aboard and ask the captain."

But at that moment the captain and the purser came down the gangplank, tired, haggard-looking men in their blue uniforms, with charts and the logbooks under their arms.

Mr. Linden stepped up to them, asked in his dignified voice, "I beg your pardon, sir, but I'm looking for my son, Rolfe Linden. I understood he booked passage on the *Portland* this trip, but he hasn't got off yet. Is he still aboard?"

"Rolfe Linden?" asked the captain, and he glanced quickly at the purser. The purser looked first at Mr. Linden and then at the pale, tense, elderly woman with her hands tightly clenched in black silk gloves at her sides. Both men looked serious and distressed. Neither of them seemed to see the girl in the white linen suit, listening intently.

"Yes," repeated Mr. Linden. "My son—Rolfe Linden. You know the name?"

The captain nodded, paused, then took Mr. Linden's arm and walked a little way off from his wife, but not too far for Annie, every sense alert, to hear his words.

"This will be a shock to you, sir, and I had hoped you'd already been notified," began the captain with the awkwardness of a man of action when confronted with a delicate situation.

"Notified of what, sir?" cried Mr. Linden in a startled voice.

"Your son did book passage on the *Portland*, but it—it was canceled." The captain's face looked tired and worn and he seemed to be fumbling for the right words.

"Canceled? You mean he's not on the ship? He didn't come back?" cried Mr. Linden sharply.

The captain shook his head, put his hand on Mr. Linden's arm. "Sir, I hate to be the one to tell you. But—your son is—dead."

Mr. Linden stepped back as if he'd been struck. His face got suddenly red as if in anger. "What's that you say, sir?"

"He was killed, Mr. Linden. Killed for his gold. His body was found in a crevasse, frozen solid. They won't be able to get it out for another month."

Annie stared at the men, unable to understand what they were saying. Were they talking about Rolfe? No—no, they couldn't be. Rolfe was coming home—to her. She'd put on her best clothes, her new hat. Rolfe—Rolfe!

"Dead? Killed for his gold?" repeated Mr. Linden dully. He rubbed his hand over his face, as if to brush away the thought, as if the captain's words were cobwebs.

"No!" cried Annie in a strangled voice, running up to the captain and pounding him with her fists. "No, he's not dead. Say he's not. Say it's a lie. It's not true. Rolfe's alive. He's coming home!"

The captain patted her shoulder even as she was pounding his broad chest with her frantic hands. Presently she stopped crying, let her hands fall to her sides.

"I'm sorry, miss," said the captain comfortingly. "Was he your fellow?"

Annie shook her head, her eyes dull. "No. Just a friend." He wasn't even my fellow, she thought. But I loved him. He was good. If he'd come back he might have loved me too. But now he's gone, like Mae. I'll never see him again. They killed him and threw his body into a crevasse up in the North, in the ice and snow, with the bitter northern wind howling over him. Oh, Rolfe. *Rolfe!*

She clenched her fists again and bent her head against the anguish that twisted her heart. Mr. and Mrs. Linden were walking away from the dock toward their waiting carriage. Mrs. Linden looked crumpled and her husband supported her drooping body with his arm about her waist. But there was no sound of weeping, no outcry, no wild display of grief like Annie's.

Annie stood woodenly, staring out across the bay, not seeing the steamer rolling slightly from the swells, nor the gulls wheeling above the ship, nor the sparkle of the sun far out on the blue water.

The captain touched her shoulder. "You'd best go home now, my dear."

She nodded and began to walk slowly away from him. He stood a moment, looking after her, his big red face worried, his pale blue eyes pitying. Then he shook his head, sighed, and glanced at the purser.

"Hardest thing I ever had to do, to tell those people about that boy," he muttered.

The purser nodded. "Wonder who the girl was? She's some punkins."

"Looks like Kit Jordan's girl, Annie. I can remember when she used to dance on the tables at her mother's saloon," said the captain. "She was only a kid then."

"She's sure grown up now. Wonder what Rolfe Linden was to her?" The purser stared after the girl's tall, drooping figure.

The captain shrugged. "She said he wasn't her fellow, but the way she carried on, I'd say he was more than just a friend."

"She was pretty cut up, all right."

"I hope she'll go home. Maybe I'd ought to take her over to Kit's. I'm going by for a drink after I turn in the books." The captain took a tentative step after the girl, but the purser said, "Aw, leave the kid alone. She don't want to go home now. Not to that hole, feelin' the way she does."

"But she—you don't think she might do something desperate?" The captain frowned.

"You mean, jump in the bay?" The purser shook his head. "She don't look like the type. She's all cut up now, but she'll be all right."

"Well, it's none of my business, I guess. Come on." The two men went into the office and the captain looked tired. It had been a hard trip and he was glad to be in port again. He thought he'd go over to Kit's and get good and drunk. It'd help him forget Rolfe Linden and the things he'd seen in Nome.

Annie didn't go home. She walked slowly, with heavy steps, along the waterfront, past the warehouses and chandler shops and docks. The sun was still hot and bright on her neck and shoulders, but she didn't feel it. She was cold all over. Inside she was numb. Her heart, that had ached so sharply, felt dead and empty now. Presently she stopped and sat down on the edge of a dock, leaning against a pile. She unpinned her bright little hat with the cherries and held it in her hand. She stared down at the dark, oily water. It looked deep and evil and she shuddered.

It never occurred to her to throw herself into it. Death horrified and frightened her. She hated it. Never in all her life, in spite of pain, sickness, grief, shame, would she ever turn to death as a release from struggle and life. Life was her lover always; though it treated her shabbily as a lover may do, still she was eager for it, she clasped it close, she gave herself up to it. Whatever gifts it gave her, whether of ecstasy or bitterness, she accepted, sometimes in joy, sometimes in anguish or rebellion. To stop living, to leave the world with all its sights, sounds, smells, its beauty and its ugliness, to cease to be able to feel, to laugh, to cry, love, fight—that was the worst thing that could happen.

She was dimly aware of this, through the fog of pain and shock that encompassed her. Rolfe was dead but she was alive. Even if her heart was broken and her dream shattered, the knowledge that she ached with life filled her. She looked at her big, strong hands, turning them over and over, thinking how even now, limp and heavy as they were, they were alive, their flesh was sweet, blood ran through them, they could clasp a man's hand, caress a piece of silk, strike a blow at an enemy. But Rolfe's hands were cold, frozen stiff in the icy crevasse. They would never touch a girl's warm arm, clasp a friend's hand, double up into a fist again.

It was nearly dark when she stumbled into the rooming house and went upstairs to her room. She laid her hat on the golden oak dresser, sat down on her bed, her shoulders sagging. Suddenly she was exhausted. She fell back on the pillow limply and went to sleep.

She wakened with a lamp shining in her face, her mother bending over her, shaking her.

"Annie—Annie, wake up!"

Her eyes flickered open and she stared blankly into her mother's sharp, frowning face.

"Go away, Ma," she whispered. "Let me be."

"You get right up and fix your hair. There's somebody down-stairs wants to see you," cried Kit Jordan impatiently. "You fix yourself up nice, now. I want you to look good. Go wash your face; it's all streaked, and your good suit's all wrinkled from lying on it. Go put on another dress."

Annie sighed deeply, rubbed her eyes, and got to her feet. She looked at her mother with an odd expression, as if she were a great way off. Mechanically she did as she was told, washed her face, changed her dress, brushed her hair. Her mother stood watching her in silence. Annie didn't ask who it was that she was getting fixed up for. She didn't care. She was too tired, too terribly tired.

When she was ready she turned to her mother without a word. "You look all right, but you're awful pale. Not sick, are ye?" her mother questioned sharply.

Annie shook her head.

"Come along then," and Mrs. Jordan took her elbow and guided her out of the room. The girl submitted as if she were a sleepwalker. "Now, Annie, you be nice to him. He's just back from Alaska and he's got a poke of gold that'd choke a horse. He's brought you a present, too."

Annie said nothing, only sighed again, a deep, shuddering sigh that made her mother glance curiously at her. They went downstairs and into the hideous little parlor where the hand-painted lamp with the beaded fringe was lighted. A man was sitting on the leather settee and he got to his feet quickly when they came in. He looked at the girl eagerly, then glanced at Mrs. Jordan, who nodded shortly.

"Hello, Annie," said Fred Carew with a nervous smile. He held out his hand and Annie put her limp one into it. A look of surprise and pleasure went over his heavy, bearded face. "My, you're looking mighty fine tonight," he cried, laughing and try-ing to be hearty. "Pretty as a picture."

Annie looked at him, wishing he'd go away so she could go back to her room.

"I've brought you a present, little girl." He fished in his vest pocket, put his hands behind his back, and winked at her. "Which hand do you take?"

Annie stood looking at him and made no move to answer, so

he took one hand from behind his back and dangled something before her. She glanced at it incuriously.

"Ain't that nice of Fred, Annie? Look at it—it's pure gold," said her mother eagerly.

"Yep—pure gold nuggets made into a necklace specially for you, Annie, for the prettiest girl in Seattle," cried Fred Carew. "Come over here and I'll fasten it around your neck."

Mrs. Jordan gave Annie a little shove and she moved obediently forward. Carew put the necklace around her full white throat and his clumsy hands fumbled nervously with the catch. His face was red and there were beads of perspiration on his forehead. Annie could feel his hot, whisky-scented breath on her cheek. When he'd fastened the necklace he started to put his hands on her shoulders, but Mrs. Jordan gave him a quick, warning frown and he let his hands drop.

"Well, what d'ye say, Annie? Like it?"

"Speak up, girl," cried Kit. "Say thanks to Fred. Lord, that's not just a string o' glass beads. It's pure gold and worth a lot of money."

"I'll say it is," chuckled Fred, his eyes flickering over Annie's impassive face.

"It's very pretty," she said in a low voice. "Thanks." Then she turned to her mother. "Now may I go to my room?"

Fred Carew's face darkened. "Look here, Kit Jordan," he said impatiently. "Didn't you tell her?"

Mrs. Jordan flushed, wet her lips. "Not yet, Fred." She took Annie's hand and led her to the settee, sat down beside her. "Honey, Fred struck it rich this time and he wants you to have everything you want. Pretty dresses, trinkets, maybe a nice house."

Annie gave her mother a puzzled look. "Why?" she asked simply.

"Because he's in love with you. He wants to marry you."

The girl stared at her as if her words made no sense. Then she looked at the red-faced man standing over her, watching her hungrily but uncertainly.

"I don't want to get married," she murmured wearily. "I'm tired. I want to go to bed."

"Plenty of time for that later," laughed Fred, with a sly look at her mother.

Mrs. Jordan frowned at him. "Listen, Annie, I'm your mother. I want to do what's best for you. You're going to marry Fred. Now. Tonight." She got up swiftly, opened the door leading into the dining room. "Come in, Mr. Hotchkiss."

A dried-up little man in a shiny black suit stepped warily into the room. He darted nervous looks at Kit, the girl, and the heavy-set, bearded man. Annie recognized him as the man who ran a small real estate office, was a notary public and justice of the peace on the side.

"Mr. Hotchkiss is going to perform the ceremony," said Mrs. Jordan.

Annie got up suddenly with a strange, frightened look on her white face. She was tired and sick and she wanted to go up to her room and be alone. She didn't want to marry Fred Carew for his pots of gold. She didn't want to marry anyone, ever. Her love, her heart were dead. But there was no escape. And if your heart was dead, what difference what happened to you?

"I want to go upstairs," she said.

"In a little while, deary," said Mrs. Jordan cajolingly. "Just as soon as Mr. Hotchkiss reads the lines. Now you stand here beside Fred and it'll be over in a few minutes."

Mr. Hotchkiss cleared his throat. "I must say, I don't like seeing a young girl get hitched to a man your age, sir. But under the circumstances, there's no way out."

"I explained the way things are with you and Annie," said Mrs. Jordan quickly, and gave Fred Carew a wink. He raised his eyebrows and laughed.

"That's right, Kit. I want to do the right thing by Annie. Well, let's get on with it." He stepped up to Annie and took her hand. She looked at him in distaste, but she didn't pull away.

Mr. Hotchkiss opened his little book, began to intone the service.

Annie looked at her finger with the thick gold band that Fred Carew had slipped on it, and then at Mr. Hotchkiss.

"You can kiss the bride now. That'll be two dollars, please," he said in his flat voice.

Fred Carew bent toward Annie, but she drew away quickly. He flushed and laughed and dug into his pants pockets for two silver dollars and dropped them into the justice of the peace's open palm.

Annie started for the door. "Hey," cried Fred, "where you going?"

"Let her be, Fred," said Mrs. Jordan sharply, with a queer guilty look after Annie. "She's goin' upstairs. You'll see her later."

"You're damn right I will," he cried. "Well, Kit, how about a little drink to celebrate?"

"Sure," said Kit, "and there's a matter of a little business, too, eh, Fred?"

Annie ran upstairs and shut the door. She was still numb inside, but the fog was lifting a little. She'd said some words, prompted by Mr. Hotchkiss, because she was tired and wanted to get away, and now she had a ring on her finger. A wedding ring. She'd married that awful old goat—that was what her mother had planned all along. She knew that now. She looked at the ring under the lamplight. It was gold, but it was ugly and thick. It was tight on her finger. She tugged at it to get it off. She got it as far as the knuckle and then it stuck, and the flesh began to swell around it. Frantically she poured water into the washbowl and soaped her fingers. The ring slid off and dropped into the washbowl with a sharp clatter. She left it there, dried her hands, and rubbed the swollen knuckle.

Then she put her hands to her neck and felt the heavy nugget necklace. It was ugly, too, even if it was pure gold and worth money. She pulled it off, not bothering to unfasten the clasp, and dropped it on the dresser. Fred Carew—that squatty, red-faced man with the hungry look. She didn't want his presents. She didn't want him either. What had her mother done to her?

Suddenly the door burst open and she turned startled eyes to see him standing there looking at her. As she watched in horror he closed the door and came toward her.

"What do you want?" she cried. "This is my room. Get out."

He laughed and kept coming. "What d'ye think I want, honey? What d'ye think I married ye for?"

Of course—she was married to him—she'd said the words because her heart was dead and she didn't care what happened to her. But now she was alive again, alive and frightened, but certain of one thing—she had to get away.

"Get out," she cried, backing away.

"Now, sweetheart, be nice to me," he laughed, grabbing her

and pulling her roughly against him. "Stop the coy stuff, Annie. You're a big girl now. You belong to me and I won't stand for any nonsense."

She tried to push him away but he held her fast, pressed his hot face against her throat and mouth. She fought him with her hands that suddenly were no longer limp and weak but hard and strong. The numbness was shocked out of her, anger and horror ran like fire through her body. He kissed her greedily and she kicked him, beat him with her fists. At last he stumbled backward, his face distorted by anger and desire.

"You hellcat! I'll show you who's boss around here. You're my wife. I paid your mother plenty to get you and I'm goin' to get my money's worth."

He started for her again, but she put out her feet and tripped him. He fell heavily and lay still, groaning. The fall and the whisky he'd consumed before and after the wedding had stunned him. She grabbed the silk scarf Maizie had given her off the dresser, her coat from the hook in the closet, and while he was still struggling to get to his feet she ran out of the room, slamming the door.

No one stopped her in the hall. Kit Jordan had gone into the saloon and Mrs. Bellows was in the kitchen, sneaking a swallow of gin. Annie ran out of the house and down the dark streets. She didn't know where she was going. Terror blotted out everything but the desire to get as far away as possible from the rooming house and Fred Carew. Tears of shame and rage at what her mother had done to her ran down her cheeks. Men stared at her curiously, some spoke and called out to her, but she didn't see or hear them.

All at once she looked up and saw the dark bulk of the Catholic church before her, with the rectory beside it. There were lights on in the rectory and through the window she could see the priest, Father Donegan, bent over his desk. He'd been good to her when Mae died. Perhaps he'd help her now. There was no one else—Rolfe was dead; she wouldn't go to the Variety girls: they'd think it was a great joke that she'd been taken in like that.

She banged the knocker of the rectory door and presently the door opened and the thin, gray-haired priest in his black cassock stood looking at her.

"Why, it's Annie Jordan," he said in surprise.

"Oh, Father! Father!" she gasped, breathless, and she began to weep stormily.

"Come inside, my child," said Father Donegan kindly. He took her arm and led her into the house. "Come into my study and tell me what's troubling you."

Chapter VI

Mrs. Conway, the father's housekeeper, knocked on Annie's door while it was still dark.

"It's six-tharty," she grumbled, "and Father's already gone over to church for mass. Git up, girl, and git dressed. 'Tis no more'n right that you should make your communion in thanksgivin' for what ye've been spared."

Annie opened the door and stood in the dark hall, fully dressed, with her bright hair wound round her head in two great braids and her white face scrubbed and shining, the lamplight behind her.

"I'm ready, ma'am," she answered shyly. "I've been up and dressed for nearly an hour."

"H'mph, so ye are. And ye look quite respectable, too, at that." The housekeeper's sharp eyes darted over the girl's tall, big-boned, sumptuous body that even the hideous dark green serge dress with its absurd big sleeves and high-necked bodice couldn't restrain entirely. "But ye've no hat. Ye can't go to mass hatless with that mass o' red hair blazin' like a flame."

"I've got a scarf, ma'am." Annie held out the gold scarf with the shiny black sequins that Maizie had given her.

Mrs. Conway shook her head and stuck out her lower lip disapprovingly. "That won't do. I'll let ye wear one o' mine. Ye look clean enough, so I guess 'twill be all right."

Annie felt the hot blood in her cheeks. The woman had no call to say that, to suppose that because she came from the waterfront she might have bugs in her hair. She didn't imagine even Mrs. Conway, neat as she was, spent as much time and care on her tight knob of scraggly, mouse-colored hair as Annie did on her rich mane, washing and brushing and combing till it shone!

"My hair's just been washed, ma'am," she said in a tight voice, restraining the sharp words that pricked her mind.

"Come along into my room and I'll get a bonnet for ye," said Mrs. Conway, and Annie followed her.

The housekeeper's room was high-ceilinged and pleasant, not like the small, bare closet that Annie had been occupying. The bed was already made and loomed immense and downy, a white-painted iron one with a crocheted white spread whose fringe reached to the floor. There was a towering dark oak dresser covered with photographs and snapshots of Mrs. Conway's relatives and friends. The walls bore cheap, vivid religious prints and in a corner was a table with a small, brightly colored statue of Our Lady with a nosegay of paper flowers and a flickering votive candle before her.

It all looked very holy, very Catholic, and eminently respectable. Annie was awed and hardly dared to look around, until Mrs. Conway disappeared into the clothespress to rummage in boxes for a hat. There was a faint scent of camphor and lavender water and Baume Bengay in the room that made Annie's nostrils tickle.

"Here, see if this will go on over all that hair," mumbled Mrs. Conway, backing out of the clothespress and waving a black velvet bonnet with a seedy-looking ostrich tip at Annie.

She took it and tried to cram it down over her braids, but it was much too small. "I don't think——" she started to say, but the housekeeper took the hat out of her fumbling hands, perched it on top of Annie's hair, pulled a long jet hatpin out of the red apple pincushion on the dresser, and jabbed it through the crown of the hat and the heavy braided coronet. Annie felt that she might have jabbed it straight into her head if the braids hadn't been there to stop it.

"There, that will do very nicely," said Mrs. Conway approvingly. "It's my second best hat and a bit out of style, but 'tisn't fitting to care about your looks when you're goin' to church."

"No, ma'am. Thank you, ma'am," murmured Annie meekly. She didn't dare look at herself in the mirror. It wouldn't do for her to burst out laughing in the good lady's face, and from the way the bonnet wobbled as she walked, she knew it must look a fright. She kept her eyes carefully averted as Mrs. Conway put her best hat on her own head, flicked a speck off her sober black poplin, and buttoned her plump hands into gray silk gloves. Then, picking up a Key of Heaven from her bedside table and looking to see that her money was in her purse, she nodded to Annie to follow and whisked out of the room.

The church was next door to the rectory, but they had to walk outside to get to it. There was a sort of tunnel affair, an enclosed walk from the priest's study, that led into the sacristy of the church, but it wouldn't have been fitting for the two women to use it.

Annie was glad of the chance to walk a few steps in the dark, foggy morning. She breathed in the pungent, rank smell from the tide flats gratefully. It cleared her head of the odor of sanctity that pervaded the rectory: the scent of soap, furniture polish, candle wax, and camphor that from this time forward she would forever associate with the cloth. Just as she followed Mrs. Conway through the heavy church door a foghorn boomed out in the harbor and a ship's deep voice answered. Somehow that lifted her drooping spirits immeasurably.

Inside, the dim church was half filled, mostly with women in sober dress, though, to her amazement, Annie saw Maizie and two of the other girls from Considine's Variety Theater on their knees in a back pew. Their heads were bowed and she couldn't see their faces, but as she passed their pew she heard a muffled sound of sobbing. She didn't feel quite so much of an intruder and outsider after seeing them there too. But she wondered about the sobbing. It was somehow very exciting and made her heart thump. Remembering her early training when the nuns had tried to make a good Catholic out of her, she genuflected before slipping into the pew after Mrs. Conway.

The housekeeper immediately sank to her knees on the kneeling pad, crossed herself, and with fingers deftly manipulating her rosary, began to pray silently. Annie, sneaking a glance at her, saw her lips moving and her face screwed up as if in secret pain.

The girl, emulating her companion, sank to her knees, too, and crossed herself clumsily, trying to remember the prayers she'd learned at the sisters' school when Pop was alive. He'd been the one who'd sent her to the nuns and had insisted upon her being confirmed and attending church. But Pop had been dead a long time—since she was seven—nine years ago, and Ma hadn't bothered with religion since. In fact it had been Pop's funeral that had ended Mrs. Jordan's churchgoing. The hundred dollars she'd paid the undertaker to prepare his "remains" for burial had been bad enough, but a practical necessity. However, when she found out she'd have to pay the priest fifty dollars to say a requiem mass for the repose of his soul and another fifty to bury his tired bones in consecrated ground, she'd decided religion was too expensive a luxury for a widow woman trying to make her own way in the world. She'd taken the girls away from the nuns and sent them to the public school and neither one of them had been to mass since then.

Annie fumbled in her mind for the right words. "Our Father," she said, and then the rest came tumbling out of the past in a great rush. There was a tight cord bound about her heart and through her mind went images of dear old Pop taking her by the hand and walking along the waterfront, to watch the gulls, pointing out the fishing boats coming in from the straits, and of kind Sister Mary Elizabeth, who'd given her a little holy card of the Sacred Heart of Jesus.

By the time Annie had finished one Hail Mary, the warm rush of memories overflowed her heart, dissolved the tight cord that made it hard to breathe, and the tears gushed down her face. Mrs. Conway, glancing at her, saw the tears and said another Hail Mary herself in thanksgiving for the sinner returned to the fold. And then the red-cassocked acolytes and the priest in chasuble and biretta came in, the mass began, and Annie, on her knees, stared in awe and delight at the shimmering blaze of the altar, the dancing candle flames, the priest's rich vestments. The strange tongue, the sanctus bell, the faltering responses of the people, the solemn moment when she, kneeling gingerly beside Mrs. Conway at the altar rail, received the Host on her tongue, engulfed, overwhelmed her. She let the housekeeper lead her, limp and shaken, back to the rectory and to breakfast. And though she thought she couldn't swallow a bite, she found that Mrs. Conway was right: mass had given her a terrific appetite.

After breakfast Father sent for her. She hastily wiped her hands (she'd been helping Mrs. Conway with the dishes) on the roller towel behind the kitchen door, smoothed her dress, patted her shining hair, and glanced at the housekeeper with wide eyes. Mrs. Conway nodded and motioned for her to go to the priest's study.

At her timid knock the tired, cultured voice told her to come in and she entered shyly, her eyes cast down. After seeing him celebrate the mass, Annie could hardly bear to lift her gaze to Father Donegan now. But when she did, her frightened awe left her and a small pang of disappointment smote her. Without the impressive vestments and back again in his shabby old black suit, the priest looked small and thin and human. He glanced up from his letter writing and nodded at her.

"Well, Annie, you were at mass this morning, I see."

She nodded and swallowed hard.

"I'm very happy about that, my child," went on Father Donegan, and his keen gray eyes softened, a slow smile lit up his bony, ascetic features, and she suddenly realized that he meant what he said. He *was* happy because she had gone to mass. "There is nothing that pleases Mother Church more than for one of her little ones, who has gone astray, to return to her bosom. I'm sure you received great comfort from your Communion."

"Yes, Father," whispered Annie, feeling the tears pricking her throat again.

"I hope you will go every Sunday from now on," continued the priest, clasping his hands and gazing at her steadily. "Even though you are to be living in a Protestant household, you must remember always that you are a Catholic. I have spoken to Mrs. Carlton about the importance of your attending mass each week and she has agreed to give you time off on Sunday mornings."

Annie said nothing, feeling at once a deep excitement and a sense of dread. It was very strange, having one's life settled for you by another person, especially someone like the priest whom you couldn't disobey as you could your mother. She'd helped Ma at the rooming house, but this would be different. She'd be working for a stranger, she'd be the *hired girl*. Her bosom heaved and she had the horrible feeling that she was going to burst into tears in front of the priest.

"Mrs. Carlton is a good woman and a Christian, though not of our faith, I'm sorry to say. She attends the Episcopal church. But she will be kind to you and you should be happy there, provided you do your work well, are respectful, obedient, and well behaved." The priest paused and his steady gaze pulled her eyes up to his face. "I don't suppose I need to tell you to stay away from the waterfront, from your mother's rooming house and all your old associates."

Annie shook her head and set her lips against the swift protest that rose to them. What right have you to tell me where I can go and what I can do? she cried out within her. Suddenly her mother, in spite of what she had done to her, seemed dear and familiar. She longed to rush out of the room, to run every step of the way until she was back on Yesler Avenue, back in the rooming house, hearing the familiar laughter and coarse voices of the men below in the saloon, the clatter of glasses, the high voices of the girls from the Variety Theater.

"Because you realize," went on Father Donegan, "that your mother is very angry with you and if she gets a chance she may force you to live with Fred Carew until I am able to get the annulment."

"Oh no! No!" cried Annie, frightened quite out of her rebellion and her longing for home. The ugly face of the miner, his groping, insistent hands, the reek of liquor and sweat upon him, came before her in a sickening vision and she began to sob wildly, forgetting where she was.

The priest came around to her and patted her shaking shoulders. "Don't cry, Annie. I'm sorry I had to speak of that man again, but I wanted to impress upon you the necessity for keeping away from your old haunts. Just stay with Mrs. Carlton, go only where she gives you permission to go, and you will be quite safe."

"Yes, Father, I'll do anything you say," she promised, and now Mrs. Carlton's house seemed to her like a haven, a sanctuary, a place of grateful refuge.

"Now go wash your face and get your things and we'll be on our way. I told Mrs. Carlton I'd bring you over at nine."

It was a long walk and a steep climb from the rectory to the

First Hill. It made the priest puff and sigh and he had to pause often to rest. But Annie could have run all the way without even getting tired. After her outburst in Father's study she'd suddenly lost her fear and dread; all her old exuberance and vitality had rushed back into her. A deep excitement possessed her and she had said good-by to the housekeeper gaily and stepped along beside the priest with light, springy steps.

The fog had lifted now and whenever Father stopped to rest she turned to look back at the bay where the sun glittered on the choppy blue water and glistened on the snowy Olympics that rose white and majestic out of the glittering bay. The town looked smaller and smaller as they climbed the hill, and the bay, the giant mountains, the wooded islands, and the great blue sky grew bigger and bigger. The air was fresher and cleaner up here, and Annie breathed it in deeply, her heart swelling with delight in the fine morning and the sense of adventure, the feeling that for all her pangs of homesickness for the waterfront, her fears about the new life that lay ahead, she was reaching out for something better. She was coming up in the world, and not merely physically either.

No wonder the people on the First Hill seem better than us down on the waterfront, she thought. Even the air they breathe is better. And how could anyone help but be good with such a view to look out upon every day! All we can see from the docks is the oily, mucky green water with refuse and dead fish floating in it, gulls screaming over garbage, bilge water pouring out of fishing smacks and island steamers. But up here you don't see that, you see the fine blue sweep of Elliott Bay in all its shining beauty and on clear days the wooded green islands, the Olympic Peninsula, and the snow-white, glistening mountains. For the first time in her life Annie sensed perspective and it expanded her soul.

The Carltons' new expensive house was a monstrosity of nineteenth-century bad taste, with cupolas and bay windows, gingerbread and ironwork, but to Annie's dazzled gaze it was most imposing and elegant.

"Someday," she burst out, gazing at the priest with starry, bemused eyes, "I'm going to live up here on the hill too. In my own house!"

The priest smiled at her and shook his head. But he said

kindly, "Who knows, child? This is a city of promise. Stranger things have happened here. Maybe, someday, you will. If you work hard and are a good girl," he added cautiously as he pulled the doorbell.

Annie's face was still shining and her lips were parted in an expectant smile when the door opened.

The girl standing in the hall, with one hand on the door-knob, seemed to her the prettiest thing she had ever seen. She was small, dainty, and blond. Her fluffy yellow hair was swept off her delicate white forehead in a pompadour, caught at the nape of her neck in a cluster of little curls held by a stiff black taffeta ribbon. She had on a sheer white batiste shirtwaist, tucked exquisitely with a tiny turned-back collar fastened by a small black bow. Her black serge accordion-pleated skirt was daringly short, stopping just at the top of her high laced pointed shoes. Little as Annie knew about style and fashions, she was sure that this girl was fashionably dressed and that she hadn't bought her clothes in Seattle. The girl's blue, long-lashed eyes met Annie's appraisingly for an instant, then she turned to the priest.

"How do you do?" she said politely in a high, sweet, affected voice.

"How do you do. I'm Father Donegan," replied the priest, taking off his wide-brimmed black hat and smiling at her. "Is Mrs. Carlton at home?"

"Yes, she is. Oh, you must be the Catholic priest and this"—her gaze swept Annie again coolly—"this must be the new hired girl," she finished with a condescending smile.

Annie flushed and averted her gaze. She felt awkward, big-boned, ill dressed. The girl's voice, her smile, sent a pang of despair through her. Hired girl—from now on that's what she would be. And girls like this would look at her without seeing her, as if she were a piece of furniture, without face, feelings, entity. The blood surged to her face and her heart burned. If she could she'd have turned at that moment and run back to the waterfront. But Father Donegan had taken her arm and was stepping over the threshold with her. For a moment she stiffened, hung back, but he gave her a quick glance and she meekly followed him into the house.

The girl led them into the parlor, pulling aside the portieres and showing the priest to a chair. Annie she ignored, left to find herself a seat. In an agony of embarrassment Annie sat stiffly on the edge of a straight-backed cane-bottomed chair, holding her purse and the little bundle of clothing the father's housekeeper had got together for her, since she dared not go back to the Nugget for her things and it was certain her mother would never send them.

"I'll call Mother," said the girl charmingly to the priest and, without a glance at Annie, switched out of the room. If she'd only smiled at me, or looked at me as if I were a human being, Annie thought bitterly. She bit the inside of her lip and stared straight ahead, not looking about the room that she was to know so well and to hate.

"It'll be all right, child," said Father Donegan kindly, with his gentle smile. "Just keep a stiff upper lip and think how much better your life will be here than on the waterfront."

Annie wanted to cry, "I love the waterfront. I'm a person there. Ma treated me like a person, even if she did yell at me and box my ears. But here—here, I'll be nothing." But she only nodded and looked down at the floor, blinking back the tears.

With a rustle of skirts and a bobbing of garnet eardrops, Mrs. Carlton hurried into the room, trailing a scent of lavender. Annie, staring at her, remembered all at once the pretty, soft-voiced woman in the sealskin jacket who'd smelled of lavender as she bent to comfort a weeping little blond girl the night of the fire. She was older-looking, of course, but still pretty, the same silver combs in her brown hair, though the hair had a streak of gray running through it now. And the little blond girl—what had been her name? "Will Carlton's daughter," Ma had said.

"My daughter Emily told me you were here, Father Donegan," Mrs. Carlton was saying as the priest rose to shake hands with her. Annie rose, too, clutching her belongings, thinking, Emily—that was her name. She was scared of the fire and bawling something awful and I dried her tears with my skirt and she said I smelled bad. Emily—Emily Carlton. Now she's grown up and a fashionable beauty and I'm to be her mother's hired girl.

"Annie, Mrs. Carlton is speaking to you," she heard Father say patiently and she colored, looked quickly at Emily's mother.

"Yes, ma'am?" That was how you addressed your mistress, Annie supposed, and it seemed to satisfy both the woman and the priest, but somehow it was a hard thing to say and there was a note of reluctance in it.

"Father Donegan tells me that you're used to working hard and to waiting on table," said the woman, looking a bit dubiously at Annie's full figure and flamboyant hair. "Can you cook?"

"I worked for Ma—for my mother—at the Nugget," replied Annie. "But I never did the cooking. Mrs. Bellows did that, or Ma—Mother."

"I see." Mrs. Carlton glanced at Father Donegan, a little color rising in her pale cheeks. "The Nugget—is a—er—boarding-house?"

"No," said Annie candidly, "it's a saloon. Ma runs a rooming house too."

"Oh." The color in the pale cheeks deepened. "Well, you understand, of course, Annie, that working here will be quite different from working for your mother. Mr. Carlton is very particular. He insists upon absolute cleanliness, won't tolerate a poorly done job. Also serving at our table will be different from—er—what you've been used to."

"I'm sure that Annie will learn your ways quickly, Mrs. Carlton," said the priest impatiently, and from the sharp glance he gave the woman Annie was sure that he was annoyed at her and felt a warm wave of gratitude toward him. "She is very quick and intelligent and a conscientious worker."

"Oh, I'm sure of that, Father, or you wouldn't have recommended her to us," cried Mrs. Carlton in a conciliatory tone.

The priest got up, put his hand on Annie's shoulder, and said with his worn, kind smile, "I'll leave you now, my child. Do your best always and you will be well treated. I shall expect to see you at confession next Saturday. Good day, Mrs. Carlton. I know I am leaving Annie in good hands."

Mrs. Carlton went to the door with the priest and Annie stood awkwardly in the parlor where they'd left her, her heart like a stone, her throat dry. She stared at the oriental rug, the highly polished floor, and thought, It'll be me who'll beat these rugs and wax these floors from now on. And if I don't do a good job I'll catch it from Mr. Carlton, who's so particular.

The door closed behind the priest and the sound was like the clanging of a prison door to the girl. She jumped when Mrs. Carlton called to her from the hall. "Come along, Annie, and I'll show you what your duties will be."

Annie followed her in silence down the long, dark, narrow hall that led to the back of the house, the kitchen, the back stairs. Mrs. Carlton opened a door off the kitchen.

"This is your room, Annie. You may put your things away and then I want you to try on one of Hilda's uniforms—she used to work for us—and see if they fit. I do hope so, as they're practically new and it'd be such an extravagance to get new ones."

"Thank you—ma'am," murmured Annie, and went into the room. Mrs. Carlton left her there and she closed the door and looked around her. It was a small, spare room with only one window and a vine growing outside made a perpetual green gloom. There was a big golden oak dresser with a mirror, a plain iron bed, a clothespress, and a commode with bowl, pitcher, and chamber pot, hidden discreetly in the lower cupboard.

On the bed lay a black poplin uniform, white ruffled apron, little ruffled white cap. Annie touched it with scornful fingers. Not only was she to be a hired girl, but she was to wear a badge to show everyone what she was, to remind her to keep her place. She hoped it wouldn't fit, so Mrs. Carlton would have to go to the expense of buying new ones.

Annie slowly unpacked her few belongings, hung her clothes in the press, laid out her comb and brush on the fresh white bureau scarf, tucked the little holy card of the Blessed Mother in the edge of the mirror.

Then slowly, reluctantly, she took off her street dress, hung it up, and put on the black uniform of the departed Hilda. It didn't fit exactly; Hilda had been thicker-waisted, narrower-busted, than Annie, but she knew it would satisfy Mrs. Carlton. She tied on the white apron with clumsy fingers that fumbled the knot, smoothed her hair, and pinned the ridiculous little cap on top of her braids. Miserable as she felt, she couldn't help smiling when she saw herself in the mirror. She looked a perfect sight and she was glad. At least I'm not made for a hired girl's uniform, she thought, and swept into the kitchen, her head held high, a dangerous, defiant glint in her eye.

Mrs. Carlton was talking to a delivery boy at the door and she beckoned Annie to her. "Joe, this is Annie, our new hired girl. Joe delivers groceries for Augustine and Kyer, where we trade."

Joe, a rabbity youth with a mop of sandy hair, gave Annie a bold stare and grinned. "Glad to meetcha, Annie. You and me'll be friends, 'cause red's me favorite color."

"That'll be all, Joe," said Mrs. Carlton with a frown, and Joe, with a sly wink at Annie, clattered down the back steps. The woman turned to Annie. "Joe is apt to be a bit fresh, I'm afraid, so you'll have to be firm with him. Mr. Carlton won't stand for any nonsense, you understand."

Annie's eyes blazed. "You don't have to worry about that," she replied indignantly.

"I hope not. And now I'll show you where things are in the kitchen and try to explain to you how I want things done. It may be hard at first, but you'll catch on in a few days. Mr. Carlton wants his breakfast at seven sharp, but I'll help you with all the meals until you learn to cook."

When at last Mrs. Carlton had told Annie what would be expected of her, how she liked things done, all in a crisp, businesslike way, as if Annie were not a very bright child, she left her alone in the kitchen to do the breakfast dishes, polish silver, scrub and wax the kitchen floor, and peel the vegetables for the noon meal. Annie was deep in soapsuds at the sink when there was a light, quick step behind her, a cool voice said, "I'd like to have you press this waist for me, Annie. Be careful not to scorch it and do it as soon as possible. I'm going to a luncheon and I want to wear it."

Annie turned slowly and faced Emily, who stood holding an embroidered white shirtwaist. The dark, defiant violet eyes met the cool, impersonal blue ones in a long stare, and it was the blue ones that looked away first.

"I said I wanted you to——"

"I heard you. I'm sorry, but I don't know how to press waists. And I'm busy. Your mother told me what she wanted me to do and she didn't say anything about pressing your clothes."

Annie's voice was quiet, steady, firm. She turned her back on the pretty blond girl and began to rattle dishes noisily.

"Well, of all things!" breathed Emily. "I'll certainly speak to Mama about this," and she switched out of the room, her heels clicking angrily.

Annie rattled the dishes, her own anger hot within her. Hired girl I will be, but not lady's maid to Emily Carlton. If her mother makes me iron that waist I'll leave. I'll go back to the waterfront. But Mrs. Carlton didn't make her do the waist. Later she overheard her telling Emily that just because she'd been to boarding school she needn't put on airs and expect people to wait on her hand and foot.

Emily never asked Annie to press anything again, but she dropped clothes all over her room, left her dresser in a mess every morning, and Annie knew she did it on purpose to make more work for her. Mrs. Carlton was exacting but fair, always giving Annie her day off no matter what came up. Mr. Carlton was fussy, but he liked having a handsome girl in the house and he treated her more like a person than his wife did. But between Emily and Annie, from that day, ran a deep, smoldering hostility.

Chapter VII

Sounding her foghorn every few minutes, the *Island Queen* felt her way cautiously through the fog that wrapped Prince William Sound in heavy white wool. The water hissed against her keel and Hugh Deming, standing in the bow, could see no farther than the ship's stained prow parting the waves into curling snow. He wondered how the pilot knew where he was going, what to steer for, how to avoid reefs and sand bars. They seemed to be moving through a dream, and the wail of the whistle had a wild, lost sound like a tortured spirit.

Hugh leaned his arms on the rail and breathed the wet, salty air deeply. He'd been in Nome for a year and now he was on his way home with just enough money to get him there and one gold nugget attached to his watch chain to show for his adventure in the gold fields. Even that he hadn't found himself but had won in a poker game at the Red Dragon saloon. He certainly hadn't made his fortune, but then he hadn't really expected to. The whole business of the gold rush had seemed fantastic and unreal to him, like a gigantic amateur theatrical that he'd gone into for a lark.

Incredible things had happened. He'd seen filthy, tattered skeletons stagger into town with hundreds of thousands of dollars' worth of dust sewed into their rags. He'd seen men lose more money at faro and poker than most people have in a lifetime. He'd seen men paying a dollar for a cup of coffee, twenty dollars for a plate of scrambled eggs. He'd watched a miner draw a gun and shoot dead the man sitting across the card table from him because he thought he'd been cheating. He'd seen men lying in dark alleys with knives in their backs, their money belts emptied and thrown beside them, mute testimony of greed and lawlessness and the violence that springs from the thirst for gold. Once he was almost trapped in a dance hall that burned to the ground, taking a block of flimsy buildings with it. He'd bought drinks for painted dance-hall girls and been amused at their frank coarseness, their surprise and annoyance when they failed to seduce him. "Oh, so I'm not good enough for you mister," one of them, a black-eyed, fiery little devil from a New Orleans brothel, had flared at him. And when he'd smiled his slow, amused smile at her, she'd flown at him like a wildcat and scratched his face. He touched his cheek now, where the blood had trickled, and smiled.

Oh, he'd had his adventure, he'd seen the rip-roaring, hell-raising, wide-open, fantastic show and that was what he'd gone for. He wouldn't have missed it for the world.

The captain came down from the bridge, smoking a cigar, and spoke to him. "Bit thick, eh?" he said, pausing at the rail.

"I've just been wondering how your pilot finds his way through this pea soup," remarked Hugh.

The captain laughed. "He's been sailing these waters since he was a kid. He could steer a course with his eyes shut. You needn't worry, son. We'll get you home safe."

Hugh smiled. "I wasn't worried. Just amazed. I'd like to be a sailor myself. I'm crazy about boats."

"It's not an easy life, but I wouldn't swap places with anybody. There's money in it, too, for the owners," the captain chuckled. "Matter of fact, after this trip I'm going to buy a ship of my own. If I can raise the capital, I might even start a steamship line. There's a big future in shipping in the Pacific Northwest."

"I wouldn't be surprised," murmured Hugh with an interested look at the captain. "How much do you make on an average run, sir?"

The captain, sensing a sympathetic listener and eager to talk, after his long hours on the bridge, put his hand on the young man's arm. "Come down to my cabin with me, son, and join me at breakfast. I haven't had but a cup of coffee since last night."

"Glad to, Captain. This sea air gives me an appetite." Hugh, having eaten, at seven, a badly cooked breakfast of soggy wheat cakes, bitter coffee, and none too fresh eggs, was hungry again and hopeful that the captain might fare better than the passengers.

His hopes were justified. The captain had his own private store of delicacies that the Filipino steward prepared for him. There were oranges—"Bill Thompson, skipper of the *City of Pueblo*, an old friend of mine, has the San Francisco run and he brings me a crate every month." There were crisp, sizzling slices of Virginia ham—"My brother sends me a ham every so often from the East." There was fresh coffee that bore no resemblance to the thick, bitter brew Hugh had been served hours earlier—"I have my own blend, especially roasted for me in San Francisco. I make Willie grind it fresh every time he makes it for me." Hugh sat back, sighing happily after a really excellent meal. The captain knew how to live.

"You were asking me about the profits from an average run, eh?" Captain Blaine poured dark, pungent Jamaica rum into two small glasses and handed one to Hugh. It slipped down the throat, fiery, full-bodied, smooth as satin. A glow spread through the young man's insides and he felt warm for the first time since they'd run into the fog. "Well, I'll tell you, young feller. The *Island Queen* clears from two to five thousand a month. The *City of Pueblo*, on the San Francisco run, cleared a million dollars in one year. No small potatoes, eh, boy?"

"Lord, no." Hugh's eyes were bright with interest. This was the sort of thing that made sense. Not fantastic tales of striking fabulous Golcondas and picking a million dollars out of the ground, and getting a knife stuck in your ribs for your trouble. There was adventure in it, too, and sweep. There was the flavor of the sea, of busy ports, of trade, of planning. Shipping—it spoke of expansion, the destiny of cities. This was something with a future in it. Say a man owned one ship—he might clear a thousand dollars a month. Say he owned two, three, a fleet. Say he had a steamship line operating up and down the coast, from Los Angeles to Nome. Hugh sipped the hot, sweet liquor and listened eagerly to the old sea dog unfolding his dreams.

"How does a fellow get into this game?" he asked.

"How do you get into anything, son? Capital, the right connections, smart planning, knowing the ropes."

"You said if you could raise the capital you might start a line of your own," said Hugh, feeling him out.

Captain Blaine nodded. "That's right. I've got enough to buy one ship already."

"How much would you need?"

"That depends."

"Let me put it this way, sir. How much would a fellow have to put up to get into business with you?"

The captain sized him up carefully, taking his time about answering. He puffed on his cigar for a while, then he said, "Fifty thousand dollars."

Hugh didn't flicker an eyelash. His slender, handsome face maintained its thoughtful calm. He nodded, as if quite used to thinking in large figures, but he was casting madly about in his mind for someone who would lend him fifty thousand dollars on the strength of his charm and the intensity of his dream. His father? Not likely. He didn't have it, to begin with. He'd sunk twenty thousand in a bakery in Nome that had been gutted by fire. Who then? There was Mrs. Maurice Crawford, whose husband was a railroad company official. She'd taken quite a shine to him and he'd beaued her around town while her husband was East on business. He knew she was intrigued with his looks and his Southern manners. Then there was J. J. Hill, one of the biggest men in Seattle, a man of vision and enterprise. Hugh had met him once, but his father knew him and another meeting might be arranged. There was Will Carlton, who'd grub-staked poor Rolfe Linden, whose body the *Island Queen* was bringing down to Seattle now. Hugh didn't know Carlton, but he'd heard that he was approachable and dead sold on the great future of Seattle and the Pacific Northwest. I'll bet I *could* raise fifty thousand, thought Hugh.

"Were you thinking of investing in my steamship company?" asked Captain Blaine with a twinkle in his blue eyes as he looked at the slim, aristocratic, well-mannered young man across the table from him. He certainly didn't look shrewd or particularly aggressive. He looked more like a ladies' man than a prospective business partner. Still, you couldn't tell. The captain never made snap judgments. He took his time.

"I might, sir. I have some very good connections in Seattle.

My father's Judge Deming. I'm acquainted with Jim Hill and Maurice Crawford."

The captain pursed his lips and nodded.

"I'll think it over and get in touch with you before you ship out of Seattle again," said Hugh easily.

"I'll be in town for a month, at least. You can reach me at Kit Jordan's rooming house." The captain got up, consulted the barometer on the wall, pulled his heavy gold watch out of his vest pocket. "Time I was getting back on the bridge. You think over my proposition, young fellow. If you go in with me you'll be getting in on something good. This country's just beginning to open up. In ten, twenty years shipping will be booming. Shouldn't wonder but what we'd have a big trade with the Orient by then."

Hugh went up on deck again to smoke, to lean on the rail, to stare at the water, to plan. The fog was lifting now, sun striking obliquely through, sparkling on the waves. The ship's engines throbbed faster, since the need for caution was past; the prow dipped and rose as it plunged merrily through the water. Wooded green mountains rose sharply from the cold darkness of the sea. Hugh saw a whole fleet of steamers plowing through these waters, fine ships that he had sent out, whose destinies were linked with his.

The *Island Queen* steamed into Elliott Bay on a bright, clear afternoon, followed by an escort of screaming, wheeling gulls. She brought a fortune in gold, men who'd made their stake and were going home to spend it, men who'd lost everything but their shirts and would have to go back to commonplace, drab jobs, if they could find them. She brought poor young Rolfe Linden, sealed in a pine box, and Hugh Deming, flat broke but full of vitality and eagerness, possessed by a dream and all ready to use his charm, his social position, and his friends to raise fifty thousand dollars.

He walked jauntily up the steps of his father's house and smack into a tea party his mother was giving. Not at all nonplused, he dropped his battered suitcase and duffel bag in the hall for Jason to take up to his room, tossed his hat on the deer antlers that served as a hatrack, and walked smiling into the parlor where his mother in gray lace, with a black velvet ribbon about her throat, was pouring tea.

"Ah, tea!" he cried humorously, rubbing his hands. "Just what I need. Of course it's a bit stronger than the stuff we drink in Alaska, but I reckon I can take it."

"Hughie!" screamed his mother shrilly, dropping a silver tea-spoon and nearly breaking one of her best Lowestoft cups. "Where in the world . . . ?"

" 'Home is the sailor, home from the sea, And the hunter home from the hill,' " he quoted, grinning, and he bent and kissed her charmingly, while all the ladies clucked approvingly and began to fuss over him.

"But why didn't you let us know you were coming, Hugh baby?" cried his mother, doting on him, patting his hand and beaming.

"I didn't know till just before sailing time whether I'd win enough money at poker to get passage aboard," he said, and all the ladies squealed with delight and pretended to be shocked.

"Oh, Hughie," gasped his mother in horror, being a good Southern Methodist, "you gambled!"

"It was either that or become a squaw man and let my Eskimo wife support me spearing fish." His eyes had found Erica Craw-ford sitting by herself on the gold plush love seat and he gave her an ironic smile over the plumed heads of the other ladies.

"Hugh, the way you talk. I declare! You'll shock my friends," sighed his mother. "Here, take a cup of tea and go sit down and behave."

"Yes, Mama," he replied in mock humility, and he crossed the room and stood before Mrs. Crawford, cup in hand. "May I?" he murmured. She gave him a long, cool, amused look and made room for him on the love seat.

"So you're back, young man," she said. "We've missed you."

Mrs. Deming was giving them a faintly speculative glance. She hadn't been sure whether she should ask Erica Crawford, since there was talk about her being a bit fast—oh, nothing really damaging, but she entertained freely while her husband was away and she liked to be seen with the younger men. How-ever, she'd invited Mrs. Deming to a musicale and Hugh's mother never failed to repay social debts. But she was annoyed at Hugh for making a beeline for her. Now the ladies *would* have something to talk about. Hugh was a dear boy and he could wind her around his little finger, but she did wish he'd marry soon and settle down. His father, the judge, though no one would ever think it to see him now in all his dignity, had been a devil with the women until she married him.

Erica Crawford saw her hostess's glance and knew exactly what she was thinking. It amused her no end, just as it amused her that she was talked about. She could afford to be: her money and her position in society, plus her immense chic, made such talk seem like envious babblings. Also Hugh Deming amused her—no, that wasn't all he did to her—perhaps "intrigued" was the word. She was glad he was back from Alaska, safe and sound and even more charming, with a racy little edge of masculine arrogance that appealed to her. Thank heaven, nothing horrible had happened to him like it had to poor Rolfe Linden.

"I missed you, too, Erica," he said. "Particularly those superb little suppers you used to give. One night in Nome, trying to eat underdone fish, I remembered the pheasant and wine you gave me the last time I was at your house. Do you still feed hungry young men pheasant?"

She laughed, quite aware that he was teasing her by mentioning her dinners instead of herself. "Certain hungry young men. If they're amusing as well as hungry."

He pulled down his mouth at her. "You mean I shall have to earn my supper if I'm to be invited?"

"Of course. Come Thursday night and tell me all about Alaska and the wild dance-hall women." She swept long lashes over the glitter in her eyes and rose to go, giving him her teacup. With her tall, willowy, full-bosomed figure, the swan neck, the poised head with the black hair done in a low chignon, the large, rose-decked hat, she was the epitome of the Gibson Girl, the ideal of the young set.

"Really, Hugh, must you pay so much attention to Mrs. Crawford?" complained his mother after the ladies had gone.

"Well, darling, since she was the only woman in the room under sixty, and since she's invited me to supper Thursday and since I mean to interest her in my career, yes, I think I must." Her son squeezed her shoulder and went up to his room, whistling "Camptown Races."

Hugh bathed, shaved, put on fresh, beautifully laundered linen, a gray flannel suit that had been hanging carefully swathed in a muslin bag in his closet, awaiting his return, and stood admiring himself in the mirror, trying to decide what he should do with his first evening home. Dinner with his family, of course, but after that, what? Since he was seeing Erica Crawford on Thursday and had seen her at tea, he couldn't very well call on her. She might get bored with him if he seemed too eager. There were the Ferry girls, but they were a bit too fresh and dewy-eyed from boarding school. Perhaps Anita Fairchild; but no, she'd been a shade too possessive just before he went away. He could drop into the University Club and play cards. He rubbed his clean-shaven jaw that was leaner and harder-looking than when he went away.

His father was glad to see him, in his dignified, restrained way, amused and not surprised that he'd not discovered a fortune in Alaska, glad that he'd come back with his shirt and none the worse for his adventure. Hugh was never quite sure that his father approved of him. He had a way of studying him when he thought his son wasn't looking. The young man sometimes wondered what his father was thinking then. Hugh always maintained toward the judge a respectful manner, almost of humility, which was quite sincere. He knew the profound integrity, the wisdom, the strength of the man and he admired him deeply. But he knew, too, that he'd inherited few if any of his father's sterling qualities except, perhaps, his charm and wit and a real friendliness toward all sorts of people.

"Well, young man," said the judge over their port, "now that you've had your fling, what do you mean to do? Go into your brother's law office?"

Hugh flushed, turned his glass round and round, watching the light make the deep purple of the wine glow. "I don't quite know, sir. I'd like to go into the steamship business if I can find some capital. I was talking to the captain of the *Island Queen*. He tells me there's a lot of money in shipping."

His father took off his pince-nez, polished the lenses with his napkin, adjusted them on his thin, hawklike nose. "H'm," he said at last, "shipping. Interesting. Of course the men in our family have always chosen a profession, the law usually, or the Army. But there's no reason to stick to the pattern. Where are you going to raise the money?"

"I don't know yet, sir. I have a few ideas. Maybe until I see how things work out I'd better read law for Beauchamp."

"An excellent idea. Do you know anything about shipping?" His father gave him a steady look.

Hugh smiled deprecatingly. When he was with his father, he felt that he knew very little about anything. "Not much. But I can learn."

The judge nodded as if that were a profound statement. "Quite right. When I told people I was going West they said, 'Do you know anything about the West?' and I said, 'No, but I'll find out.' An inquiring mind is a good thing. So is courage and so is persistence. Just so you don't get to flitting from one thing to the other, my boy. Make up your mind what you want to do, then stick to it."

The judge finished his port, pushed back his chair, and went into the living room where his wife already sat with her knitting. "Read to me, Molly, will you?" he said, stretching out in his easy chair. "A bit of Bobby Burns, if you please."

"But, Robert, I thought Hugh might like to sit and talk to us," said his wife, putting down her knitting and reaching for her husband's favorite volume on the table beside her.

"We've talked. Now he wants to go out and impress his friends with all his exciting adventures in the North. Can't you see he's all dressed up?"

Hugh laughed, his face coloring. He was both grateful and rebuffed. His father always made him feel young and slightly foolish. He kissed his mother, took his bowler hat from the hall, and started out the door. "There's a band concert in Volunteer Park, Hugh," called his mother. "You might enjoy that."

He smiled as he went down the path between the shiny green of the madroña trees. A band concert! After the Red Dragon saloon and Klondike Kate's Palace of the Dance. Still—why not? He was suddenly restless, a little sorry he'd come home. He didn't want to call on any of the girls he knew, the well-brought-up, fashionable daughters of the first families. He didn't feel like the University Club either. He wanted a girl, not too well bred a girl, but not a bad girl, either. In the park, listening to the band concert, he might be able to find one to josh with, maybe steal a kiss, have a mild flirtation, not one that might get him over his head like Erica Crawford. Not a woman of the world, but not a hothouse flower, either.

Annie Jordan had been to confession and as she walked past the park on her way back to the Carltons', she suddenly didn't want to go back to her little room and sit on the bed. Mr. and Mrs. Carlton had gone out to a program at the Episcopal church and they'd not be back till ten. Emily was with her friend, Marguerite Brookes, for the night. The night was cool but clear and there was going to be a moon. She wanted to walk in the park and smell the fresh scent of grass and flowers and look at the moonlight.

She turned into the park with a delicious feeling of adventure. There were a few couples wandering arm in arm, some sitting close together on benches. She didn't mind being alone, she had such a wonderful feeling of freedom. Since she'd gone to live with the Carltons, she'd been bound by her promise to Father Donegan to go straight home after confession, never to wander or give her mistress any worry. But tonight—tonight she'd stay out just a little while. She'd get back before the Carltons did.

There was an empty bench under a maple tree and she sat down, took off her hat, and leaned back against the seat, closing her eyes and letting her thoughts wander. She wondered what was going on down at the waterfront tonight. The Alaska boat was in, she'd seen it coming in when she went marketing for Mrs. Carlton. It had taken great will power not to go down and watch it dock. The Nugget would be full of sailors and men from the Klondike. The Variety girls would all be there, Maizie pounding the piano, the others laughing and drinking with the men. "Casey would waltz with the strawberry blonde," she hummed softly. She was grateful for her sanctuary, but oh, how dull and flat it was after the waterfront. Nothing exciting ever happened.

"May I share this bench?" said a slow, quiet voice, and she nearly jumped off the seat.

"Oh!" she gasped, staring at the elegant young man in gray flannel who stood with his hat in his hand, smiling down at her.

"I'm sorry. I didn't mean to frighten you." What was it about his voice that made her heart leap in recognition? It wasn't dark yet and she stared at him curiously.

"Perhaps you'd rather not have me," he said, and bowed as if to leave.

"Don't go," she cried involuntarily and then was covered with confusion. Nice girls, according to Mrs. Carlton, didn't speak to strangers. But this young man wasn't a stranger. His voice—she knew his voice and his slightly ironic smile, the gray eyes flecked with gold. "I know you," she blurted in her frank, quick way.

"Do you now? Then it's all right for me to sit down." She nodded, moved over for him, and he sat beside her, looking as intently at her as she had at him. He was sure he'd never seen her before or he'd certainly remember. You don't forget hair that color, eyes like purple pansies, skin that looked good enough to eat, a figure like a young Juno.

"You're Hugh Deming, aren't you? The judge's son," this amazing, forthright beauty was saying.

"Yes." He was still smiling, trying to place her, deciding that she certainly wasn't one of the fashionable young debutantes he'd called on or met at cotillions. But she wasn't one of the actresses he'd met at gay supper parties, either. She had none of the coyness, the artificial manners of society nor yet the cheap boldness of the theater girls. Suddenly he realized she was just what he'd been looking for, a simple, direct, friendly person he could be himself with, who might not be averse to a little innocent spooning, from the soft ripeness of her.

"You don't remember me," Annie went on eagerly, as if he were an old friend. "I just saw you once, when I was only thirteen. On the dock. You came down to watch the boats come in. You'd just come to Seattle."

"You taught me the Siwash word for 'friend' and gave me a caramel," cried Hugh, suddenly remembering the gangly, unkempt, red-haired adolescent with the amazing violet eyes. "*Tillicoom.*"

Annie laughed. "Yes. *Tillicoom.* You gave me a ride home in a carriage. It was the first time I'd ridden in one."

"But you can't be the same girl. She was—well"—he laughed—"not a beauty. And you are."

Annie blushed, then she tossed her head. "You said I might turn into one. You said Cleopatra had red hair too."

"Good Lord, did I? And you haven't forgotten."

She shook her head. "I always remembered it when the kids teased me about my hair."

"I wish my memory were as good. You did tell me your name then, didn't you?"

"Oh sure, but I wouldn't expect you to remember it. After all, I was only a kid and it was four years ago. It's Annie Jordan."

He liked her. She was the most natural girl he'd ever met. And Lord, what a beauty. No taste in clothes, of course. A daughter of the people. Probably from the waterfront, since she'd been hanging around the docks that day. But that didn't mean he couldn't enjoy her.

"I thought there was going to be a band concert tonight," he said, looking at the soft curve of her cheek.

"There will be, later, I think."

"I've been away for a year, so I don't know what's going on in town." He put his arm casually over the back of the seat, but she didn't seem to notice. She looked at him with interest and he went on, "I've been in Alaska, seeking my fortune. But I didn't find it." He laughed.

Her smiling face changed and she looked away. "I—I knew a boy who went to Alaska for gold," she murmured. "But he didn't come back. He was killed."

"I'm sorry," said Hugh softly, and pressed her shoulder gently.

She turned and smiled gratefully at him. The sorrow for Rolfe lay deep and she'd never mentioned it to anyone. It was nice for Hugh Deming to be sorry, but she wasn't going to burden him with her troubles. Still she had the impulse to talk about Rolfe to someone.

"He was engaged to my sister Mae. Maybe you knew him. His name was Rolfe Linden."

"The banker's son? I knew him slightly. The boat I just came in on today brought his body home."

Annie gasped and her face went white. Her whole body stiffened and he pressed her a little closer, bent toward her. She sat perfectly still, staring straight ahead, and tears began to roll slowly down her cheeks. She seemed quite unaware of them; she said nothing, and, conscious that she was lost in some private grief of her own, he volunteered nothing. But he took out his pocket handkerchief and quietly wiped the tears from her face.

She turned at that and looked at him with dark, wide eyes. "You see, I loved him too," she said simply.

There was a silence and then Hugh said softly, "What rotten luck. I'm sorry, Annie."

"Thanks," she murmured. "I've never told anyone before." She sighed. "Let's walk a bit, shall we?"

"Yes." They got up and Hugh took her hand. They walked slowly down the path to the sunken gardens, hand in hand, and Annie's stride matched his.

"Rolfe Linden was a lucky fellow, if you loved him, Annie," said Hugh at last.

"He never knew. No one did." The deep, shocking spasm of grief was gone and Annie's face was calm again.

"You're very young, you know. You'll love someone else and it will be all right."

Annie looked at him and smiled. "Yes," she answered, "I will. I'm all right now. I'm sorry I cried."

Now the band concert had begun; the strains of the Poet and Peasant Overture came to them through the trees. The air was sweet with dewy grass and heliotrope. They walked slowly and Annie's hand was strong and warm in Hugh's. He told her about some of his experiences in the North and she listened eagerly, her face turned to his, glowing and alive.

"I wish I'd been there," she said once. "If I were a man I'd have gone too."

"I'll bet you would," he laughed. "You'd probably have done better than I did. You wouldn't have come home empty-handed."

"Oh, I wouldn't care about the gold. It'd be the adventure, the excitement I'd be after. I like things happening. That's why I liked it on the waterfront."

"Don't you live there now?" he asked. Where do you live, you strange, unself-conscious, exciting girl? he wondered. There's no placing you—what world do you belong in?

"No." Her face darkened a bit. "I live on the First Hill now."

He wanted to ask where, but he knew if she'd wanted him to know she'd have told him. There was a strange quality to his meeting with her—a mixture of familiarity and restraint, of naturalness and mystery. He didn't want to spoil it.

The band was playing a Brahms waltz now and she swayed slightly, her body unconsciously moving to its rhythm. What a beauty she was and how unaware of it she seemed. She doesn't really know she's beautiful or what power she could have over a man. She's completely unawakened, in spite of her having been in love with Rolfe Linden.

"Look," she cried in sudden, childlike delight, "there's a new moon." The slim silver moon hung breathlessly suspended in the deep night blue of the sky, attended by the evening star.

"Close your eyes and make a wish," murmured Hugh softly.

She laughed and, turning her face to the moon, she did as she was bid. Hugh suddenly caught her to him, kissed the warm, sweet curve of her cheek. Her eyes flew open and she looked at him in sudden confusion.

"Oh," she cried, trying to push him away. "Please let me go. I have to go home now."

"Not yet, Annie—please, it's early." His voice was urgent and he pulled her closer.

She struggled for a moment and then, her eyes dark and wide, her cheeks flushed, she put her arms impulsively about his neck, lifted her mouth to his. His arms tightened around her, a warm, wonderful excitement went through her, but she pushed him away at last, laughing, her face hot, her hair tumbled.

"Annie!" he cried, but she tore her hands from his, grabbed up her hat, and escaped up the path, leaving him standing there, looking after her.

Hugh sat down on the bench to light a cigarette, but to his surprise he found that his hands were trembling so that it was hard to hold the match steady. The feel of her warm body, the clean, fresh scent of her skin and hair, the frank, impulsive pressure of her lips were still with him. He'd kissed girls before but it had never been like this. She was ardent, she was sweet and natural, and he'd swear she was good. Will I ever see her again? he thought. I've got to see her again. Be careful, boy, she's not the kind you can flirt with, and is she the kind you want to marry? Don't forget, you've got a career to carve out for yourself and if you get mixed up with that girl you may not be able to give her up.

Chapter VIII

The work at Carltons' was hard, the hours long. Annie was up at six every morning and, if Mrs. Carlton was entertaining, she didn't get to bed sometimes till midnight. But Annie was strong; she'd worked hard at the Nugget, too, and she had every Saturday off, after the work was done in the morning. She was allowed Sunday mornings from ten to twelve to go to mass, which she attended faithfully as she'd promised Father Donegan. Mrs. Carlton, having found out that Annie was honest and a shrewd buyer, let her do the marketing twice a week. Annie loved marketing days. It gave her a chance to get away from the house, to take the streetcar downtown, to mingle with the crowds on the street, look into store windows, to sweep into Augustine and Kyer's in her best hat and coat and chaff with the clerks.

The clerks, most of them brash young fellows with a quick line of talk for a pretty girl, would brighten the minute they saw her tall, handsome figure swinging in the door with the hearty, free step that always made people turn to look at her.

"Here comes our wild Irish rose," they'd say, grinning at her. "Sure and she looks like the kiss of spring this mornin', too."

"None of your fresh talk now, boys," she'd answer, tossing her head, her eyes sparkling. "I've got no time for fooling and me with a list to buy as long as your arm."

"Whose arm? Mine?" laughed the assistant manager, a sturdy, likable fellow named Ed Bauer whose brown eyes always managed to give her a long, deep look over the counter and who kept her talking longer than the others, even when plushy dowagers like Mrs. Terry or Mrs. Green were waiting to give their orders. "It's a long arm, Annie, long enough to go around that waist of yours. Want me to show you?"

"Indeed and I do not," she cried, but her cheeks were rosy and her laugh was warm. "You keep your long arms to yourself, Ed Bauer, and measure me out five pounds of tea—orange pekoe and the best in the store. Mrs. Carlton's very particular about her tea."

The clerks made her feel good, like a person again, not just a hired girl. The one she liked the best was Ed, and until she'd met Hugh Deming in the park she'd dreamed about him once or twice. He had a kind of healthy, blunt, manly good looks with ruddy cheeks and nice, honest eyes. But he couldn't hold a candle to Hugh, with his fine features and his ironic eyes.

She gave her order, which would be delivered by Joe, the delivery boy, the freshest of the lot, but he kept his hands to himself after Annie had slapped him a good one once in the kitchen. It was ten-thirty and she had to be back by eleven to start the midday meal. She felt wonderful, and a little smile hovered over her mouth and made her eyes bright as she swung along the street, glancing now and then at herself in shop-windows.

It was a fine, early summer day with air as mild and sweet as baby's breath. The sky was a pure high blue with only a few soft clouds like puffs of white smoke. The teasing admiration of the store clerks, Ed's long, searching look as he said good-by, the memory of Hugh Deming's kiss the other night in the park all merged together inside her in an exhilarating feeling of warmth and power. What was it her mother had said once, looking sharply at her ripening body? "You'll have the men crazy for you."

Annie's smile deepened as she thought of that and a well-dressed, middle-aged man stared at her a moment, then smiled and raised his hat to her as she passed. It would be something to have men crazy for you—no, not men, but one man. But in order to have the one man, the one you wanted out of all the men in the world, you'd have to have the others crazy for you, too, so that he would notice and want you. Besides, how could you know which was your man unless you got to know a lot of them? And would you know for sure, even then? Yes, she thought, I'd know. When it happens, I'll know. Something deep within her told her that he would know, too, or that she could make him know.

"Annie," said Emily, coming into the kitchen after lunch with the placating little smile and the soft, wheedling voice she used when she wanted something, "Marguerite Brookes is coming to tea this afternoon. Would you be an angel and make some of those wonderful coconut dreams of yours?"

Annie glanced at her coolly. She knew how to handle Emily now. She simply treated her as an equal or, if she got on her high horse, as a sulky child who should be ignored. "Why, yes, Emily, I'd be glad to, but I'm not sure there's any coconut left."

"Oh dear, I *do* hope so. I've boasted so *much* about your coconut dreams," cried Emily.

"Suppose you run down cellar, then, and see if there's still a coconut in that box your father sent away for," said Annie calmly, continuing to polish silver at the sink.

Emily flushed and then, with a laugh and a toss of her blond head, opened the cellar door and went down the steps. She returned triumphantly, bearing a coconut. Annie had known all along there was one, but she had to maintain her independence with Emily.

"Here it is, Annie, and since Marguerite's coming at four and it's nearly two now, you'd better let the silver go and start the cookies."

"Your mother wants the silver polished for her musicale tomorrow and I'll be too busy getting the house ready and making sandwiches to do it then. I'll finish the silver and then I'll make the cookies," said Annie firmly.

Emily shot her an irritated glance and with a sigh of exasperation flounced out of the kitchen. Annie took her time doing the silver, then washed her hands, dried them, and started the cookies. She hadn't known how to cook anything but fried eggs and very black coffee when she came to the Carltons', but her mistress was an excellent cook and a good teacher and Annie liked good food, so it hadn't taken her long to learn. She still couldn't make baking-powder biscuits or bread like Mrs. Carlton's, but her cakes and cookies were always successful.

At four the doorbell rang and as Annie was just taking the cookies out of the oven, she didn't answer it. Mrs. Carlton was out, calling on the new Episcopal minister's wife, so Emily had to let her caller in. Annie could hear the two girls' voices chatting, or at least Emily's high voice, in the hall as Marguerite took off her wraps. In a minute Emily appeared at the kitchen door, her eyes bright, her cheeks flushed. She loved company and always sparkled when friends came in, but today her color seemed higher than ever and her manner more excited.

Annie heard her say just before she came out to the kitchen, "Go into the den, Marguerite, and I'll be right there. I have the *most* exciting news to tell you." At the door she said to Annie imperiously, "You may bring in the tea right away, Annie. And please put on your white cap to serve it."

"The cookies are still too hot, Emily. I'll bring it in in a few minutes. And my white cap is in the wash."

Emily gave her a hard, angry stare but at that moment Marguerite came to the doorway. She was a tall, cool-looking brunette and had none of Emily's airs and graces; she always acted amused when her friend put on what Marguerite called her "finishing school manner." It annoyed Emily that Marguerite was so democratic with Annie and always made a point of coming out to the kitchen to talk to her, would even stop her on the street, as if they were friends and Annie as good as she was.

"Hello, Annie," she said now with a friendly smile. "How have you been?"

"Fine, Marguerite. How are you?" Annie knew quite well what Emily thought of Marguerite's attitude toward her. She knew, too, that the tall, dark girl whose mother ran a select boardinghouse liked her and considered her as much of a person as Emily.

"I've brought you some books. They're on the hall table."

"More Graustark stories?" cried Annie eagerly.

"No," said Marguerite, "a different one. *The Prisoner of Zenda.*" They exchanged a smiling look. Both of them were devotees of the romantic novels of the period, and since Marguerite had found out that Annie liked to read, she always brought her a book when she came to see Emily.

"Come along, Marguerite," interrupted Emily, putting her arm through her friend's possessively. "I've *so* much to tell you. We're having tea in the den, Annie," she added coldly.

Annie made the tea, arranged the dreams on a silver dish, sliced lemon, got out Mrs. Carlton's second best tea set, and put it all on a tray. She liked handling the thin china, the silver spoons, the delicate tea napkins. She had a quick eye for detail, for the right way of doing things, thinking always, When I have my *own* house on the First Hill and invite people to tea or dinner, I'll know what to do.

She pushed back the long, narrow leather strips that covered the doorway between the living room and the den and served as portieres. The den was a snug little room with a Franklin stove, bookcases, a leather Morris chair, and a soft divan piled high with leather and plush and beaded cushions. The leather cushions had interesting pictures burned or painted on one side. One was of an Indian chief in a bristling war bonnet, one was of Mount Rainier with a pink glow on its snowcap, and another, more sophisticated and cosmopolitan, was of New York's sky line.

Emily and Marguerite sat on the divan with piles of cushions at their backs. Annie came in sedately, with the white apron on if not the cap, and put down the tea tray on a low table near the divan. Emily paid no attention to her, went on babbling to Marguerite. Annie, arranging the cups and saucers, couldn't help but listen.

"I've been simply dying to tell you, Marguerite, but Mama kept wanting me to do things. Finally I decided I'd have to get you over here."

"What have you been dying to tell me?" Marguerite's smile was aloof, amused.

Emily pulled out a card from her bodice. Annie, her back turned, was busy pouring the tea, but she heard Marguerite's gasp as she read out loud, "Mr. Hugh Deming requests the pleasure of Miss Emily Carlton to the Nesika Club Ball to be held at the Denny Hotel, the sixteenth of June, 1900."

"Oh *no*, Emily!" breathed Marguerite. "Not Hugh Deming! Not Seattle's most dashing and eligible bachelor!"

"Oh yes, darling. Do you wonder that I'm thrilled?" She leaned forward, her eyes sparkling. "He's so handsome, has his boots made in New York, I've heard, and everyone knows he was the first man to smoke cigarettes in Seattle. Now half the men at the University Club are smoking them!"

Annie poured the tea, passed the cups, the lemon, the sugar, the cookies to Emily and her guest. The slow, painful color burned in her cheeks and her eyes had a bright, glittering look. She didn't once glance at either Emily or her guest, but Emily, suddenly looking at her, wondered at the strange expression on her face.

Annie managed to maintain the proper poker face of the well-trained servant as she served the tea and passed the cookies. But her throat was dry and her heart beat heavily and slowly. Marguerite's easy friendship had made her forget the difference that lay between her and these girls from the First Hill. But now the gulf seemed to stretch between them, abysmal, fixed.

"You could be a beauty," Marguerite had told her once, and when she brushed her heavy hair before the mirror at night, in her corset cover and petticoat, the line of her creamy throat and round, white shoulders was both queenly and seductive. Her forehead was pure and clear, the eyebrows that arched above her deep, violet eyes were as delicate and perfect as if they'd been penciled. Her skin was white as new milk, her lips full and strawberry-red.

Yes, she was a beauty, she guessed, but what good had it ever done her? It had made lecherous Fred Carew want her enough to pay a bag of gold dust for her and it had made Hugh Deming kiss her in the summer darkness of the park, Ed Bauer flirt with her in the store. It hadn't been able to get Rolfe Linden for her, though if he'd come back from Alaska alive and found Mae gone, she knew with all the passionate surge of her blood that it might have.

If she'd been born on the First Hill instead of the waterfront, if her mother had been the wife of a banker or a mill owner, or even the proprietor of a genteel boardinghouse like Mrs. Brookes's, she could have been somebody in Seattle. She could have backed pink-and-white-and-gold Emily Carlton right off the map. Maybe all men were created free and equal, and ambition and ability might be able to carry an emigrant's son up to the presidency or to be a railroad executive, but that didn't hold for women. Not in the tight, respectable, self-conscious society of a pioneer town just becoming aware of its destiny. Annie Jordan came from the docks, she was a hired girl and, beauty or no beauty, the doors were shut upon her.

Marguerite and Emily chattered away about the ball. "What are you going to wear?"

"Oh heavens, I don't know. Everything I have is so frightfully young and schoolgirlish."

"I could make you a dress, Emily. If you'll get the material, we'll pick out a pattern from Godey's and I'll copy it."

"Oh, Marguerite, if you would! If you would I'll let you dance at my wedding!"

"To Hugh Deming?" laughed Marguerite.

Emily giggled, her cheeks flushed. "Silly! I haven't even gone out with him yet. Besides, I expect to have hundreds of beaux before I marry. No self-respecting girl would marry the first man who came along."

Annie handed round the lemon and the cookies and went back to the kitchen, got out the ironing board and some clothes she'd sprinkled, took one of the sadirons she kept on the back of the big coal range that never went out, winter or summer, and began to iron doggedly.

She could hear the murmur of the girls' voices and occasionally a burst of laughter from Emily. Why was it that she was in the kitchen, ironing other people's clothes, and Emily was in the den, drinking tea and planning her ball gown? For a while the hopelessness that had suddenly engulfed her weighed down her heart and mind. Was she a fool to think that someday she'd have a fine house and a man who loved her? Was she a fool to remember Hugh Deming's kiss, to think about him, when a girl like Emily could dance with him, meet him as an equal?

After supper Annie had permission to go to confession. Ever since she'd come to the Carltons' she'd done exactly as she'd promised Father Donegan. She'd asked her mistress for permission every time she stepped out of the house. She went only where she said she was going, to confession, to mass, once in a while she went shopping, on rare occasions she took in the show at the Third Avenue Theater. Never once had she gone back to the waterfront, to Considine's or Yesler Avenue. In all the time since the dreadful night when she ran away from Fred Carew, she hadn't seen her mother.

Mrs. Carlton, who'd been a bit uneasy about her at first, had no cause to worry now. Annie was well behaved, obedient, trustworthy. She never stayed out after ten even when she went to a show.

When Annie left the house that night she had every intention of doing as she'd told her employer. She meant to go to confession, perhaps stroll up Boren Avenue, where some new houses were going up, maybe drop in on a girl she'd met at church who also worked out. She didn't know why she'd put on her new foulard dress and the little straw sailor she bought with her first pay. She'd been saving them for church. But suddenly as she'd stood at the mirror in her little room, a deep feeling of anger and bitterness and hatred for her life surged over her. What was she getting out of it? Security, perhaps, safety from her mother's schemes, the friendship of Marguerite, the kindness of Mrs. Carlton. But oh, it wasn't enough. Tonight, with the blood beating in her cheeks and throat, it wasn't near enough. She wanted some fun again, some excitement.

"I want to see Hugh Deming again," she whispered, and her eyes glittered at her from the mirror. The encounter with Hugh in the park had been the only thing that had happened to her that the Carltons didn't know about, and she hugged it to her in secret, thrilling delight. She closed her eyes and felt his arms about her again, insistent and strong, the excitement of his sudden, unexpected kiss that had ended in laughter and escape, but that had lain in her memory ever since. "He doesn't mean a thing to me. I don't care if he is taking Emily to the ball. But I want to see him again!" she whispered, and pinned the smart little sailor jauntily on top of her head.

Chapter IX

On Saturday nights in summer, weather permitting, there were band concerts in Volunteer Park. In the warm, sweet dark, with stars twinkling overhead, the music floated dreamily through the trees and couples strolled along the paths or over the cool grass, arm in arm, murmuring together, their laughter disturbing the older people who'd come to hear the music.

Annie liked the band concerts. She loved the music that stirred her heart and set her to dreaming. But even better than the music she loved the excitement, the secret, deep thrill of expectancy that possessed her and made her cheeks burn, her heart beat fast. Walking alone down the little paths or sitting on the grass under the trees, with the strains of a Strauss waltz floating through the dusk, she would half close her eyes and see herself in a shimmering ball gown, with jewels in her hair and at her throat, waltzing in a lighted ballroom with crystal chandeliers and potted palms, one dainty gloved hand on the uniformed arm of the handsome hussar who had fought a duel over her, the other holding up the train of the gown. The hussar looked like Rupert of Hentzau and she, in her dreams, was the proud, full-bosomed swan-necked heroine of the illustrations in the romantic novels that Marguerite let her borrow.

But since her encounter with Hugh Deming, her hussar had borne the aristocratic features, the gray eyes, the half-tender, half-ironic smile of the judge's son. Tonight, as she strolled slowly under the trees, conscious of her new foulard and the saucy little sailor perched on her pompadour, she tried to recapture her dream, but instead of herself, waltzing in Hugh's arms, she kept seeing the elegant blond figure of Emily Carlton. She saw him bend toward her, smiling and murmuring, and Emily's pink-and-white face with its dainty features laughing up at him. Suddenly she hated the lilting music, the soft, treacherous enchantment of the summer twilight, her own foolish dreams.

I'm nothing but a hired girl, she told herself. My mother runs a saloon. The only waltzing I'll ever do will be in a cheap dance hall with a sailor.

But her rebellious heart refused to listen. Pride and anger swelled up in her. You're a beauty, Annie Jordan, no matter where you come from. Remember what Hugh said when you were thirteen? With that hair and those violet eyes you'll be a fascinating woman. You don't have to be a hired girl all your life. Someday you'll live in a fine house on the First Hill—your own house—and you'll give balls and cotillions and Hugh Deming and Emily Carlton will be proud to come to them.

"Waterfront rat!" she heard her mother say. She heard her harsh, brittle laughter. "Don't be puttin' on airs, my girl." "Pride goeth before a fall, my child," she heard Father Donegan warn her. "Keep your place. Obey your mistress and the Church and be satisfied with what God has given you." "But God gave me my red hair and my white skin and the heart that burns in my breast. God gave me a thirst for life, didn't He?" she whispered to herself.

The band began to play a Strauss waltz and a couple, arms entwined, passed her, humming the tune. Annie cast them an envious glance. On a night like this, dressed in her best, she should be strolling with a man too.

Two fellows in dapper straw hats and Norfolk jackets were coming toward her, their eyes bright and interested as they glanced her way. One of them paused as they came abreast and tipped his hat. "Lovely evening, isn't it, miss?"

She didn't answer; her cheeks burned and she kept her eyes averted. But she walked more slowly, her heart beginning to thump under the tight bodice. It was all she could do to keep from turning her head to see if they were following her. Why didn't you speak to them, you ninny? she scolded herself. No harm in being civil, is there? No harm in maybe strolling through the park with two nice-looking fellows. Why should you go home and sit in your room this fine summer night, when you might have a little fun?

There were footsteps behind her, someone whistling the tune the band was playing. Involuntarily she quickened her own steps and there was a laugh and the steps behind her quickened too.

"She's a lady, can't you see?" said a laughing voice. "Maybe she don't talk to strangers when they're not properly introduced."

"Oh, is that all that's wanting?" said another voice. "I'll fix that up right now." The footsteps were hard on her heels and she had to bite her lips to keep from smiling.

"Pardon me, Miss Brown."

Annie stopped, tilted her head, and glanced over her shoulder, trying to look stern, but her heart was beating with excitement and she knew her cheeks were pink. The young man who had tipped his hat to her came up now, hat in hand, and made a short bow.

"My name isn't Miss Brown," said Annie coolly, but the dimple beside her mouth gave her away.

"Oh, I'm so sorry. I thought you were Miss Brown from Chicago." The young man gave her a sly smile and his eyes were bold and dark. He had a small black mustache which gave him a very dashing air. "May I introduce myself and my friend?" Then, without waiting for her answer, he went on quickly, "I am Ned Weaver and this is Benjy Olsson."

"How do you do?" said Annie demurely, smiling at the other man. He wasn't as good-looking as the dark one, being stolid and blond with a mouthful of teeth. But he had a ruddy skin and china-blue eyes that stared in frank admiration at Annie.

"Pleased to meetcha, Miss . . . er . . ." He grinned and she hesitated.

"Oh, come now, aren't you going to play fair and tell us your name?" said the dark one softly. "We told you ours."

"I didn't ask you to," retorted Annie, bridling. Suddenly she didn't care. Mrs. Carlton would be shocked and Father Donegan wouldn't like it, but how was she ever to meet any young men unless she picked them up in the park or at the theater? "My name's Annie Jordan," she said. "Of Seattle."

"Charmed to meet you, Miss Jordan," laughed the dark one,

Ned Weaver, and he took her arm. "May we have the pleasure of your company for a stroll?"

"And maybe a glass of beer later?" put in Benjy, grinning.

"I guess there's no harm in that," replied Annie, laughing, and she set off down the path, a young man on each side of her. The band was playing a lively air now and Ned began to whistle it. Annie hummed the tune, her eyes sparkling, her cheeks warm. This was something like it. This was better than mooning around alone, dreaming impossible dreams. Ned was no hussar, but he wasn't unattractive and she could feel the pressure of his arm against her body now and then, and that gave her a nice, warm, tingly feeling.

" 'While strolling through the park one day,' " sang Ned, with a sly glance at her, " 'in the merry, merry month of May, I was taken by surprise, by a pair of roguish eyes.' " Here he definitely squeezed her arm and she reproved him with a frown, but she couldn't help smiling. " 'In the merry, merry month of May.' "

"Do you walk in the park often?" he asked.

"Quite often. I like to hear the band play," she replied.

"Ah-ha, the musical type. I'm crazy about music myself. So we've got that in common. What's your favorite tune?"

"Oh, I don't know. I like them all, I guess. The waltzes best. 'After the Ball' is nice. I like sad songs. It's the Irish in me, I suppose." Now her tongue was loosed and she found it easy to talk to the two strange young men. In fact she found herself chattering and laughing like a silly. She couldn't seem to stop. Maybe it was being with just women so much and not ever having a chance to talk to young men. She was hungry for the company of men.

Ned monopolized her, though Benjy tried to put in a word now and then. He tried to squeeze her arm, too, but Annie gave him a cold look and he stopped, though she pretended not to notice now when Ned did it.

"Listen here, Ned," he burst out at last, "you're doing all the talking. How about giving me a chance?"

"Can I help it if Miss Jordan and I have so much in common? Can I help it if I am such a sparkling conversationalist? Run along and find yourself a young lady if you don't like it, my boy," cried Ned, winking at Annie.

"Say, who saw her first, I want to know? I did. I said, 'There's a pippin. Dare you to speak to her.' Now you're trying to freeze me out."

"I leave it up to the young lady. Since it seems that at this point three is a crowd, one of us must go. Let her choose." Ned relinquished Annie's arm and winked at her again. Benjy, red in the face, stared at her, his eyes hungry. Something about him reminded her of Fred Carew. A shudder went through her, though she smiled at both of them. Her smile lingered on Ned's face the longest, but she laughed, "I wouldn't dream of breaking up your friendship. If three's a crowd, I'd better go myself. Toodle-oo." And she turned and walked quickly down the path, leaving them staring after her.

She couldn't help smiling at the way their faces had dropped when she left them, but she was a little sorry to lose Ned. He'd been fun, gay and teasing and quite attractive. There was something so rakish about his little black mustache. Yet in a way she was glad to be rid of them both. After all, she didn't know them from Adam. There was no telling just what she'd have got herself in for. Well, she'd had her little adventure and she felt the better for it. Her cheeks were still warm and there was a faint smile playing over her lips as she settled herself on an empty bench half hidden by shrubs to listen to the band.

"You can't get rid of me so easily, me proud beauty."

Annie jumped as Ned sat down beside her. He was smiling triumphantly and his black eyes sparkled. His face was so close to hers she could see the small brown mole on his cheek and smell the pungent barbershop scent of bay rum and eau de cologne. She edged away from him a bit, embarrassed by his sudden reappearance.

"What did you do with Benjy?" she asked, unable to keep from smiling back at him.

"Strangled him with my bare hands and stuffed his body under a gooseberry bush," he whispered melodramatically.

"Poor Benjy. That wasn't a very nice way to treat him," she said, laughing. Now that Benjy wasn't with them she felt both more constraint with Ned and a greater sense of intimacy. She was sure that the way she'd smiled at him when she left them had emboldened him to follow her.

"Benjy is a good enough sort. But I don't like the way he eyes a girl," said Ned with a little frown.

Annie shuddered again, remembering the way he'd looked at her.

"Neither do I," she confided, then blushed, thinking how improper that sounded. A lady wouldn't be expected to know what Ned meant.

"I thought you didn't," said Ned quietly. He took her hand and pressed it. "I could tell you weren't that kind of a girl."

Annie drew her hand away, her cheeks burning. She didn't know just what to make of that. It sounded fresh; it wasn't the sort of thing a young man should say to a lady. She'd learned that much at the Carltons'. There were nuances in the attitudes of men toward women that she'd never been aware of down on the waterfront. There they were simple and direct, but up on the hill there were many shadings and refinements that she had unconsciously absorbed. So she drew away from Ned Weaver and held her head proudly.

"I beg your pardon, Mr. Weaver," she said haughtily. "But I haven't the faintest idea of what you are referring to." She sat stiffly, her chin out and her shoulders back, the very picture of offended modesty.

Suddenly Ned's arm went around her waist, she was pulled roughly against him, and though she struggled valiantly he kissed her on the cheek.

"Oh!" she cried, breathless with indignation, pushing him away at last. "How dare you!" In the struggle her sailor hat had tipped over one eye, the pins came out of her heavy knot, and her thick, sumptuous red hair spilled down her back.

"I couldn't help it," he whispered ardently. "You look so pretty when you're mad."

The proper thing for her to do would have been to get right up and sweep away from him, but she had to straighten her hat and pin up her hair and while she was retrieving her hair pins with Ned's help there were footsteps along the path, a murmur of voices. She glanced up and there were Emily Carlton and Hugh Deming staring at her.

She sat with the pins in her lap, awkwardly trying to twist her hair into a knot, while Emily's cool, amused gaze took in her, Ned, and the whole situation. The hot color washed up into Annie's cheeks and she wished the earth would open up and swallow her.

"Why, Annie," said Emily patronizingly. "Fancy seeing you here." Then she smiled up at Hugh, put her hand on his arm, and minced gracefully down the path. Hugh glanced back over his shoulder while Annie was staring after him and their eyes met and clung for a brief instant. Then he turned, said something to Emily, and they both laughed.

Annie straightened her hat and faced Ned angrily. "Now see what you've done!" she scolded.

"What have I done?" He was grinning unashamedly and she had to restrain herself from slapping his face.

"What will they think of me?" she went on hotly. "I was never so mortified in my life."

"What for? Because your friends caught you spooning with a fellow in the park?" Ned laughed. "Go on with you. They'll be doing the same thing, as soon as they find an empty bench."

"Oh, you—you cad!" she cried, using the words of her favorite romantic heroine. "Don't you dare talk like that about them." She grabbed her purse away from him, got to her feet and, with all the dignity she could muster, stalked across the lawn.

Her cheeks were still hot with shame and anger, but what made her heart burn with anguish were Ned's words. "They'll be doing the same thing, as soon as they find an empty bench." Of course he was right. For what other reason did young couples come to the park on a summer evening? But not Hugh, cried her heart, not Hugh and Emily Carlton. She could see him bending toward her, with that tender, mocking smile, only for Emily it would be all tenderness and no mockery. She could see him take her plump, pretty little hand, not big and bony and red from dishwashing like Annie's. He wouldn't grab Emily and kiss her roughly like Ned, he'd only touch her fingers to his lips and murmur something lovely and romantic, like Rupert of Hentzau. And Emily, cool and dainty, would drop her eyes and blush sweetly. Not a hair of her head would be ruffled, not a bow on her pale blue lawn dress go awry. Emily was the right kind of girl for Hugh Deming, not big, awkward, red-haired Annie Jordan who picked up strange men in the park and was treated like—like the waterfront rat she was. But why had Hugh turned and given her that strange, direct look before he went down the path with Emily? What did he mean by it?

She hadn't realized she was sobbing until she felt a hand on her arm and heard Ned Weaver say, "Aw, honey, what're you crying for? Are you mad at me?"

She looked at him through the tears that suddenly welled up in her eyes and spilled down her cheeks, but she couldn't answer him.

"I'm sorry. Honest Injun, I am," he said softly, and he took out his pocket handkerchief and wiped her eyes very gently. "I guess I put my foot in it, Annie. But if you'll forgive me I promise I won't do it again. I won't even hold your hand unless you want me to."

His voice was earnest and pleading and his black eyes were no longer bold. He wasn't such a bad sort, really. It was only that compared to Hugh Deming . . . But she might as well stop dreaming about Hugh. Emily Carlton had him now and all she had was—Ned. She lifted her head proudly. Well, she might as well make the best of it.

"I guess I'm not mad at you any more, Ned," she answered, smiling at him.

"That's the girl," he cried eagerly. "What do you say we take in the show at the Third Avenue Theater and then maybe a bite of supper afterward? Will that fix things up?"

She nodded. "That will be very nice," she said demurely, and she put her hand daintily on his arm, as Emily had done with Hugh, and they walked sedately up the street to the car line to take the horsecar downtown.

The play was *East Lynne*, very sad and very beautiful, about wonderful, noble people with refined, high voices. Annie loved it and Ned lent her his handkerchief to weep into. As they came out of the theater they could hear a boat out in the bay whistle in the darkness. A nostalgia for the waterfront came over Annie. Since she'd left it, she'd never been back. Someday soon she was going to slip down to the docks and watch the boats come in. There'd be no harm in that, surely. Even if she should see her mother, she had nothing to fear from her. Father Donegan had fixed everything for her. Maybe, on my next day off, she thought.

"A penny for your thoughts," said Ned, taking her arm gingerly, still fearful of offending her again.

"I was listening to that boat. I love them, don't you?" she said, her eyes dreamy.

He shook his head. "I'm a landlubber myself. Boats and the water are fine to look at. But give me old terra firma every time."

Hugh liked the boats, she thought. He'd rather have been a sailor than study law. I wonder if he ever took the trip up the sound he was talking about that day I first met him?

"Hey, come out of it," laughed Ned, waving his hand before her eyes. "You were miles away."

"Yes," she answered. "I guess I was."

"How about something to eat? I'm hungry." He jingled coins in his pocket and Annie frowned unconsciously.

"So am I," she said, and to her surprise she found she really was. Any kind of emotion gave her an appetite and when she had eaten she always felt better again.

They went to King's Oyster House and had cracked crab and beer, a whole big Dungeness crab apiece. Annie ate hers greedily but remembered her table manners, even to crooking her little finger the way she'd seen Emily do, and dabbing the tips of her fingers daintily in the finger bowls to wash off the smell of crab. But Ned ate the way the men who came to her mother's saloon did, noisily and untidily. She tried not to notice it, but she made up her mind then and there to one thing. She'd never marry a man with bad table manners.

The beer tasted good. It was the first she'd had since she left the waterfront. But when Ned ordered another glass for himself, she declined. One glass was fine, made you feel warm and relaxed, but more than that and she might forget that she was trying her best to become a lady. More than that and she might forget Ned's bad table manners, forget that he wasn't her hussar.

It was after ten when Ned took her home and only the hall light was burning. Annie was glad of that. She'd not like to meet Mrs. Carlton or Emily with beer on her breath. Ned was impressed that she lived in such a nice house on the First Hill. She didn't tell him that she worked there as a hired girl.

At the door he squeezed her hand, gazed at her pleadingly. She knew he wanted to kiss her good night, but she only smiled at him, murmured politely, "Thank you very much for a very pleasant evening," and turned to go in. He caught her arm.

"Listen. When am I going to see you again?" he whispered ardently.

"Oh, I didn't know you wanted to," she said, bridling.

"You know darn well I do," he answered sharply.

She smiled softly. It was nice having a young man, even if he wasn't what you wanted. It made you feel warm and proud, it gave you a sense of power. Besides, he wasn't bad-looking and if he wasn't a gentleman—well, she wasn't a lady, *yet*.

"Saturday night," she whispered, "after confession. Meet me at the Catholic church at seven thirty."

She went in then, turned down the gas in the hall lamp, undressed in the dark in her little room. She felt more alive than she'd felt in months. She felt like a person again. It was very nice. Ned was nice, too, she thought, brushing her hair in the darkness, feeling its weight and texture on the brush. Ned was very nice, but . . . When she slept she dreamed, and she smiled in her sleep, murmured a name, pushed down the covers, exposing her rich, full throat and swelling breasts. She dreamed, not of Ned, but of Hugh Deming and it was his name she murmured in her dream. And in the morning when she awakened she was wondering how and when she could see him again and what he'd meant by that strange, intent look he'd given her over his shoulder.

By the time Hugh had seen Emily safely to her door, pressed her hand fondly, cautioned her to let nothing keep her from the ball the next week, it was quite dark and the band concert was over. But he went back to the park, found the bench behind the rhododendron bush empty, walked up and down the paths and over the lawns, peering curiously at murmuring couples. But he didn't find Annie. He knew now that she was the Carltons' hired girl. Emily, laughing at catching her with a man, had told him. But somehow it made no difference.

Even when he was quite certain that it was useless to look for her any longer he didn't go home. Instead he did a curious thing for such an elegant young gentleman of fashion. He walked all the way down to the waterfront and leaned against a tarry pile, watching the oily dark water wash in and out under the pier and the stars faintly glimmering in their depths, until a brisk wind blew in off the bay and a few raindrops began to spatter on the water where the stars had been. Then he turned up his coat collar and walked home.

Chapter X

The Denny Hotel was the biggest, most imposing and fashionable hotel in Seattle in the early 1900s. Later the new Butler Hotel was to become the gathering place of the "smart" people in town, but until the Denny Hotel and the hill it crowned were torn down, the big square building with the veranda running along three sides of it, with its magnificent view of the bay and the mountains, perched on the steep ascent of Denny Hill, was the favorite place for all the large, solid, important functions. Here it was that the town feted Theodore Roosevelt with a lavish banquet. Here it was that the social clubs entertained, the Again Club, the Not Again Club. Here it was that the Nesika Club cotillion was being held.

Here it was that Emily Carlton, breathless and starry-eyed, went to her first cotillion with Hugh Deming. Just going to the cotillion with any personable young man would have been enough to thrill her. And going with the dashing Hugh was marvelous beyond words. But going, as she did, through intrigue and conspiracy, was doubly exciting. She smuggled her clothes into Marguerite's house disguised as fine laundering Annie had done for Mrs. Brookes, in case she met her strait-laced father, who considered her too young to attend parties with a young man in gay Seattle society. She dressed in a delicious fever of excitement and terror lest somehow her father find out and come marching over to prevent her going. Then she was whisked away in a hansom cab by Hugh as if they were eloping. Marguerite and her escort, Rolly Collins, one of Mrs.

Crawford's young men whom Marguerite's patroness had prevailed upon to take her, went along in the cab, too, but that only added to the fun and the banter. Emily, secretly, would have been terrified to go alone in a cab with Hugh.

But now she was actually at the ball, in the great ballroom where dizzily circling couples waltzed breathlessly to a six-piece orchestra. She was there in a ravishing white moiré gown that Marguerite had copied from a Godey's fashion plate, and Hugh, tall and slim and elegant in tails, was holding out his white-gloved hand to her, smiling his queer little smile and murmuring, "You look like the princess in a fairy tale." And then she was lightly in his arms, floating away, away to the strains of a Viennese waltz.

Before the next waltz started her program book was filled and Hugh was besieged by urgent young men to share more of the dances he'd saved for himself. But he was adamant. Six of the dances were his and he refused to give them up. Emily, standing by Marguerite against the potted palms, heady with excitement and delight, tried to pretend a vast indifference to the whole business. Oh, it was a glorious night and even Marguerite seemed to be having a good time. She was looking uncommonly attractive and her dark poise, coupled with the fact that Rolly was well liked among the men, had filled her program too.

Emily went from one admiring young man's arms to another's, laughing, fluttering her lashes, accepting compliments as charmingly as if she'd been in society all her life.

"You're the belle of the ball, princess," said Hugh when he claimed her again.

She laughed up into his eyes, put her hand on his arm, then stiffened and gasped. Across the ballroom floor, bearing down on them like a man-o'-war, was her father, his full face bursting with color, his blue eyes snapping. Somehow he must have found out. Her mother must have weakened and told him. Hugh felt her hand tighten on his arm, glanced inquiringly down into her terror-stricken face. Then he saw Will Carlton.

"Yoicks!" he whispered. "It's the Papa Bear himself. Shall I hide you in a palm?"

"Don't joke, Hugh. This is going to be awful," said Emily in a choked voice.

For a moment Will Carlton simply stood before his daughter, breathing hard and boring her with his eyes. Then he put out his hand. "Emily, I've come to take you home."

Emily put her hand slowly into his. "Yes, Papa. . . ."

Hugh stepped forward, his jaw tight. "But, sir——"

Mr. Carlton vouchsafed no answer. He merely turned and glared at him. Emily gave Hugh a despairing look, shook her head, formed the words, "I'm sorry," and, with her blond head held high and her chin trembling, let her father lead her out of the ballroom, under the astonished gaze of the assemblage.

"Phew!" cried Rolly Collins, coming up to Hugh and patting his shoulder. "What an ogre. I'll bet he eats babies."

"I wouldn't have believed it if I hadn't seen it," muttered Hugh, his face scarlet.

"I think you need a drink, brother," said Rolly. "The punch isn't bad and I know where we can find a stick to put in it. Come along."

After the third drink Hugh felt better. He could even laugh about the capture of Emily. He made a number of quite clever jokes about it—did an excellent imitation of the Papa Bear carrying off his cub. But deep inside he was humiliated, outraged.

"Come on back to the party," urged Rolly. "I'll let you dance with Marguerite. She's not bad. A cool little piece and too brainy, but a good dancer."

Hugh smiled, shook his head. He had other ideas. He got his coat and top hat and started for the door.

"Where are you going?" demanded Rolly, trotting after him like a worried puppy. He knew that his friend was deeply wounded in spite of his nonchalance.

"Going to get a girl. A wonderful girl. Better-looking than the first one," said Hugh with the bright, clear edge of intoxication in his voice.

"Oh, Lord," groaned Rolly as Hugh went out, calling a cab.

Annie was brushing her long hair in front of the little mirror when the doorbell rang. She had been thinking about Emily and Hugh at the ball. She'd caught a glimpse of Emily, radiant and glowing, with the box containing the ball gown, whisking out of the house to Marguerite's before her father got home. She'd overheard the girl persuading her mother to let her go in spite of Mr. Carlton's strictness. In her mind she saw the

dancers, heard the waltz music, and the doorbell cut sharply
into her fancies. She had on a faded cotton kimono over her
chemise and petticoat, but since she thought it was probably
Mrs. Carlton returning from the Literary Society meeting, she
didn't hesitate to go to the door. "Probably forgot her key,"
she murmured as she wrapped the kimono tightly about her
waist and hurried into the front hall.

For a moment neither of them spoke. Hugh stood, faintly
smiling, standing very straight, staring at her loose, heavy hair
tumbling about her shoulders. Annie had drawn in her breath
in sharp surprise when she saw him, but she said nothing, only
looked at him dumbly, waiting.

"Have you got an evening gown?" he said at last, in the most
casual way imaginable.

For just a moment she hesitated. Of course she hadn't an
evening gown, but there was one of Mrs. Carlton's that she
secretly coveted. It was nile-green satin and Annie had often
looked at it, fingered it, while cleaning her mistress's room, and
pretended it was hers.

"Go get it on. You're coming to a ball with me." Hugh's
voice wasn't demanding or imperious. It was low and matter-
of-fact.

Annie looked at him to see if he was making fun of her.
But his face was without any expression, except the faint,
amused smile that she knew so well.

"I'll wait in the cab for you. Will it take you long to dress?"

She shook her head and he turned and hurried down the
steps. There *was* a cab at the curb and he got into it, after speaking to the driver. She closed the door, leaned against it, suddenly
weak, her heart smothering her. The palms of her hands were
wet and she wiped them slowly down her sides. All sorts of
thoughts tumbled through her mind. What if Mrs. Carlton or
her husband came home? What if it was all a joke? How could
she get in again if she did go? What had happened to Emily?
But slowly, irresistibly, she moved toward the stairs, ran up
to Mrs. Carlton's room, took down the green satin from its
hanger, hurried back down to her little cubicle, unfastened her
kimono, struggled into the evening gown. This was perhaps
not happening at all. It was a dream and she could not let it
go. "Don't let me wake up," she whispered, twisting her thick

red mane into a knot like the heroines wore in her favorite
novels.

The gown was tight on her—Mrs. Carlton's figure was not
so opulent as hers—but she managed to get it hooked. She had no
jewels to wear, no flowers, but instinctively, as she caught a
fleeting glimpse of herself in the mirror, she knew she didn't
need adornments. In the queenly dress with her magnificent
hair, her white skin, she was like a jewel herself, fabulous and
shining. She draped the gold silk scarf with the black sequins
about her shoulders, turned down the gaslight, and hurried out
the door.

When he saw her coming down the steps Hugh sprang out
of the cab, tossing away his cigarette, and took her arm as
gallantly as if she'd been the Queen of England. He couldn't see
much of what she had on in the dark, but the way she walked,
the proud, free carriage of her head, her dark, calm eyes as they
looked into his, gave him a queer turn. By God, hired girl or
no hired girl, she carried herself like a queen.

They hardly spoke during the drive to the hotel. Hugh
suddenly felt very far away from her, unable to banter with
her as he had in the park, unable as well to pay her the lighthearted compliments he gave Emily's kind. The truth was, she
baffled him and he was suddenly ashamed of the mean impulse
that had made him ask her to go to the ball.

She sat in her corner, with her face turned away from him,
her hands lying loosely in her lap, perfectly still. She was glad
he didn't try to talk. She didn't want to speak lest the spell
break. She was in a dream, savoring its strangeness and beauty,
and she was content to be still. Just before they reached the
hotel Hugh leaned over and took her hand. At his touch, she
turned, looked at him, and smiled. Gravely, with no answering
smile, Hugh lifted her hand to his lips.

The orchestra was playing "The Blue Danube" when Hugh
and Annie stepped out onto the floor. The ballroom was a
kaleidoscope of whirling figures, shimmering gowns, white
arms, black shoulders. For a moment shyness overcame Annie
and she hesitated, with Hugh's hand outstretched to her. Then
she lifted her head, drew herself up to her queenly height,
which nearly matched Hugh's, put her hand in his, and stepped

out onto the dance floor. The dream held, she was its heroine. She was dancing at a ball in a gorgeous gown with her handsome hussar. As long as the spell lasted, why should she be afraid?

"You look utterly magnificent," whispered Hugh, smiling at her with eyes that glittered. "Cleopatra!"

"I'm glad you came for me," she said, and her eyes looked deeply into his, candid, without guile.

Rolly Collins, dancing with Marguerite, suddenly saw them. He squeezed his partner's hand. "Good Lord, look at that gorgeous creature with Hugh. He said he was going to get a better-looking girl than Emily, and by George, he has. Who is she?"

Marguerite looked over his shoulder, caught her breath, and then smiled. This was too perfect! Wouldn't Emily be furious! Then she frowned. What if someone should find out who "the gorgeous creature" was and be unkind? If she could help it, no one was going to spoil Annie's lark. "She's a Miss Jordan, I believe."

"Good heavens, why haven't I seen her before? Where did Hugh discover her?" Rolly was so intent on Annie that he bumped into another couple, also staring at the red-haired girl in the nile-green gown.

When the dance ended Annie and Hugh stood together by a palm. "Is it all right? Are you having fun?" he asked.

She sighed deeply. "I've always dreamed of going to a ball like this in a lovely gown with a—a handsome man."

Hugh flushed, feeling guilty again. "Thank you for the compliment, my dear."

She looked at him, her eyes shining. "I dreamed of going to a ball with you."

He said nothing, only pressed her arm against his side, unable to tear his eyes away from her. Then he saw the stag line descending on him.

"Here come the boys, wanting dances with you," he laughed.

Annie's eyes darkened with fright. She caught his hand. "Oh no. Please don't give them any. I—I can't dance with anyone but you."

Hugh gave her an odd look. Then he squeezed her arm again.

"Don't worry. I wouldn't dream of letting you get away from me."

The stag line pleaded, then turned away, disgruntled. Rolly Collins, with Marguerite on his arm, came up.

"My dear boy, I want to be introduced," he cried.

Annie looked at Marguerite and her face went white, her hand trembled on Hugh's arm. But Marguerite only smiled reassuringly.

"Miss Brookes, Miss Jordan," said Hugh gravely, not batting an eye and hoping that Annie would be able to carry it off.

"Miss Jordan and I have already met. It's a pleasure to see you here tonight," said Marguerite, giving Annie her hand and trying to tell her by the pressure of her fingers that she was on her side.

Annie flushed, then returned Marguerite's calm smile. "It's nice to see you, too, Miss Brookes," she replied quietly.

The orchestra struck up "And the Band Played On," and Hugh, smiling, led Annie out on the floor again.

All over the ballroom, people were looking at them, whispering about them, wondering who the unknown beauty was. Everyone had seen or had been told about Will Carlton's snatching his daughter literally from Hugh's arms; now they buzzed with curiosity over this new prize Hugh had brought. At first no one but Marguerite recognized her. After all, there was little resemblance between the quiet-mannered, badly dressed Irish hired girl and this exciting and magnificent girl in the perfectly cut satin gown. Then Essie Keating gasped and whispered something to her partner. The word spread, the whispers grew, the glances flashed. There was laughter.

But Annie was sublimely unaware of any of it. All she heard was the music, Hugh's low voice telling her how beautiful she was, how divinely she danced. She cared for nothing else, she heard nothing else.

During the intermission they walked out onto the veranda, gazed at the bay, quiet and sparkling under the white summer moon. Hugh brought her punch and they sipped it, laughing softly. With his sharpened social sense, he knew that they were being talked about and that the mystery of his beautiful partner had been discovered, but he realized he didn't care. The punch or his pleasure in being with Annie had made him quite reckless.

They went in to supper with Marguerite and Rolly, and either Rolly hadn't been informed or else Marguerite had forbidden him to show it, for they talked and laughed together pleasantly.

Nothing happened to spoil Annie's dream. She and Hugh danced until the ball was over. His manner toward her was all she'd ever dreamed of, gentle, tender, almost ardent. If she hadn't been sure it was a dream and that in the morning she'd wake up and know it hadn't happened, she might have thought he was even a little bit in love with her.

When the cab stopped at the Carltons' house he leaned toward her, his eyes and mouth eager. She looked at him gravely, but with a strange smile he took her hand again and kissed it.

"Thank you, my dear," he murmured. "You were perfect. You are a great lady, Annie Jordan." And he got out and handed her out of the cab.

The house was quite dark when Annie let herself in with her key. Everyone must be in bed, she thought, and breathed a sigh of relief. Then, as she opened the door at the end of the hall that led into the kitchen, she gasped. There was a light in the kitchen and Emily, in dressing gown and slippers, her eyes red and swollen from weeping, was sitting at the worktable, eating a piece of chocolate cake and drinking a glass of milk.

For a moment the two girls stared at each other as if they were strangers. Then Emily's eyes widened with incredulity as she suddenly recognized this vision in the green satin.

"Annie Jordan!" she whispered hoarsely. "Where have you been? Where did you get that dress?"

Annie said nothing, but her eyes were enormous and her face had gone white.

"Why, that's Mama's dress, isn't it?" Emily had got up from the table and Annie stood in the door as if transfixed. "You go take it off this minute," cried Emily furiously, her face red.

"All right, I'll take it off. And if you want to know where I've been, I'll tell you. I've been to the Nesika Club Ball with Hugh Deming!" Annie burst out at last, lifting her chin proudly and starting to go into her room.

Emily rushed at her and for a moment Annie thought she was going to slap her. Then Emily laughed contemptuously. "I don't believe a word of it. Hugh take *you* to the ball?"

"Ask Marguerite," said Annie coldly. "And you don't need to run tattling on me to your mother. I'll tell her myself in the morning. If she fires me, that's all right too."

Annie swept past the girl and into her room, haughty and proud as a queen, but once inside with the door shut, she began to tremble. She had difficulty unfastening the green satin gown, her fingers were shaking so. But it wasn't fear that possessed her. It was a white rage at Emily. So Hugh wouldn't take me to a ball, she thought, pulling off the dress savagely and with it her hairpins, so that her hair came tumbling down. I'm not good enough, that's what she means. We'll see if I am or not, Miss Emily Carlton. We'll see.

By the time she was undressed and had brushed her hair, said her prayers, the anger was gone and she lay quietly on her narrow bed, her eyes parted in a soft smile. What Mrs. Carlton would say or do when she told her in the morning didn't concern her. She refused to think of tomorrow, of any future, hugging only the splendid memory of this shining and perfect night, dropped like a miracle into her hands. If she never saw Hugh Deming again, she would be grateful to him for tonight. But somehow, in spite of Emily, the Carltons, her own humble station, she knew that she was going to see him again.

Mrs. Carlton was quite taken aback by Annie's forthright confession the next morning and from her surprised look Annie knew that Emily hadn't tattled.

"I hardly know what to say, Annie," she gasped.

"If you want me to leave I will, Mrs. Carlton. I'll go right now." Annie faced her squarely, her eyes very bright.

"Leave? Oh no—no, I don't want you to leave. Goodness, I wouldn't know what to do without you. But I—I can't have you wearing my clothes, you know."

Annie flushed. "I'm sorry about the dress. I'll have it cleaned for you, Mrs. Carlton."

Mrs. Carlton shook her head. "It isn't that. And I never did like that dress on me, the color's too bright. No, I'll give you the dress, if you'll promise never to do anything like this again."

You understand, I'm sure, that your coming to me and telling me the truth is why I'm not going to punish you."

But Emily wouldn't speak to Annie for several days and she managed to leave her room so untidy that it took Annie a full hour to straighten it up every morning.

Chapter XI

It was three-thirty on Sunday afternoon and Hugh Deming was calling on Erica Crawford to find out what luck she'd had in persuading her husband to lend him twenty-five thousand dollars to go into the shipping business with Captain Blaine.

He'd tossed the smaller figure at Erica when they'd talked about it, because he couldn't quite bring himself to mention fifty thousand. He knew Maurice Crawford was wealthy; they had an imposing house on Boren Avenue, and Erica gave fabulous parties, went to New York twice a year for her clothes, but he wasn't sure that it all represented solid, gilt-edged securities. He'd seen enough magnificent houses in the South, which seemed to exist mainly on their debts, to be skeptical, even here in the West where people hadn't yet learned to fool the world about the state of their bank accounts.

He wondered whether Erica had heard about the incidents at the Nesika Club Ball. She hadn't been there, since it was strictly a young, unmarried crowd's affair, but by now he supposed it was all over town. He rather hoped she'd be amused and not annoyed at his taking a hired girl after Emily's departure, but he dreaded talking about it with her. Annie had been so wonderful. He'd been proud of her and ashamed of himself. He hoped Mrs. Crawford would have the good manners not to mention it.

Thinking about Annie and remembering her beauty and dignity, the simplicity with which she'd accepted his curious invitation, her candid, clear, violet eyes meeting his as they danced, he suddenly wanted to see her again. The Carltons' house was on the way to Crawfords'.

He paused as he neared the place, glanced up at the windows, half expecting to see Annie looking out of one of them. But no one was about; Sunday afternoon languor drowsed over the lawn, the rosebushes, the golden-glow hedge. The rockers on the porch were empty and the blinds half drawn to keep out the blaze of the westering sun. Besides, how could he see her? He couldn't very well go around to the back door, and what would Emily and her parents think if he presented himself in the front parlor to see their hired girl? Already the audacity and impulsiveness that had made him take her to the ball seemed ridiculous and foolish to him.

I must have been three sheets to the wind or I'd never have done it, he thought. But damn it, I had a good time with her, a better time than I had with Emily. I'd like to see her again. But what kind of an ass am I, mooning after a servant girl?

Moodily he walked on past the house. No wonder his father always seemed to be half laughing at him. He *was* an ass, thinking about a girl from the waterfront when he should have been preoccupied with whether or not his career was to be grub-staked.

But as he neared the Crawfords' house he forgot Annie and Emily, too, and a tenseness took hold of him, tightening his stomach and making his palms sweat. It was all very well to be the amusing companion for Erica's bored leisure, but that was hardly the basis on which to swing a business loan. I ought to have gone to Maurice Crawford myself, he thought. What will he think of me for using his wife as an intermediary? But as soon as he'd broached the subject to her, Erica had taken it out of his hands. "I think it sounds like a wonderful opportunity, Hugh. You've got brains and enthusiasm and people like you. I'm sure you'll be a success. Let me talk to Maurice about it for you. I can handle him better, I'm sure."

Erica was one of those women who love to arrange other people's destinies, to have a finger in their pies. Her tremendous energy, which made her such an original hostess, should have been used to further some great cause or the fortunes of a statesman. She was the kind of woman who might have intrigued with cardinals and prime ministers to change the course of empires. People said she'd had a great deal to do with her husband's success, and Hugh, looking now at her vibrant face, not beautiful because the line of the jaw was too square and heavy, but fascinating, arresting with its full, sensual mouth, high cheekbones, large, luminous eyes, and wide, intelligent brow, was inclined to believe it.

She leaned toward him, her gray eyes searching his face, and patted his hand. "My dear boy, I'm so frightfully sorry. I've not been able to get anywhere yet with Maurice. For some strange reason he's being most stubborn. He insists that he has no way of knowing that you'd be able to make a success of this thing. He asks what experience you have had in the shipping business, what securities you could give—oh, so many stupid, practical things. I'm quite put out with him."

Hugh smiled easily, masking the little shock of dismay her words had given him. He realized that he'd counted heavily on Erica's influence with Mr. Crawford. "Perhaps he's right, Erica. After all, one doesn't just go to a man and say, 'I've an idea I can make a lot of money in a steamship company—hand over twenty-five thousand, please.'"

"Not anyone could, but you're different, Hugh, with your father's position in town, your intelligence and connections. Besides, this Captain Blaine of yours is well known as a very clever and able man. But Maurice just wouldn't listen to me." She laughed, gave him an arch look. "I think he's doing it just to spite me. I'm afraid, my dear, that he's jealous of you."

Hugh raised his eyebrows, laughed with her. "But, of course, he's got no reason to be."

She colored faintly, dropped her eyes. "None at all. He doesn't seem to realize that you're very young and have dozens of charming girls on the string and that I'm an old woman with only the most platonic interest in you."

Hugh protested that she was far from being old, that she was far more attractive than any young girl, and that as far as platonic interest went—well, he shrugged as if to dismiss such a dreary thought as impossible.

"No, I'm quite right, darling. And, as your friend, and an older woman, I do think I must tell you what a naughty boy you were to play such a trick last night at the ball." She had been playing with a little ivory fan, opening and shutting it with her long white glittering fingers. Now she closed it with a snap and rapped him gently across the knuckles.

For some reason this annoyed him sharply. He could not endure sitting there another minute, alternately being flirted with and scolded like a small boy. Suddenly he saw their relationship for what it was—a shallow, silly, even wicked thing, since it had neither the honesty of passion nor the sincerity of friendship.

Looking at her with the cold eye of disappointment and wounded ego, he saw her clearly as a restless, vain, unsatisfied woman who had probably brought neither love nor dignity to her marriage. He saw her for the frustrated egoist she was, hungry for drama and attention, longing possibly for physical satisfaction but too cowardly to take it, nibbling at passion through such artificial flirtations as theirs had been. Knowing that she could never keep an older, more demanding lover at arm's length, while she fed her strange vanity with his devotion, she surrounded herself with the young, baffling and intriguing them with a vision and a promise, both unattainable and provocative.

"I've taken too much of your time," he said stiffly, rising and bowing coldly. "Thank you a thousand times for your kindness, your efforts in my behalf."

She leaned back on the soft, luxurious nest of pillows in her chair and looked at him through her long lashes for a moment without speaking. Then with a sigh and a shrug, both of regret and dismissal, she murmured, "I'm sorry I was unable to help you, dear boy. Come soon again, won't you? I shall be having a little supper next Tuesday. If you are free, I should be so glad . . ." Her voice trailed off. She gave him an indolent hand as if indifferent whether he took it or not. They both knew that he would not be coming to see her again. There was nothing now between them—perhaps there never had been.

With a little ironic smile, conscious that he was making a melodramatic gesture and doing it quite deliberately, both for his own satisfaction and hers, he took her white, jeweled hand and bent over it, pressed it lightly, almost insolently, to his lips and left her.

As he went down the street he was cold with anger; his mind and heart seemed to be giving off sharp splinters of bitterness and disgust. To appease her wounded vanity at having lost him, or whatever she may have thought she possessed of him, she would probably decide that he was a mercenary person who dropped her because she couldn't get him the money he wanted. Actually, he hardly thought of that at all. He had suddenly been awakened to exactly the role he played in her mind and it revolted him.

He knew perfectly well she could have persuaded her husband to let her have the money for him. She chose not to, she chose to punish him for having been attracted to Emily Carlton and for having taken Annie Jordan to the ball. Undoubtedly people had told her of Annie's magnificent beauty. Out of pique she had given him this blow, counting on his infatuation to hold him in spite of it.

Perhaps she had a suspicion she was being used and was determined to prove to herself and to him that she could keep him dancing attendance because of her charm alone. Quite possibly this was to be only a warning and if he were a good boy and amused her by telling her about his conquests, laughing about them to prove they meant nothing to him and were only evidences of youthful wild oats, she would eventually relent and reward him for his devotion by presenting him with the money, after all.

"No, thanks," he muttered, kicking savagely at a pebble. "No, thanks, Erica. Keep your money and your little suppers and your sly glances, your provocative remarks, for somebody else. I've had all I want of you."

Suddenly he felt quite free, as if a subtle chain that had bound him, half unconsciously, but none the less tightly, had been snapped. Maybe it would be a good idea to get drunk to celebrate. He turned down the corner of Eighteenth Avenue and Madison.

He was passing an ornate square house with an iron fence around its wide lawns, a brown dog guarding the gate. It always amused him to see the house here on the First Hill, flanked by the homes of the eminently respectable and the socially elite. For it belonged to Lou Graham, the madam of the fanciest sporting house in Seattle. This, of course, was not her place of business, but a sort of rest home for her girls, to which she sent them for two weeks' vacation, in rotation, every year. Storms of protest, petitions, indignation meetings on the part of irate neighbors did no good. The mayor refused to do anything about it, and Lou's girls continued to relax in the best surroundings.

"Why not?" Hugh's father had surprisingly said when a delegation of townspeople had gone to him about the "situation." "They cause no disturbance of any kind up there. No one is allowed to visit them while they're on vacation. They're as quiet and well behaved as any of the young ladies from our best families. Lou's girls are the handsomest and the best-dressed women in town. I fail to see that it's any of our business."

The delegation had been stunned and had gone away baffled by his frankness. Even the young ladies in Emily Carlton's set knew who Lou Graham's girls were and secretly envied them their chic. Lou sent to the best shops in New York for their hats and it was even rumored that their gowns and suits came from Paris. "I wouldn't be surprised," Hugh's mother had said. "The French are an immoral people."

Passing the house on Eighteenth and Madison, Hugh thought scornfully that Lou and her girls were at least honest about their dealings. Erica Crawford might learn something from them. Lou was a shrewd businesswoman, but she had a reputation for having a generous heart. Hugh stopped dead in his tracks. He stared up at the discreetly curtained windows and gradually a mischievous smile spread over his face.

"I'll ask Lou Graham to stake me to that money," he said softly. "By God, I'll bet she'll do it, too." He burst out laughing, and a woman in a carriage going by glanced at him curiously, then, noticing the house he was staring at, turned her head quickly away and set her lips disapprovingly.

Lou's business establishment was in a tall, three-story frame house on First and Main, on the same block as Rae McRoberts's, which, as everyone knew, ran second best to Lou's.

Hugh rang the doorbell and a pretty café-au-lait maid in a black alpaca uniform with a little white apron and ruffled cap, as correct as Erica Crawford's maid and much prettier, answered the door.

"The ladies aren't receiving this early, sir," she said politely, with a smile. "Come back around seven."

Hugh returned her smile, pressed a silver dollar into her pale brown palm. "I didn't come to see the girls this time. I want to talk to Lou on a business matter."

"Yes, sir. I'll see if the madam is free." She stepped back decorously and ushered Hugh into the long dark hall. He took out his cardcase and, with the same dignity that made him the favorite on the First Hill, gave her his card. She showed him into the ornate, overfurnished parlor that would have surprised the matrons of the First Hill, whose idea of a brothel embraced red plush hangings, voluptuous divans, and gaudy pictures.

There were a stiff black horsehair sofa, several straight-backed golden oak chairs, two rather good Empire settees, a dark red leather Morris chair, a round marble-topped table with a begonia in a Chinese flowerpot, a Japanese screen with white and blue butterflies, several hassocks, a gramophone with a large horn, a cabinet full of records, and a player piano with a silk scarf draped over it. The pictures would have done credit to the public library: a steel engraving of the Acropolis, Rosa Bonheur's "Horse Fair" and a tinted photograph of Mount Rainier. It was as stuffy, decorous, and in as bad taste as the most respectable, bourgeois home in Seattle.

Hugh sat with his hat on his knee, smiling at his thoughts. Erica Crawford's drawing room, with its subtle, pale gold hangings, nest of little pillows, and luxurious deep divans and chairs, was far more in keeping with the popular idea of a house of ill fame.

"Hullo, young man," boomed a deep, hearty voice.

Hugh got quickly to his feet as Lou Graham swept into the room. She looked like the headmistress of a select girls' school, only a shade more chic. Her iron-gray hair was piled up in a pompadour; she wore a pince-nez on a black ribbon; her dark gray foulard was severely tailored and she wore a little white piqué turned-back collar that gave her a prim air. But she was smoking a black cheroot and the hand she offered him was strong and hard, like a man's.

"Dolly said you wanted to see me on a business matter. What can I do for you?" she said, coming straight to the point.

"You know who I am, Lou?" Hugh gave her his slow, ironic smile and she looked him over with a deliberate air, then, her keen blue eyes a trifle warmer, she nodded.

"You're Hugh Deming, the judge's son. You've only been here once before, I think." She puffed on her cigar, observing him through the cloud of smoke.

"I've been in Alaska." He gave her a deprecating little smile, indicating that only urgent business could have kept him from the charms of her establishment.

"Find a gold mine?"

He shook his head. "No. Came back flat broke. But I had a lot of fun."

She laughed harshly. "Good for you. Gold is where you find it, I always say. I don't need to go traipsing off to the Klondike."

"Why should you? You've got a gold mine right here."

"I do all right." She shrugged, sat down on the sofa, and he sat down beside her.

"You're a smart businesswoman, they tell me, Lou." His manner was a subtle combination of the casual and the admiring.

"Thanks. There are those in this town who'd like to put me out of business." Her jaw tightened and a hard glint came into her eyes. Generous she might be on occasion, if you got on the right side of her, but get in her way and she was granite clear through.

"Well, Lou, I guess you can't blame them. People have to do what they think is right." He met her shrewd eyes coolly. One thing he had inherited from his father was the utter necessity of speaking his mind no matter how it might damage his own interests.

"Did you come here to preach to me? Or what's on your mind?" snapped Lou.

"I'm no reformer. I'm not good enough to tell anyone else he's wrong. I've got a business proposition to make to you."

"Well, what is it?" Lou put down her cheroot and folded her arms.

"You know, Lou, it's not a bad idea to have two strings to your bow. Now, say these people who want to put you out of business should succeed. What would you do then?" Hugh took his time, crossed his knees, and lit a cigarette, glancing at her casually.

She gave him a quick, guarded look. She knew who his father was and that, if a movement were afoot to run her out of Seattle, Judge Deming would know about it.

"I've got plenty in the bank. Plenty to fight with and, if I lose, enough to get along."

"But wouldn't it be smart to invest some of your money in a paying business—have that other string to your bow?"

She snorted, blew a cloud of smoke at him. "You trying to sell me mining stock or gold bricks, young feller? I'm no sucker for that kind of a touch."

Hugh ground out his cigarette in the ash tray, got up as if to leave. "I'm sorry I bothered you, Lou. It never occurred to me that you'd think I was a con man or a slick promoter."

"Hey, wait up, my young buck, don't fly off the handle. I know your father and I guess you've got good stuff in you. Sorry I riled you. What's the deal?" She put her hand on his arm, led him back to the sofa, and sat down beside him.

"I'm going into the shipping business with Captain Blaine, skipper of the *Island Queen*. He's bought one steamer himself, the *Kitsap*, and I've got to raise fifty thousand dollars to go in as a full partner. How'd you like to be a silent partner, a part owner, say, for twenty-five thousand?"

She searched his face, chewing the end of her cheroot. Then she burst out into a guffaw that would have done credit to Captain Blaine himself. "You're a cool customer. Drops in casual like of a Sunday afternoon and asks for twenty-five thousand dollars."

"I'm not asking you for anything, Lou," snapped Hugh tartly. "I'm giving you a chance to get in on something big. Shipping's going to boom in a few years. Now's the time to get established to grab off the trade with the Orient. Blaine's no fool and he knows the shipping business. That's why he's starting his own line."

"I know Harry Blaine. He's a good man. Hardheaded, too." Lou gave him a twisted smile. "But what would people think if they found out one of your partners was Lou Graham?"

Hugh laughed, but he had the grace to blush slightly. "I think it'd make a wonderful story, don't you? It'd give all the debutantes something to whisper about behind their fans and would probably make me twice as popular as I already am."

When Hugh hurried down the steps of the house on First and Main he was smiling and a portly gentleman in gray clothes going by in a carriage gave him a disapproving frown. The young man was too bemused by his success to notice that it was

Will Carlton, who was on his way downtown to a meeting with a big Eastern steel man interested in Will's tide-flat property for a factory site. But Will recognized him.

At Kit Jordan's rooming house a toothless old crone showed Hugh upstairs to Captain Blaine's room, wheezing and groaning at every step. The captain answered Hugh's knock stripped to the waist, the mat of grizzled red hair on his chest like the pelt of a bear. He stared at the young man without recognition for a moment, then a surprised smile spread over his weather-beaten face.

"Hello, bucko!" he cried. "I'd forgotten all about you. Come in and sit down. Throw that gear off the chair. What's your name, now? I never was any good at remembering names."

Hugh told him, then added with a rueful laugh, "If you've forgotten me, I hope that doesn't mean you've forgotten the proposition you made me coming down from Nome."

"Proposition?" The old salt's eyes twinkled and he scratched his head. "Now you just go over the details of this here proposition for me, so's to refresh my mind, son."

Hugh's face was red. The cockiness was oozing out of him just as it did when his father laughed at him. But he pretended a coolness he didn't feel. "Well, sir, I came here prepared to invest twenty-five thousand dollars in your steamship line as a junior partner. I expect to raise another twenty-five thousand for a full partnership."

Captain Blaine's jaw dropped an inch or two and it was his turn to redden. He gave the young man with the casual manner a sharp, appraising glance.

"However," went on Hugh coolly, "if you're not interested, I'll take my investment elsewhere and start a rival company."

The older man laughed and grabbed Hugh's hand in a crushing clasp. "I never thought you could do it, son. My error. I apologize. Where's the money?"

"Naturally I haven't got it with me. But I can get it as soon as we draw up the partnership papers and the letters of incorporation."

The captain eyed him shrewdly. "Where'd ye raise it, son?"

Hugh smiled, shook his head. "From a friend who prefers to remain anonymous at the present."

"We'll have a spot of grog on it now," cried the captain,

pulling open a drawer of his bureau, "and tomorrow we'll go to a lawyer and draw up the papers." He took out a bottle and poured rum into two tumblers with a generous hand. "Here's to the North Star Steamship Company, Incorporated." They drank solemnly and Blaine sat down on the bed and leaned toward Hugh. "Know why I call it the North Star, son? Because that's the sailor's star. As long as ye steer by the North Star, ye can't go wrong."

As Hugh descended the dark, musty-smelling stairs of the rooming house, he was flushed with rum and the bright future he felt sure lay ahead of him. As he opened the door with its colored glass panes, he heard a woman's angry voice raised in a tirade. On the porch of the rooming house stood a tall, raw-boned woman with wisps of gray hair flying about her hatchet face. Her hands were on her hips and she was bending forward to pour a stream of invective on a girl standing at the foot of the steps.

"Don't come hangin' around here, ye cheatin', sneakin' little bitch!" screamed the woman. "Made your own mother a laughing stock! Run out on yer lawful wedded husband! You and that snivelin' priest! I shoulda thrown him out when he come sneakin' around whinin' prayers over poor Mae's dead body! Fine priest he is, turnin' a girl against her own mother, takin' her away from her husband and hidin' her in his own house, while Carew was breakin' up my furniture and threatenin' to kill me. How do I know what went on between you two whilst ye was stayin' with him?"

"Ma!" cried the girl in a shocked voice. "Don't talk like that. Don't dare to say anything against Father Donegan."

"Father Donegan, is it? I'll father him. Pretendin' to be so holy and keepin' a young girl in his house for three nights. Had your marriage annulled, did he? What'd ye pay him to do it, eh, my girl? I can guess. Too good for Fred Carew, who'd have given ye anything ye wanted. Had to take up with an old man in skirts!"

"Shut up, you dirty old woman!" cried the girl, and she started up the steps, her face white and blazing.

The old woman backed up and Hugh saw to his amazement that the girl running toward her with fists clenched was Annie

Jordan. "Keep away from me, you whore!" shrieked the woman.

"Annie!" cried Hugh.

The girl stopped, her fists raised to strike her mother. She turned her suffering, distorted face to him and suddenly all the anger and fire went out of her. Her hands dropped limply to her sides and she hung her head.

"I'll take you home," said Hugh quietly and, stepping past the woman on the porch, he took Annie's arm and led her down the steps.

"Get out!" screamed Annie's mother. "Get out and don't you ever come back!"

"That's telling her, Kit," called an insolent voice. Somebody laughed and clapped. Hugh saw that there was a small crowd beginning to gather, waterfront loafers, a Chinaman in pajamas with a bundle of laundry on his head, grinning like an idol, a raddled creature in a feather boa with hectic spots of paint on her sunken cheeks. Annie stared at the woman who had spoken.

"Well, well, if it ain't Annie," the creature said with a grimace. "Long time no see. Heard you were livin' on the First Hill now. Guess you think you're too good for the waterfront now that you're a hired girl!" She burst out into hideous laughter and Hugh could feel Annie's arm tremble under his hand.

"Hello, Maizie," she said in a queer, flat voice. "You still around?"

"Don't make no cracks at me, ye little snob!" cried Maizie, sneering at her, and elbowed her way toward the white-faced girl.

Hugh put his hand in his pocket, took out a silver dollar, and tossed it at Maizie. "Here," he said lightly, arrogantly. "Catch! Now you won't have to work tonight."

The ex-Variety girl gave him a look seething with hatred, but she put her foot on the dollar when it spun at her feet.

"Come on, Annie, let's get out of here." Hugh pushed through the crowd, hailed a passing hansom cab, and put her into it.

She sat rigid in the seat, her eyes wide open, her face white. Only the rise and fall of her bosom indicated the tumult in her breast.

"It's all right, Annie," he said softly, taking her hand. "Forget it."

"I shouldn't have come back," she whispered. "But I had to. I was lonesome for the waterfront." Suddenly she put her face against his shoulder and began to cry, her body shaken with sobs.

She told him she'd had the day off and how she'd smelled the bay, standing on Madison Avenue looking toward the sound. Suddenly she thought she couldn't stand it if she didn't walk along the docks, see the gulls, the ships, smell the tar and the bilge and the salty, pungent air. So she'd walked all the way to the waterfront, she'd seen where they were filling in the tide flats to make solid ground for factories and warehouses. She'd peered in the ship chandler shops, gone into Ye Old Curiosity Shop, where the same old man in his black alpaca jacket and skullcap sat among his jumbled treasures. Then, irresistibly, she'd been drawn toward the Nugget Saloon and the rooming house.

"I wanted to see Ma again," she said simply. "She's the only relative I've got, now that Mae's dead."

Hugh pressed her against him and she sighed deeply. Then she sat up, wiped her eyes with the handkerchief he'd given her, and smiled shakily at him. "Well, I'll never go again. They don't want me and I guess I don't want them, either. But I miss the waterfront, Hugh, and the docks. I like to see the boats come in." She was like a child who has been scolded and deprived of its dearest toy.

"I didn't know you'd been married," said Hugh thoughtfully, looking at her with quickened interest. What a strange girl she was—how little he knew about her.

She laughed bitterly. "It wasn't a real marriage. I didn't know what I was doing and I ran away from him as soon as the ceremony was over. That's why Ma hates me so. Fred Carew promised her a lot of money, I guess, to get me. She hates Father Donegan, too, because he took me in and found me the job with Mrs. Carlton."

"What happened to the man?" asked Hugh, his face dark, his voice, though he didn't realize it, edged with jealousy.

"I don't know. Father Donegan had the marriage annulled. I hope I never see him again. He was horrible." She shuddered and looked away.

"Don't think about it, Annie. Don't think about what happened back there today, either. I'll take you home now." Hugh squeezed her strong, cold hand, but there was no answering pressure.

She gave him a steady, clear look. "Home?"

"Aren't you happy with the Carltons?"

She looked straight ahead. "It's all right there. But it's not home. I have no home. The Nugget wasn't much, but I belonged there once. Now I don't belong anywhere."

Her voice, calm, steady, with no trace of emotion or self-pity, moved him curiously. He thought he had never known anyone who seemed so completely alone.

He tapped on the window, spoke to the driver. "Go down by Colman Dock." He turned to Annie. "Let's see what boats are in. I want to take a look at the *Kitsap*, Captain Blaine's boat. He just acquired it."

"Captain Blaine was a friend of mine when I was little. He always said he'd take me for a trip on his boat." She smiled at him. "But he never did."

"I'm going into business with Blaine," said Hugh, the excitement of his success creeping over him again, warming him as the rum had. "That's how I happened to be at your mother's rooming house. He's staying there. We're starting a steamship line together."

Annie turned to him eagerly. "You never did want to be a lawyer, did you? I remember the first time I saw you, you said you wanted to be a sailor."

Hugh laughed. "You don't forget anything, do you, Annie? Maybe I won't ever be a sailor, but at least I'll be mixed up with boats and the sea. That's better than spending my life in a musty law office."

The cab drew up at Colman Dock and they got out. Annie leaned on a pile, gazing out over the choppy blue bay, smelling the pungent air eagerly. Gulls screamed and wheeled above them and she said wistfully, "I used to feed them. When I was a child I was always getting a licking for hanging around the docks. I wish I'd been a boy. Then I'd have been a sailor."

Hugh glanced at her full breast, slim waist, the soft white curve of her neck where tendrils of red-gold hair curled in the damp air. He laughed softly. "I'm glad you're not a boy, Annie."

She met his gold-flecked gray eyes and a slow blush spread over her face. A little pulse began to beat in her white throat and she looked away in sudden confusion.

The *Kitsap* lay in the slip, stained with bilge. A sailor was washing down her decks, whistling loudly. Farther out in the bay two squatty gray freighters were anchored. The Tacoma boat was coming in at another dock. She had a high, falsetto whistle. They could hear the throb of her ancient engines as she churned past them.

"Do you still want to take a boat trip up the sound, Annie?" asked Hugh suddenly. He didn't look at her and when she glanced quickly at him his face was withdrawn and stern.

"Yes."

"Then I'll take you." He looked at her gravely. "When can you get away to go?"

"I'll have next Saturday off, from twelve noon on." She didn't know why, but she met his gaze as gravely as he was gazing at her. There was something between them as they looked at each other that she didn't understand. It made her almost stop breathing.

"Good," he said, taking her arm and leading her back to the waiting cab. "I'll meet you here at twelve-thirty next Saturday." She got into the cab and sat in the corner, staring out the window. Something had been said that was not put into words. Something had been settled that her mind could not reach. But her heart began to pound and she did not want to talk any more. She closed her eyes and suddenly she knew that she was deeply in love with Hugh Deming.

Chapter XII

She was waiting for him, sitting on the pier, when he got there. He was late, but she had been early. As soon as she'd done up her work she'd left. The Carltons had been invited on a yachting excursion by Mrs. Crawford and were to be gone for the week end. Mrs. Carlton had hesitated at leaving Annie alone, but finally, after innumerable instructions and exhortations about locking the doors, not staying out late, and being careful to bank the coal range, she'd decided to leave Annie in charge of the house.

The minute the Carlton family had gone, Annie rushed into her room with the teakettle of hot water she'd kept on the back of the stove. She stripped off her house dress, tossed it into her closet, washed herself all over with a bar of lavendar-scented soap she'd been saving, changed her underwear, and put on a sprigged brown-and-white poplin she had made herself. A fleeting sense of disloyalty went through her mind as she was brushing out her long hair, but she refused to think about it.

Why should she stay alone in the house all day? Nothing could happen to it if she locked it up tight. She knew in her heart that nothing could make her stay. Even if she knew the house was going to walk away the minute she was out of it, still she would go to meet Hugh Deming at the dock. If Mrs. Carlton found out and punished her afterward, that was all right.

Since her rebuff by her mother at the waterfront she'd felt desperately that she was really alone, she belonged nowhere—she was only a hired girl on the First Hill; she'd been repudiated by her own kind. Or were they her kind? No, now she knew they never had been. She'd loved the waterfront, its life, its variety, its vigor and crudeness, but she'd not been entirely part of it. Always in the back of her mind was the determination to get away, to get above it. Now she was suspended between two worlds. And as the Carltons' hired girl she had no true life of her own at all. But she meant to have.

The noon whistles were blowing as she took a last quick look at herself in the mirror, picked up her purse, locked the front door. As she turned to go down the steps a man was coming in at the gate. He had quick, dark eyes, a black mustache, and he wore a straw hat with a jaunty striped ribbon. It was Ned Weaver.

"Hullo," he called, beginning to smile.

"Why, Ned," she cried, trying to keep the impatience out of her voice. Oh, dear Lord, if he makes me late . . . if I miss Hugh because of him . . . !

"Surprised to see me, honey?" His voice was warm and familiar. She felt hot with embarrassment. How had she ever thought him attractive? His cheap, ready-made clothes, his vaudeville mustache, his jaunty assurance filled her with distaste.

"Yes, I am, Ned. I thought you'd given me up as a bad job," she laughed, furious at herself for lapsing into his own easy familiarity. The truth was she didn't know how to snub anyone, particularly someone who was fond of her.

"I been out on the road. Got a new line. Ladies' corsets. Very fancy." He winked at her. "Soon as I got back to town I said to myself, 'I got a little unfinished business to take care of up on the First Hill.'" He laughed and squeezed her arm. She stiffened and tried to draw away from him, but he bent closer. "Maybe this ain't the time nor the place, but a drummer learns never to miss a chance. Look what I brought you." He opened his hand and showed her the little white leather box he'd been holding. Annie stared at it and then at him. "Go on, Annie, take it. It's for you."

When she still made no move to take the box, he opened it himself by pressing on the button which made the top spring up, exposing a small diamond ring that glittered faintly in the sunlight. She stared at it, unable to lift her eyes to his face.

"Well, kiddo, what d'ye say? Not bad, eh?" He lifted the ring from the white satin bed on which it lay and grabbed her hand. "Course it ain't no sixteen-carat diamond. But it ain't glass, neither. I got it from another drummer I met on the road, a jewelry salesman. He gave me a good buy on it."

Annie wished she could run away without ever having to look at him or answer the eagerness in his voice. She was deeply ashamed to think that in her loneliness she'd led him on to thinking she'd accept a ring from him. She didn't know what to say.

He tried to slip the ring on the third finger of her left hand, but the knuckle, swollen from dishwater and strong soap, was too big.

Annie laughed, suddenly relieved. "It's too small for me, Ned. Better find a girl with dainty hands."

His face got red and he frowned. "I'll have it made bigger for you, Annie."

"No," she said quickly, "don't do that, Ned."

He pressed his arm tightly about her waist. "I don't want any other girl, honey. I want you."

"Ned," she managed to say, "please don't. I like you very much, but I don't want to marry you. We've only been out a few times together. We hardly know each other."

"I know you're the one for me," he whispered. Then he grinned. "But I won't rush you. Take your time. I'll have the ring fixed and then I'll take you to the park under the moon and maybe you'll change your mind." With a confident smile he slipped the box with the ring back into his pocket. "How about going out to Luna Beach with me today?"

"I can't, Ned. I've got an engagement at twelve-thirty."

"Oh." He frowned. "So I've got a rival, eh?"

She blushed swiftly and shook her head. "He's just a friend. But I'll have to go now, or I'll be late."

"May I escort you to the trolley, Miss Jordan?" He swept off his hat and bowed extravagantly. He took Annie's arm and held it tightly as they walked to the cable-car line. "I'm making good money now," he boasted. "Five per cent commission on every sale. Expense account, too, when I'm on the road. Sometimes I make as much as twenty-five or thirty dollars a week. You'd be able to get along on that, I guess, eh?" His jauntiness had returned and he kept squeezing her arm and grinning at her.

At the car line Annie turned and looked at him squarely and candidly. "Ned, you're a nice fella and some girl will be lucky to have you for a husband. But it won't be me. I don't love you and I'll never marry you." She hated like poison to have to hurt him, but it wasn't honest to keep him dangling.

He flushed and his grin faded but he said doggedly, "I won't take no for an answer, Annie. I'll just keep on trying."

She shook her head. "No, Ned. It's no use. I'm in love with someone else."

The cable car rocketed around the corner just then and Annie stepped forward to get on. "Allow me," said Ned gallantly, and he helped her on, dropped a nickel in the box, then got off, hat in hand, and watched the cable car lurch down the hill. He was smiling cockily when Annie looked back and he lifted his hat in farewell.

She felt bad about Ned, but she couldn't help the way she was. At least she had told him the truth. She was quite sure he wasn't the sort to die of a broken heart. He'll probably have another girl in a week, she thought, but she was touched by the tribute he'd given her in wanting to marry her, in buying her the brave little diamond. Maybe it wasn't the kind of romantic love she'd dreamed about, but it was good and clean. It wasn't like Fred Carew, bargaining with her mother for her body.

The cable car swayed from side to side as it plummeted down the hills, straight toward the bay. Annie loved riding in the cars; it was like flying. You had the feeling that they couldn't possibly stop until they plunged into the blue, shimmering water of the harbor. It was a very fine day, sunny and bright. It was so clear that you could see right across the bay to Vashon and Bainbridge islands hooded in green woods; you could see the little island steamers plowing along, leaving a white wake on the blue water like the silver trail left by a snail.

Annie's heart quickened as she watched the steamers. She forgot about Ned and his proposal. Hugh! I'm meeting Hugh. He's taking me on a boat trip! How lovely it will be standing beside him at the rail, with the sea breeze in our faces and the dancing water below us. But will he be there? Sudden panic gripped her. Did he really mean it? He's Judge Deming's son and I'm just a hired girl. When she lived on the waterfront, such distinctions meant nothing to her, but since she'd been on the First Hill she was very much aware of them. But the way he looked at me—the way he said, "I'll meet you at twelve-thirty." That sudden, breathless moment between them—yes, he'd be there. She knew he would.

He wasn't there when she reached the pier, but she knew she was early. The West Seattle ferry was just coming in with a great churning of water, clanging of bells, and jockeying to make the ferry slip. What a fuss those old side-wheelers made! She sat on a pile of neatly wired hay, watching it dock. The *Kitsap* was in again and on the other side of the pier the *Rosalie*, trim little steamer with a red-and-black smokestack. She made the Bellingham run, stopping at points on Orcas Island—Friday Harbor, Eastsound, Orcas. Steaming into Elliott Bay, far out, proud and beautiful, one of the San Francisco boats smudged the clear sky with her black plume of smoke.

Annie sat clasping her knees, seeing it all, smelling the tarry, rotting smell of the wharves, the pungent smell of fish from the nearby market, her face eager and delighted. There was no place like the waterfront.

"This is how I first saw you," said Hugh quietly, coming up behind her. She hadn't seen him; she'd been too absorbed in watching the boats, the gulls, the longshoremen. She turned her smiling face up to him with her head cocked on one side like a child.

"Yes," she replied. "I've been having such a fine time sitting here. I told you the other day that I didn't belong anywhere. But I do. This is where I belong." She laughed. "Ma always said I was a waterfront rat. I guess I am."

"Then you didn't mind waiting?" He smiled, wondering whether she were a child or a woman.

"Oh no," she said, meeting his eyes gravely. "I knew you'd come."

The smile still hovered over his lips, but his eyes were sober and piercing. "You knew I'd come," he repeated. He put out his hand and helped her up. She stood quietly beside him, looking up into his face. "We'd better get aboard. The boat leaves in ten minutes."

"Which one are we taking?" she asked eagerly.

"The *Rosalie*."

Her face broke into a delightful smile. "Oh, she's a fine little boat. I've been looking at her while I waited. She goes all the way up the sound, as far as Bellingham."

He nodded. "It's a beautiful trip. We'll see all the islands. She puts in at a number of little towns. They serve meals aboard, too, so we'll be able to get lunch."

"Oh, Hugh," she cried suddenly, tucking her hand under his arm and pressing against him impulsively, "you're so nice to take me. I'm so happy!"

He smiled at her, the gold flecks in his eyes dancing. "We'll have a fine time, Annie. I'm happy too."

They hurried across to the other pier, where passengers were boarding the *Rosalie*. Annie laughed and chattered like a child and Hugh seemed to be enjoying himself as simply as she was. The thing that had been between them Sunday afternoon was gone; Annie forgot that it ever had been. Hugh found two deck chairs and they sat in the lee of the smokestack, protected from the wind. Annie took off her hat and her little Eton jacket and held them in her lap. The whistle blew, so close behind them that they both jumped; Annie screamed and covered her ears and Hugh laughed at her.

They steamed out into the sound and Hugh and Annie left their chairs to stand in the stern and look at Mount Rainier, rising like an unearthly vision from behind the city, eternally snow-capped, noble, majestic, rarely visible in such clarity as this day because of the fogs and mists, the smoke from summer forest fires. But today the great mountain seemed to soar above the bay like the Great Spirit of the Northwest.

"It looks just like a big dish of ice cream!" cried Annie.

"No wonder the Indians worshiped it. It looks like a god—some eternal, prehistoric deity brooding calmly over its people. Too bad they changed the name to Mount Rainier—the old name, the one the Indians gave it—is much better—Tahoma," said Hugh.

Annie laughed. "No true Seattleite would ever admit that, though."

"No, because it would give Tacoma too much honor. If we'd lived here in medieval times, those two cities would probably have made war on each other." He looked at her profile, strong and yet tender, the white forehead, the proud, slightly aquiline nose, the full, warm mouth, the strong, stubborn, softly rounded chin, the sweet, long throat. In a way it was not a beautiful face, not in the classic sense, the nose a bit too long, the mouth too large, but it was alive and warm and glowing.

"You have a beautiful mouth, Annie," said Hugh suddenly as she turned her face from the mountain to smile at him. Her eyes darkened and a little cloud of pain went over her face. She seemed to be searching his eyes for something. My God, he thought, she's in love with me.

He'd been in love several times himself, he'd flirted with and pursued any number of girls, but this was the first time he'd been aware that someone was in love with him. Looking into her grave, dark eyes, he knew that love to Annie would never be a casual, easy, fleeting thing. She was completely honest. She was wholehearted. She was generous. She had no idea of how to hide her emotion, nor would she have tried if she could.

Suddenly Hugh realized that he was trembling, that he wanted to take her in his arms, that he wanted her aliveness, the honesty and truth that were in her. He took her hand, and her fingers tightened over his. At the touch of her warm, strong hand a little shock went through him. Perhaps he was falling in love with her, or perhaps the strength of her own emotion was enough for them both. He didn't know. He had never felt quite like this before and he didn't know how to proceed. There was no rule in his superficial romantic code to cover something as real, as forthright, as vital as Annie Jordan.

"Annie," he said in a low, surprised voice, "I want to kiss you."

"Yes," she answered quietly, and she put her free hand on his arm.

They were alone in the stern for the moment, but he felt that it wouldn't have mattered to her, she would have turned to him as simply if there had been a crowd beside them. He bent and softly kissed her lips. Her arms went around his neck and she sighed and held him close. His arms tightened about her and he kissed her again, for a long time. When he let her go, they were both pale and trembling.

She moved away from him and stared down at the white foam boiling behind the boat. He looked at the soft curve of her neck, that looked as tender and defenseless as a child's. A pang of pity smote him sharply and he had to look away. What would happen to her? He knew instinctively that it was in his power to hurt her.

Those kisses hadn't been like the quick, stolen one in the park where a lonely girl lifted her lips for a taste of life, for a lark, and could escape, laughing and disheveled, into the night. These had been the kisses of a woman in love, who gives her lips to her lover and, with them, herself.

Some deep dissatisfaction, some sudden realization of his own weakness and selfishness, depressed and humbled him. He could not speak to her or touch her just then. He turned away, leaving her standing at the rail, and went below into the dining salon, looking for a drink.

Annie stood looking at the water, trying to compose herself. She knew now that the love she'd had for Rolfe Linden had been a good and pure thing; perhaps if he'd lived it might have been all that she wanted out of life. But Rolfe was dead and with all the vigor of her passionate being she was in love with Hugh Deming. The love of her adolescence had been part love, part hero worship for a person out of her experience and background, a person she saw always with a kind of incandescence about him. But in Hugh she found the response to the vital, half-understood yearning of both flesh and spirit. Shaken and moved by the thing that was between them, the thing that her instinct recognized but her intellect wondered at, she knew only that his arms, his lips had been urgent, that he had met her yearning with his own. He loves me too, she cried in her heart. He loves me as much as I love him.

She turned to search his face again, to touch his hand, to give solidity and certainty to her conviction. But he wasn't there. Suddenly she was frightened. She must not lose him as she'd lost Rolfe. Where had he gone? Why had he left her? Had he meant anything by that desperate embrace or had he done it for a lark and been put off by her ardent response? She who never whimpered under her mother's harsh punishments was all at once weak and close to tears. She struggled with herself to keep from sobbing.

Some people were coming with deck chairs and a picnic hamper and she averted her face and hurried past them toward the bow where Hugh had left their chairs. But he was not there either. She sat down and waited, her heart bleak.

He was gone for half an hour, and in that time she knew anguish, loss, humiliation, anger, and, at last, resignation.

He cannot possibly love me because I am not good enough for him. He is for girls like Emily Carlton, not me. He only took me on this trip to be kind and he kissed me because— because maybe I'm pretty or he thought I wanted him to. It didn't mean anything to him. I mustn't let him know that it meant anything to me either.

Then suddenly he was beside her, followed by a steward carrying a covered tray. "I've brought you lunch," he cried gaily. She could only look at him, unable to speak. She took the plate of food the steward served her, she ate, she swallowed, but she was unaware of what it all tasted like.

"What's the matter?" asked Hugh at last. "You've hardly eaten a thing."

She looked at him. "I—I thought you'd gone and left me," she said honestly. "You were gone a long time."

He tried to laugh. She kept looking at him, her violet eyes hurt and dark. Suddenly he took her hand and pressed it to his cheek. "I'm sorry," he whispered. "I went away because I—I didn't know what else to do. Forgive me."

She didn't say anything for a moment. She put down her plate on the deck and wiped her lips with the paper napkin.

"It's all right," she said quietly. "I guess you didn't mean it when you kissed me."

He didn't answer. He put down his plate, too, got up, went to the rail, clutched it, stared at the sparkling blue water, lit a cigarette with shaking hands, then wheeled and stood before her, gazing at her with earnest eyes.

"You're wrong, Annie. I did mean it. I've never meant anything so much in my life."

She began to smile slowly, incredulously, suddenly she stood up, stretched her arms wide, did a little waltz step, reached out and caught his hands and, laughing, whirled him along with her. He laughed, too, he clasped her waist, they began to waltz wildly, madly, round and round, their heads back, smiling into each other's eyes. An elderly couple rounded the lifeboats, stopped short, and stared at them, popeyed. Annie and Hugh saw them at last and stopped dancing, flushed and laughing.

The elderly woman smiled, made a tentative gesture toward

them. "Oh, don't mind us. I love seeing young people enjoy themselves."

"Thank you, madam," said Hugh gaily, bowing, and clutching Annie's hand, he ran with her along the deck. Her cheeks were hot, her eyes sparkled, her whole body seemed glowing and alive. At last they came to a stop at the stern where they'd kissed. Hugh took both her hands, gazed ardently into her uplifted face.

"Annie—Annie," he cried, "I think I'm in love with you!"

"I'm glad," said Annie simply, smiling into his eyes. "I love you, Hugh."

Afterward he tried to justify himself as a man will do. He tried to say to himself that he hadn't planned it that way. All he'd wanted was a simple, innocent little excursion up the sound and back again the same day. But he knew in his heart that he'd hoped and intended that things should turn out as they did.

Actually, it was Annie's fault. At Port Madison she'd asked how long the boat stayed there. The steward had said airily, "About twenty minutes."

She'd looked wistfully at the little white town clustered about the dock, at the wooded green hills stretching beyond.

"Would you like to get off and stretch your legs?" asked Hugh casually. But even then he'd had the strange, hard, insistent core of purpose inside him.

She turned her bright face to him. Ever since he'd told her he loved her she'd been like a spirit, like a child, happy and soft and eager. "Oh yes, Hugh."

They went ashore, while the boat disgorged passengers and mail and waited at the pier. The curving white beach intrigued Annie. "Oh, have we time to walk on the beach?" she cried. "I want to find some shells."

"If I find an agate I'll have it made into a ring for you," he promised. They ran the length of the wooden dock, then Hugh jumped down onto the sand, held out his arms, and Annie, laughing, jumped into them. He released her quickly because there were people watching them, but the swift, dark look he gave her made her heart turn over. She could feel it pounding, and it seemed as if he must hear the tumult it was making.

The tide was going out, leaving the wet sand dark and smooth for the sandpipers' delicate footmarks. The smell of drying kelp and seaweed was strong and pungent, and Annie breathed it in deeply. She found three frail pink scallop shells, dainty as mermaids' fans, a big curved sea snail shell with gleaming purple inside, a gooey duck shell, pure white and unbroken, and a hermit crab with his old man's claws scrabbling frantically around the edge of his tiny spiral house, like the fingers of a prisoner signaling for help.

Hugh found a lucky stone, smooth and black, with a white ring around it, and two agates, but neither clear nor unusual enough for her ring. He gave her the lucky stone. They walked slowly on the beach, exclaiming over what they found, showing each other their treasures like children. The sun was benign on their necks, the air fresh and heady. They didn't realize how far they'd wandered from the dock until the boat whistle blew. Even then they didn't notice it at first because Hugh had put the lucky stone in Annie's palm, had closed his fingers over her hand, and was gazing deeply into her eyes.

The whistle blew again and Annie pulled her eyes from his to stare back at the dock where the *Rosalie* was beginning to churn the green water.

"It's our boat!" she cried. "It's leaving without us!"

They ran back along the beach, shouting at the boat. Several people on the dock waved to them, but the *Rosalie* backed away from the pier, pointed her bow toward the straits, and the space widened between her and the land.

Hugh and Annie, out of breath, stopped and stared at her in consternation. "What will we do?" gasped Annie, pressing her hand to her side. Her eyes were wide and bright, but she didn't look frightened, only excited and wondering. She wasn't frightened, but she shivered inside with a curious little tingle of expectancy. Now what was going to happen? she thought. Whatever did, it would be better than having to go back to Carltons'. All at once, meeting Hugh's ironic little smile of concern and bafflement, she began to laugh. It was fun being left in the lurch by the boat. It was a real adventure!

Hugh laughed too. "I guess we're stuck here for a while."

She nodded. "I guess we are."

"You're not scared?" He looked at her in admiration.

"No. What's there to be scared of?" She looked away from

him at the water sparkling far out, she lifted her head eagerly and breathed the salty air. "I love it here."

"But we may have to wait till tomorrow for another boat."

She nodded. "I don't care. I'd like to stay here forever."

"What about your job? Won't Mrs. Carlton be angry?"

She met his eyes fearlessly. "What if she is? I'm not afraid of her. If she fires me I can get another job."

He squeezed her hand. "You're wonderful, Annie. Most girls would be furious or hysterical."

"I think it's fun." She bent, picked up a smooth, flat stone, and skipped it over the water.

"Well, let's go up to the town and find out what to do."

The little white town dozed under the summer sun. A dirt road ran up from the dock to the "business district," a cluster of frame buildings, general store, post office, blacksmith shop, harness maker, saloon, and a warehouse. There were wooden sidewalks on each side of the street. Another road wandered up the hills where scattered white houses nestled among the firs and spruces. On the hill overlooking the bay there was a small weather-beaten building, with a belfry, swings, and two out-houses, that looked like a school, another with a steeple and a cross and one large square house painted white with a veranda running along three sides of it that Hugh decided must be the hotel. He went into the general store to make inquiries.

Annie stayed outside, looking at the assortment of merchandise in the store window: garden tools, sacks of flour and sugar, men's overalls, china dishes, straw hats, chick feed, a child's red wagon, striped candy sticks in a glass jar. The store cat, an orange tabby with white paws, slept languorously, pressed against the window.

Presently Hugh came out. "The next boat to Seattle leaves at eleven-twenty tomorrow morning." He gave her a quick, sharp glance.

In spite of what she'd said about not being afraid, a little pang went through her. If the Carltons should get home before she did, there'd be the devil to pay. Then her heart lifted again. What of it? This was the most exciting thing that had ever happened to her. She loved the little town and the beach. She and Hugh would have the whole beautiful day together. Why shouldn't she enjoy every minute of it? She lifted her eyes to his and smiled. "We'll pretend we're castaways on a desert island. I've always wanted to spend the night in the woods."

He glanced away and a slow flush warmed his slender face.

"I don't think we'll have to do that. The storekeeper says that big square building on the hill is a hotel. He says we can get supper there and rooms."

"Oh, let's have our supper on the beach," cried Annie eagerly. "We can make a fire and buy something at the store. Maybe the storekeeper will lend us a hoe to dig clams with and we can have a clambake."

He smiled at her, wondering how she could be at once so womanly and desirable and so childlike and simple too. "All right. We'll do whatever you say. But I think I'd better go and arrange for our rooms now."

"And I'll get the things for our supper, and the hoe. The tide's just right now for clam digging. I'll meet you on the beach."

Hugh started up the hill to the hotel and Annie went into the store. The storekeeper, a spidery little man with a bald head, a pencil behind his ear, and a bright blue eye that gave her an appreciative glance, lent her a hoe and a pail. She bought bread, butter, salt, six ears of corn, a coffeepot, coffee, matches, and a pound of Black Republican cherries. She put her purchases in the pail and shouldered the hoe.

She started off up the beach, singing "The Band Played On," oblivious of the stares of the young men hanging around the dock, aware only of the wonderful, singing excitement within her, the warmth of the sun on her face, the smell of the tide flats, the blueness of sky and water, the cries of the gulls.

She left the town behind, passed the point, and came to an empty stretch of beach with no houses. The tide was far out here and the trees grew to the edge of the shore, hanging over the bleached logs, white as bone, tossed there by high winter tides and left to whiten in sun and spray. It looked as wild and untouched as it must have at the dawn of creation. Syringa bushes exhaled their cloying sweetness, and wild rose, tart and spicy, smelled like incense.

Annie took off her jacket, rolled up the sleeves of her blouse, turned her skirt back, and fastened it with a safety pin. She took off her shoes and stockings and, barefooted, ran with pail and hoe to the water's edge to dig clams, the sand wet and cool under her bare toes.

When Hugh came back from the hotel she had half a pailful already dug and she turned to wave to him, her cheeks streaked with mud, her hair tumbling about her shoulders. He was so entranced by the sight of her, bare-armed, bare-legged, unashamed of the tumult of flaming hair blowing about her face, that he took her suddenly in his arms and held her against him.

She had already started a fire, to heat the rocks for the clambake. He watched her rake away the coals when the rocks were red-hot, spread a layer of damp seaweed over them, then the clams which she waded out into the water to wash, then the sweet corn. She covered it all with another thick layer of seaweed, and a piece of an old sail she'd found on the beach.

"It won't be ready to eat for a while," she warned him.

"Where did you learn to do all this?" he asked, staring at her in admiration and astonishment.

"From the Siwashes out on Alki Point," she laughed. When her preparations were finished, she washed her face and hands in the sound, unpinned her skirt, and sat beside him on the beach, combing her hair. She couldn't bear to put her shoes on; she sat digging her toes into the warm dry sand.

"Don't pin up your hair yet," Hugh whispered when she was about to knot it again at her neck.

"Why not?" She glanced at him with her head on one side, her eyes bright.

"It's so lovely loose. Let me look at it awhile." He put out his hand and took a handful of it, pressed it against his face. "It's like silk," he murmured, "and it smells like wood smoke and wild roses."

She leaned back on her palms, smiling lazily at him. She felt so good, full of sun and wind and the smell of the sea. She felt like herself, like Annie Jordan, a person, for the first time since she'd left the waterfront. A surge of power went through her when she saw Hugh's hand shake, lighting a cigarette. He loved her; he wanted her; she'd make him forget Emily Carlton. "Oh, I'm happy!" she laughed, and lay back on the sand and closed her eyes.

Hugh sat looking at her for a while, one hand still caught in the meshes of her glorious hair. His face was pale and a muscle jumped in his cheek. "You're the strangest girl I ever knew, Annie Jordan," he said suddenly. He bent over her and she opened her eyes and gazed steadily up into his. With all her soul she wanted him to kiss her. Her lips curved, full and provocative, and her eyes were soft. But he stood up and said sharply, "I think I'll go for a swim. Do you mind if I leave you for a while?"

She shook her head and he walked quickly up the beach. She sighed, stretched her hands above her head, and smiled. He'd wanted to kiss her, too, she knew. He would be back. She turned on her side, cradled her cheek in her hand, and went to sleep.

It was sundown when they ate their supper. The clams, the corn, were like ambrosia.

"I never tasted anything so good," sighed Hugh, taking out his handkerchief and wiping his mouth. "Maybe I should have been a Siwash."

"Anything tastes good on the beach when you're hungry and happy," said Annie cheerfully.

"And in love," said Hugh under his breath, but she heard it and blushed.

They scattered the clamshells and corn husks at the water's edge for the tide to take away. The fire was long out, the sun disappeared, flaming, into the sound, the tide was nearly full, and there was only a strip of beach left for them to walk back on. Hugh carried the pail and hoe and Annie carried her shoes and jacket and purse. The lights were on in the little town when they climbed up the trail from the beach. Annie stopped and put her shoes and stockings on. "They wouldn't let me in at the hotel barefoot, I guess," she laughed.

Hugh said nothing, only smiled at her, and the thing that had been in his face that Sunday on the Seattle dock was there again. Annie suddenly felt queer—not frightened, but as if a hand were pressing, pressing on her breast. She took a deep breath and followed him up the trail.

They left the pail and hoe at the store and climbed the hill, hand in hand, to the hotel. When they'd reached it and were about to go up the steps, Hugh suddenly turned to Annie, his face tense and strange.

"Annie," he whispered.

"What is it, Hugh? Why do you look like that?"

"I told them we were married. They've given us the same room."

Annie looked at him and felt her heart struggling in her breast. His eyes were dark and passionate and uncertain. His lips were set as if in pain.

"If you don't want to go in—I'll find you some other place to stay," he said in a choked voice.

She put her hand on his arm. "How much do you love me, Hugh?"

"Better than anyone else, Annie," he whispered, and at the moment he meant it. She was in his blood, like strong drink. He was weak with desire for her, but his instinct made him give her the opportunity to escape.

"That's how I love you too," she said softly, and she went up the steps before him, her red-gold head held high.

Chapter XIII

The birds woke her at dawn; the birds, that have awakened lovers in city and country, in every land, since time out of mind; the birds, that to St. Francis seemed to be chanting a canticle of praise to God their Maker, and to Annie, suddenly wide-eyed in the dark room, with her hair spread out like rippling flame on the pillow, were telling the world that she was loved, that she loved, that love was what life was created for, that it was the beginning and the end.

It was still gray outside, the sun had not yet risen, but the birds knew it was dawn; they had their cue, they burst into the clear, high, poignant chorus, they seemed to fill the room with their songs.

The birds sang, called, twittered; they announced that the night was past, that the lonely sufferers to whom the hours of darkness are torture could be released from their agony, and that those to whom the night was so short that it was like the time between a sigh and a kiss must wake, must tear themselves from each other's arms, must face the world without each other.

Annie lay, listening, a sweet, troubled ache in her breast. It was dawn. The night of ecstasy, of discovery, of warm darkness, of passion, and of tenderness was over. The day's urgency and demands would soon be upon them. There was only this short time, this waking, bird-haunted hour for each to turn to each, to gaze into each other's eyes, to whisper the things they would never say when the sun was high.

Annie turned to look at Hugh. He lay on his stomach, with

his face on his arms, and as she looked at him, he stirred, sighed, turned away from her. Oh, darling, she said in her heart, don't turn away from me. Her heart smote her with sudden sharp anguish, the swift, fleeting moment of intuition and prophecy, the knowledge that, no matter how close lovers may come in the warm, dark night, the day, the world, the years will inevitably separate them.

A little cry went out from her and suddenly he turned toward her, his eyes bright and searching. For a moment he gazed at her without speaking, as if surprised to find her there beside him. Then he smiled; his eyes were full of gold flecks, his lips were tender. "Annie! Oh, Annie, you're really here," he whispered sharply, and caught her roughly to him.

"Yes," she sighed, and her heart seemed about to burst with love, with sorrow, and with joy. "Yes, I'm here, Hugh." Tears sprang to her eyes, fell down her cheeks, fell coldly on his face, pressed to hers. He didn't speak. He didn't ask her why she was crying, but with infinite tenderness he wiped the tears away with his hand and then he kissed her eyes, the fluttering, closed lids, her white brow and cheeks, the little pulse beating in her throat, and finally her warm, eager lips.

When they slept again she was in his arms and that was how she wakened the second time, with the sun streaming in through the open windows, gulls crying out on the water, a whistle blowing somewhere, the clatter of dishes coming up from the dining room below, and Hugh smiling at her and saying, "It's nearly ten, sweetheart. We'll have to get up if we want our breakfast before we catch the eleven twenty back."

The boat back! She shivered suddenly, pressed her face against his shoulder. The night was really over now. It was broad day and time to go back. "I don't want to go back," she murmured like a child.

He kissed her cheek lightly and laughed. "Neither do I. But . . ." He pushed off the covers and she knew he wanted to get dressed, to eat breakfast, to get started.

I don't want to go back to Seattle, to the Carlton house and kitchen, to not seeing him again except by accident or perhaps in the park. She knew he loved her and that she was in his blood. But she knew with a strange clarity, for all of her inexperience, that this had been an adventure for him; not just a lark, but something that, however much it meant to him, would not lead to anything more except, perhaps, another night or two together, in secret, in some little hotel hidden away from all who knew him.

Even as she accepted this certainty she knew it made no difference. Whatever happened, she would always be glad of the night they had had together. She wouldn't have done anything differently. What was to come after would be separate and apart, something else to be dealt with. They had had a whole night together and if it was to be all, then it would last her for a lifetime. Whenever, afterward, she woke at dawn and heard the birds heralding the new day, she would see again his dark head on the pillow, his eyes, bright and urgent, searching her face.

They had breakfast in the clean, white, impersonal dining room overlooking the sound. There was a wonderful smell of bread, clean linen, and good coffee in the room.

"I'll bet the food is good here," she said to him across the table, her eyes sparkling. Her moment of sorrow and acceptance was past; she was full of gaiety and life. She was happy as she had never been before. She seemed to be on the crest of a great golden wave.

"What makes you think so?" He smiled at her, his eyes dark with the memory of how she had lain in his arms, of her white, sumptuous body naked beside him on the bed. He had been anxious to get down to breakfast, to catch the boat, to get started on the business of the day. But now, looking at her eager, flushed face with the little sailor perched so charmingly over her forehead, he suddenly wished they were back upstairs with the door locked. He suddenly wanted to take off all her clothes, the tight-bodiced dress, the Eton jacket, the long, confining skirt; to have her again, naked and warm and shivering with excitement under his caresses. The curve of her cheek, the soft, full lower lip seemed achingly sweet and desirable. Her eyes, bright and clear, shone with love and confidence and a curious childlike joy.

He had expected to feel remorse and shame in the morning; to be angry at himself for having seduced her and at her for having yielded and thus exposing him to his guilt, but in the face of her happiness and simplicity it was impossible to feel anything but wonder at her and gratitude for what had been so freely and beautifully given him. He suddenly reached across the table and caught her hand. "Hello, my darling," he murmured, and he loved her then more than he would ever love any other woman, except his daughter.

"Hello," she answered, and gave him a soft, melting look that made his loins ache with desire, tenderness, pity. She was so completely his and yet so completely herself that for a moment she took on the stature of a queen, a legendary woman, generous, passionate, but essentially untouched. In a flash of clarity he knew that whatever came of their relationship—and he was utterly unable to see what would come of it—Annie Jordan would never lose her innate dignity, courage, strength. For a fleeting second he recognized her as stronger, braver, more deeply rooted in some timeless source of strength and integrity, than he was or would ever be.

Then the waitress came with the steaming bowls of thick, nutty oatmeal, a pitcher of rich yellow cream; later, there were poached country eggs and sausage, big squares of coffeecake with crumbs on top, strong, fragrant coffee. They ate ravenously, laughing at each other. The good, hearty food was somehow all of a part of the fulfillment of their love and they were not ashamed of their appetites. There was only just time to check out of the hotel, run down the hill in the fresh, salty, sunny air, and catch the boat. The *Rosalie* was already hooting a warning as they reached the dock, and Annie's sailor was askew, her cheeks rosy, her eyes sparkling as Hugh handed her aboard.

Not once on the trip back did Annie let herself think of what lay ahead for her, or wonder whether she could get in without being caught by Mrs. Carlton. Her holiday, her adventure, her taste of life and love, were nearly over, but she was going to savor it to the last, enjoy every drop. She laughed, chattered, beamed at Hugh with no shadow of regret or doubt in her voice and eyes. She caught him up in her mood, so that it was only as the boat was docking in Seattle that he began to feel nervous and depressed, to examine his conscience and wonder what price they must pay for their irregularity.

Annie sensed the change in him and suddenly the cloud, the weight, the knowledge of what she had done. descended on her.

Her gay spirits dissolved, her face paled, her eyes were dark and heavy. She stood beside him at the rail, fidgeting with the clasp of her purse. She felt lost and cold, very far from him. And he seemed like a stranger, someone who wanted to be rid of her.

"Perhaps it would be better if we weren't seen getting off together," he murmured, avoiding her eyes, his sense of guilt growing as the boat maneuvered for the landing.

"All right," she answered in a tight voice. She immediately moved away from him and stood beside the two stout ladies in linen suits with market bags. She did not even look his way as the boat whistled, docked, and the gangplank was run out. Her hands were cold and it was hard to breathe. She had known instinctively it would end like this, but she had not been prepared for the feeling of desolation that swept over her.

But her head was held high and she strode down the gangplank proudly, unaware of the admiring glances of the deck hands and the male passengers. The sky was overcast and it had begun to drizzle as they came into the harbor. It seemed fitting that even the weather should have become sad and gloomy. He didn't even ask when he could see me again, she thought. Maybe I'll never see him again. Maybe he's ashamed of me now and wants to forget me.

But as she reached Front Street and stood looking up the street for a streetcar, a hansom cab drew up at the curb and Hugh leaned out the window, beckoned to her. With a sharp, sudden constriction of her throat, she ran to him, got into the cab, and sat down beside him. She didn't look at him, nor he at her. But he caught her hand and held it tightly all the way through town.

"You'd best let me off at the corner of Boylston Avenue," she said at last.

He nodded and then he looked at her. They sat gazing at each other for a long moment and then Annie's eyes filled with tears and she had to turn her head away.

He didn't put his arms around her or try to kiss her, but his hand gripped hers so tightly it hurt. "Annie," he whispered tensely, "I do love you. Don't forget that. It was—wonderful, being with you."

She couldn't speak: she was too intent on trying to blink back the treacherous, silly tears. He took out his handkerchief and very gently wiped them away, as he'd done that morning when they were in bed together. Already that moment seemed years past, in another life.

"I hope this hasn't hurt you—that you'll be all right." He paused, drew a sharp breath as if a knife were being thrust through his breast. "I don't want you to be hurt by anything I've done, Annie."

"I'll be all right," she said faintly, drawing away from him, though she longed to throw herself on his breast and weep. "Don't worry about me."

"We'll see each other again, won't we?" There was an edge of urgency, almost of despair, in his voice. He was torn between the desire to keep from being involved in something that he sensed might be too powerful for him to control, and the sudden realization that he could not bear to let her go.

"If you want to," she said humbly.

"I'll write to you. I'll drop you a note," he went on, his mind quickly making plans, leaping ahead to another rendezvous, making arrangements. "Yes, that would be the best way. If I phone, they might get suspicious, but a letter—I'll write you a letter."

She got off at the corner and walked quickly up the street toward the Carlton house. Her mind was empty of everything now but the desire to get there before the family returned. She had put Hugh out of her thoughts as soon as she stepped out of the cab. She did not even look back as it rattled away. With her heart pounding like mad and her palms wet and cold, she hurried up the steps and unlocked the door.

The house was still; there was the smell, the feel of emptiness in it. With a sigh of relief she shut the door and went down the hall to her room. Just as she was about to go in she heard a sound from the kitchen. Her heart was beating hollowly in her breast as she turned and walked carefully through the living room and pushed open the kitchen door.

Through the window in the back door that led to the porch she saw a man's face, heard him rap again against the pane. It took her a moment to recognize Ed Bauer, the assistant manager at the grocery store. He smiled at her through the glass and she let him in. He had a package in his hand.

"Hello, Annie. Surprised to see me?"

"Yes." She stared at him as if he were very far away. It must have been in another world, another life, that she had laughed and joshed and flirted with this man.

"Well, I discovered this package of bacon that hadn't been delivered yesterday with your order. I figured you might be needing it, so I brought it out on my way home from the store." She took the package, wrapped in heavy brown butcher's paper, and stood holding it.

"You work on Sundays?" she asked.

"Not usually, but we're taking inventory, got a lot of new stock in, so I came down this morning to help the boys." He glanced at her hat and jacket. "You going out? To church maybe?"

She flushed, shook her head. "No. I just got back. The folks are away and I—I spent the night with a friend."

"Oh." There was a silence. He gave her a long look and she found herself unable to meet his eyes. She had the feeling that she must look different, that her love for Hugh must have changed her so much that anyone could tell that she'd spent the night with him. Ed's dark warm eyes seemed to be searching her face for something.

"Do you like trout?" he asked suddenly.

"Trout?" she asked stupidly.

"Yes. I'm going fishing in a couple of weeks, up the Elwha on the Olympic Peninsula. I thought if you liked them I'd bring you some."

She smiled at him. He was very nice and he had an eager, almost humble look, not fresh and teasing the way he was in the store. "That'd be fine, Ed," she answered.

"I'll bring enough for the whole family," he said, pleased. "The biggest Rainbows in this part of the country are in the Elwha."

"Fine." She wished he'd go. She wanted to get out of her good clothes and into her uniform, air the house, and put the Sunday roast on. Mrs. Carlton had said they'd be home in time for dinner.

He sensed her uneasiness, for he turned to go. With his hand on the knob he said, "They say the vaudeville show down at the new Seattle Theater is pretty good. Like to go sometime with me?"

His voice was so eager and expectant, she smiled at him, said, "Why, yes, Ed, I'd like to," though she had no idea of ever going with him. How could she go out with another man when all she could think of was Hugh?

"Swell. Maybe next Friday?"

"Maybe."

"Well—I'll see you at the store before then and you can let me know."

He went out the door reluctantly, as if he'd like to have her ask him to stay. As soon as he was gone she hurried into her room, took off her good clothes, and got into her uniform. When the Carltons came back she had the dinner table laid, the roast and potatoes cooking, and a lemon pie in the oven. Mrs. Carlton seemed pleased, but Annie kept her eyes downcast, afraid of what she might read in them.

Mrs. Deming didn't know what had got into her son Hugh lately. Ever since he'd gone up the sound on an excursion, "to look into the steamship business," he'd been difficult and restless and morose. He didn't eat much, just sat at the table fiddling with his fork, and he drank more port with his father after dinner than she thought he should. He'd sit in a corner with a book, pretending to read, and then he'd toss the book onto the table, get up, light a cigarette, and stand at the dark, rain-swept window, staring at the night and jingling coins in his pocket.

She'd put down her knitting and gaze anxiously at him and frown at his father, who'd give him a brief glance over his book and then shrug and forget him. But his mother couldn't forget him. Something was wrong, something was troubling him, and she didn't know what to do about it. Of course there was no use asking him. He wouldn't tell her and she didn't believe in prying into menfolks' affairs. When the time came for her to help, they'd tell her. But somehow she knew Hugh wouldn't come to her with this problem. Oh dear, she sighed to herself, counting stitches with her lips pursed, I do hope he hasn't got himself mixed up with a woman. Was it Mrs. Crawford? But she knew he hadn't seen her for weeks. At least he never mentioned going there, and she knew Erica had given a number of parties to which he'd not been asked. But maybe he's seeing her secretly, she thought. Hugh baby, why won't you tell your mother?

Hugh tossed the volume of Shakespeare's sonnets onto the library table, got up, and walked up and down the room, his hands in his pockets, his face closed and dark. Poetry, that had been his bulwark and delight, was no comfort to him now. Poets couldn't get off the subject of love, or was it that he masochistically sought out the love poems with which to torture himself, to send the knife deeper into his heart?

"Being your slave, what should I do but tend Upon the hours and times of your desire?" "Shall I compare thee to a summer's day? Thou art more lovely and more temperate." "Take all my loves, my love, yea, take them all." On and on, sonnet after sonnet—praise of the beloved, longing for the beloved, jealousy, fulfillment, the agony of separation. Even John Donne, metaphysical and obscure as Browning, must cry, "I wonder by my troth, what thou, and I did, till we loved!"

The rain blew sharply against the pane, the wind shook the shiny red branches of the madroña tree. A boat whistled lonesomely out in the bay. Where were the blue skies and the warm yellow sunshine of the day when they'd taken hands and run laughing up the beach? Suddenly, as if conjured up by the wind and the rain and the tumult in his own heart, he saw her face turned to his as it had been on the boat, the large violet eyes dark with pain and love. Oh, Lord, Lord, he groaned, I love her. I want her.

He'd thought he could take her, enjoy her, and go lightly on his way, back to his old, gay, social life. She'd made no demands, asked no questions except that he should love her. She'd left him free as the air, and thereby had bound him like Prometheus to his rock. She was in his blood, his flesh, his heart, his mind. He was being eaten up with longing for her. He knew that if he asked her to go away with him again she would go. Why didn't he? Was it because he didn't want to hurt her, or because he was afraid that if he saw her again he could never let her go? I could marry her. He stopped pacing. I could marry her and she would be mine forever.

He turned and looked at his father and mother sitting quietly under the lamplight, at his father's distinguished gray head, his mother's thin, aristocratic features, the slender black velvet ribbon about her throat. What would they say if he suddenly announced that he wanted to marry a hired girl, daughter of a waterfront saloonkeeper? He could imagine the shock of such a statement exploding in the quiet room like a bombshell.

He could imagine the way his friends, his social acquaintances, would take it. The Crawfords, the Greens, the Carltons, the Fishers. There wouldn't be a door in Seattle society that would be open to him and his wife, if his wife were Annie Jordan. He'd never be able to go to his club again. Where would they find their friends? On the waterfront? Captain Blaine was counting on his social connections to help set up the steamship line. It would mean the end of his social life and it might hurt his career. Were Annie's warmth and ardor and sweetness, her white body, her eager mouth worth the cost?

But he didn't have to marry her to have her. She was his already. No one knew about their trip to Port Madison; no one need know about their other trips, other meetings. He was keenly aware that this was Friday night—tomorrow was her day off. All he had to do was put a note in the mail tonight and he could be with her tomorrow. It had been a week since they'd been together.

"I want her," he murmured to himself. "I've never really wanted a woman before. If this is love, then I've never been in love before." Suddenly he wished Seattle were still a frontier fishing town where society had never set foot and all that mattered was to find a woman you wanted for the mother of your children. Then he could marry Annie and be proud of her. What beautiful children she would give him, too!

"My goodness, Hugh," cried his mother at last, with a nervous little laugh. "You're as fidgety as a cat this evening. Why don't you go out and see some of your friends? Or settle down here with your father for a game of chess?"

"If you'll excuse me, Father, I'm not up to chess tonight. But if I'm making you nervous, Mother, I'll go out," he said with unwonted sharpness, took his hat from the hall, and slammed out the front door.

"Oh dear, what's the matter with him?" sighed Mrs. Deming. "He's been like this for nearly a week."

His father laughed. "He'll be all right directly. Young men get like that sometimes."

His wife blushed and bent to her knitting. She knew what the judge meant but it embarrassed her to think about such things in connection with her sons. Thank goodness, Beauchamp, Hugh's brother, was safely married and anchored with a new baby.

The night was wet and chilly for July. There was a wind that blew the raindrops in Hugh's face. He walked quickly down the street with his head bent against the wind and rain. He didn't know what to do with himself. There were any number of attractive debutantes he could call on, but he wouldn't have been able to listen to their silly prattle or to pay them the charming compliments that made him so welcome in their homes. Their coy glances and little airs and graces would have made him think of Annie's direct, honest gaze, her simplicity and candor.

He walked downtown and, passing the new Seattle Theater on Third and Madison, on the site of the old Corday Theater, he stopped and stared at the billboards. There was a vaudeville show playing there now. He decided to go in. He was at that point, that emotional impasse, when one welcomes the stupefying effect of the vulgar and the commonplace.

The theater smelled of cheap incense, cheap powder, and perspiration. The music was loud and tinny. As he found his seat the orchestra was playing "Swanee River" and a blackfaced singer trotted onto the stage. He sank into his seat, gave himself up to the sentimental songs, the cheap humor, the worn-out routines. He laughed at all the tired jokes, applauded the syrupy singers, gasped at the gold-painted acrobats. When it was over he walked as if in a daze out into the foyer and as he paused to light a cigarette he looked up and saw Annie on the arm of an earnest-looking, rugged fellow with honest brown eyes and a hand-me-down suit. He was so shocked he could only stand back and stare at them. Annie looked very smart in dark blue poplin and a hat with red cherries on it. She clung to the man's arm and smiled gravely up at him as he talked. She didn't once look Hugh's way. She seemed to be unaware of anyone in the foyer but her escort.

The shock he'd had at first seeing her, when he'd been thinking about her for days, even imagining her longing, too, for him, left Hugh quite cold. His first impulse had been to speak to her, to compel her to look into his eyes, to make sure again of the love she'd shown him such a short time ago. Then when he saw her kindly, sober escort and the gentle, earnest way she was playing up to him, he could do nothing. Maybe this fellow wanted to marry her. What right had he to spoil her chances?

She moved gracefully and with dignity out of the theater, onto the street. Her escort took her arm firmly, hailed a cab, and they were gone. Hugh stood looking after them. He had never felt like this in his life. He was only glad there had been a crowd and that he'd not come face to face with the earnest young man who'd been with her. Tonight he felt equal to murder with his bare hands. And yet he knew he was acting like a madman. At best, he could make her nothing but his mistress. He couldn't marry her. He knew suddenly that he lacked the courage or the doggedness or the arrogance to pull it off.

And the next day Emily Carlton telephoned him and asked him to a party that she and Marguerite Brookes were giving at Marguerite's house. "Papa is in Chicago," she said enthusiastically. "I think we'll have fun."

Papa is in Chicago and the little bird can flutter out of the nest. No, that wasn't a good simile. The Papa Bear's away, so Goldilocks can play. He smiled ironically, feeling suddenly quite calm and poised again. He went into his mother's room, kissed her soft, wrinkled, very fine cheek, and asked her if he had a clean dress shirt and if his evening clothes had come back from the cleaners.

His mother smiled happily at him, relieved to see him gay and casual, the dark brooding look gone from his face. "Oh, you're going to a party, Hugh?"

He nodded. "Emily Carlton and Marguerite Brookes are having a small dance at Marguerite's house tonight. It ought to be amusing. It's Emily's first social function."

"How nice. Your dress shirts are in a box in the linen closet and your evening clothes are in a dust bag in your wardrobe." Mrs. Deming listened to him whistling a waltz tune as he went into his room and sighed with relief. Whatever had been bothering him seemed to have been put out of his mind or solved. Perhaps it was Emily Carlton he'd been worrying about and now that she'd invited him to her party all was well again. Emily was a sweet girl, very pretty, and her family was solid and well-to-do, as good as families were apt to be here in the West. Of course, if they'd stayed in Virginia, that would have been another matter. I just hope, she said to herself, that Hugh gets married soon.

As he was dressing for Emily's party he suddenly remembered that last night, in his pain and loneliness, he'd scratched off a note to Annie, asking her to meet him at Pier 6 that afternoon at two. He couldn't remember whether or not he'd mailed it. He put down his bow tie and went through the pockets of the suit he'd worn yesterday. But he couldn't find the note. For a moment he felt guilty and ashamed. He knew she'd have kept the appointment. Perhaps she was still there, waiting for him. He had a sudden impulse to chuck Emily's party and dash down to the waterfront to find her. Then he shook his head. No—he'd seen her with that fellow last night. She'd been at peace and happy with him. She'd not been thinking about Hugh then. Perhaps he'd been mistaken about her all along. Maybe the night at Port Madison had been simply an adventure to her too. Anyway, she'd made him suffer. He'd lain awake for hours last night, thinking about her and hating the man she'd been with. Let her suffer now. Let her wait for him and wonder, as he had.

He went to Emily's party, but on the way he made the cabbie drive him down to the waterfront. The pier was deserted and after half an hour's fruitless searching for Annie, he gave up, stopped in a First Avenue bar to fortify himself against the black despondency that had settled over him. Whether it was the whisky he drank there, or the champagne Emily recklessly served—or her prettiness and grace, or the fact that once he'd toyed with the idea of marrying her—at any rate, before the night was over, he found himself engaged to Emily Carlton, his signet ring, miles too big, on her white finger, her cool, unresponsive kiss of promise on his lips.

Chapter XIV

The moment she saw the white envelope with her name and address in the dashing black hand, Annie knew it was from Hugh. It came Saturday morning, the one morning she hadn't flown out to snatch the mail from the postman as soon as she heard his step on the porch. All week she'd waited and watched for some word from him, but by Saturday she'd given up hoping. She'd really given up Friday night, which was why she'd said yes when Ed Bauer asked her to go to the vaudeville show with him.

Mrs. Carlton had given her a speculative look when she asked for permission, then she'd nodded and said thoughtfully, "Why, yes, Annie, I think that will be quite all right. Mr. Bauer is a very steady young man, I'm sure." She looked intently at the girl's handsome figure, her lovely face. "Besides," she went on, "you don't have much fun. It will be good for you to go out with a nice man like Mr. Bauer. But please be in by ten."

"Yes, Mrs. Carlton." Annie had suddenly flushed under her employer's pleasant, kind smile, thinking of last Saturday. What would she think if she knew where Annie had been all that day and night! The girl turned quickly away lest the woman read the truth in her eyes. She knew that every time she thought of that night her face changed—she could feel it changing.

She dressed carefully, after doing up the dinner dishes. She didn't really care how she looked, since it wasn't Hugh she'd be with and she wasn't vain enough to care for herself. But she

liked Ed Bauer and she felt rather guilty for having accepted
his invitation. It wasn't right to let a man take you out when
you belonged heart and soul to someone else. So to make up to
Ed for wishing he were Hugh, she dressed as nicely and as re-
spectably as she could, knowing instinctively that he would
prefer her dark blue tailored poplin to the little white suit with
the Eton jacket. Besides, she'd worn that suit for Hugh and she
couldn't bring herself to wear it for another man. But she wore
the hat with the red cherries because her spirits were low.

Ed was just as nice as he could be to her and under his kindness, his hearty, unaffected liking for her, she began to feel less
lost and abandoned. She enjoyed the show as she always did.
The theater in any form had fascinated her since she was a little
freckle-faced kid, sneaking into the Variety Theater down on
Occidental Avenue. She laughed at the jokes, grew dreamy
over the husky blonde in spangles who sang "My Wild Irish
Rose," applauded the acrobats and the jugglers.

She liked the way Ed turned to her when something appealed
to him, she liked the way his eyes shone when the lights went
up and he said, "That was a darn good show, I think. I hope you
enjoyed it. The acrobats were great, weren't they?" He was a
thoughtful, likable fellow; intelligent, too, and wholesome. He
wasn't cheap and sporty like Ned Weaver and he wasn't like
Hugh Deming—no one was like Hugh. For just a moment she
closed her eyes and saw Hugh's slow, ironic smile, the little gold
flecks in his intense gray eyes, and it was hard to breathe. Ed
was good and kind, and she respected and liked him.

They had spaghetti at a little restaurant on Third Avenue Ed
had found and then he took her home, thanked her for having
gone with him, said he hoped they'd go out together again, and
left her in the hall. He'd made no attempt to hold her hand or
get fresh in any way. Annie went to bed, not excited or stimulated, but oddly at peace. It had been a pleasant evening.

Her feeling of peace, that serenity that comes only after intense feeling, bitter longing, and then the final abandonment of
desire, the reluctant but conclusive resignation, persisted the
next morning when she awoke and lay for a moment wondering what was missing. She had a vague sense of something being gone, but she didn't realize that it was the sharp ache in her
heart. Instead her heart felt quite dead and that was better; at

least that made it easier to breathe, made it possible for her to consider calmly the fact that Hugh didn't want to see her again, that she had nothing now to wait for and therefore she'd best be about the business of picking up the pieces of her emotional life and fitting them into a different pattern.

She dressed quickly, brushed her hair without looking in the mirror, washed her face and hands, and went quietly into the kitchen to get breakfast. Her body felt light and springy as she waited on table, carried out the dirty dishes, washed, dried, and put them away. All week she'd felt heavy and slow, and the weight of her heart had been almost too much to bear, but now, now that she knew it was all over between her and Hugh, she was as light as an empty shell. It was not the lightness of a gay heart or an untroubled mind. It was the almost disembodied lightness that comes with the cessation of pain.

She was dusting the parlor when Mrs. Carlton called from upstairs, "There's the postman, Annie. Would you go and get the mail, please?"

"Yes, ma'am," said Annie, entirely without that quick wave of excitement she'd had every other day at the postman's arrival. She put down her dustcloth on the Duncan Phyfe table and went to the door.

"Nice day, miss," said the postman, a stooped little man in a faded gray uniform and eyeglasses. His heavy leather pouch seemed almost too big for his thin, drooping shoulders.

Annie smiled. "Yes, a fine day." She looked at the day, smelling the pungence of marigolds in the late summer gardens and the freshness of the bay. "The first nice day all week."

"We're gettin' our rains early this year." He handed her a sheaf of letters and the *Ladies' Home Journal*. "Lotsa mail today." He grinned. "Folks always like to get mail, seems."

Inside the hall, she sorted the letters. Three for Mr. Carlton, two for his wife, a letter for Emily from Chicago, probably from a boarding school friend, and, suddenly, under her hand, the square white envelope with her own name on it—Miss Annie Jordan.

With deliberate, steady hands she tucked her letter inside her bodice, laid the rest of the mail on the table. Emily, whisking downstairs, cried, "Oh, Annie, anything for me?" just as she was hiding her letter.

"Yes," she replied, her cheeks warm, hoping Emily hadn't seen her put her letter in her dress.

"Is that all?" Emily gave her an odd look.

"All but a letter for me," said Annie, and went upstairs to do the bedrooms. She made the beds, dust-mopped the floors, and tidied the dressers, carefully and without haste. She seemed to be putting off the moment when she would be free to read her letter, though the feel of it against her flesh, the crackle it made as she bent to make the beds, sent shivers of excitement over her body.

At last the upstairs work was done. She went back down to the parlor, finished dusting, taking more time over the carved legs and arms of the chairs than she ever did, dusting even the picture frames. Then she shook the dustcloth out the back door, hung it up in the broom closet, washed her hands at the sink, and went into her room, closing the door.

For a moment she stood in the middle of the floor and stared at her white face and enormous dark eyes in the mirror. Then with slow, trembling, uncertain hands she fumbled in her dress for the letter. She held it in her hand, feeling the smoothness of the heavy white paper. Then she sat on her bed, tried to open the envelope with her thumb, but it was sealed tightly. She reached for a nail file on the dresser, slit it cleanly, and took out the one folded sheet of paper. It was dated Friday night.

"ANNIE:

"I have to see you again. This week has been hell for me without you. I don't know if it's right or wrong, but I don't much care tonight. Meet me tomorrow afternoon at two o'clock on Pier 6. I don't know where we'll go, but at least we'll be together."

It wasn't signed, but the words he'd written in his bold, impatient hand were as real and urgent as if he were standing before her, frowning, his mouth set, saying them to her in his low, intense voice.

She read the brief note over and over and then she lay back on the pillow, her eyes closed, her breast rising and falling in sudden turbulence. She was suddenly weak, trembling, undone; all her serenity, her resignation, her emptiness were gone as if they had never been.

"Oh, Hugh—Hugh, oh, my darling," she moaned, her heart aching, aching with love and sorrow for her doubt, joy in his need for her, gratitude that it was all to begin again, that what she had thought dead was alive. She pressed her hands to her breast to press deeper the sting of happiness that was almost as sharp as the pain that had pierced her before. She read his letter again, then put it back in her dress against her breast. The edges of the envelope were sharp against her soft skin, and she liked the feeling.

Her little alarm clock said eleven o'clock. There was the kitchen floor to be scrubbed, the back steps to be swept, a pie to be baked for supper, vegetables to be cleaned and peeled— oh, a hundred little chores still to be done before her afternoon off would really begin. "What am I doing lying here then?" she cried, and jumped to her feet, smoothed her hair, smiled at herself in the glass, hurried out to finish her work.

It went as fast as lightning. The piecrust turned out light and flaky. Everything she did seemed easy and she was careful not to be slapdash about anything. She scrubbed the kitchen floor till it shone. She cleaned out the icebox. She watered the rubber plant and cleaned the canary's cage. She sang softly at her work and, when Mrs. Carlton came down to inspect what she'd done, she praised her for the extra care she'd taken.

She put on the white suit with the Eton jacket and the little sailor hat he'd found so pert and charming. She thought the cable car would never get down the hill. It seemed to stop at every corner and the motorman got out once and bought a bottle of milk while the passengers waited and Annie tapped her foot in her new tan, laced walking shoes.

The day was fine with an intense blue sky, no clouds, and the sun skipping off the waters of the bay. There was a fresh, washed coolness from the week of rain that seemed to give depth and clarity to everything. Annie thought it was wonderful that whenever she was to meet Hugh the weather should be so perfect.

She got off the cable car at the foot of James Street and walked along the busy streets toward the docks, gazing at all the shopwindows. There were so many fine stores now in Seattle. It made you feel that it was really a city—Frederick & Nelson's on Second Avenue, MacDougall and Southwick, the Bon Marché, Turrell's fine new shoestore. The horsecars had given way to trolleys that clanged along the tracks, very fast and important, and went clear out to the Ravenna district, which was nearly the country. The streets were all paved, many with red brick, and already the town had earned the name of the cleanest city on the coast. Street cleaners were busy all day, cleaning up after the cab and delivery horses, picking up papers and trash, and the water sprinklers washed the streets night and morning. Oh, it was an up-and-coming place, Seattle, and Annie swelled with pride in it, glad to have been born here, to have seen it grow from a sprawling fishing and lumbering town to a first-class coast city with a growing shipping business and, recently, a railroad terminal. There was something in the air that stimulated you, an aliveness and vigor, a feeling that people were going places, that nobody was going to stop its lusty, steady growth.

Annie remembered the fire and how she'd stood on the First Hill, watching the smoke roll out over the bay. She remembered the tent city that had sprung up like magic overnight and the way everyone had buckled down to rebuild, not in the same meager pattern, but bigger and better.

She thought of Hugh and the steamship line he and Captain Blaine were starting. Already they had the *Kitsap* under way, between Seattle and Vancouver, and another ship bought and being overhauled. Hugh had told her that day on the beach about his dream of an Alaskan run, of maybe even a line to the Orient, stopping at Honolulu and the Philippines. As he'd talked, she could see the boats steaming up and down the coast, small and white against the immensity of the Alaskan shore, the smudge of black smoke staining the broad blue sky of the vast Pacific. She could see the strange Eastern ports with the quick little yellow and brown men scurrying to unload their cargoes, reloading them with spice and silk and rice and ivories.

She was glad that Hugh was a part of all this vision and progress, that in spite of his casual, ironic manner and his elegance he had the quick mind and the courage to plunge in and take hold. Suddenly she wished with all her heart that he would marry her, that she could be with him always, that she could help and encourage and bolster his dreams. In some strange way she realized that she was the woman he needed—she wasn't from the First Hill, she wasn't a lady, but she was strong and unafraid and she loved adventure and life and growth. But whether he married her or not, she would always be his in soul and body—whatever he did or wherever he went, she would be beside him with all her hopes and dreams.

A San Francisco steamer was docking as she reached Pier 6. She stood and watched the passengers mincing off, then the stevedores unloading the cargo. The gulls screamed and wheeled, circling above the boat. She had no watch, but she asked one of the deck hands the time and he told her it was three-thirty. Hugh was already an hour and a half late.

She began to walk toward the street to see if he were coming or if she'd mistaken the pier. He was not coming up the street and he was not at the next pier. She fumbled in her dress for his letter and read it again. There was no mistake. He had to see her. He'd meet her at two on Pier 6 today. She went back to Pier 6 and sat down on a box to wait.

At six o'clock a longshoreman asked her if she'd missed her boat. She looked up at him with dark, bewildered eyes and nodded. "Yes, I guess I have."

"Well, you'd better go home then, sister. The next one don't leave till tomorrow morning." The red-faced, burly fellow stared at her speculatively, but she barely glanced his way, got up, and walked slowly toward the street. A trolley passed her but she didn't hail it. She walked dully along Front Street, not seeing anyone, though plenty of men turned to look at her and several spoke to her and smiled. She walked up the hill, hardly noticing how steep it was, not aware of her own weariness until she let herself into the house and sank down on her bed. Then she was suddenly engulfed in fatigue so deep and complete that she could only take off her hat and shoes. She fell back on the pillow and fell into a sleep that was like a stupor.

At four in the morning she woke, shivering. The fog was rolling up from the bay through her open windows. She got up and undressed slowly. Her white suit was wrinkled from having been slept in, but she hung it carefully in the closet. Then she unbraided her hair, brushed it, washed her face and hands, knelt by her bed, and said her prayers. She got into bed and pulled the covers up to her chin, but she couldn't stop shivering. She was cold, cold clear through. She wondered whether she'd ever be warm again.

The next morning as Annie served breakfast, setting the platter of eggs and bacon before Mrs. Carlton, because Mr. Carlton was still in Chicago, Emily surprised her by smiling sweetly and saying good morning without the little patronizing edge that was usually in her voice. Annie answered politely and passed her the cup of coffee Mrs. Carlton had poured.

"Mother, when is Papa getting back from Chicago?" cried Emily.

"Tomorrow night unless he is delayed, dear. Why?"

Annie stood at Mrs. Carlton's side, waiting for her to serve the eggs and bacon. With her serving fork poised over the platter, Emily's mother smiled across the table at her daughter, whose eyes seemed even brighter than usual and whose cheeks were suddenly very pink.

"Because I have some terribly exciting news to tell you both, and I want him to be here when I tell you."

Mrs. Carlton gave her a startled look, then put an egg and two strips of crisp bacon on her plate. Glancing at Annie's impassive face, which seemed very pale this morning, she handed the plate to her and Annie started around the table.

"For goodness' sakes, child, don't be so mysterious. Tell me now. After all, I'm your mother!" exclaimed Mrs. Carlton.

Emily laughed and pushed back her chair, rushed to her mother, and flung her arms around her neck. "Of course you are, darling! And girls always tell their mothers first, don't they? Besides, I'm bursting to tell. I can't wait a minute longer. I'm engaged, Mama! To Hugh Deming. He asked me last night."

While Mrs. Carlton was gasping and Emily was half laughing, half crying, Annie set the plate of eggs and bacon down very carefully at Emily's place, walked quietly out to the kitchen, and closed the door.

For a moment she stood in the middle of the floor, seeing nothing, her hands tightly clenched at her sides. Then she began to shiver so violently that her teeth chattered and her knees knocked together, just as if she were having a chill. The sharp pain in her breast made her catch her breath and hold onto the kitchen table. She sat down on the kitchen stool and folded her reddened, work-roughened hands on the table, staring at the wall with dry, aching eyes.

So it was all over. That was the reason he hadn't met her yesterday. She'd probably never see him again. She'd known from the first that it would end like this, that someday he'd marry a girl of his own sort. But not Emily Carlton! Not that little . . . ! Suddenly black rage swept over her, loosening the tight band that made it so hard to breathe. For a moment she hated them both, Hugh as much as Emily—Hugh even more than Emily because she loved him so terribly.

The bell tinkled from the dining room faintly, but Annie didn't hear. All right, you can have her if that's what you want. I wish you joy of her, Hugh Deming. She's pretty and silly and she can play Chopin's "Butterfly Etude" on the piano and flutter her eyelashes and she'd never stay all night with you at Port Madison. Oh no, not Emily—not till it was all legal and she was sure of you, not till it was all tied up with tulle and satin bows and a gold wedding ring. Do you think she'll give you what I can give you? Do you think she'll make you forget me and that night at the beach and in the hotel room?

She closed her eyes and saw his face bending over her, white and drawn with desire. She remembered his hands touching her breasts in wonder, his mouth urgent and seeking hers. She remembered waking in the cool dawn, with the birds talking outside the window and Hugh's eyes as he turned to clasp her in his arms.

The bell jangled violently this time and Annie pushed herself up from the table, stood a moment, pulling back her shoulders. The trembling had ceased. She was quite calm. As she went into the dining room there was a strange little smile on her pale lips and when Emily glanced up at her she gave her a cool, mocking stare.

The next time she went marketing she dressed very carefully, put on a new ruffled blouse and the hat with the cherries. When Ed Bauer looked at her across the counter with his dark, ardent gaze, she smiled deeply into his eyes. And when he shyly asked her if she'd go out with him that Saturday afternoon, canoeing on Lake Washington, she blushed and murmured that she'd be delighted, she was sure.

Chapter XV

The morning after Emily Carlton's party Hugh woke with the sun in his eyes and a splitting headache, a bad taste in his mouth and a curious sense of guilt that made his stomach feel hollow. For a while he lay with his arm over his eyes to shut out the sun, groaning. There was a discreet tap on the door and Jason tiptoed in, a solicitous frown on his black face. "Mr. Hugh, sir," he crooned softly, "I brung you some black coffee."

Hugh sat up slowly, his head reeling. Jason pushed two pillows to his back and Hugh grinned feebly at him. "Thanks, Jason. I must have had a drop too much last night. Just a drop, mind you."

"Yassa." Jason grinned back. "Just a drop. You couldn't seem to find the keyhole, so I got up and let you in. You was sure feelin' good, sir." He chuckled and held the cup of coffee to Hugh's lips.

Hugh gulped it down and shuddered, lay back against the pillows. "You had to put me to bed, did you?"

"We-ell, I just helped some. You wasn't so awful drunk."

"Jason, you cheerful liar, you know damn well I was drunk as a lord. Good God, my head's as big as a house." He lay for a moment with his eyes shut, trying to remember what had happened, why he should feel so sick inside, so certain of guilt. "What did I do last night, Jason? Did I tell you?"

"You mean you disremember, sir?" The butler's eyes rolled and he clucked in wonder.

Hugh shook his head. "I don't remember a thing, except that

I went to a party and drank champagne. Tell me quick, Jason. Did I do something awful? Knock somebody down? Insult people?" He stared at Jason's worried face. "Lord, Lord, I didn't commit murder, did I?"

"Mr. Hugh, you done worse'n that." Jason sighed. "You done got yourself engaged to be married."

Hugh groaned, shut his eyes. The wave of guilt swept over him again, black and cold. "Oh, my God, I didn't do that, Jason!"

"That's what you tole me, sir. You say last night, 'Jason, I'm the happies' man in the worl'. I done got myself engaged to the purtiest gal in Seattle, Washington.'" Jason puckered his lips, shook his head. "But, Mr. Hugh, you sho' didn't look happy."

"Now I remember. I tried to find Annie. I couldn't, so I stopped in at a saloon and had a couple of drinks. Then I went to Emily's party at Marguerite Brookes's house. They served champagne punch, and I drank it down like water, because I was thirsty and it didn't seem to have any effect. Emily *was* pretty, devilishly pretty, all gold and silver, and gay. We danced and laughed and flirted. Then she suddenly felt faint, so I took her out on the veranda. The damn perfidious moon was shining. She leaned against me with her eyes shut and I kissed her. That seemed to revive her more than the fresh air. She fluttered those long lashes at me and laughed and said, 'When my mother was young, if a man kissed a girl that meant they were engaged.' And I kissed her again and said, 'I wish it still meant that.' And she looked very serious and pushed me away and said, 'Oh no, you don't. You don't want to be engaged to me.' And the poor fish rose nobly to the bait and insisted it was exactly what he wanted, that he'd been wanting it ever since he first laid eyes on her but he never dreamed, he never hoped . . . 'Oh, Hugh, I should be so proud to be your wife,' she said, and there I was, caught, netted, done for. So I gave her my signet ring and she kissed me and her lips were cool and matter-of-fact. It wasn't a kiss, it was the seal to a bargain. So now I'm engaged to be married. God damn it to hell!"

"Yassa," said Jason sympathetically, and Hugh stared at him, realizing he'd been thinking out loud. He sighed, turned over, and pulled the covers up to his chin.

"Go 'way, Jason. I'm sick."

"But, Mr. Hugh, sir. You got an appointment downtown to-day. You got to see Captain Blaine, sir. He already telephoned once to see why you late," protested Jason, laying a gentle hand on Hugh's shoulder.

"Oh, Lord."

"When you have some bre'fus you gonna feel better. You lie still and Ah'll bring you a tray."

Jason went out softly as a cat and Hugh lay with his head whirling, the sickness in his heart making him forget his headache. Oh, Annie, Annie—what have I done to you—to us? I don't love that little piece of fluff and chatter. She's pretty and amusing, but I don't want to live with her the rest of my life. It's you I want, Annie. You're the one I should have. I need you—your strength and courage and honesty. Why didn't I tell my family and friends to go to hell and marry you? You'd have won them over—they'd have given in. Look how you carried off the ball I took you to—you were a sensation. Beauty like yours can always win people over. Oh, God, what a fool I am. What a coward and a snob. Annie darling, forgive me.

He ate his breakfast, got up, dressed, and went downtown to see Captain Blaine. The office of the newly organized North Star Steamship Company was in a warehouse on the docks. It had once been a coal and wood office and it was large, bare, unimpressive. The bright light of the bay shone glaringly in the big dusty windows. The captain roared at him for being late, chuckled with delight when Hugh told him what had happened the night before.

"It's just what you need, bucko. A smart woman to hog-tie ye and keep ye in line. Ye'll be a better businessman for it. Ye'll have to keep your mind on your work. No more redheads for ye from now on."

Hugh choked on his glass of rum. "What do you know about any redheads in my life?"

The captain guffawed, slapped his thigh. "Ye can't keep things like that from the waterfront. Ye went up the sound on the *Rosalie* with Kit Jordan's daughter and ye didn't get back till the next day. Ye was supposed to meet her yestiddy, but ye stood her up. The poor kid waited till nightfall, too. It's a shabby way to treat a fine-lookin' gal like Annie, but I guess you know your business." The captain tossed off his glass of rum, coughed, spat into the spittoon. "If I'd been in your place, I'd have got myself engaged to Annie in place o' Will Carlton's daughter."

"I wish I had," said Hugh gloomily, and poured himself another jigger of rum.

"Still an' all, love don't make the world go round, no matter what they say. It's cold cash that does that, bucko, and Will Carlton's got it and makin' more every day. I oughta be glad ye had sense enough to get tied up with his daughter. It'll be good for our business. Ye ought to be able to talk him into putting some money into the North Star Steamship Company."

"He hates me. The thing I'm counting on is that he'll refuse to give his consent to Emily's marrying me."

"I wouldn't bank on that, lad. She's the apple of his eye, and a pretty woman can always wind a man around her finger. If she wants you, she'll get you, whether her old man likes ye or not."

Hugh stared moodily at the wall. "I could go to her and tell her it was all a mistake, that I don't love her and don't want to marry her. I could tell her I was drunk last night."

The captain nodded slowly, cut off a slice of chewing tobacco from a big black chunk, and stuck it in his cheek. He chewed for a while, like a cow ruminating on its cud. "You can. But I'll bet you won't." He patted Hugh's knee with his large, red, hairy paw. "Ye're a gentleman, son. In your world there's rules about a thing like this. Ye'd never go against the rules."

No, thought Hugh, I wouldn't. It would have been going against the rules to marry Annie. Spending a night with her was all right; that's just a young gentleman having his fling. But to marry the girl—not in the rules, son. You think when you're a youngster and subject to your parents' will that the great thing is to be twenty-one and your own master. That then you'll begin to live your own life, do as you please, be free. But then you find yourself subject to the will of the society in which you live, with a thousand more rules, regulations, restrictions than the simple prohibitions of your childhood. Wherever you turn, there are walls, barriers, people shaking their heads at you. You can't do this or that because it's against the rules. You must do the other thing because that's what's expected of you.

"But what if I said the devil with the rules and did as I pleased?" cried Hugh, jumping up and pacing about the room.

The captain shook his head, pushed out his lips. "Ye'd be a goner, son. Ye'd belong nowhere and ye'd be miserable. Trouble with you is, ye was brought up too well. Now me—I'm like Annie—I been knocked about since I was a little shaver. Nobody ever told me right from wrong. I had to make my own rules. No matter how you live, there's gotta be rules, bucko. Either someone else makes 'em for ye or ye make yer own. But ye can't live without rules and ye can't get anywhere unless you stick to 'em."

Hugh reached for the rum bottle again, but the captain took it out of his hand, corked it, and stowed it away in a drawer of his big roll-top desk. "No more fire water for you today, son. We got to get down to business. I just heard last night that the *Sioux City's* gonna be sold. Suppose we mosey down to the dry dock and take a look-see at her. We could use another steamer on that Victoria run."

"Where are we going to get the money to buy another boat?" asked Hugh dispiritedly. Today all the enthusiasm in the steamship company was gone. What difference did it make whether they had a dozen ships on the coast? What did he really care about making money when you came right down to it? What was the struggle worth if at the start you'd messed up your chance for personal happiness?

"Now that's a thing you might talk over with your father-in-law to be," said Captain Blaine slyly, putting on his seaman's cap and rolling down the top of his desk. He went to the door and Hugh followed him, his hands in his pockets, his face dark and moody.

But as they walked along the waterfront and he smelled the tarry, fishy air, his spirits began to rise. The bustle of the docks, the freighters being loaded, the steamers refitted and painted, the sense of vigorous, hearty life and activity stung him again, touched that deep core of desire to be a part of it, to leave his mark here. He matched his walk to the captain's rolling gait and soon they were in a deep discussion of freight rates, cargoes, ways of beating the competition of the rival company that was already running boats up to British Columbia.

The *Sioux City* was a sturdy little steamer, but as she lay in dry dock it was obvious she needed repairs, painting, refitting. Blaine talked to a short, stocky man in hound's-tooth-checked tweeds, smoking a pipe, who was standing on the dock looking at the boat. He turned out to be Captain Tom Williams, skipper of the *Sioux City*. He was down in the mouth because the boat was going to be sold and he'd lose his berth unless the new owners decided to keep him on, but he brightened considerably when Blaine told him that if the North Star Steamship Company bought her they'd want him to sail her.

"I'd like that fine," said Williams, taking his pipe out of his mouth. "Not that I couldn't find me another ship, but I like the *Sioux*. She's got class. She's dependable and she's fast. I can beat any other steamer on the Vancouver run in the *Sioux*."

"Why is she being sold, then, if she's so good?" asked Hugh.

"Because the owners have taken considerable losses last year and this. They lost the *Potlach* off Cape Flattery and they've mismanaged things in general. My guess is that they're going out of business," said Williams sharply, taking quick umbrage at Hugh's suggestion that his ship might be at fault.

"They're the Northwest Shipping Company," mused Captain Blaine. "They've got good offices at the foot of Yesler Avenue. Maybe we'd better have a talk with them, Hugh. If they're going out of business maybe we could take over their offices."

There was something in the scope of Captain Blaine's vision and enterprise that made anything seem possible. The North Star Steamship Company didn't amount to a hill of beans yet, with only two island steamers and a dingy office in a warehouse; it was ridiculous to imagine that they could take over not only the *Sioux City* but the Northwest Shipping Company's offices and other ships. But why not? The fact that Northwest couldn't make money and was going out of business meant nothing. After seeing and talking with the dried-up, futile men in their office, Hugh wondered how they'd ever got into the shipping game at all. They might know boats, but they had no imagination, they were hamstrung by caution; they couldn't see Seattle as the gateway to the Orient and Alaska, a great, teeming port that would outshine San Francisco; Seattle, the Queen City, the Pearl of the Northwest.

"Hell," cried Captain Blaine as they left the shipping office, "what've we got to lose? I'm an old man with a good life behind me, no one to take care of, and you're a young buck just starting out. Even if you do marry this Carlton girl, there's always her old man to fall back on in a pinch. We've made money already on the *Kitsap* and the *Olympic*, on just them little passenger and freight runs up the sound. With the Northwest Company's fleet, we can give the Alaska Steamship Company a run for their money."

"I'm willing to take a chance," said Hugh. "I've got a lot of ideas I want to work out. We could put on a big campaign to get people to take excursions and trips up the sound and to Alaska. We could fix up the cabins better, so the ladies would like them. We could have orchestras aboard for dancing. Cut prices. Serve excellent food instead of the bilge you get on the other boats."

He was so full of himself and his revived enthusiasm that he forgot Annie, he forgot he was engaged to Emily, he even forgot to be afraid of Will Carlton, whom he was to face in the capacity of a future son-in-law when Carlton returned from Chicago. A week later Emily summoned him to dinner. The Papa Bear was back, roaring to meet the young whippersnapper who'd dared to become engaged to his pearl beyond price. Hugh knew he should be nervous about the encounter, but his mind was too full of plans for the North Star to dwell upon it. Only at the door after he'd rung the bell did he remember that Annie worked here and that he might have to come face to face with her. But the door was opened by a big, red-faced Scandinavian girl he'd never seen before. And then he was ushered into the parlor before he had time to wonder where Annie was. He strode into his fiancée's house like a man with a purpose and he wrung Mr. Carlton's hand, looked him firmly in the eye, and accepted the Havana cigar he was offered. Then Will asked him to go into the study with him and Hugh agreed quickly. Emily hadn't appeared yet and her mother had beamed at him most hearteningly. There was an enormous moose head on the wall above Mr. Carlton's desk and its shiny black eyes under the drooping lids regarded Hugh sardonically.

"Now, young man," said Will Carlton as soon as they were seated, "my wife tells me you've asked my daughter to marry you!"

"Why, yes, Mr. Carlton, I guess I did," answered Hugh, smiling. It was funny how unconcerned he felt about Mr. Carlton's reaction, considering how nervous he'd been the first time he came to call. But that was before he fell in love with Annie and became a partner in the shipping company that was going to make Seattle the biggest port on the coast. A calm confidence, a sense of ironic acceptance enveloped him. This will be the sign—if Carlton doesn't kick me out, I'll have to marry Emily and make a success of the North Star Steamship Company. If he does, I'll be free to marry Annie, step out of my world, and get a job on a freighter or something.

"You *guess* you did!" sputtered Mr. Carlton, eying him fiercely. "Either you did or you didn't."

"I did, sir." Hugh's voice was respectful but unawed.

"And how do you propose to support her? What's all this talk my wife's been getting off about a steamship company?"

"I am vice-president of the North Star Steamship Company which Captain Blaine and I have recently organized. We own two steamers, the *Kitsap* and the *Olympic*, and are now negotiating to buy the *Sioux City* and possibly the entire fleet of the Northwest Shipping Company." Hugh puffed slowly on his cigar, which was too heavy for his taste, and regarded the blue smoke nonchalantly. There, that ought to hold you, you old pirate.

"I'll be damned!" Will Carlton leaned forward, his blue eyes snapping. "Tell me some more about it. How much profits have you shown so far? How are you going to take over the Northwest Company's holdings?"

Mrs. Carlton had broken the news to Annie in the morning that they were having a dinner guest that night. "Emily's fiancée, Mr. Deming," she'd said with a simper. "So I want everything to be particularly nice, Annie."

Annie stared at her without a word and the color came and went in her cheeks.

"We'll have a roast of beef—prime ribs. Men always like good beef, don't you think?"

Annie nodded.

"Or do you think roast chickens would be nicer? With a sage dressing." Mrs. Carlton pondered, and Annie said nothing,

but her mind was in a turmoil. So I'm to cook the dinner and
serve it to Hugh Deming and his bride-to-be. I'm to answer the
door and take his hat and show him into the parlor. He'll see me
in my uniform and he'll wonder why he ever thought he could
love a hired girl.

"No, I guess the beef is better. But you tell Ed Bauer you
want the best cut in the house," went on Mrs. Carlton. "You'd
better go right now, Annie, and pick it out before the best ones
are gone."

Annie nodded again and went into her room to change for
the street. When she walked into Augustine and Kyer's, Ed
came quickly forward to meet her, smiling. She tried to smile
back at him, but her heart wasn't in it. He'd been so nice on
Saturday. They'd had a real treat, canoeing on the calm blue
waters of the lake, eating a picnic lunch at Leschi Park, then
dancing later at the pavilion. Ed had pressed her hand as they
danced, and on the way home she'd let him kiss her on the
cheek, had been grateful for his admiration and devotion.

"You don't look well today, Annie," he said in a low, worried
voice, and put his hand over hers as it lay on the counter.
"Don't you feel good?"

She shook her head. "I have a headache, Ed."

"You're not coming down with the grippe, I hope? Two of
the boys here at the store are out with it." He gave her hand a
quick squeeze. "I hope you didn't take cold Saturday on the
lake."

"Maybe that's it," she said, suddenly seeing the way out for
her that night. "How do you know when you've got the grippe,
Ed?"

"Well, your head aches and your back aches—I guess you
ache all over—and you're tired and feverish." He gazed at her in
concern. "Gee, honey, I sure hope you're not going to be sick.
I was hoping you'd go to the Potlatch with me."

By the time she'd carried the huge prime rib roast home—
Mrs. Carlton wouldn't entrust it to the delivery boy for fear it
might not arrive in time—Annie was convinced that she ached
all over and that she was quite unable to be on hand for the
dinner.

"I'm afraid I'm coming down with the grippe, Mrs. Carlton,"

she said weakly, her hand to her head, which did indeed throb and pound now. "I just ache all over."

"Oh dear, how awful—and with Mr. Deming coming to dinner, too!" cried Mrs. Carlton.

"I hate to upset your plans. Maybe I could get dinner started, if you can get someone to serve. Couldn't you borrow Martha from Mrs. Terry for tonight?"

"I'll try. And of course I don't want you to feel you have to do any work, Annie, if you're sick. I must say, you don't look well. You haven't for several days."

"I know. I didn't pay any attention to it. I thought it'd pass, but today—oh, I just feel awful," said Annie with sincerity. She did. She felt sick at heart. Hugh would be here in this very house, under the same roof, and she wouldn't see him or speak to him. He would be here to see Emily and her family, not her. How would he feel, knowing she was there? Would it bother him, or didn't he care at all?

She got the vegetables ready, a pie baked, the roast in the oven, and then Martha took over, big-boned and competent, so sympathetic about Annie's illness she wanted to run home and get some camphor to rub on her chest. But Annie assured her she could doctor herself and that the best thing she could do for her was to let her go to bed and be alone.

Annie went to her room, shut the door, and undressed in the green twilight. It seemed strange to be going to bed so early, with all the kitchen noises still going on, the footsteps in the hall and up- and downstairs. But everything was strange. What could be stranger than for her lover to be engaged to the daughter of the house where she was a servant?

She lay on her bed in just her corset cover and ruffled muslin petticoat, with an arm over her eyes. The doorbell rang and it pierced her heart. Hugh. He was here now. He was standing on the veranda waiting for the door to be opened. Martha's heavy steps echoed down the hall. Now she's letting him in, taking his hat. Now she's showing him into the parlor.

Suddenly Annie couldn't stand it another minute. She had to see him, even if he wouldn't look at her or speak to her. Even if he treated her as a hired girl. She couldn't just lie there in her dark little room, thinking about him. It would be better to be doing something. She struggled into her uniform again, brushed and braided her hair and wound it around her head. But she wouldn't put that ridiculous little starched white cap on, no matter how Mrs. Carlton glared at her.

"I'm feeling better, Martha," she said as she went out into the kitchen. "I'll be able to help serve."

"You should stay in bed ven you got a chance," scolded Martha.

"It makes me nervous to lie still when something's going on." She tied her apron around her waist, opened the oven, and basted the roast. Presently Mrs. Carlton came rustling out in her good gray silk, with her garnet earrings in her ears, to see how Martha was getting on. She was surprised but relieved to find Annie in charge again.

"If you're sure you feel up to it, Annie, I'd like to have you serve and Martha can dish things up and help with the dishwashing afterward."

"I'm all right now, Mrs. Carlton."

There was a touch of color in her cheeks and her eyes were very large and bright. She looks feverish, thought Mrs. Carlton, but she serves so much better than that big clumsy Martha. I'll let her stay in bed all day tomorrow.

"You may announce dinner as soon as you're ready," she said graciously, as if she were conferring a favor on the two maids, and rustled off again.

There was the tinkle of piano music from the parlor. Emily was playing Chopin's "Butterfly Etude." Annie smiled grimly and started to ladle out the soup from the kettle into the big delft soup tureen. Mr. Carlton always served the soup himself. Martha said she'd carry in the tureen and Annie could bring the plates. At the door of the dining room Annie hesitated a moment, then stepped through, put the soup plates at Mr. Carlton's place, and twitched back the portieres leading into the parlor. Emily had just finished her piece and was swinging around on the piano stool, flushed and laughing. Annie caught Mrs. Carlton's eye. "Dinner is served," she said calmly, looking at no one else, though someone had got up from a chair in the corner when she appeared.

"Thank you, Annie," said Mrs. Carlton with a smile.

She had not meant to, she had meant to stare straight at Mrs. Carlton, then turn and go out, but she knew it was he standing by the chair in the corner, she knew he was looking at her. Mrs. Carlton had turned to her husband, Emily was fluffing her hair at the mirror above the sofa, and Annie lifted her eyes and gave Hugh a long, burning look across the room. For the space of a heartbeat they gazed at each other as if there were no one else in the place and then Annie disappeared into the dining room. She didn't look at him again that evening.

She served the dinner as quietly as ever; she helped Martha wash up afterward, and then she brewed herself a cup of tea, having eaten no supper herself, and took it into her room to drink. She sipped it slowly and the hot tea eased the throbbing in her temples. She was glad she'd seen him, that he'd seen her waiting on the table, answering Mrs. Carlton's bell. Because in that one moment when his eyes met hers she knew that he loved her, that, though he might marry Emily, he still wanted her, even if she was a hired girl.

For a week Hugh worked feverishly, without the time or energy to think of either Annie or Emily. All his thoughts, energies, talents were thrown into consummating the deal with the Northwest Shipping Company. With Will Carlton's money and name to support him, he had no trouble effecting a sizable loan from the Dexter Horton Bank, and by the end of the week the offices and the six ships in the Northwest fleet had been transferred to the North Star Company and he and Captain Blaine, ensconced in dignified, modern offices with a staff of secretaries and clerks, got roaring drunk on Saturday afternoon with the door locked and the staff sent home. When he awoke the next morning with a hangover, Hugh realized he had a career on his hands. He'd made his choice. His elegant, casual, lighthearted youth, his romance, his dilettante days, were over. From now on he was doomed to respectability and, quite possibly, success.

He was so engrossed in work that it wasn't until he went downtown one morning and saw the streets decorated with banners and flags, fake totem poles set up on every corner and signs announcing the big clambake on Alki Point and the pow-wow at the circus grounds on the tide flats out in South Seattle, that he remembered this week was the Potlatch and he'd promised to take Emily to see it one night.

When he went into Captain Blaine's office with a list of figures, the old salt was sitting at his desk with an Indian war bonnet on his grizzled head. He greeted Hugh with a hand upraised Indian style and a stream of guttural Siwash.

"Goin' to the Potlatch tonight, bucko?" he asked, chuckling. "There'll be big doings. Princess Angeline's goin' to be there and the mayor's to make her a speech and present her with a gift from the city. Say, you haven't got your Potlatch button yet. Here, better put this one on, or you'll be stopped on every corner. I bought a handful this mornin'." He handed Hugh a button with a grinning beaked face, half eagle and half man, and Hugh with a shrug pinned it on his lapel.

"I suppose so. Emily wants to go."

"I remember when I was a young feller I used to sneak into the real Indian potlatches. That was a show. Drums and rattles going it hammer and tongs, ritual dances, a long speech from the chief and then the God-damnedest feed ye ever saw. Dried salmon, dried clams, and the special dish was a concoction of rotten salmon eggs. Whoof! You never smelled anything like it. Then the chief gave away all his possessions to the members of the tribe—blankets and tomahawks, spears, baskets—the whole kit and kaboodle."

"Why did he do that?"

"Oh, that was what the potlatch was for—a sort of good-will business—to show the tribe what a hell of a fine guy the chief was, how he loved the tribe like his own children, that he was such a big chief he could afford to give away his stuff, I guess. Anyway, that's what the real Indian potlatches were like."

Hugh took Emily to the Potlatch, or rather, he was absorbed into the Carlton family group that went to the Potlatch. He had a sudden premonition, as Will Carlton took over the situation and shepherded them all into the special streetcar that was being run to the circus grounds, that if he didn't watch out he would in the end discover that he had married Emily's family or that they had married him. It gave him an uncomfortable, hedged-in feeling that Emily's extremely charming prettiness, her soft little proprietary glances, her secret squeeze of his hand, did nothing to dispel.

There was a crowd at the circus grounds; there was a hubbub, an air of deviltry and mischief. Grown men whisked about in

Indian war bonnets emitting war whoops. Matrons blew feather-tipped whistles at people that shot out and tickled their noses. Children darted about like wild Indians with hideous masks, clackers, horns, balloons, and food. Confidence men had set up their booths and were skillfully fleecing the unwary with shell games, shooting galleries, weight guessings. It was a carnival with a Siwash and clambake flavor.

Long tables were set up, and clam chowder, steamed clams, corn, baked beans, and beer were being served free to one and all. There was a wooden platform upon which in due time the flashily dressed, rusty-voiced mayor made a long, flowery speech about the glories of the Siwashes (while the stinking, impassive, uninspiring representatives of their noble tribe stood or squatted beside their kelp and reed baskets, scratched themselves, ate smoked salmon, or chewed desiccated clams hung around their necks as ornaments and tidbits). Then Princess Angeline, wrinkled as a winter apple, toothless and coldly black-eyed as a snake, but resplendent in buckskins, blanket, and beaded slippers (a gift of the city fathers, since the rusty black skirt and shawl some white woman had given her were too filthy for such an august occasion), was escorted to the platform, there to receive the homage of the city whose early settlers she had saved from massacre by her father, Chief Sealth, and a gift of a house fit for the princess of the Siwashes, the patron saint of Seattle, to live in. The deed to the house was handed to her, she grinned malevolently at the mayor, and squatted again beside her uncouth subjects. They might better have given the princess a side of bacon, a plug of tobacco, or a bolt of calico, for she refused to live in her neat new cottage and continued in the broken-down hogan on the waterfront to the end of her days.

After the mayor's speech, when the band began to play, the crowd thickened so much that Hugh became separated from Emily and the Carltons. Suddenly finding himself cut off from his party, Hugh, instead of trying to find them, let the crowds sweep him farther and farther away. He was washed up in front of a shooting gallery that displayed cheap, gaudy blankets as the prize of marksmanship. Hugh paid his dime and took up the rifle the concessionaire handed him. He was an excellent shot and, to the man's chagrin, knocked down every one of the revolving ducks. There was applause from the crowd watching him and the shooting-gallery man reluctantly took down one of the blankets and handed it to Hugh.

As he turned to go away with the blanket slung over his shoulder Mexican style, he had a glimpse of a magnificent head of red hair, a white cheek being turned away.

"Annie!" cried Hugh, pushing his way through the crowd. The red head went proudly on, never once turning in his direction. All at once he had to stop her, talk to her, make her turn her face and look at him. He remembered that long, dark look she'd given him when he came to dinner at the Carltons'. "Annie!" He caught her elbow, held her fast.

She stopped, stared straight ahead, and then slowly, unwillingly, she turned to face him. The crowds surged around them, pushed them together. They were practically breast to breast, and they stood in a pool of silence, gazing helplessly into each other's eyes. Hugh held her by both arms, bending his intent, fierce gaze upon her.

Her face was pinched and white and her violet eyes blazed at him. He forgot where he was, that several hundred people were milling around them, he forgot Emily and her father, he forgot everything but that they had come together again, as if by a miracle, and that his longing for her had never once ceased, and that, seeing her again, it seemed to swell like a deep, tragic chord of music until he thought his heart would burst. Without a word he clasped her to him, the fragrance of her clean hair and skin sharper than the myriad odors of the carnival, the warmth of her body enfolding him in sudden peace. In that moment, in the midst of the crowd, she was his more perfectly and completely than she had ever been and he knew that he would never possess anyone as wholly as he did her. How long they stood there, breast to breast, her hair against his cheek, scarcely breathing, not in this world of time and space, but in an eternity of their own, he did not know. They might have stood there forever if an angry, shrill voice, that he later realized had been calling him several times, hadn't impinged upon his consciousness. Annie stiffened, dropped her arms with a muffled sob. He let her go, turned and saw Emily staring at him over a man's shoulder.

For a moment Hugh had the wild impulse to take Annie's

hand and escape into the crowd. He turned back to her, but she was gone. The crowd had swallowed her up.

"Well!" said Emily in a voice like ice.

He went slowly toward her but in spite of his anguish, the sense of loss, the feeling that he would never again know peace and fulfillment, his mind was busily forming a plausible excuse for his outrageous behavior.

Chapter XVI

Hugh faced Emily, waiting for the tirade that seemed ready to burst from her lips. "I've been looking all over for you," she said in a strained voice.

"I've been looking for you too," he lied, meeting her accusing blue eyes steadily. "But the crowd was so thick I got carried away."

"I see." She seemed to be waiting for more. But he took the gaudy blanket from his shoulder and draped it over her arm.

"Here," he cried, "I won this for you at the shooting gallery."

She looked at it in distaste and her cheeks were hot. "Thanks very much, but I really wouldn't know what to do with it."

"Do whatever you like. Give it away if you don't want it." His voice was suddenly sharp and she gave him a quick glance. His face was pale and withdrawn and there was a tight look about his mouth. His coldness frightened her. She didn't know what to think of what she'd seen, or thought she'd seen. It had *looked* like Annie Jordan and it had *looked* as if she was in his arms, but in the crowd . . . so many people . . . after all, he was *engaged* to her, Emily. But men had been known to break engagements, girls had been jilted with the trousseau all made, the announcements sent out. Oh, heavens, if that should happen to her, she'd simply die.

"Of course I won't give it away, Hugh dear," she said softly, her face all smiles, her eyes tender. She put her arm through his and gave it a little squeeze. "I think it's too clever for words of you to win it for me. I'll keep it always, as a souvenir of our first potlatch together."

He looked down at her with a puzzled frown. He'd have sworn she was about to have a row with him and for a fleeting moment he'd hoped she would. He'd hoped she'd be angry enough at what she'd seen to give him back his ring, break off their engagement, set him free. But she began to chatter gaily about the potlatch, to call his attention to the clowns performing on a raised platform, and she kept her arm tightly in his. So she's going to pretend she didn't see Annie at all, he thought, and the feeling of being trapped came over him again. When Emily led him back to her family, like a lost sheep gone astray, her father boomed heartily, "Well, well, my boy, so she found you, did she? We thought we'd lost you. Come along, the trolley's about to leave. We're all going back to the house for a little supper." The Carltons closed in on him and he was borne away in their midst.

The wedding was in St. Mark's, in October instead of June. Emily was taking no chances on a long engagement. Now that she had decided to marry Hugh, she wasn't going to let anything happen.

She had become an Episcopalian at boarding school and had kept at her parents until they submitted to confirmation and became members of St. Mark's.

It is quite impossible to say that this was exactly the moment she had foreseen when she was confirmed—the altar festive with candles and white chrysanthemums, the venerable Dr. Calhoun in cassock and surplice, the rustling, well-dressed congregation, the swelling tones of the new organ rolling out Mendelssohn's Wedding March—but at least she had a devout moment of gratitude that she was being married at St. Mark's, the most fashionable church in Seattle, and not at home in the awkwardness of the parlor, with the long staircase to negotiate.

Hugh was pale, nervous, and elegant in cutaway and striped trousers. But Emily was the bride every woman longs to be. Her filmy tulle veil floated like mist about her charming golden head; her wedding gown, of white mousseline de soie, embroidered and tucked exquisitely, had a high, boned lace collar that gave her the air of a stately queen about to be crowned. Her train was carried by two little boys in white velvet Lord Fauntleroy suits with stiff lace collars. Her bouquet was white roses and lilies of the valley. Her bridesmaids were only a shade (but the proper shade) less charming than she. Many a feminine eye was wet as she floated up the aisle on her father's arm, her face serene, her eyes downcast, her whole demeanor full of grace and tender maidenly decorum. Even Erica Crawford, casting a slightly sardonic glance at Hugh, had to admit that he was getting the cream of the season's belles.

Marguerite was maid of honor and very stately and smart she looked, too, in pale yellow organdy and a drooping Leghorn hat. Essie Keating and a Southern girl Emily had known at boarding school were bridesmaids. The handsomest and most personable young men in Seattle were ushers. Beauchamp Deming, Hugh's distinguished-looking older brother, was best man. There was a tremendous reception and supper afterward at the Denny Hotel, with everybody who was anybody invited, and even a few, perhaps, who were not.

Emily, in a fine gesture of democracy not unmixed with spite, had invited Annie to the wedding, though not, of course, the reception. Annie had thanked her quietly but had said, since it was her day off, she had made another date and couldn't go. Instead, she went to the trotting races at the fairgrounds with Ed Bauer and to supper at the Lion Oyster House afterward. She had a very good time and, if sometimes she seemed not to be listening to what Ed was saying, he didn't notice. She smiled at him whenever she lost herself in her reveries and the sight of her lovely, kind, open countenance, the way she clung to his arm in the crowd, which was something she hadn't done before, was enough for Ed. For now he realized that he was head over heels in love with her and just to be with her was enough to make him feel happy and proud.

That night he asked if he might kiss her and she looked at him gravely, unsmiling, unruffled, but very kind, and said, "Yes, Ed, you may kiss me." He kissed her very gently and her response was warm and satisfying. She liked Ed tremendously; he had been kind to her, and tonight his devotion was something to cling to. The tenderness in her kiss was out of gratitude, respect, and honest affection. To Ed, it was the encouragement he'd been hoping for.

"Annie," he whispered, "I love you. Do you think you could care for me a little? Enough to marry me?"

She met his eyes gravely. "Ed, I'm very fond of you. But I . . ." She frowned, because she didn't want to hurt him, and turned away.

He pressed her arm. "I can wait, honey. You think it over. I'm going into business for myself soon. I'd take good care of you."

"Yes, Ed, I think you would," she answered, and suddenly that seemed a wonderful thing, to be taken care of by a good man who loved you. What more could a girl like her, a hired girl from the waterfront, expect? "But I can't give you an answer now."

"I'll wait. You take your time, Annie." But his voice was vibrant with hope and assurance.

Annie didn't go to bed at all that night. For a time, after Ed took her home, she sat in her room, staring at the wall. Then she put on her coat, let herself quietly out of the house, and went for a long walk that took her to the waterfront. She sat on a bale of hay on the deserted pier, looking out over the wide, dark water with the fresh night wind on her face, the smell of the sea and the rotting pier in her nostrils, watching the riding lights of ships anchored out in the bay, until it began to grow light and the gulls flew in, hungry-eyed and raucous-voiced. Then she went home. She didn't weep, because it would have done no good. She had wept the night she saw him at the potlatch; she had gone straight home, bearing with her the pressure of his hands on her arms; she had shut herself up in her room and wept as if her heart would break. But she didn't weep on his wedding night. Only her body felt sore all over, as if she'd been beaten, and her heart was like a heavy stone in her breast. It was no comfort to think of Ed Bauer, no comfort at all.

Emily and Hugh spent their wedding night at the Denny Hotel. It was a delicious coup, because everyone thought they were going to Victoria and waited around outside the hotel where the carriages stood for hours. Then they decided the newlyweds had sneaked out the back way and escaped them, so they all went back into the living room where the reception was being held and drank more champagne and danced till dawn.

Emily had been very gay when they ran away from the reception; her eyes had shone with excitement, her cheeks had been flushed. But when they reached their suite and the door closed behind them, her gaiety took on a feverish quality. She giggled, she picked things up and put them down, she kept going to the window and exclaiming about the view. Hugh, watching her while he smoked a cigarette and talked lightly about the wedding, the guests, the quality of the champagne, began to feel stiff and embarrassed, as if he'd got into a silly schoolgirl's room by mistake.

Suddenly she turned to him and said in a queer, tight voice, with a little laugh, "Would you be awfully shocked if I asked you for a cigarette?"

He stared at her, then said easily, "No, of course not." He held out his case, filled with imported English cigarettes, and her fingers, white and rosy-tipped, reached for one, fumbled, dropped the cigarette on the floor. He picked it up for her, tossed it in the watesbasket, took out another one, and gave it to her. She held it awkwardly, not knowing quite what to do with it, and when she held the cork tip toward the match he'd struck for her, he smiled, took the cigarette from her shaking fingers, and turned it around for her.

"You light this end, Emily."

She flushed, met his eyes, looked down at the match flame. "I never smoked one before," she whispered, and he knew that she *was* just a schoolgirl and that she was scared to death of him, of the great, canopied, white bed of love, of her wedding night.

He felt a sudden rush of tenderness for her. Almost, in that moment, he loved her. He put his arms around her gently, wanting to comfort her in her loneliness and fear, wanting to reassure her, to let her know he could wait, he would be tender, he would insist on nothing that she didn't want to give. But her body stiffened in his arms, she seemed to steel herself for the inevitable, she lifted her face to him for his kiss and her lips were set and cold as if waiting for a blow.

Suddenly he was blind with anger, hurt pride, rage at her for having tricked him into marriage when she knew nothing about love, when obviously she was only willing to offer herself up as a sacrifice for man's desire in return for his name and the social position of being his wife. If she had been soft, trembling, if she had wept a little, he would have kissed her gently and told her to go to bed in peace, while he slept on the couch in the sitting room. But this frozen acquiescence stung him into brutality. His arms tightened cruelly about her. He forced her head back, kissed her lips, throat, bosom harshly, determined to shake that icy resignation. The lace at the neck of her pale blue going-away gown tore and she gave a little exclamation of distress. Not, he was sure, a cry for mercy, but of irritation at having her frock spoiled. He let her go, saying coldly, "I'm sorry I tore your dress."

She went to the mirror to view the damage. "You might have been a little careful, Hugh," she said, pouting.

"Ah, but, darling," he cried, his eyes glittering with irony, "you shouldn't be so beautiful, so desirable. How can a man be careful with you in his arms?"

She turned and stared at him with wide, frightened eyes. A nervous little smile played over her lips and a hot blush swept her cheeks.

Hugh did not spare her. His eyes met hers and then traveled over her throat, breast, body, insolently. "It's getting late," he said coldly. "We'd better get to bed. I'll undress in the sitting room. Don't take too long, will you?" And with a strange little smile that terrified her, he picked up his suitcase, went into the other room, and shut the door.

They took their wedding trip two weeks later, on one of Hugh's newly acquired boats on its first run to Victoria under the North Star line's flag. It was a gala excursion celebrating the official opening of the expanded new company.

The steamer glistened in its new white paint and polished brass; it was brave with pennants. Each stateroom was filled with flowers and every lady was presented with a box of candy, courtesy of the company. A ten-piece orchestra played at dinner and later for dancing. The cuisine was superb, Hugh having imported the French chef from the Palace Hotel in San Francisco at a fabulous salary.

Every stateroom was taken, with as many as four people sharing a cabin. It was perfect, blue October weather, with sun every day, no fog, and only a hint, a breath, of fall in the air. The passengers were very gay and enthusiastic, filled with the sense of holiday. The stewards were happy because of the lavish tips; they hurried about the deck with steamer rugs, deck chairs, drinks for the gentlemen, bouillon for the ladies. The captain was happy because the fine weather held; the ship responded like a sensitive woman to every turn of the helm. It was undoubtedly a most successful voyage.

Emily was very happy. She had a chance to wear her wonderful new clothes, to bask in the admiration and envy of her unmarried friends, and to flirt with all the men in perfect safety, being a young matron now. Hugh was quite satisfactory, too, now that he'd got over the idea of making love to her and contented himself with being merely charming and attentive when they were with people, and mildly ironic when they were alone. Most of the time his irony went over her head, so it didn't bother her. Sometimes she recognized the sarcasm, but pretended to ignore it, so they got along well enough.

When they got back to Seattle they moved into a little bungalow in a new residential district and Emily was the perfect little bride, making curtains, hanging pictures, arranging her wedding presents, learning to cook, and entertaining her women friends at luncheons and teas. She felt very important, shopping for cuts of meat and instructing the butcher about the thickness of steaks for her husband.

Hugh found her good company in a light, relaxing way, though half the time he hardly heard her chatter, but he enjoyed being the center of attention, being asked what he wanted for dinner and whether he liked her new frock. There was something very satisfactory about marriage, even if you weren't in love with your wife. It was good to have a pleasant, well-kept house to come home to after a busy day and it was good to have a pretty wife to take out to parties and the theater. His gay bachelor days were over and he was getting on with the business of making a living and establishing a home. If sometimes when he sat in the evening reading, while Emily crocheted her interminable table mats and tidies, a line of poetry struck him to the heart and he was suddenly swept with longing, he simply got up and went outside for a walk. He was done with all that. He had put Annie out of his life and he would do his best to keep her out of his mind and heart.

Annie never saw Hugh, though Emily was always running

over to her mother's for help about recipes or sewing, and once Mrs. Carlton sent Annie over with a mince pie for her daughter's supper. Emily was very cordial, asked Annie in, though the girl tried to refuse.

"Oh, but I want you to see our dear little house, Annie. I've put new curtains in the kitchen and I've crocheted a spread for our bedroom," cried Emily gaily.

"It's very nice," said Annie quietly, standing in the middle of the living-room floor looking at the chairs that Hugh sat in, the pictures he looked at, the rugs he walked on. "But I have to get back. I've got bread in the oven."

"Oh, fiddlesticks!" laughed Hugh's wife, and she caught Annie's arm, led her from room to room, chattering all the time about Hugh and his funny tastes, as if Annie were an old friend.

"You must be very happy," said Annie all at once in a strange voice.

Emily looked at her with a curious smile. "Of course. I love having my own house and doing as I please. Why don't you get married, too, Annie? Why should you stay there at Mama's working so hard for someone else? I'll bet you have lots of beaus. Isn't there one of them you'd marry if he asked you?"

"One asked me," said Annie suddenly, not knowing why she should be telling this to Emily, whom she didn't like. "He's a nice fellow, too."

"Do you like him?" Emily's eyes were bright with curiosity.

Annie nodded. "I like him a lot."

"Then why don't you take him? If he's nice he'll give you a good home and you won't have to take orders from anyone. You'd be much happier than working for someone else." Emily seemed to be looking at Annie as if she were a person for the first time. She almost acted as if she were interested in what happened to her.

"Maybe I will," said Annie, and laughed and went out the door. She hurried up the street, terrified that she might meet Hugh coming home from his office. She didn't want to meet him now; she didn't want him to know she'd been in his house.

The next Saturday she had a date with Ed. He took her to dinner at the new Butler Hotel and she wore her best dress and the kid gloves Mrs. Carlton had given her for Christmas. There was music, and Ed ordered wine with their dinner. Annie felt very elegant and she was pleased at Ed's solicitousness. He really did make her feel wonderful. He looked very nice, too, in blue serge, white shirt, and polka-dot bow tie. His manners were good without being foppish and his brown eyes, meeting hers across the table, were shining with admiration for her.

After dinner they went to the Moore Theater. In the darkness of the theater she wept a little over her lost dreams, and Ed, sensing her sadness, put his hand over hers. It was a large, warm, masculine hand and it was very comforting. In the hansom cab going home (an extravagance, but one Ed insisted upon, which secretly pleased Annie) the hand captured hers again and she sat back with her eyes closed, feeling protected and cared for. Before they reached Boylston Avenue, Ed turned to her and said shyly, "Have you thought about what I asked you last time?"

"Yes, Ed," she answered with no attempt at coyness.

"Can you give me your answer now, Annie?" His voice was so humble and gentle it brought tears to her eyes. How good he was and how much he seemed to love her!

"Yes, Ed." She looked at him, her dark, wide eyes on his face, candid and unflinching. "I'll marry you, Ed, if you still want me to."

"Darling!" he cried, and started to take her in his arms.

She held him off, still searching his face. "Ed dear, I must tell you this and I hope it won't hurt you. I'm terribly fond of you and I respect you. But I'm not in love with you." He met her eyes bravely, though she knew from the way he set his jaw that it had hurt him. "But I think I can be a good wife to you."

He pressed her against him. "You'll be the most wonderful wife in the world, Annie. You're all I want, even if you don't love me the way I love you. Just give me a chance. I'll make you happy."

"You're so good," she whispered, "so good and kind" and she let his strong, kind arms enfold her, she let his lips find hers, she gave herself up to his joy in her. I'm a lucky girl to have a man like Ed Bauer want to marry me, she told herself, and she blinked back the tears and smiled at him.

That winter there was a great banquet at the Denny Hotel to which everyone went who had the price of a seat at the long tables set up in the vast ballroom. It was a memorable occasion, the last great event to be held at the old Denny Hotel, for the next spring the hill on which it stood was to be washed away by hydraulic pressure to make way for the expanding business district. The President of the United States, the beloved Teddy Roosevelt, a man after the West's own heart, was making a tour of the Pacific Coast with a stopover in Seattle.

The speaker's table was crowded with notables; the governor of Washington, Seattle's mayor, and leading citizens, the President's party, which included the Secretaries of Commerce and the Interior, and the President himself, like a plum, in the center. Ladies, elegant and dazzling, in evening gowns and jewels, their bare white shoulders gleaming under the lights from the great crystal chandelier, lent the occasion grace and beauty. Emily Deming and her mother were at the President's table, as wives of two of Seattle's most progressive businessmen.

There were speeches from everyone, but the speakers, on turning to the guest of honor to deliver flowery compliments, nearly forgot their next lines when they discovered the President's seat empty. The irrepressible T.R. kept dashing out onto the veranda to drink in the wonderful, heady air and gaze raptly at the magnificent view of the bay and the Olympics. However, his own speech, delivered, of course, without notes and with much flashing of teeth, quite made up for these derelictions in its enthusiasm for the beauty of the Northwest and his faith in Seattle as the greatest, most up-and-coming city in the West.

After the banquet, the President stood for two hours, shaking hands and flashing his famous smile that never seemed to become mechanical. All the First Families were presented to him, as well as the Second and Third Families. Annie Bauer and her husband, Ed, shook the great man's hand, and the President's eye twinkled behind his glasses as he looked at Kit Jordan's red-haired girl.

"I can see, ma'am," he said gallantly, "that the Olympics and Mount Rainier are not the only beauties of this magnificent country."

Annie blushed, Ed squeezed her arm, and they passed on.

"That's something to tell our children, honey," Ed murmured as they went toward the cloakroom. "The President of the United States paid you a compliment."

Annie smiled and her eyes were bright. She was wearing the nile-green ball gown that she'd danced in with Hugh Deming in this same ballroom. Her eyes searched the crowd but she didn't see him. She'd caught glimpses of him at the President's table during the banquet, and her heart swelled with pride. He looked the very picture of success, and handsomer, more elegant than ever, in his dinner clothes. He was going to be an important man and she was glad. She was glad, too, that Emily, by his side, was so beautiful and well dressed. It was right that he should have a lovely wife who was a lady and knew how to act at important functions. There was just a moment when, as she watched them from her table in the corner, she saw herself as the woman by his side and imagined that if she'd been the one he'd not have paid so much attention to the lady on his left. But the moment passed when Ed, reaching for her hand, whispered, "You're the best-looking woman in the room, Annie. There's not a one can hold a candle to you." His honest eyes were soft with love and pride, and a rush of gratitude for him and for his devotion warmed her heart. She squeezed his hand and moved her chair so that she couldn't see Hugh and Emily.

"And you're the nicest man in the world," she replied with deep sincerity. He was. He was the best husband a girl could want. She *was* happy in a quiet, serene, unecstatic way, and perhaps that was the best way.

Hugh and Emily were standing in a group with the Crawfords and Marguerite and Philip Lorimer, a New York lawyer for one of the railroads, when Annie and Ed went by to get their wraps. Hugh had been deep in a discussion of Seattle shipping with Lorimer when, without knowing why, he broke off, turned, and saw Annie across the room. Her glorious head was lifted, there was a smile on her lips as she moved with the grace and quiet dignity of a young queen through the crowd. "Cleopatra," he whispered, and Lorimer turned, glanced at his face, and followed his strange, intense gaze.

"By Jove, what a handsome woman!" Lorimer said.

"Which one?" asked Emily quickly, always jealous of her own laurels.

"The red-haired beauty in the green dress over there."

Emily glanced over her shoulder. Her lips curved in an exquisite little smile, but her eyes were sharp and cold. "Oh, that's our ex-hired girl. Her mother runs a saloon down on the water-front."

Philip Lorimer raised his eyebrows. "Amazing!"

"Yes, isn't it?" murmured Emily sweetly. "But we're frightfully democratic here in Seattle, you know. And at an affair like this, you're apt to rub shoulders with almost anybody."

"Yes," said Hugh in a cold voice, "the lady sitting on my left at dinner once ran a dance hall in an Idaho mining town, but now she's one of the town's stuffiest social leaders. And my wife's mother was born on a farm and was apprenticed to a tailoress. Here in the great West there is opportunity for all."

Emily was biting her lips and staring at him in fury. Marguerite smiled her amused smile and Lorimer listened in genuine interest while Hugh went on in his flat, ironic voice. "As a matter of fact, I'd like to have you meet the distinguished-looking woman in black coming toward us now. Excuse me just a moment." Hugh bowed to the ladies and, with an icy smile playing over his lips, advanced toward the woman with iron-gray hair and her pince-nez on a ribbon. She saw him, but pretended not to recognize him. He stopped in front of her, bowed, and extended his hand.

"Hello, Lou. It's a pleasure to see you here tonight."

Lou Graham lifted an eyebrow and with a speculative gleam in her eyes shook hands with him. "What's the idea, Hugh? Are you drunk?"

He laughed. "Sober as a judge. Come along. I want you to meet my wife."

Lou frowned and hesitated. "She won't want to meet me."

"Any friend of mine is a friend of my wife's," said Hugh acidly.

Lou shrugged. "I don't get it, but I'll meet her."

The little group was watching them as Hugh came up with Lou Graham on his arm. Several other people stared in astonishment as he presented her first to Emily—"I want you to meet an old friend of mine, Emily. This is Mrs. Graham." Then to Marguerite, the Crawfords, and finally Philip Lorimer. "Mr. Lorimer, Mrs. Graham, one of Seattle's most successful businesswomen, who happens to be one of my partners in the North Star Steamship Company."

With perfect aplomb and a mischievous glint in her keen eye,

Lou bowed, murmured sedate greetings, then swept on her way.

Maurice Crawford's face was suffused; Erica gazed at Hugh in frank admiration at his audacity; Marguerite looked bewildered, and Emily was white-faced.

"What an interesting-looking woman!" exclaimed Philip Lorimer innocently. "She reminds me of an aunt of mine who is headmistress of a girl's school in Massachusetts. What sort of business is she in?"

Hugh offered him a cigarette and, while he held the match for him, answered casually, "Lou? Oh, she's the madam of the most select sporting house in Seattle."

There was dead silence and Philip Lorimer choked on his first draft of cigarette smoke. Emily sunk her nails into Hugh's arm. "Take me home," she gasped.

"Gladly, my dear," said Hugh.

Halfway home in the cab, Emily suddenly broke her frozen silence and turned on him in white-hot fury. "How dare you! How dare you insult me by introducing that—that person to me?"

"It was a little lesson, darling. I hope it will teach you not to be such a nasty little snob," said Hugh coolly.

"You did it to get even for what I said about Annie Jordan, didn't you?" she spat at him, trying to see his face in the dark.

He smiled at her ironically. "Now whatever put that into your pretty little head, sweetheart?"

But that night as he lay beside Emily, unable to sleep for thinking of the girl in the nile-green dress, he was disgusted with himself. What good had it done except to embarrass his friends, hurt Emily, and satisfy some curious sense of justice in his own mind? Nothing that Emily could say about Annie could hurt her as much as he had already done by his cowardice, selfishness, and his own snobbery, which was deeper and more unyielding than Emily's could ever be.

Chapter XVII

Nearly every day Annie walked downtown from their little house on Twenty-third Avenue to watch the washing away of Denny Hill. The hotel had gone first, torn down and carted away, all its glories of banquets and balls reduced to a heap of rubble to make way for the upward progress of the expanding city.

The powerful streams of water pounded at the hill, eating it away, foot by foot, gradually bringing its proud crest down. Annie would stand by the hour watching the tons of water battering the hill, the crews of men working. Ed came with her sometimes, when he could leave the store for an hour or so, and while he was fascinated in a masculine way at the skillful engineering, he was amused at Annie's intense interest.

To her, there was drama in the whole thing—the drama of elemental forces unleashed by man's intelligence to accomplish his will. She was sorry to see the great hill, that had commanded the bay and the city for so long, humbled and destroyed, but it was an exciting thing to watch. She felt that, by watching, she became part of the progress of the city. She came even as the months advanced and her child grew heavy and unwieldy in her body.

She had married Ed knowing that she was deliberately doing the best she could for herself. He was a good man, he loved her, he would be good to her. He wasn't rich, but he was hard-working and he had a good, solid future. The store was doing well and he was talking of expanding. She could leave the Carltons, have a home of her own, be cherished and cared for.

It wasn't a fine house on the First Hill and soup out of thin white china, but it was a big step up from the waterfront. She knew that she loved Ed for his goodness and simplicity, for his rugged manhood; the very quality of his love for her, full of tenderness and devotion, made her content to be his wife. There was none of the anguished joy, passion, ecstasy that she'd had with Hugh. She was grateful that she had known those things and now she was grateful for Ed. You had to take things as they came in this life, the good and the bad. You had to get on with the business of living.

Once she thought she ought to tell Ed about Hugh, but then she decided against it. If Ed should ask her whether she still loved him, she'd have to say she did. That would hurt Ed, spoil what she had to give him. And she had much to give him. She knew she could make him happy. Wasn't that all a man could expect from a wife?

After their marriage at St. Anne's Catholic Church, with Father Donegan officiating and looking pleased that his waterfront girl was doing so well for herself, she and Ed went on a fishing trip up the Elwha River. Ed was an expert woodsman and fisherman. He could make a fire out of damp wood, a comfortable bed from fir boughs. Annie was proud of Ed on the trip. She liked to watch his tall, well-built body, sturdy legs apart, braced against the swift current, standing in the river, casting for trout. She liked lying wrapped up in blankets beside their campfire, looking up through the dark, murmurous fir boughs to the white stars, listening to him talk about hunting and fishing or about his work. She had married a real man and they would have a good life together and that was the purpose of existence, wasn't it?

They moved into the little bungalow, bought furniture, and Annie settled down to the first real home she had ever known. She had never liked doing housework for her mother or Mrs. Carlton, but in her own house it was fun.

One morning when she was in the kitchen, frying bacon, with the door open to let the sun and air in, she heard a sea gull scream. She set the pan of bacon on the back of the stove, went out on the back steps, and watched the white gull sweep overhead, toward the bay. The air was fresh and there was a smell of the sound in it that made her breathe it deep. Suddenly she laughed. "I'm happy," she cried. "I'm happy clear through."

Ed came up behind her and put his arm about her waist. "What makes you so happy, honey?" he asked, smiling at her radiant face.

"I don't know, Ed, but maybe it's because you're so good to me and we have such a nice house and it's a fine morning." She smiled at him, her eyes thoughtful. "Or maybe I'm going to have a baby."

His arm tightened about her and his face was suddenly tense and awed. "A baby!" he whispered. "Oh, Annie. Oh, my little wife."

She looked at him. "Would you like that, Ed?"

"I'd be the happiest man in the world," he cried in a voice rough with emotion. His mouth trembled and Annie pressed her face against his shoulder, suddenly ashamed at the painful joy and humility in his eyes.

"You go to the doctor today and find out," he said sternly, holding her away from him to look at her. "And if it's true, I'll buy you anything you want. I don't care how much it costs."

"You can buy me a set of thin white china," she laughed.

Ed's joy in her pregnancy satisfied whatever doubts she'd had about her marriage. And as the days went by and her body became heavy, and the pile of baby clothes she was making grew, she was aware of a sense of fulfillment so deep that she wondered how she had ever wanted anything else out of life. She seemed to be moving in a deep, sweet dream of contentment. Ed was pathetically tender and devoted to her, waited on her hand and foot, treated her like a queen.

The baby was born on a bright, wind-swept morning with the smell of the sound very strong as it came through the open window. Mrs. Hopkins, the nurse Ed had got for her, disapproved of the open window, but Annie insisted on it. She'd been in labor all night and she thought the dawn would never come. Whenever the waves of darkness and pain seemed about to engulf her, she'd turn her head toward the window and breathe the fresh, cool night air deeply and the darkness would clear away and she would go back to her struggle again.

She heard the faint, angry cry and then she closed her eyes

and went to sleep, glad it was over, glad that the child was born, but weary, weary to the bone.

When she wakened, Ed was bending over her, stroking her hair. "You've given me a son, darling," he murmured tenderly. "A little boy with red hair."

She smiled. "Red hair? You'll have your hands full, Ed, with two redheads to handle."

Mrs. Hopkins rustled in, starched and bony-faced, and laid the blue-blanketed bundle beside her. Annie looked at the tiny, wizened red face with the fuzz of pink hair, and laughed out loud. He was the image of her father. Suddenly she felt very proud and so happy that the tears rolled down her cheeks. I wish Hugh could see him, she thought. She smiled up at Ed but it was Hugh's face she saw bending over her, the gold lights in his gray eyes, the little ironic smile on his lips.

"What are we going to call him, Annie?"

"Hugh."

"Was that your father's name?"

"No. It's just a name I like."

"Whatever you say, honey. Hugh Bauer. That's a good name."

Annie's second son was born just eleven months after little Hugh. He had brown hair like Ed's and in a few months his eyes were brown, too. They named him Joseph, for Ed's father. Hugh and Joseph were healthy, gay little boys and their father adored them.

Annie loved them with a deep, primitive feeling of pride, devotion, and selflessness. She often looked at them and wondered how it had happened that she had borne them. They were so perfect, such individuals. It seemed incredible now that she had ever carried them in her own body. She knew that she would cut off her hand or gladly die to save them one moment's sorrow or pain. And yet she had no feeling of maternal possessiveness. She didn't want to keep them bound to her. Each sign of independence or assertiveness delighted her. They kept her hurrying; they were into everything; they had no fear and they could take punishment with the same acceptance that their mother had.

Ed was doing well enough. The store was a good, steady, paying business and he was respected as an honest, capable businessman. But he'd never set the world on fire or be able to build Annie the house on the First Hill she'd once set her heart on. These days, though, Annie had too much to do, running her house and keeping track of her two boys, to think of things like that, or to miss the waterfront, or to wonder how she'd feel if she came face to face with Hugh Deming again.

When the boys were five and six, Kit Jordan died. Her lawyer notified Annie, and for the first time since her mother had sent her packing the day she went to see her, Annie walked up the steps of the Nugget rooming house, into the musty-smelling, ugly rooms with their dark brown wallpaper and hideous furniture. For a moment as she went up the steps she'd had a vision of Kit standing on the porch, her gray hair in wild locks around her angry hatchet face, shaking her fist and calling her daughter every vile name in her talented repertory. It was saddening to have only that memory and others, almost as coarse and brutal, of your mother.

Oh well, she's dead and gone now, poor Ma. She had a hard life. Maybe she'd have been different if Pop had lived or if she hadn't had to run a waterfront rooming house and saloon, said Annie to herself. It was no good thinking hard thoughts about the dead. They were gone, they couldn't defend themselves or explain why they had done what they had done while they were still on earth. Best to think as kindly as possible of them, whisper a prayer for the repose of their souls, and cross yourself as you came into the room where all that was mortal of them reposed in grim state.

Kit's casket was in the same little dark parlor with the horrible red curtains and the marble-topped table where she'd entertained Fred Carew, where the unholy marriage service had been read.

Annie stepped reluctantly toward the casket and looked at her mother. She didn't want to, but it was expected of her, it was the courtesy due the dead. The hatchet face was sharper than ever and it poked grotesquely upward from the gray satin lining of the casket. The undertaker had curled the wispy gray hair and it reminded Annie of the night Kit had fixed herself up for Fred Carew and she'd told Mae she was afraid her mother was going to marry him. She never did know whether that was Kit's first plan and when that fell through she had decided to marry Annie off to him instead. Well, it didn't matter now. It was all water under the bridge. Her hatred, her fear, her disgust were all gone and here she was, alive and well and happy, and Kit Jordan, bad or good, was cold clay. It was impossible to hold a grudge against the dead when you were still bursting with life. And her mother looked very quiet and old, dead.

Annie was tired when she and Ed got home from the cemetery. She took off her hat and unpinned her heavy braids and let them swing loose. Her head ached and there was a weight on her breast. Death was a horrible thing and it would take her days to shake off its gloom and depression. She didn't pretend to be overcome with grief for her mother. They hadn't seen each other for years and the last time had been fraught with bitterness and recriminations. But Kit Jordan had been her mother, the last one of her own blood left, the last link with her past, with her childhood and the waterfront. She sat on her bed and shivered, bowed down with loneliness and a nameless, primitive sorrow for all the lonely, forgotten dead.

She felt so utterly and bleakly alone that when Ed came into their room and tried to comfort her she couldn't bear it. She pushed him away, told him she was all right. His good brown face looked hurt and bewildered and she had a flash of anger—at herself and at him for not being clever enough to know what made her do that. Hugh would have understood, she kept thinking, and she stopped pacing the floor and stared at herself in the glass. It was the first time she'd thought of Hugh since Joseph was born, but now she knew that the thought of him, the need for his quick responsiveness and subtle understanding, had lain deep all the years, had lain under the forgetfulness of him, under her almost animallike contentment with her home and family.

She sat on the bed and buried her face in her hands, weeping bitterly, not for her mother's death, but for the death of the perfect thing that she and Hugh might have had together, and the hot tears ran down between her fingers.

Ed, that night in bed, wanted to love her, to be tender and sympathetic, but for the first time she deliberately turned away from him, rejected his love, which was really all she had now.

Ed didn't understand and he was hurt and she wondered if she'd done the right thing, after all, in marrying him and bearing his children. But the next day she was all right again, subdued and thoughtful, but loving and warm with him, and he put it all down to the funeral and a woman's deeper emotions.

Kit Jordan left a very large estate and when her will was read it was found that she'd willed it all to the Roman Catholic Church in a gesture of great irony and revenge upon Annie. But Ed was determined that Annie should have what was rightfully hers, so he went to Judge Deming. Kit, in her determination that Annie should have no part of the money she'd worked so hard for, hadn't left anything to the girl, not even enough to satisfy the law. So the will was broken and Annie came into nearly a hundred thousand dollars, after the saloon and rooming house were sold, along with several lots on the tide flats that an Eastern manufacturer wanted to buy. In 1908 tide-flat lots were bringing a fabulous price, and Ed persuaded Annie to sell at once.

The first thing Annie did with her money was to buy the Lathrop house, a great white mansion with Ionic columns on Capitol Hill. Ed couldn't understand what she wanted such a big place for, but Annie simply said, as she took possession of the house and stood in the enormous, paneled living room, "I've wanted a house like this ever since I was six years old."

Standing there, with a curious smile on her lips, Annie thought of the night of the fire when she'd looked in awe at Rolfe Linden's plush-curtained dining room, of the day she'd stood at the Carltons' door with Father Donegan and said, "Someday *I'll* have a house on the First Hill." Well, she had one now, a much finer, more imposing one than the Lindens' or the Carltons', and she thought that maybe Kit Jordan would have been pleased, after all, with what she had done with her money.

Chapter XVIII

Emily was ripping a perfectly new hat to pieces because she didn't like its lines. She was going to make the brim smaller and sew an enormous pink rose on it. It would be very smart and Frenchy-looking when she finished. She couldn't make clothes worth a darn but she had a gift for hats. Hugh came in from the office, looking tired, tossed a rolled-up evening paper on the table, and gave her a peck on the cheek. She smiled at him brightly.

"Who do you think is giving a New Year's party and has asked us?"

He yawned, bit the end off a cigar that James J. Hill had given him at lunch. Hill had finally agreed to lend Hugh and the North Star Steamship Company half a million dollars to expand the line.

"Who?"

"Annie Bauer. She used to be Annie Jordan, remember? Mama's hired girl." Her voice was light as fluff, innocent as a kitten's purr.

He lit the cigar, puffed on it steadily, and slowly raised his eyes to hers. "Yes, I remember Annie Jordan," he replied quietly.

"She came into her mother's money, you know."

"Did she?" He looked vague and uninterested and sat down on the sofa, crossed his legs, and unrolled the paper.

"You know perfectly well she did. Your father was the one who broke Kit Jordan's will and got the money for Annie."

"H'm." He held the paper before his face but he was not looking at the print. He was staring into space, into the past perhaps, seeing the wide, soft violet eyes, the creamy throat, the flaming red hair spread out like a fan on the pillow.

"Anyway, she and Ed—he used to work for Augustine's but he has his own store now—have bought the old Lathrop place and you should see the way she's fixed it up. Marguerite helped her with the decorating and I was over there for tea this afternoon. It's simply lavish; she's spent a fortune on it. Thanks to Marguerite, it's in surprisingly good taste." Emily laughed, a little icy bell that tinkled in the warm room. "I can imagine what it'd be like if Annie'd tried to do it herself. It would probably be a glorified Nugget Saloon."

Hugh looked at her over his paper. "Why are you women so catty about each other?"

"I'm not being catty. It just amuses me to see Annie Jordan, brought up on the waterfront, buying Aubusson carpets and Empire love seats and Chippendale chairs. Of course she doesn't know a thing about them and she's honest enough to admit it."

"She would be. I've never known a woman as honest as Annie," Hugh said thoughtfully. "Is she still as beautiful as she used to be?"

Emily's face sharpened. She gave him an odd look. "Well, she's still flamboyant-looking, if you call that beauty. And she's learned how to dress. But there's still the flavor of the waterfront about her, in spite of her New York gowns and her custom-made shoes."

"Thank God for that. I'd hate to see Annie lose her flavor." Hugh smiled.

"You ought to see her shoes. She's got dozens of pairs. And she's had a cabinet for them built into her closet, and hatstands for her hats. She said she'd always wanted lots of shoes and hats." Emily laughed. "She's really like a child with a new toy. I'll bet she spends all her money in a couple of years and ends up back on the waterfront."

"You wouldn't be envious of her, would you?" asked Hugh with his ironic smile.

Emily tossed her head. "Envious? Heavens, no. In fact, I've always felt that she was envious of me. She's come quite a ways from the Nugget Saloon, with her nice husband, her two little boys, and her fine house, but I've got something she's never had and always wanted."

"What's that?" Hugh's eyes narrowed and he looked at her; he seemed suddenly to be waiting.

"Background. Breeding. I was born on the First Hill and she was born on the waterfront and she'll never live it down!" she flashed triumphantly.

"Oh, is that it?" He smiled and the expectancy died out of his face. "So she has two children now? What are they like?"

"Cute little boys. One has red hair and looks like her. The other is dark like his father. Their names are Hugh and Joseph." Suddenly Emily drew a sharp breath. She glanced quickly at her husband and the color rushed into her cheeks, but he only smiled.

"I'm glad she got a good break at last. She was a nice kid and she had an old harridan of a mother," he said calmly.

But Emily couldn't let it pass. She lowered her gaze to the hat she had in her lap and said in a light, casual voice, "I wonder why she named her first boy Hugh?"

"Why not?" he replied as casually. "It's a good name. So she's giving a New Year's Eve party. Are we going?"

Emily hesitated, met his eyes. "Why, of course," she said slowly. "I wouldn't miss it for the world. You see, poor Annie is trying to get into society and Marguerite and I are supposed to help her. I think it will be heaps of fun, getting Kit Jordan's daughter into the First Hill crowd."

Hugh threw down his paper, got up, and began to pace. "Look here, Emily, give Annie a chance, will you? She's had plenty of hard knocks in her life and now she's getting somewhere. Don't do anything to spoil things for her."

She stared at him, her pretty, petulant mouth open. "For pity sakes, Hugh, what's the matter with you? I just *told* you I was going to help her get into society, didn't I?"

"I didn't like the way you said it. There was a mean note in your voice, as if—as if you were making fun of Annie, as if you knew she'd get hurt and you were glad." He stopped in front of her, gave her a hard, cold look. "Don't let Annie get hurt, Emily. Don't do it!"

For a moment they stared at each other like angry strangers, then Hugh turned and went out of the room. Emily's lips quivered, her cheeks were hot, tears sprang to her eyes. She longed to jump up, run after him and cry, "Why do you care what happens to her? What is Annie Jordan to you?" But she didn't dare. She had a curious feeling that he might tell her the truth and the truth might crumble her superiority, her pride, to bits. But she made up her mind then and there that Annie would never get into First Hill society if she could help it.

Hugh went into the dining room, poured himself whisky and seltzer water, and took his drink up to his room. He shut the door, sat down in his big chair by the window, and drank his whisky slowly. Every nerve in his body was jangling. He'd been working like the very devil, it was true, expanding the company, coping with the competition of the Northern Pacific lines, floating that big loan from Hill, but until now his only reaction had been a certain aloof satisfaction in the success of the business he and Captain Blaine had built on a shoestring. He often wondered why he'd been so successful when he had such a strange attitude toward business. Actually, the reasons other men had for pursuing success meant nothing to him. He didn't want money, he had no ambitions for power or respect. He didn't want to impress Emily. It was more like a game to him, that he played with a kind of unconcern over winning or losing, but with a detached pleasure in his own skill. Yes, it was a game that sometimes he wearied of, in which there was no purpose other than the playing.

It wasn't his work or the competition or the loan, it wasn't his life with Emily, which was another game he enjoyed playing skillfully and gracefully, that made his hand shake as it lifted the glass to his lips. They were all outside of his real life, and only the things that touch the core of a man's being can really disorganize and shake him. You can do that, Annie, because the only real life I ever had was through you. Even now, years later, you can come into the empty shell of my heart and quicken it with pain and longing and despair.

Ed came into Annie's dressing room and found her staring at herself in the long mirror, her hands clenched at her sides, her face pale. She was all in white, with her lovely shoulders bare and a froufrou of white net enclosing her bosom. She turned as he touched her arm and lifted wide, frightened eyes to him.

"Gee whiz, honey, you look like a million dollars!" he cried happily, and kissed the tip of her ear.

"Oh, Ed, do you think I look all right? Not too dressy? Should I wear these earrings and the necklace, too? I'm so afraid I'll look too flashy."

"Say, your hands are like ice and you look scared. What's the matter, sweetheart?"

She leaned her head against him. "Oh, Ed, I am scared. Scared green that everything won't be right. That I won't look right or the party won't be right. I've never given a real party before in a fine house with nice people, real society people, coming."

"Everything's going to be just dandy, honey. You'll be the finest-looking woman here. The house is swell, and with the money you've spent on the food and drinks, the party ought to be a rip-snorting success. Besides, with Marguerite and Emily to help you, how can you fail?"

She sighed and relaxed. "Oh yes, I'm so glad they're coming. Marguerite's been so wonderful and she's persuaded Mr. and Mrs. Crawford to come, and Emily—Emily's been wonderful too." She hesitated just a second and her face looked a bit puzzled. "I was afraid at first Emily wouldn't come; she's sort of funny. I mean, she's never forgotten I used to work for her mother and I had a feeling she wouldn't want to accept me socially just because I'd come into money and we live on the First Hill now. But she's coming and she's bringing Essie Keating and Rolly Collins and she was just as sweet as she could be about it."

"Then what have you got to worry about, Annie? Come on downstairs now and taste the punch. I made it myself; wouldn't trust that butler you hired. I may not know much about society, but I know something about liquor, and the better the punch, the better the party."

Annie went downstairs, holding up her skirt carefully, and as she walked through the rooms her confidence returned and her face grew warm with anticipation. The house was perfect, far grander than the Linden house that had once been to her the symbol of perfection. Wine-colored velvet, not plush, curtains hung at the tall windows; rich, soft rugs in exquisite colors covered the polished floors; the furniture gleamed softly, all beautiful old pieces that Marguerite had helped her find. Marguerite had carefully steered her away from the golden oak and the ugly Mission furniture that was the rage, from the Maxfield Parrish prints that bloomed on every wall, from beaded, agate lamps, from the meaningless bric-a-brac that cluttered so many houses. The result of Marguerite's taste and Annie's humility was a house of dignity and charm. Instinctively Annie recognized it as such and was happy in it.

The house was Marguerite's product, but for tonight Annie had added her own mark—flowers in every vase, with extra ones bought to hold the tremendous chrysanthemums in gold and white and bronze. Flowers bloomed in the hall, on the mantel, on every table, and the centerpiece in the dining room was made of the most exotic and expensive flowers she could find: tiger-colored orchids in a nest of maidenhair fern. Warm, rich, effulgent, the flowers brought the quiet dignity of the rooms to life and said to the world, The woman who lives here can't be bound by convention because she is too richly, gloriously alive. Walking in her lovely rooms, among her profligate flowers, Annie was all at once happy with fulfillment.

The party was a great success. The Crawfords and Emily's friends, whom she'd subtly led on to expect something gauche and amusing, were enchanted by Annie and her unaffected joy in their presence. The food was superb, the punch authoritative, and their hostess's manner charming.

Only once did Annie falter and that was when she took Emily into the dining room and whispered diffidently, "Is everything all right? Is the table set right? Have I forgotten anything?" And Emily paused, surveying the room, the exotic flowers, the sumptuous silver and crystal, and in that pause Annie thought she was finding something wrong and that the light, patronizing laugh meant that she was tactfully covering it up. Actually Emily was overwhelmed with the table's perfection, with the grace with which Annie assumed the role of the perfect hostess.

"Everything's too wonderful," she said at last.

The moment Annie had dreaded and yearned for was simpler and more quickly over than she could have hoped, the moment when Hugh came into the drawing room where she was receiving her guests. He entered with Emily, Essie Keating, and Rolly Collins, all talking and laughing together, and when Annie

went up to welcome them, he held out his hand, met her eyes
for one brief glance, smiled, and said cheerfully, "It's wonderful
to see you again, Annie. You're looking splendid."

"It's good to see you, Hugh. It's been a long time," she
answered, her voice quite steady and only a little pulse in her
white throat giving away her feeling of joy at seeing him and
hearing his voice. Ed was at her elbow and she turned. "You
haven't met my husband, have you? This is Hugh Deming, Ed,
an old friend of mine."

Ed shook hands heartily, and Hugh stood talking to him
while Annie escaped to her other guests.

Just before supper, at midnight, as the clock began to strike
and the bells outside pealed in the New Year, Annie, who had
sent Rolly Collins to bring her a glass of punch, found herself
standing beside Hugh. Someone began to sing "Auld Lang
Syne" and everyone took it up. Rolly, halfway to the punch
bowl, reached for Marguerite and kissed her. Ed, a little the
worse for having sampled too much of his own brew, bowed
elaborately to Erica Crawford and she laughed and held up her
cheek to be kissed.

Hugh looked at Annie and she met his eyes. He said, "For
Auld Lang Syne, Annie," and put his arms around her and
kissed her lips softly. For a moment she clung to him, weak and
frightened. She forgot she was the hostess in her fine house at
an elegant party, she forgot that this was her bow to society,
that her husband and his wife were in the same room. Hugh's
arms were around her, his lips on hers, nothing had changed, it
was all there, the joy, the ecstasy, the anguish of love. And
from the way he reluctantly let her go, she knew it was there
for him too.

"Happy New Year!" "Happy New Year." The laughter, the
voices, the glasses raised. "Everybody needs more punch,"
cried Ed. "Everybody must drink to the New Year." Emily,
coming smiling up to Hugh to give him her wifely kiss. Rolly
Collins putting a glass into Annie's icy hand. "Happy New
Year!" It was over in a moment, it was over before anyone
noticed, even sharp-eyed Emily, who'd watched her husband
and Annie every time they spoke to each other. Miraculously
she hadn't seen them kiss. Only Erica Crawford had, and she,

remembering the incident of the Nesika Club Ball, was coolly amused.

When they'd toasted the New Year Hugh was standing beside his wife and Ed had his arm around Annie, and the world, that had stopped spinning for that long moment, was back on its axis. Annie, with her head held high, led the way into the dining room where supper was waiting.

After the party was over and Annie lay beside Ed in bed and the lights were off, he patted her arm and murmured, "It was a bang-up party, honey. Couldn't have been better. I was real proud of you." Annie smiled and pressed his hand, but before she went to sleep she thought, I still love Hugh. He loves me. It's as strong as ever. I don't know whether to be glad or sorry. I don't know what to do about it.

The next time she saw Hugh was quite by accident. Emily, determined to keep her promise to herself not to help Annie get into First Hill society, but nevertheless bound by social convention to repay her hospitality, asked her to luncheon at her house with Marguerite, Essie Keating, and a neighbor of no social prominence.

Annie had arrived in her red motorcar, which was the object of much talk and, in Emily's set, amusement as well as envy. She'd told her chauffeur to return for her at four, but when the others were ready to leave he still hadn't come. Marguerite, Essie, and the neighbor, Mrs. Peabody, were within walking distance of home, so they set out. Emily, both amused that Annie should be kept waiting but a bit annoyed at having her on her hands, had excused herself to speak to her maid about dinner, and left Annie sitting with her coat and hat on in the parlor.

Annie had enjoyed the luncheon, though whenever Emily rang for the maid she had a queer feeling that she was an impostor, that she should be out in the kitchen in a white apron and a ruffled cap. She had a feeling that Emily sensed that, too, and made every excuse she could for tinkling the little silver bell by her plate. But still, it had been pleasant, and Essie and Marguerite had been most complimentary about the New Year's Eve party. Now, however, she felt embarrassed and uncomfortable. She wished she hadn't come in the automobile at all and could take a streetcar home. She sat staring at the pictures on the wall, at the flowers in the rug, opening and shutting her new seal leather pocketbook. The bungalow had long since given way to a smart new stucco place in the Denny Blaine district and this was the first time Annie'd been there.

It was a curious feeling, being in Hugh's house. In a way she couldn't think of it as his, so permeated was it by Emily's personality. Yet perhaps he sat in the evening in the very chair she was sitting in. She tried to picture Hugh sitting there with Emily on the settee, sewing or chatting with him. She could not. It had been easy to imagine the gold-and-blue Emily dancing to a Strauss waltz with him, laughing conquettishly up into his eyes, but she couldn't picture them as a married couple, living together, sharing the same house.

The front door opened and she sprang to her feet, thinking it might be John, her chauffeur, but surprised at him for not ringing the bell. She started toward the hall, then stopped short. Hugh was standing there, taking off his coat. He turned and saw her, stared at her in surprise.

"What are you doing here?" he said in a low, queer voice.

"Emily asked me to lunch. I'm waiting for my car."

He came toward her like a man in a dream, his hands held out for hers. She stood quite still, waiting for him, and when he caught her to him hungrily, she gave herself up to his embrace.

"Annie, I've got to see you again," he was whispering against her cheek. "I love you. I'll always love you. Nothing has changed between us, has it?"

"No, Hugh, nothing," she murmured. But it had. They were both married. She had two children. Everything was changed except the one thing that might release them and give them peace.

"Meet me somewhere tomorrow. I have to talk to you. Ever since the night of your party I've thought of nothing but you."

There was a light step in the hall. "Tomorrow in the park at five," he murmured, and let her go. Emily came in from the kitchen just as John rang the doorbell. Annie turned quickly toward her hostess.

"There's my car now, Emily. Thank you for a lovely time.

Good-by." She couldn't trust herself to look at Hugh or speak to him again.

He opened the door for her, and John was there with an umbrella to shield her from the light drizzle, and she, who loved to walk in the rain with no hat, with her face lifted to its damp caress, walked docilely out to the car, with her chauffeur's hand on her elbow, and got into the tonneau. The park, tomorrow at five. Where could he mean but Volunteer Park where they'd met so long ago, where he'd first kissed her? What could she do but meet him there?

It was a dark, overcast day, and the grass and shrubs were an intense, unearthly green. Clouds hung low over the bay, and though it didn't rain, there was a smell of rain in the air. Annie walked to the park with a light step, feeling suddenly young and eager and excited. She remembered the nights when she was a hired girl and used to escape from her little room to the wide lawns, the fragrance and mystery of the park. She remembered the time she met Ned Weaver there and had been so chagrined when Emily and Hugh caught him kissing her. She remembered the first time Hugh had kissed her there, the laughter, her pounding, excited heart, her escape.

The park was almost deserted at five. Children still straggled after their impatient mothers, who urged them on toward home and supper. A few men sat on benches, staring into space or reading newspapers. They glanced up with vacant, incurious stares as Annie walked past.

She found the bench beside the rhododendron bush where they'd met that first night when she was an awkward, romantic girl of seventeen. Now she was twenty-five, a wife and mother, mistress of a fine house, wearing a sealskin jacket, custom-made shoes, soft kid gloves, handmade embroidered underwear. But her heart still ached with the old longing, the scent of grass and heliotrope was still as poignant. Sitting there, waiting for Hugh, she was as frightened and abashed, as fearful that he'd not come, as the day she'd waited so long for him on the dock.

She heard his quick step on the gravel path and sprang to her feet, the blood rushing away from her heart, leaving her weak and trembling.

"Annie, forgive me for being late," he cried, taking her

hands. He held her tightly for a long moment, then he kissed her, held her away to look deeply into her eyes, caught her to him again. At last she stirred in his arms and he let her go. They sat down on the bench and looked at each other.

"I didn't mean to keep you waiting. But I was in a meeting," he said.

"I didn't mind waiting," she said, happy just to be near him, to hear his voice. "It isn't the first time I've waited for you, Hugh."

"If it'd been Emily, she'd have worked herself up to a tantrum," he said, frowning. Then he took her hand. "Annie, I want you to know something. All these years I've been sorry that I let you go."

"But you wouldn't have got ahead so fast in your business, Hugh. You had to think of your career and I was only a hired girl then," she said, her violet eyes steady and candid.

"And now that I've got ahead, what does it mean? Not a damned thing. It hasn't made me happy. I haven't really been happy since we parted. I've cursed myself a thousand times for what I did." His eyes were dark and intense; there were fine lines about his mouth that hadn't been there eight years ago. There was none of the lightness, the mockery, the secret amusement at himself and the world. Yes, he was an unhappy man.

But I've been happy, she thought, I've been happy with Ed and the children. And yet I think I loved him more than he loved me. There wasn't anything I wouldn't have done for him. And I love him now. It hurts me to see him unhappy. There's nothing I wouldn't do to take away that look on his face.

"It's over now, Hugh. You musn't think about it," she murmured, and laid her hand over his tenderly.

"It's not over, Annie. It'll never be over. Ever since that night at your house I've been thinking about it and trying to figure out what to do." He pressed her hands suddenly to his lips. "Annie, I want to marry you."

She drew a sharp breath. "But we're both already married, Hugh."

"I'll divorce Emily. You can divorce your husband."

"Divorce!" she cried in horror. She wouldn't have been so shocked if he'd asked her to become his mistress. "Oh no, Hugh,

we couldn't, we couldn't do that." There was something ugly
and bitter and exposed about the very word. She'd never known
anyone who was divorced. It seemed far worse than infidelity.
Society, the Church, spoke of divorce with horror and condemnation. Even on the waterfront she'd never known of a
divorce. Women dragged out their lives with brutal, drunken
husbands who beat them and let them walk the streets for a
living. Men put up with slovenly, promiscuous wives and took
to the bottle to forget their shame. But there were no divorces.

"Why not?" he cried. "Why is it wrong to divorce a woman
you don't love and never did love so that you can marry the
woman who can make you happy?"

"Emily would die of shame, Hugh. She'd never let you do
it."

"Would she rather have me leave her and take you as my
mistress?" he retorted harshly.

"Yes. Yes, I know she would."

"And what about your husband, Annie? Would he rather
have you ostracized and living in what is commonly called
'shame' than my cherished and lawful wife?"

"Ed would do whatever I asked him to," said Annie slowly,
her voice flat, her face spent and white. "But it would break
his heart."

Hugh got up with an exclamation, began to walk up and
down before her. "Then what are we to do?"

She didn't answer right away. She sat very still, thinking, Oh,
why couldn't this have happened eight years ago? Why
couldn't he have found out how much he needed me when we
were both free? For she knew now that there *was* something
she couldn't do to make him happy. She couldn't break Ed
Bauer's heart. He'd done nothing for which he deserved to
suffer. But they had. They had sinned and this was their punishment.

"We musn't see each other again, Hugh. We must go back
to those who love and trust us and try to make them happy,"
she answered at last, wearily, and she pulled her gloves on,
buttoned them, and got up.

He started to take her in his arms, but the look on her face
stopped him. They stood gazing at each other in silence and
then she said quietly, "Good-by, Hugh."

He said nothing at all. His face was like stone and he stood and watched her go up the path.

Joseph and little Hugh were swinging on the gate, watching for her, when she got home. They both rushed at her at once and caught her around the middle. Their faces were wildly excited and they couldn't get their exciting news out fast enough.

"Darlings, darlings, don't both talk at once," she laughed. "Hugh, you tell part of it and then Joseph may tell the rest."

Little Hugh gave his younger brother a triumphant look. "Daddy's bought us a sailboat."

"A real sailboat, Mother, that you can go sailing in!" cried Joseph.

"It's big enough for all of us to go on and it's got a real cabin," shouted Hugh, jumping up and down.

"It's name is the *Water Sprite* and it's got big white sails!"

"And Daddy's going to teach us to sail it."

"And we're all going out in it tomorrow," finished Joseph in a rush.

Ed, hearing the commotion, came out on the porch, grinning with pleasure. "Well, I guess you've heard the news."

Annie smiled at him. Sometimes she was afraid that the depth and intensity of her feeling for Hugh must show on her face, or in her voice or actions, and that Ed would see it and be hurt. She was almost afraid to look at him now. But with the children jumping all about her, she didn't have to do more than hold up her cheek for his kiss and pat his hand lovingly. At least she'd never played a part with Ed. She gave him the affection and the tenderness that she felt for him freely, and it was honest. It seemed to be all he expected. Looking at him now, with a boy under each arm, she knew she'd made him happy.

They went sailing in the new boat the next day. Ed wasn't an expert sailor, though he'd sailed a bit on the Great Lakes in Wisconsin, so they took along a young fellow from the boatyard to give him pointers. Annie had put up a huge box lunch for them, with beer for the men.

It was a bright day with a spanking breeze that made the waves slap the *Water Sprite's* sides and filled her white sails. The sound was a deep, live blue flecked with whitecaps. Ed was as eager and excited as the boys, who both wanted to steer. Larsen, the sailor, smiled and shook his head. "Not till you've listened to me tell ye how. Come sit here by me and I'll show ye the hang of it."

"But I've been watching you!" cried Hugh impatiently. "I *know* how. All you do is move that stick in your hand and the boat turns any way you want it to."

"Oh, so you know how, young fella," cried Larsen, with a wink at Annie. "Very well. We'll see how much ye know. Come back here by me and take the tiller."

Hugh scrambled to the stern, grasped the tiller, and the boat swerved sharply to leeward. The wind went out of her sails and they flapped loudly against the mast.

"Ready about!" shouted Larsen, and Hugh looked at him wildly, swung the tiller over so far that the wind hit them, and they heeled over close to the water.

"Tell me what to do!" cried Hugh in terror. "She doesn't do what I want her to."

"You ready to learn how to sail, young fella?" asked Larsen quietly, making no move to take the tiller. Annie was trying not to look frantic and Ed was trying not to smile at his son's discomfiture. Joseph was shouting that his brother was going to wreck the boat.

Little Hugh bit his lip, gave his mother a direct, quick look, and nodded, his chin set to keep it from quivering. "Yes, sir."

"Good enough. And on a boat it's 'Aye, aye, sir,'" drawled Larsen, taking the tiller and expertly setting the boat right again.

"Aye, aye, sir," said Hugh humbly, and sat very still, his bright blue eyes fixed on the sailor's face while he explained the handling of the tiller.

At first Annie sat in the bow, loving the wind and spray on her face, but after lunch she began to feel very nervous and uneasy, and descended to the cockpit. At each dip of the boat she felt worse. Good heavens, she thought, I'm going to be seasick. She'd never been seasick in her life. She tried to catch Ed's eye to signal him her distress, but he was leaping about, pulling ropes and shouting to Larsen. Suddenly she could stand it no more. To her shame, she was violently sick over the side.

They put in at the boatyard and Ed insisted upon taking her

home. She protested, not wanting to spoil the day for him and the boys, but he was firm. He wouldn't let her take a streetcar and it was John's day off, so the car wasn't there.

A week later she understood why she'd been sick. Dr. Fuller told her she was pregnant again. She didn't know how to feel about it. Her first thought was thankfulness that she'd told Hugh they couldn't see each other again, and that she'd rejected any relationship with him. To go to him carrying Ed's child would have been unthinkable. Then she thought, So I have to go through it all again, the three months of nausea, the heaviness, then the awful pain. But all at once she felt warm and happy at the knowledge that she was carrying a new life. She told Ed that she was very happy about the new baby and he kissed her tenderly and said he was too. "I hope it's a girl this time, honey." She smiled. "It doesn't matter. Whichever it is, we'll love it."

But now she certainly couldn't join the family sailing parties. And though Ed protested that they wouldn't leave her alone, she knew that he was longing to go. Sailing was becoming a passion with him, and the boys could hardly wait to be on the water again. So she insisted that they go without her and resigned herself to spending every week end alone. It was no hardship for her. She had always liked to be alone and now she had sewing to do for the new baby, her fine house to run, an occasional friend to have in for tea. Marguerite was in Europe with Mrs. Crawford, but Emily dropped in now and then, as if she were impelled by some inner compulsion to keep track of the woman she feared and patronized. Annie didn't know what, exactly, Emily felt for her, but she knew it was not the simple, frank affection that Marguerite had. Sometimes she wondered whether Emily knew anything about Hugh and her.

Now that she was going to have another baby, her longing for Hugh, the anguish that their recent meetings had brought her, was pushed into the background. It was as if nature or God had sent her the new life to crowd out her yearnings, to turn her back from the impossible and dangerous path of desire, and set her straight on her purpose in life again. She spent the days Ed and the boys were sailing happily and quietly and was always at home to welcome them when they came back, tanned, weary, and ravenous.

The boys had been hounding their father to take them on an overnight cruise. They couldn't bear not to use the wonderful little cabin with the four neat bunks. At last he gave in. They were to be gone Saturday and Sunday, to sleep on the boat, to cook their own meals in the tiny galley, to sail across to Vashon Island and anchor in one of the little inlets.

"Are you sure it's safe, dear?"

"Lord, yes, Annie. The sound this far down is safe as a lake. Besides, she's a seaworthy craft and the boys and I have become really good sailors. Even Larsen says so. And the boat-yard has given me charts."

"Well, take care, and if a storm blows up, you make for the shore," she warned. "Don't try to bluster it out, mind!"

He laughed at her, kissed her good-by, and loaded himself down with supplies. Joseph and Hugh pattered after him, their arms piled to their eyes with blankets and food. Annie saw them to the car, smiling and waving, but as the red car disappeared around the corner, she felt uneasy. They'd never attempted such a long sail before. They'd never been away all night. She felt lonesome going back into the big, quiet house. All at once she realized there'd be no way of knowing they were safe until they got back.

John brought the automobile back, reported the sound was "just a bit choppy, mum. Enough wind to give them a good sail," and that he'd stayed and watched them get under way, the boys working like beavers as crew for their father. "They're right good little sailors, too, mum," he chuckled. Annie wished she'd driven down to see them off. For about an hour she was nervous, going to the window to look at the sky, worrying whenever the sun went under a cloud.

But finally the sun came out full and strong, and though there was a brisk breeze that rustled the lacquered dark green madroña leaves outside her bedroom window, her uneasiness vanished and she told herself it was her condition that made her so nervous.

She was busy all day, working on curtains for the baby's room, since she'd decided the boys had a right to the nursery and that it would be better for the baby to sleep in the little sewing room next to Ed's and hers. Already there was a charming bassinette in readiness, draped in long ruffles of dotted swiss, lined with pink satin with a pink satin bow on the canopy. Few of the boys' baby clothes would do for the new baby: they had seen hard wear and many washings in their less affluent days. She and the maid, a pretty, jolly Irish girl with black hair and a lively tongue, hung the curtains when they were finished and then Nora made her lie down on the chaise and drink a cup of tea.

"Ye mustn't overdo, mum. 'Tis the early months that are the delicate ones, my mither used to say. She lost her first two hoein' p'tatoes when she was but three months along."

So Annie lay on the chaise, drank the tea Nora brought her, sewed for a while on a tiny tucked dress, and then went to sleep.

Nora wakened her for dinner, but she couldn't sit in the big empty dining room alone. She asked to have a tray brought up and she ate in her room, feeling queer and lost. After dinner she tried to read, but she was too restless to get any sense out of the words and sewing made her head ache. She went into the nursery and looked at the two little empty beds and a great pain came to her heart. Her eyes filled with tears and she went out, closing the door. Suddenly she realized it was the first time her babies had been away from her all night. She wandered up and down the house, with the ache in her heart.

She couldn't understand it. "I've never been a doting mother, afraid to let my kids out of my sight. It's good for them to be independent and free. Besides, they're with their father. He'll take care of them." A rush of gratitude for Ed's strength and protectiveness, for his devotion to the boys, swept away the uneasiness and the ache and she went to bed at last and slept peacefully. Ed would take care of them.

The next morning was dark and cloudy. The sun tried vainly to come out all day but the clouds prevailed and toward afternoon the wind came up, a strong sou'wester. Annie telephoned the boatyard, but they told her not to worry; there might be a storm later in the day, but other boats were still going out. Ed had promised to be back for Sunday dinner at six. But at six dinner was ready and they hadn't come. Annie telephoned again. There had been no word of the *Water Sprite* and all the other boats had come in. The proprietor's voice was calm and soothing, but Annie sensed that he was disturbed. She paced up and down her room, listening to the wind and the rain that had now begun to spatter against the windows, until she could bear it no more. She ordered John to bring the car up and to drive her to the boatyard. Nora begged to go along, frightened out of her Irish wits by Annie's white, tense face, her enormous eyes, nearly black now with fear and pain. All the way to the waterfront she grasped her hand tightly, but Annie wasn't even aware of her.

At the boatyard the proprietor came out to meet her, his face grave, his manner solicitous. He took her inside and she sat amid the sailing gear, ropes and spars, sails and anchors, while he and Larsen tried to minimize the danger to her. "Now, ma'am, the Coast Guard's been sent out to look for them and they'll be towing them in before long, I'm sure."

"Sure, ma'am. Probably they had a busted halyard or maybe even the mast went in the wind. But Mr. Bauer's a good sailor. He'll bring her through it."

She said nothing, only looked from one face to the other and nodded. Then she got up and paced, peering out the windows, until the men were nearly crazy. Larsen went outside in the rain, leaving his boss and John and Nora to try to talk to her or get her to rest. Finally she went outside herself, deaf to their entreaties, and stood on the dock with her cape blowing out behind her, the rain and wind lashing her face and body, plastering her hair to her head.

It was dawn by the time the Coast Guard cutter got in. Annie stood rigid as a statue, unable to speak or move while the men in slickers and sou'westers climbed out of the cabin and onto the dock. They looked at her and then buried their necks in their slickers and stamped into the boatyard office. Two men came last, carrying a man wrapped in blankets. Annie gave a cry and started forward.

"Ed!" she cried. One of the men nodded. She couldn't ask him the question, but he answered for her.

"He's alive, ma'am, but he'll need a doctor."

Annie's gaze went back to the cutter, but there were no more figures swathed in blankets being taken off. She ran after the men carrying Ed, plucked at their arms. "But the boys, my two little boys? Where are they? Didn't you bring them too?"

The men looked queer, as if they were going to be sick. They shook their heads. "This was the only one we picked up, ma'am. He was hanging onto a broken spar. That was all that was left of the boat."

Nora and John came running out of the boatyard office in time to see Annie pitch face forward onto the dock.

Chapter XIX

The nurse nodded to the man in the hall, her face stern with pity. "You can go in now for a few minutes. She's awake. But she may not talk to you. Remember, she's had a great shock and she's very weak after the miscarriage. Don't tire her."

Ed shook his head and walked woodenly into his wife's room. She was lying on her back with her arms fallen limply onto the counterpane, and her eyes were closed. Her red hair, parted in the middle and braided in two heavy braids, gave her the look of a little girl. Her face was chalk-white.

He stood in an agony of awkwardness, staring at her, swallowing and trying to speak her name. Her eyes fluttered open, but she didn't turn her head, she stared like a sleepwalker at the wall.

"Annie," he groaned, but she gave no sign that she had heard. Only her fingers began to pluck at the counterpane. Ed, his face ravaged with grief, stumbled to the bed, went down on his knees, and pressed his cheek on her hand. It was icy cold and it lay like a stone under his flesh. Suddenly he burst into terrible, heartbreaking sobs. His shoulders shook convulsively and his tears poured onto her hand.

She sighed and tried to pull her hand away, but he caught it in both of his, kissed it desperately. "Annie, Annie, speak to me. Don't hate me. I can't stand that too. It wasn't my fault. I tried to save them, but they were swept away. I'd a million times rather it'd been me—you know that, don't you, Annie? You don't blame me, do you? Annie, speak to me."

Her lips parted and tears dropped slowly down her cheeks.

"My boys," she whispered. "My little boys. Both gone. Both drowned."

Choking, Ed got to his feet and stumbled out of the room, his face contorted and working. The nurse gave him a swift, anxious glance and then hurried back to her patient. Ed groped his way downstairs and into the dining room. There was a decanter of whisky on the sideboard and he poured himself half a tumblerful, drank it slowly, one hand clutching the buffet for support. "She hates me," he mumbled. "She blames me for being alive when the boys are dead."

When the whisky in his glass was gone the sharp pain in his heart was eased a bit. He filled his glass again and went into the library and sat down, but the white, terrified faces of his boys just before the wave swept them overboard and Annie's unrelenting eyes kept flashing into his mind to torture him. He drank the second glass of whisky in a few gulps, choking as the fiery liquid burned his throat. When the nurse came downstairs, intending to suggest that he take a sedative, he was slumped in his chair. She hurried across the room, fearing a heart attack, but as she bent over him she smelled the reek of liquor and saw the empty glass on the floor. With a pitying glance she shook her head and went out, closing the door so the servants would not see him like that.

Every night for three weeks he came home, went up to his wife's room, stood looking at her, tried to talk quietly so as not to upset her, found himself gripped by a passionate need for her to absolve him, to tell him she loved him. And always the pain and bewilderment and loss sent him to the only thing that gave him any ease—whisky. Oh, blessed release from agony, guilt, grief—the warmth flooding his body, softening the loneliness and pain, the warmth and forgetfulness stealing over his brain, blotting out the fearful pictures of the storm and the lost boys. By the time Annie was well enough to get up and come downstairs Ed was drinking himself into a stupor every night.

Annie was unaware of what she had done to her husband. The night he had wept by her bed she had been scarcely conscious of him at all and she didn't know what she had said. Held in the trauma of her grief and shock, she had been conscious of no one and of nothing but her pain. Then as she gradually emerged, she began to wonder why Ed had just stood there, staring at her, muttering a few stiff words, asking her how she felt. She began to long for him to hold her close, to kiss her, to give her back the warmth and strength she had lost. But when she tried to speak to him, to gaze at him appealingly, he turned quickly and went out of the room.

The first night she came down for dinner she put on a pale green negligee. She couldn't wear black in the house and she felt it would only make it harder for poor Ed, who must have had a dreadful time of it while she was so ill. She even hoped it might make him feel better to see her in something pretty and soft. But he gave her an odd glance as she came down the long, beautiful, winding staircase. He was standing in the hall with a glass in his hand.

"Aren't you glad to see me downstairs at last?" she asked, trying to smile at him.

"Sure. It's fine." He smiled queerly at her and suddenly she knew that he was slightly drunk. "Mighty fine." At first she felt a little sense of shock, then she thought, What difference does it make? After all, a drink or two probably makes him feel better.

During dinner she tried to talk to him and to make a pretense of eating though her own heart was numb. She knew she would never get over the loss of her two sons.

This is the time that I wish I loved Ed the way I love Hugh, she thought, staring at his brooding, darkened face across the table. If we were really lovers, we could share each other's grief. If I loved him as I should, I would know the right word to say.

He hardly touched his food, answered her few forced remarks in monosyllables and, as soon as the coffee was served, disappeared into the library.

Annie wandered about through the rooms, feeling oddly light-bodied and strange, after so many days in bed, shut in between the walls of her bedroom. The house was clean and orderly, but it lacked warmth; the rooms seemed dead and empty. They were silent—oh, God, so silent. Not since the night Ed and the boys went for their tragic cruise had she gone into the nursery or the little bedroom she had been fixing up for her new baby. But as she stood in the drawing room she was painfully conscious of the two empty rooms upstairs, the empty beds. Someday she would have to go in, force herself to dispose of the furniture, the clothes, the toys.

Now, she said to herself, clenching her fists so hard that the nails bit into her flesh, now is the time to do it. The longer I wait, the harder it will be. I must do it now, tonight.

Like a sleepwalker, she turned and glided out of the room. At the stair she stopped, sudden weakness overtaking her. Her knees felt as if they'd buckle under her, a wave of sickness swept over her. I can't do it alone, she thought. I have to have help and support. She went to the library, pushed open the door.

"Ed," she whispered.

He was slumped in a big leather chair and he turned slowly to look at her, his face heavy and unresponsive.

"You have to help me, Ed," she went on, pressing her hand to her heart to ease the sharpness of its pain. "I'm going up to the boys' room."

A spasm contorted his features. "For God's sake, why?" he muttered.

"It's got to be done sometime. If I wait—I don't know if I can ever do it. I have to get their things out of there—the beds, everything. If I don't I can't stay in this house." Her voice shook and it was an effort to stand erect.

"You're doing this to torture me!" he cried, gripping the arms of the chair. "You hate me, don't you? You want to punish me. My God, don't you think it's punishment enough for me to be alive when they're——" He broke off in a sob and she stared at him, not understanding his violence.

"What do you mean, Ed? Why should I hate you?" she said quietly.

"Don't pretend. Don't try to cover it up. I know how you feel. You trusted me to take care of them. I came back and they didn't. You'll never forgive me for that, will you?" His voice was thick and uncontrolled. She stared at him, shocked into coldness. He's drunk. He's babbling like a baby, just when I need him. Then suddenly his words penetrated her mind. Is that how I feel? Do I blame him? Is that why I can't reach him, say the word, make the gesture that will release him from his feeling of guilt?

She made a move toward him. In her mind she knew that she

must do it. She saw herself kneeling beside him, pressing her face against his, murmuring the words of comfort and love and salvation. She put out a hand toward him, her face white with pity, but he wasn't looking at her. He tried to rise, fell back, and his eyes closed. His breathing was heavy, stertorous—he was dead drunk.

Very slowly she moved out of the room. She felt completely alone. Instead of trembling as she had before when she thought she could count on his strength, she walked erect and still as stone. Her body felt like a rock. Her spirit was bleak, comfortless, but certain. It had to be done tonight and she must do it alone.

Dry-eyed, she dismantled the nursery. When all the clothes, books, pictures, toys were packed in boxes, she rang for John to come and take them to the attic. "Take the beds and the bureau, too, John. Tomorrow I'll call a secondhand dealer and sell them," she said in a flat, matter-of-fact voice.

John gave her a queer look but said nothing. He quickly removed all evidence that there had ever been two little boys in the house.

"I'll take care of the baby's room tomorrow," she said, and with the slow, fumbling step of a very old woman she crept downstairs. She went into the library and looked at Ed. He was sleeping soundly, snoring. His face was relaxed, vulnerable. But, for now, for as long as the liquor had effect, he was at peace.

Poor Ed, she thought as she went upstairs, not to bed, but to sit at the window, looking down at the street, wondering what was going to happen to them now. She felt no condemnation for him, only pity and a sense of futility. There was no way she could help him. She didn't love him enough, and only a deep, enduring love could reach out to him and pull him back to life and reality.

The days went by and Annie's strength returned, her eagerness for life flowed slowly back to her. The numbness that had bound her heart ebbed away and left pain and loss in its place, but she refused to bow to it. She sent Nora off on a vacation and took care of the big house herself. Though the house was always well kept and clean she worked day after day, washing woodwork and windows, airing bedding, so that at night she was bone-tired, tired enough to sleep.

Ed hardly noticed her any more, scarcely touched the good meals she cooked for him while Nora was away. He was sinking deeper and deeper into himself, into the abyss of grief and self-condemnation he had dug for himself. Annie tried several times to get him to go out with her, hoping to get back their old companionship, but it was no good.

One night after dinner she followed him into the library, put her hand on his arm as he went to the bookcase where he always kept a bottle of whisky. He turned slowly and looked at her, his eyes remote.

"Ed," she said brightly, smiling at him, "let's go out somewhere tonight. Let's go to the Moore Theater. There's a new stock company playing there now with a young actress, Laurette Taylor, who's all the rage."

He took out the bottle of whisky, poured himself a drink, held up the bottle, looked inquiringly at her. She shook her head. "Please, Ed, did you hear what I've been saying? Haven't you been listening to me at all?"

"Sure I heard," he muttered, frowning at her. "I'm not deaf. I don't want to go anywhere tonight or any night. I don't want to see some damn-fool actress mooning and prancing around on a stage. Just let me alone, can't you?" He tossed off his drink, poured another.

"Ed." Her voice was steady and low, but her eyes held his with dark, pleading intensity. "You're drinking too much and it's not good. I know how you feel about the boys. Don't you suppose I feel as bad as you do? But it won't bring them back for you to drink yourself to death."

He met her eyes, then looked away. "Why shouldn't I drink myself to death if I want to? It's as good a way as any. I know what you're thinking. You're thinking I'm no good. I killed the boys and I'm not man enough to take it standing up. You hate me like hell, don't you, Annie?"

"No, Ed. Oh no—I don't hate you," she cried, and the quick tears sprang to her eyes, softened now by pity. She tried to put her arms around him, to comfort him, to summon up the old affection she'd once known for him, but he pushed her away. "It wasn't your fault about the boys. Nobody blames you, Ed."

He laughed bitterly. "Well, I do. I blame myself and you do

too. I know. I can see it in your eyes, even though you try to hide it. You told me when I married you that you didn't love me. Now you hate me."

"No. No, I don't hate you. Please believe me, Ed." She followed him as he paced about the room, but he wouldn't turn to her. "How could I hate you? You're my husband."

Suddenly he faced her. His face was oddly shining. "Do you love me? Answer me that. Do you love me, Annie?"

She stood perfectly still, staring into his bloodshot eyes. Her heart felt like a stone. If I could say yes, she thought, if I could make him believe that I do, perhaps it would save him. "Oh, Ed, I—you know I——" She couldn't say the words, though all her being ached to be able to say them. "Oh, my dear," she whispered, putting out her hands blindly.

He took her hands, gazed intently into her tear-stained face. "No, you don't love me. It's not your fault. You've been a good wife. You gave me two fine children and I took them out and drowned them."

"Ed—oh, Ed, please don't feel like that." She swayed toward him, but he dropped her hands so suddenly she almost fell.

He went to the bookcase, poured and drank another glass of whisky, and without a word walked out of the room. She heard him going unsteadily upstairs, stumbling once or twice, and she had a sudden, wild instinct to go after him, but she had no strength, she was engulfed in a tide of apathy and weakness. Trembling and sick at heart, she sat down on the divan, leaned back, and closed her eyes. She did not know how long she sat there, not asleep, but in a state almost of suspended consciousness. The house was empty and silent and all the fine furniture she had chosen so happily with Marguerite stood about like ghosts. She opened her eyes and stared at the room, remembering how once she had thought that if she had a grand house on the First Hill she would be perfectly happy.

Suddenly she was on her feet, the apathy gone, her heart pounding. From Ed's room upstairs had come the sound, the unmistakable sound of a shot being fired. "Ed!" she cried, and panic swept her out of the library into the hall.

At the foot of the beautiful winding staircase she paused. "Ed?" she called in a strange, clear voice. Then, as she ran up the stairs, she began to scream, "Ed—Ed—Ed!"

The door to his bedroom was locked and though she beat on it until her fists were bruised, it would not open.

"Is anything wrong, Mrs. Bauer?" It was John, coming in from his room off the kitchen. He stood below her in the hall, looking up the stairs, his good Irish face puckered in concern.

"Come up quick, John. Mr. Bauer—his door's locked and I —I heard a shot."

"Jesus, Mary, Joseph," breathed the chauffeur devoutly, and raced up the stairs, two steps at a time. It took him only a few minutes to break open the door, splintering the dark wood. Ed was lying across his bed and John took one look, then pushed Annie toward the hall.

"Don't look at him, mum. For God's sake don't look," he cried in horror. He picked up Ed's dressing gown from a chair and threw it quickly over the figure on the bed.

"Is he dead?" Her voice was flat and toneless. She stared into John's ashen face.

He nodded. "He's dead. Best go downstairs, mum. There's nothing you can do for him now, poor soul."

On the floor beside the bed Annie saw the hunting rifle Ed had been so proud of, so pleased at her giving it to him for Christmas last year. Her eyes couldn't leave it as she backed slowly toward the door and fell unconscious in the hall.

The day of Ed's funeral the sun shone for the first time in a week. There had been fog, rain, and wind the first part of August, which was unusual for Seattle, as late summer was apt to be clear and sunny. That morning the sky was overcast until eleven and then the clouds rolled away like a curtain, revealing the clear blue and sunshine that sparkled on the maple leaves outside Annie's bedroom window.

The funeral was at two in the afternoon and at twelve a florist's boy brought a dozen red roses from Emily and Hugh Deming with a card in Emily's dashing hand:

"Our thoughts are with you in this time of sorrow. Deeply regret that we cannot attend the funeral. Leaving today for a cruise to Victoria with some Eastern business associates of Hugh's.

> "Love,
> "Emily"

Nora put the roses in a vase and brought them up to Annie's room. Annie looked at them while she was dressing in the black silk dress she'd had made after the boys died. Why did people send lovely, rich, alive flowers to houses where death had struck? It seemed like a mockery. Or was it a symbol that life went on, that life triumphed even over death and dissolution? At any rate, Emily's roses and her note left Annie cold. It was merely a social gesture that meant nothing. If she or Hugh had bothered to come and see her before they left on their cruise, that would have meant more than all the roses in the world.

John drove Annie to the funeral parlor and Nora, back from her vacation and shocked into white-faced silence by the tragedy in the house that had had its share of tragedy, sat in the back with her mistress, sniveling into her handkerchief. Annie sat erect and dry-eyed, but her face was drawn and haggard and her great violet eyes were sunken and lusterless.

Since Ed had been a Protestant and had never embraced Annie's faith, though he'd agreed to bring their children up as Catholics so that Annie could be married by her priest, the service was read by the Episcopal rector of St. Mark's. The Carltons had belonged to that parish and it was the only non-Roman church Annie knew much about. So far as she knew Ed had never belonged to any church, though he'd mentioned once that his mother had been a Methodist. But Annie, remembering the coldness and sterility of the service she'd gone to at the Methodist church as a child when her sister Mae sang in the choir, decided against it.

Because Ed was a suicide the service was not the full Episcopal burial service, as the rector of St. Mark's explained, but it was simple and dignified and the words "I am the Resurrection and the Life" kept coming back to Annie. Ed had been a good man and she couldn't believe that the Lord would turn His back on him because, out of his grief and desperation, he had taken his own life. Don't punish Ed for it, dear Lord, she prayed as the clergyman read a psalm, it wasn't his fault. If anyone's to blame, it's me. I didn't love him enough. It's my sin, Lord God, not Ed's. I'll take his punishment.

When the service was over and the casket had been carried out to the hearse that was to drive it to the cemetery, Annie

looked at the handful of people filing solemnly out of the
funeral parlor. The two clerks from Ed's grocery store (the
store had been closed all day out of respect for its deceased
owner), several men from his lodge (they'd wanted to have it
a lodge funeral but Annie had refused), the owner of a whole-
sale grocery house where Ed had traded, an old crone in shabby
clothes whom Annie suddenly recognized with a shock as Mrs.
Bellows, who'd worked for her mother at the Nugget, and Jim
Petley, thin and gray as a wraith—that was all, except for John
and Nora. Not a soul from the First Hill, though Rolly Collins
and Marguerite Brookes had sent handsome floral pieces.

They were glad enough to come to our house and eat our
food, thought Annie with sudden, sharp bitterness. But neither
Ed nor I really belonged to their world, after all. They didn't
even think enough of him to spend half an hour by his casket,
praying for the repose of his poor, tortured soul. Perhaps they
were shocked because he killed himself and didn't think it
proper to show him the courtesy to come to his funeral. Not
one of them came forward to help me, to comfort me, to stand
by my side.

She had not wept since the night Ed died, nor during the
service, but as she walked toward her car, leaning on John's
kind, strong arm (the arm, after all, of a hired servant, but more
loyal than any of her friends), the tears stung her throat. They
were tears for Ed, who had been snubbed by the people she
once thought so fine.

At the car Jim Petley was waiting for her, his thin face
solemn and concerned. "I'd like to ride out to the cemetery
with you, Annie," he murmured, "if it's all right with you."

She put out her hand impulsively, grateful for his kindness.
He was part of her childhood, part of the wild, free waterfront
days, and he'd come to Ed's funeral, not as a newspaperman,
she was sure, but as her old friend. "Thank you, Jim," she
whispered in a choked voice. "I'd be glad to have you."

He took her hand and held it all the way out to the cemetery
and on the way back Annie leaned her head on his thin shoulder
and wept for Ed, for her lost children, for all her fine dreams
that had turned to dust. He held her quietly and went up to the
house with her, sat awhile in the library.

"You'll want a drink, Jim," she said with a wan smile, taking off her hat and gloves and giving them to Nora, who fluttered helplessly about her. "And Nora will make me some tea."

Jim fixed himself a drink and Annie sat on the divan, sipping gratefully the hot, strong tea Nora brought her. The storm of weeping was spent and she was exhausted, but glad that the ordeal was over. It was good to be home, drinking tea and talking to Jim, who, now that she had herself under control again, tried to be cheerful.

"You were mighty good to come today," she said. "It's been years since I've seen you. I wouldn't have expected you to come."

Jim ran his hand over his unruly hair, thinner now and no longer brown. "When the story about your husband's death came into the office, I was shocked. It seemed such a dirty shame, coming so soon after—your other trouble. I was tickled pink when you got your ma's money and moved up here. I said to myself, That redheaded Jordan kid always had spunk. She knew what she wanted, and by God, I'm glad she got it."

Annie smiled sadly. "Yes, I knew what I wanted and I got it. That is—part of it. But I guess I made a mistake, Jim. I don't belong on the First Hill."

"Hell, Annie, you belong wherever you want to be," protested Jim. "You're as good as anyone."

She shook her head. "I thought that, too, once. But today at Ed's funeral I knew I was wrong. Not one of our First Hill friends was there. They sent flowers and regrets, but you came."

There was a silence and Jim finished his drink, filled his pipe. "What will you do now, Annie?"

She had been staring into space and she lifted her head and looked at him gravely. "That's what I've been thinking about just now, Jim. I'm going to sell this house and go away. I've always wanted to see something of the world. I think maybe I'll go to San Francisco for a while."

He nodded. "A good idea. You ought to get away from here until you've had time to get over all that's happened. But I'll bet you'll come back to Seattle, Annie."

"I don't know, Jim. Right now I feel as if I never wanted to see this town again."

He got up and put his hand on her shoulder. "You'll be back. You've got Puget Sound salt in your blood. But wherever you go, I'll be plugging for you. Good luck, kiddy. Remember, they can't keep a redhead down. Not a Seattle redhead."

Annie's boat sailed for San Francisco at five of a brisk, blue October afternoon. She took a taxi down to the docks, since the car had been sold, and John, along with Nora, had gone to a new job in Tacoma. She was sailing on the *North Star Queen*, and in spite of her loneliness and the knot of homesickness that had already tightened in her breast, she was conscious of a thrill of pleasure at taking a trip on one of Hugh's ships.

She reached the waterfront early and, after her baggage had been checked, walked along the docks till she came to Hugh's office, a block or so away. She had no intention of going in, she only wanted to take a last look at the place where Hugh went every day, the office that housed the dream he had made come true for himself.

I may never see it again, she was thinking, or Hugh. Perhaps I'll never come back, never see the gulls circling over the harbor or smell the tar and fish and salt of the waterfront.

Clerks were still at their desks in the North Star office and as she stared through the window one of them glanced up and smiled at her. All at once she was swept by an intense longing to see Hugh once more. He hadn't come to Ed's funeral. He hadn't come to see her afterward either. But he was still Hugh and she couldn't leave Seattle and not say good-by to him. If he knew I was going away, he'd come to see me, she thought.

With her heart beating fast and her eyes very bright, she went into the outer office and gave her name to a young man at a desk who glanced appreciatively at her handsome, well-dressed figure and asked her to have a chair while she waited. The expensive furniture and the original oil paintings of Alaskan and Puget Sound scenery on the walls made her cheeks flush with pride at these evidences of Hugh's success.

The young man came back at once, followed by Hugh, who clasped Annie's hand tightly and kept it as he led her into his private office.

"Annie, this is wonderful!" he cried when the door was shut and he stood looking down at her eagerly.

"I can't stay but a minute, Hugh," she said, smiling at him, glad to see that he looked well, that his lean face was tanned and keen-looking. "I just dropped in to say good-by."

"Good-by?" His own smile faded. "Where are you going?"

"To San Francisco first. Then—I don't know. Maybe I'll travel a bit."

"I was shocked to hear about Ed, Annie," he stammered, color touching his cheeks. "I meant to come to see you—Emily and I both did—but—I've been working like a dog."

She made a little gesture. "I knew it must be that, Hugh. I've sold the house and I don't know when I'll be back, if ever."

The telephone rang and Hugh took down the receiver. "You'll have to call me back, Tom," he said briskly. "I'm busy right now." He replaced the receiver. "Let's go somewhere and have a cup of coffee, so we can talk. That damn phone has been ringing all day."

"There isn't time, Hugh. I'm sailing at five." She flashed him a proud look. "On your boat, the *North Star Queen*."

"Then I'll walk down to the pier with you and see you off," he cried, grabbing his hat from the hatstand in the corner and taking her arm. "I wish you'd let me know before and I'd have seen that you had the best stateroom aboard, and flowers—all the fixin's."

Outside, as they walked slowly, arm in arm, along the dock, with the wind off the bay in their faces, Annie smiled up at him. "I almost didn't come to see you today, Hugh. But when I walked past the North Star office, I knew I just couldn't go away without saying good-by."

He stopped and looked down at her, his eyes dark, his mouth stern. "You wouldn't have left without telling me, Annie. That would have been hard to take."

"Would it have mattered that much, Hugh?" She met his eyes gravely, with no coquetry in her searching, honest gaze.

His hand tightened on her arm. "You know it would, Annie."

There was just time for him to put her on the boat, see that her bags were settled in her stateroom before the warning whistle blew.

"I'll have to get off now," he said in a queer, lost voice. They looked at each other strangely. "Good-by, Annie Jordan," he whispered, and he took her in his arms and kissed her. Then he was gone and Annie stood for a moment in the stateroom with her hands pressed against her breast.

There was the rumble and throb of the ship's engines, the churn of water as the boat began to back away from the pier. Annie ran out of the stateroom and out on deck. She clasped the rail with taut fingers and stared down at the crowd waving good-by from the dock.

Hugh stood to one side, by himself, and his face was lifted toward the deck of the steamer. Across the widening gap of water his eyes met Annie's in a look of longing and despair. They didn't wave or call out to each other, but as long as she could see him he stood there, with his face turned to her. Then the boat gave another long blast, the propellers churned the water into foam, and with the dignity and grace of a queen the ship swung slowly away from the harbor and headed toward the sea.

"Good-by, my darling," whispered Annie. "If I never see you again, God bless you."

Chapter XX

Nineteen-seventeen and Liberty Bond rallies in Pioneer Square. Four-minute speakers between acts at the Pantages Theater. "Keep the Home Fires Burning" and "There's a Long, Long Trail." Camp Lewis overflowing with ardent young men from the classrooms and athletic fields of the University of Washington. Shipyards paying such fabulous wages that riveters could and did pay twelve dollars for silk shirts.

The war brought boom times to Seattle, and the North Star, which had been about to expire, its throat cut by competition, suddenly came to life again.

Hugh and Emily were swept up on a tide of prosperity. They built a new house in Laurelhurst. Hugh bought a yacht. Marcia was sent to St. Nicholas School for Girls. They lived high, wide, and handsome. Hugh, being engaged in an essential industry and suffering from a slight heart murmur, didn't go to war. Besides, he was unimpressed by the propaganda of hysterical patriotism. He had developed a materialism, a cynicism, that would have shocked Annie.

But Hugh hadn't seen Annie since the day he'd put her on the boat for San Francisco and all that he had been able to find out about her was that Marguerite Brookes had seen her in San Francisco at the Fairmont Hotel, where she'd been living after traveling abroad for a year. That had been five years ago, and since then no one had heard from her. No one, except Hugh, seemed to care what had happened to her. She'd simply dropped out of sight and been forgotten.

Aside from a faint nostalgia, an inexplicable tug at his heart whenever he heard the lonesome whistle of a steamer, Hugh rarely thought about Annie now.

He was a good businessman, but when the North Star had had its back against the wall he'd known a strange apathy, a desire to cut and run, let the whole thing go to smash. He really had no passion for success, like the other Seattle businessmen, whose vigor, audacity, and drive had put the Puget Sound country on the map.

He had his business, which he conducted with a kind of academic astuteness, as if he were playing a game of chess. He had Marcia, who was a constant delight to him, particularly since he found more of himself in her than of Emily. They went on tours of the waterfront and the little girl loved, as he did, the smell of the rotting old piers, the greenish water slipping under the docks, the screaming, greedy, avid-eyed gulls, the battered, rakish island steamers with their bilge-stained hulls.

In a way, he had Emily. If there was no passion or romance in their relationship, at least, over the years, there had developed a kind of tolerance, a bond of living together. Emily was a good housewife, she ran his home to perfection, she entertained the right people, she wore the right clothes, she had the right friends. And as she grew older, she developed a humorous tenderness for the man who had destroyed forever her immature, unreal, adolescent dreams of romance. As a matter of fact, Emily was not the woman for romance. It takes fire, intensity, idealism, and a kind of blind unawareness of others to accept romance. Emily was cut out for flirtations and beaux; she was the perennial belle, too absorbed in her own success to be swept up in the desperate whirlwind of romantic love.

As she got older she grew a little too plump and then all her energies and ardor were marshaled to reduce her weight, regain the willowy figure that had floated in white net through cotillion after cotillion. These things absorbed her thoughts, the preservation of her looks, the upbringing of her child, and the maintenance of her social position. Hugh was important to her because he was necessary to the latter. When he seemed to be paying too much attention to other women at parties, it wasn't because she was afraid of losing his love that her jealousy flared and drove her to nagging him.

The war boom gradually began to slough off, but what really ruined Hugh's steamship line, along with most of Seattle's shipping, were the strikes. They started with a general strike in 1919 and from then on, from time to time, the harbor was the scene, not of the bustling, prosperous activity of earlier days, but of idle ships, idle men loitering on the docks, in the streets, in the waterfront dives where, in spite of Prohibition, a longshoreman or a seaman could get his beer or gin.

Often there were picket lines, fights, ugly mobs, occasionally a stabbing or cracked skulls. Settlements would be made reluctantly by the ruggedly individualist shipowners, who hated to budge an inch to labor's demands, but who saw cargoes spoiling, trade dwindling, the railroads getting the California passengers. The ships would move again, cargoes would be loaded and unloaded. But there was always the uneasiness that lies behind a truce. The owners were wary, worried, waiting for the next sign of unrest. The men were edgy, ready to strike at the first sign of infringement of their hard-won rights.

It was an unhealthy time for the waterfront, and this ill-health seeped upward to the rest of Seattle's business, since shipping was the heart and pulse beat of the city's life and growth.

The North Star had really only got back solidly on its feet again when the strikes began. For several years it didn't begin to feel the pinch, but by 1924 profits were way off and the once spic-and-span fleet of island steamers was beginning to look weather-beaten and dingy. Hugh's captains kept complaining about the lack of maintenance, the necessity for dry-docking and overhauling. But there wasn't the money to make repairs, except the most urgently needed ones. Worn-out boilers slowed down running time, blew up, injuring engineers and stokers. One ship, leaking badly, had to put in at Port Townsend for repairs. Paint peeled from the once trim hulls, passengers complained about the chipped china in the dining salons.

Finally, in 1925, Hugh was faced with the necessity for raising twenty thousand dollars or going into receivership. Captain Blaine was dead, Lou Graham gone too; her house long since had become a Japanese rooming house and her famous girls, those elegant and charming beauties who'd shocked the First Hill ladies, were scattered and forgotten. The responsibility was all on his own shoulders. He'd already mortgaged the house in Laurelhurst and Emily, in whose name it had been bought, wouldn't hear of their selling it. He tried to raise more money at the banks, but the shaky North Star was a poor risk and no one cared to gamble on its recovery.

One rainy October night Hugh worked late, going over the books, trying to figure out a way to save his shirt. At last, his head aching and his mind a confusion of figures, he locked the office door, stood a moment breathing in the salty air, looking at the bay. The darkness was pungent, full of small sounds, the lapping of water, the creaking of rotten piles, the cry of an occasional sea gull. He walked along, tasting the smells, the flavor of the waterfront. His ear caught every noise, identifying it unconsciously. He was a part of the waterfront as much as any deck hand or longshoreman.

What am I going to do if the North Star goes under? he asked himself, and a strange feeling of loss, of sadness, weighed down his spirit. He'd always felt that his business didn't mean to him what it did to most men, that he'd been able to view it with detachment. But now, as it was about to slip from his grasp, he realized that through the years it had become his life. He'd put more of himself into it than into anything else. The North Star was closer to him than his wife and daughter, it was closer to him than his own flesh and blood. But it *is* my flesh and blood, he thought with a wry smile. I created it, I nurtured it, and now I have to stand by and watch it die.

He walked slowly along the docks to where his car was parked. If we have to close down I'll have to look for a job, he thought. How did you go about getting a job? His brother would have no use for him now, after all the years away from the law. Besides, Beauchamp was a sour, precise individual who had inherited none of his father's gracious attributes. Hugh had no desire to ask him for a job.

The judge had been dead for years. Never once, in spite of his success, had Hugh felt that his father quite believed in him. He knew he loved him, was amused by him, but always there was that quality of irony in their relations. To the judge, Hugh was the perennial young man about town, elegant, debonair, but not to be taken seriously. Sometimes Hugh felt his father knew him better than anyone else. His death had left a big gap in Hugh's life, a feeling of resentment and loss. If he were alive I could go to him, he thought, and somehow he would be able to tell me what to do.

As he walked past the warehouses, saw the idle ships rotting at anchor, heard the hungry, questing gulls screaming, the thought of Annie Jordan came so sharply to his mind that he stopped at the Colman Dock and leaned on a pile. He was thinking about the first time he'd seen her, sitting on perhaps this very pile, chewing caramels and watching the gulls. He wished he could talk to Annie. He wished it were Annie Jordan he was going home to now; Annie's arms to hold him, warm and tender, her mouth laid in silence on his to tell him that there was more to life than the building of a business or the failure of a shipping line. With Annie, he might have found a meaning and a purpose.

A long-forgotten line of Virgil that he'd not thought of since his college days came suddenly into his mind, and he said the words out loud, while a gray-and-white gull banked against the wind and veered down to the dark water below the pier. "They walk alone under the uncertain moon." Was the old Latin poet right? Did men and women, however desperately they strove for union, for binding themselves to each other against the awful loneliness of their fate, find in the end that they walked alone—that they had walked alone always, even when the beloved, the friend, the child, was closest?

"God, I need a drink," he said out loud. He didn't want to go home. He didn't want to explain to Emily why he was late for dinner, to lie and say, No, I'm not worried about anything. He wanted to find a corner somewhere to sit by himself and get quietly drunk so he'd stop trying to figure a way out when he knew damn well there wasn't a way out.

He slid under the wheel of his car, drove toward Yesler Avenue. There ought to be some dive around here, some dark, smelly little speakeasy where he could get a drink and be alone. He parked the car and got out, walked half a block, and went into a cigar store.

"Package of Melachrinos," he told the clerk, a heavy-set man in shirt sleeves with a half-chewed cigar in his mouth. Pretty soon, he thought, I'll have to give up some of my expensive tastes.

"Anything else, friend?" asked the clerk.

"Well, I could do with a drink. D'ye know a good place to get one?" His smile was ironic and the man gave him a slow wink.

In a low voice he said, "You want a bootlegger or just a speak?"

"A speak that won't be apt to be raided. I'm in a quiet mood tonight."

The clerk leaned his elbows on the counter, pointed out the door with his cigar. "You go down to the corner, turn right into the alley. There's a sign says 'Café'—that's all it says. That's Nick's place and it's okay. Not cheap, but the liquor's the best in town. Tell him Cliff sent you and he'll treat you right."

Hugh turned off Yesler Avenue into the alley, down a flight of stairs into a basement café. It had no name, only the electric sign "Café" above the door. Inside it was warm, dim, full of tobacco smoke and good cooking smells. But it was clean, the woodwork newly painted, red-checked tablecloths on the tables. Only a few of the tables were taken and Hugh found one in a corner near the kitchen. It was the hour when most people had had their dinners and the late crowd hadn't come in yet. It was a quiet, rather lonely time and Hugh felt lonesome, sitting by himself. He wished he was with a friend who wouldn't ask questions or try to cheer him up, but would just sit and get drunk with him.

"What'll it be? Dinner's over but you can get a plate of spaghetti, maybe."

Hugh looked up at the big dark man in shirt sleeves with a towel draped around his middle and said evenly, "Cliff said I could get a decent drink here."

The big man eyed him steadily, then jerked his head in assent. "What'll it be?"

"Bourbon and soda. Make it a double bourbon and I'll put in the soda myself."

The dark man nodded, disappeared into the kitchen. Hugh lit a cigarette and watched a young couple across the room. They sat gazing into each other's faces as if under a spell. A man who'd been sitting at the counter, drinking something out of a tall glass, went over to a small upright piano against the wall and began to pick out "Chinatown, My Chinatown" with one finger. Hugh's drink came and he took a big gulp of it. It wasn't bad; better, in fact, than the stuff he'd been getting from his own bootlegger.

A woman came from the kitchen with two glasses on a tray and set them down at the young couple's table. She didn't have on a waitress's uniform, just a dark skirt and a white blouse with a V neck that showed her white throat. Maybe she was the wife of the proprietor or something. But the man who'd waited on him had disappeared and Hugh, warmed and relaxed by the bourbon, wanted another.

"Oh, miss," he said as she started to pass him. "Do you know where my waiter is?"

She paused, glanced at him. "You mean Nick? He's busy. I'll take your order."

"I'd like——" He stopped and took another look at her. Something about her voice, something about the way she walked, free and easy and sort of proud, something about her full, white throat . . . In the dim light he couldn't get a good look at her.

She came closer, leaned her hand on his table, and he looked up straight into her eyes. Her heavy auburn hair was wound round her head in a coronet.

"My God," he whispered, "Annie Jordan."

She stood perfectly still, looking down at him, and then she began to smile slowly. She pulled out a chair and sat down across from him, still gazing into his face and smiling wonderingly. "Well, Hugh, it's been a long time," she said at last, softly. "But I had a hunch that one of these days you'd walk in here."

"You don't mean you—you work here?"

"Yes, I work here. Nick and I own the place together." Her voice was amused. "Are you shocked to see me in a speakeasy?"

"I guess I am. The last time I saw you——"

"Was fourteen years ago. A lot can happen in fourteen years, Hugh, but I can see you're still the same." She laughed softly and her eyes were tender.

"What do you mean? I'm fourteen years older too."

"I mean, you still get shocked. You're still from the First Hill."

"I guess I'm pretty much of a stuffed shirt, Annie." He

laughed and put his hand over hers. The touch of her strong hand had a curious effect on him. It comforted him and made him want to tell her all his troubles. Or maybe I'm a little too drunk, he thought. Well, what if I am? Annie won't care.

"I never held it against you, did I?" She was searching his face, wondering at how haggard he looked. Something's the matter. . . .

"No. You were always wonderful, Annie." He was thinking, Annie wouldn't mind if I lost the North Star. She'd stick by me. Maybe that's the way out. Let the business go and pull out, take Annie with me. I'll bet she'd go. We could start all over again someplace where nobody knows us. By God, that's what I'll do. He didn't feel drunk now. His mind was clear as a bell and he had that feeling of strength and certainty that comes from making a decision. We were meant to be together, that's why I've found her again—it's fate, it's our destiny. Now, after all these years, we've got the right to make up for all we've missed. "Annie——" His fingers tightened over her hand. "I–I've got to talk to you. Can't we go somewhere and talk?"

She nodded. "We can go to my place. Wait here. I'll be back."

She was gone a few minutes and Hugh finished his drink. When she came back she had on a black cloth coat with a big red fox collar. "It's all right. I spoke to Nick. Peggy's on duty from eight to twelve. They can manage without me."

They went through the café, out the front door, and around to the side. An outside staircase concealed by a lattice led to an upper story above the restaurant. A narrow decklike porch went halfway round it.

"I can sit out here and look at the harbor," said Annie. "On clear days I can see across the bay to Vashon. Nick had one of the boys build me some window boxes. There isn't much left now, but in the spring I have geraniums and lobelia and wandering Jew. They're awfully pretty."

Her voice held a note of pride and satisfaction. Hugh glanced at her, wondering. The sky was clear now and it was surprisingly light, light enough for him to see her face as she stood beside him, one hand resting on the porch railing. Her head was lifted and she was gazing out above the shimmer of lights on Yesler Avenue toward the dark mystery of the bay. The strong, lovely profile of her face looked calm and curiously at peace and yet there was that quality of eagerness and wonder in it that he remembered when she'd stood at the rail of the island steamer that day so many years ago.

She turned with a smile. "This is my place, Hugh. It isn't grand, but it's mine and I like it. You're very welcome here." She opened the door to her apartment with a graceful little flourish, motioned him to precede her. Two ship's lights, red and green, were burning on each side of the mantel of the small brick fireplace. Annie snapped on a lamp and Hugh looked around the neat, pleasant room.

There were red-and-white-checked cotton curtains at the windows that ran along the side that looked out on the bay. "There was some material left after I made the tablecloths for the café, so I ran it up into curtains," she said, seeing him glance at them. "They're easy to keep clean and they're bright."

The room was long and furnished simply but attractively in plain, sturdy maple and leather furniture. There was a small table pushed under the windows, four straight maple chairs, a big armchair in dark red leather, a maple rocker, a small studio couch covered with blue denim, plain open bookshelves painted gray to match the woodwork. African marigolds in a copper bowl glowed on the window sill. Hugh turned to smile at Annie. "You've got a nice place here, Annie."

She smiled back and again he caught the look of quiet pride and contentment in her face. "I like living near the waterfront. I can hear the boats coming in and smell the tide flats. There's a little kitchen in the alcove and a bedroom and bath through that door. It's all I need."

She took off her coat and tossed it on the couch. "Sit down, Hugh. The leather armchair's the most comfortable."

She went out to the kitchen alcove, came back with a bottle of whisky, two glasses and soda. "Like a drink?"

He nodded. "A short one. I had a couple at Nick's." She poured a little whisky into a glass, added a splash of soda, and handed him the glass. "How long have you been back in Seattle? Last I heard you were in California," he said, watching her. She had an easy, graceful way of moving about, as if she knew what she was doing.

She fixed herself a drink, sat down on the couch across from him. "I came back in 1914, just before the war started in Europe."

"Eleven years ago! And you never let me know."

"No. I didn't go back to the First Hill, you see. I came back to the waterfront."

"Why? If you needed money, why didn't you come to me?" The thought that for eleven years she'd been in the same town, walking up and down the streets, going to bed at night, waking up in the morning, and he hadn't known it, made him feel queer. He'd not thought about her much in those eleven years, but there had been times, nights when he couldn't sleep, that if he'd known where to find her he'd have gone to her. Perhaps she knew that, perhaps that was why she hadn't let him know.

"I didn't need money, Hugh. Oh, I don't mean I was still rich. I traveled for a while after Ed died and I spent a lot. But I had some saved. I put it into the café."

"But why didn't you get in touch with any of your friends?"

She smiled. "I didn't want to embarrass them. After all, I never really belonged on the First Hill. I found that out at Ed's funeral. That's why I went away. There didn't seem to be anything left here for me."

"You—never married again, did you?" His voice was casual, but his eyes held hers and his heart tightened.

She shook her head. "I guess I was afraid to, Hugh. Things didn't work out very well the first time. Or maybe I never fell in love."

"What a rotten deal you've had!" he cried indignantly, and then his face reddened. He wasn't forgetting his part, the rotten deal he'd given her. "You deserved better, Annie."

Annie shrugged. "I'm not complaining, Hugh. Things may not have worked out the way I wanted them to, but it's all been part of living. We have to take things as they come, I guess. And now I'm back where I belong. I like the café. I guess you might say I'm happy."

He stared at her, at her calm, strong face, her lovely, dark eyes, her mouth still full and sweet. There was a quality of life and vitality in her that he guessed nothing would ever dim. There were shadows under her eyes and her cheeks were thinner, you could see that life hadn't dealt kindly with her, but

my God, he thought, how she could take it! "You're wonderful,
Annie. I wish I had your strength."

"Something's the matter, isn't it, Hugh? You wanted to talk
to me and here I've been talking about myself." She leaned
forward to look at him earnestly. "What is it? Is it—Emily?"

He smiled wryly. "No. Emily's all right. She's just the same.
She's been a good wife according to her lights."

"Then you're worried about your business, is that it?"

He nodded, drained his glass, and put it on the table. "The
North Star is about to set for good, I guess. The banks won't
lend me a dime and we'll have to go into receivership."

"Oh no, Hugh!" she cried. "You can't let the North Star go."

"It's a funny thing, Annie, but until I saw you tonight I felt
pretty bad about losing it. I hadn't realized how much it meant
to me. But now—it doesn't seem important." He got up, went
over to the couch, and sat down beside her. He reached out for
her hand and, after looking at it gravely for a moment, she
put it in his. He held it tightly. He was smiling and there was
that old ironical flicker in his eyes. "Do you want to know what
seems important, the most important thing that's happened to
me in years?"

She didn't answer. She continued to regard him gravely, with
a faintly worried look.

"Finding you again, Annie."

She smiled and shook her head, seemed about to withdraw
her hand, but he tightened his clasp, gazed at her so intently
that her smile faded and her face, that had been so calm and
contained, grew pale and vulnerable.

"It's a funny thing how I never could get you out of my
mind. You'd think, after all these years and everything that's
happened, that I wouldn't feel the same about you, wouldn't
you?" He sounded as if he were talking to himself and his face,
which had looked haggard to her in the café, was softened and
tender. "I won't pretend that I've thought about you all the
time. I've had my business, my family, clubs and people. My
life's been active and full. But you were always there, Annie,
waiting. Sometimes when I'd read a line of poetry I'd suddenly
remember that night at Port Madison or see your eyes looking
into mine. Or maybe I'd be walking on the docks and I'd see
your face uplifted to the wind off the bay. Whenever I was

lonely I'd wish I could talk to you. Just tonight, when I left the office feeling tired and at the end of my rope, I wanted to be going home to you."

He'd been talking as much to himself as to her and he hadn't noticed that she was crying. Now she took her hand from his and covered her face. She made no sound, just sat there with her hands over her face and her body tense with silent weeping.

"Oh, my darling," he murmured sadly, putting his arms around her and drawing her close to him. "We've wasted so many years. It was all my fault, Annie. But I was such a silly, shallow young fool. I knew all along that we belonged together. But I thought other things were more important. Now I know only one thing really mattered and that was what we had together."

He took her hands from her face and she lay against his shoulder while he wiped away her tears with infinite gentleness. Her face was white and the shadows under her eyes were like bruises. He bent and kissed her pale mouth and her lips trembled under his. With a little moan she put her arms around him and pressed her body close against his.

"The North Star doesn't matter now, you see. Emily will be all right. She has a trust fund from her mother's estate. Marcia is in school in the East. Emily insisted on sending her and paying for it with her own money. We'll go away together, maybe up the Sound, to the San Juan Islands. Make a new start. Forget everything else. We're not old, Annie, we've still got some good years before us." His voice went on and on, in a sort of dream, and Annie lay in his arms, hardly listening to his words, feeling his heart beating against her cheek, his arms holding her, thinking, How long I've waited for this, and didn't I always know that someday he'd be with me again and everything would be as it was when we first loved each other?

There were things she must say to him, but she seemed to have no will to utter them. Deep within her something struggled to be heard, but she only sighed and felt his hand stroking her hair. Was there to be a happy ending after all? Were they to be together again at last?

"Your hair," he whispered against her cheek, "your lovely hair. Take it down, Annie, and let me feel it again. Let me see you brushing it. I think one of the loveliest sights I ever saw was you with your hair down. I've always remembered how it fell along your back like a waterfall and how it felt like silk when I touched it."

With a strange, soft smile she sat up and took out the pins. The two heavy braids swung unbound down her back. She looked almost like a girl, unbraiding them and glancing sideways at him, her cheeks flushed, her lips softly curving. He watched her as she went into the bedroom, came back with a hairbrush and, standing before the round mirror that hung above the couch, brushed her hair till it shone.

How natural it seemed for him to be there, smiling at her, she thought. All the years slipped away and were as if they had never been and her heart beat hard, her eyes, glancing back from the mirror, were dark and shy. Suddenly he stood up and caught her in his arms.

"You'll let me stay tonight, Annie," he cried. "And tomorrow we'll go away together for always."

She trembled in his arms and the shadow of pain touched her face but she only whispered, "Yes, I'll let you stay," and she lifted her mouth to his.

When he wakened in the morning she was gone, but the fragrance of her hair and body were still in the room. He lay for a long time looking at the wall, thinking about her, remembering the curve of her cheek and throat, the depth in her eyes, her tender hands. He thought, How I've wasted my life and hers. There was one thing that would have made me whole and I let it go. I was meant to love this woman and she was meant to love me. Everything else has been a disappointment and a delusion. There was this one perfect, enduring woman in the world who loved me and will always love me and now that my life is more than half over I have found her again.

He didn't know where she had gone but he knew that she would be back. He lay thinking about what he would do, how he would make a living for her, where they would go. It didn't matter what kind of a job he got, maybe a job as a deck hand on some little island steamer. They would have a little house. . . .

The door opened and Annie came in with a tray covered with a white napkin. "I've brought you some breakfast from the café," she said. She set the tray down on the bed and sat at the foot, pouring his coffee from the little crockery pot and buttering his toast. He was very hungry, and the bacon and eggs and coffee tasted wonderful.

"You're not eating much," he said, reaching for her hand.

"I don't have the appetite I used to," she answered, smiling.

He ate with a relish, talking between bites about his plans for their life together. His face was eager and boyish and he realized that he felt younger and more alive than he had in years. She listened to him, watching his face and handing him more food, only sipping a cup of black coffee and nibbling at toast herself. When he'd finished his meal she put the tray on the dresser and he stretched out his arms for her.

"You haven't kissed me good morning yet, darling," he said.

She stood looking at him and then she said slowly, her eyes very dark, "I can't go away with you, Hugh." She sat down on the foot of the bed again, searching his eyes. He started to say something but she went on quickly. "I love you. I always have and I always will. I guess you know that."

"Then—if you love me . . ." His voice was insistent, harsh.

"I want you to be happy. You wouldn't be really happy if you let the North Star go and deserted your wife for me."

"Can't you let me be the judge of that?" he cried.

She shook her head. "If things had been different we could have had a wonderful life together. I think maybe we were meant for each other. But it's too late now. You can't walk out on everything you've built up. You've got to go back to your life—to your business and your family."

"My business is washed up and my family doesn't need me," he said impatiently. "But maybe you don't want to take a chance on me."

"You know that's not true. I'd go with you anywhere if I thought it was right for you. But it's not. You're a gentleman, Hugh, you're not the kind of man who walks out on his wife. You can't let the North Star go, either, without a fight. You've put too much of yourself into it. You're proud of it too—and I'm proud of it." She fumbled in her bodice, took out a roll of bills, and handed it to him. "Maybe this will help you keep it going."

He looked at the bills, frowning, then at her in amazement. "What's this for?" he cried angrily.

"There's twenty-five thousand dollars there, Hugh. I went over to the bank as soon as it opened."

"I can't take it, Annie. I can't take your money."

Her eyes, dark and intense, were fixed on his. "You've got to! I don't need it. I have plenty to live on from the café. All my life I've been proud of what you've made of yourself and of the North Star. I've always wished I could have been a part of it. Please let me now, Hugh, please let me feel that I've been able to do something to help."

He turned toward the wall, feeling impotent and beaten. He knew he couldn't change her mind about going away with him. When she'd made a decision, right or wrong, she stuck to it. He knew, too, that he was going to take her money and go back to the struggle again, try to pull the North Star together, not because it mattered to him but because it mattered to her, because it was a symbol of what she believed him to be.

"All right, Annie," he said harshly. "I'll take the money. I'll go back to the North Star and to Emily. Not because I want to or think it's right, but because you want me to. If we never see each other again, remember it was you who sent me away."

"It'll be all right, Hugh," she said gently, kneeling beside him and laying her cheek against his. "You'll see. And every time I hear a steamer whistling out in the bay I'll think, Maybe that's one of Hugh's boats, and I'll be proud. Maybe we won't ever see each other again, dearest, but don't be too sad or lonely. We've loved each other all these years and we'll keep on loving each other. You'll be on the First Hill and I'll be down on Yesler Avenue, but the love will be there between us, right to the end."

Chapter XXI

Emily had gone over to Marguerite Brookes's apartment to play bridge. She and "the girls"—Essie Keating and her sister Molly and Marguerite—had an evening bridge club that met twice a month on Thursdays. It was different from Emily's afternoon bridge that met at the Sunset Club on Tuesdays. That was a larger, smarter group where the women dressed expensively and carefully for each other, ate an enormous, fattening lunch, and played cutthroat bridge for money. The Thursday night club was a hangover from the old days when Emily was a bride and Marguerite was just starting on her newspaper career and had Thursday nights off.

Hugh ate a solitary supper in his study, having worked late at the office. Emily had fixed herself a salad, since the servants were out, and was ready to leave when he came in.

"There's cold roast in the refrigerator and I've left some salad for you in the green bowl. Martha made a chocolate pie before she left this morning, so I think you'll have enough," she said, standing at the hall mirror, adjusting a very chic hat with a sweeping feather that curled under her chin. "I'm sorry to leave you just as you get home, but I *told* you we'd eat early, Hugh. It's my bridge club night."

"I know, Emily. I couldn't get away any sooner. I was checking up on the reports from Tomlinson on the Pacific Line. I think the merger is going through all right." His voice was weary, but there was a note of triumph in it that she didn't miss.

She glanced at him over her shoulder. "Oh, really, dear? That's what you've been working for, isn't it?"

He nodded, smiling vaguely. Working for it was a mild way to put it. He'd sweated over it, night and day, managing somehow to make the whole thing appear, even to Ben Tomlinson, president of the Pacific Line, as a concession on the part of the North Star, when actually it was going to be the blood transfusion that would pull the old girl out of the dumps.

"I'm *so* glad, Hugh," she cried, brushing her lips lightly against his thin cheek. "It'll be wonderful for you to be making money again. I need just everything. And if we don't do something to this house soon, it'll fall down about our ears."

When she'd gone he went out to the kitchen, sliced off some of the roast beef, rummaged in the cupboard for mustard, piled salad onto his plate, found a couple of cold baking-powder biscuits in the breadbox, poured a glass of milk, and put the whole thing on a tray and carried it into his study.

It was a comfortable room with a fireplace, two deep armchairs covered in brown rep, a really beautiful kneehole desk, good reading lamps, and bookshelves that lined one wall completely. He sat down in one of the armchairs, placing the tray on a low table at the side. Before picking up his plate he leaned back and surveyed the room with pleasure. Emily knew how to make a home attractive and comfortable. She had good taste and she understood the things a man liked in his own room.

He looked at the hundreds of books that filled the bookshelves. He'd read them all, some of them over and over. There had been a time when he never sat down without a book in his hands. Now he seemed to have no time for reading or he fell asleep, exhausted from the strain of the day's struggle, as soon as he'd read a couple of pages. Perhaps, if the merger with Pacific went through all right and business moved along smoothly again, he'd get back to his books, his old friends, to Shakespeare and Browning and Keats, to Carlyle and Ruskin, to the wise old Latin poets with their understanding of the tragedy that underlay all human life and endeavor, their understanding, too, of the superb moments of exaltation and fulfillment that illumined men's lives like flashes of lightning.

The North Star had a fighting chance now and if the merger

went through she'd be on solid ground again. The merger had been a sudden inspiration of Hugh's, and if Tomlinson fell for it he could pat himself on the back. But if it hadn't been for Annie's money, that had pulled them out of the hole to a place where they could see light again, there wouldn't have been anything left to merge with except oblivion.

Someday, he thought as he cut his cold beef and spread it with mustard, I'll buy a new boat and name her the *Annie Jordan*. She'd like that, I think. He smiled, thinking of how her face would light up like a child's. And I'll take Annie with me on her maiden voyage, too. We'll sail up the sound to Port Madison and tie up at the dock, and we'll have a clambake on the beach and go wading in the bay. I wonder if the old beach hotel is still there? I wonder what she'd say if I asked her to spend a night with me there? His smile deepened, because he knew what her answer would be, even though he hadn't seen her since the morning she gave him the roll of bills and kissed him good-by. We've parted so many times, each time for good, but always knowing in our hearts that we'd meet again. "If the merger goes through, by God," he said out loud, "I'll make Emily throw a party and I'll invite Annie to come and I'll toast her in champagne."

He ate his supper, carried the tray to the kitchen, returned to the study to do some paperwork he'd brought home with him. Before he settled down at the desk he went to the bookshelves, ran his fingers along a row until he came to a worn limp-leather volume which he took out and sat down with. His tired, lean face, with its narrow, tapering bones and slightly bitter mouth, grew thoughtful, reminiscent, as he read the poems that he'd marked so many years ago. What tempests had raged in his breast as he'd read and reread these sonnets that seemed written expressly for *his* need, *his* passion, *his* despair!

> "Being your slave, what should I do but tend
> Upon the hours and times of your desire?"

That one he'd committed to memory and this one he'd read aloud to himself, pacing up and down his room, while the rain spattered the window and he was torn between love and ambition: "Take all my loves, my love, yea, take them all."

And this—here was one marked by the hand of his youth, but surely only half understood then:

> "Let me not to the marriage of true minds
> Admit impediments. Love is not love
> Which alters when it alteration finds,
> Or bends with the remover to remove:
> O, no! it is an ever-fixed mark
> That looks on tempests and is never shaken;
> It is the star to every wandering bark,
> Whose worth's unknown, although his height be taken.
> Love's not Time's fool, though rosy lips and cheeks
> Within his bending sickle's compass come:
> Love alters not with his brief hours and weeks,
> But bears it out even to the edge of doom.
>   If this be error and upon me proved,
>   I never writ, nor no man ever loved."

He sat with the book in his hands, looking out the window where the dusk was gathering the shapes of trees, shrubs, climbing vines into the soft, amorphous unity of the twilight. Birds were still calling, their voices sharp and clear in the silence. It was too dark to read any more and he was reluctant to turn on the lights. A sense of peace and fulfillment possessed him. It had taken him nearly half a century to come to the full understanding of that sonnet, but now he knew what the poet meant. "Love's not Time's fool . . ." Annie had taught him the truth of that. If a man somewhere along his years comes to the complete understanding of but one truth that illumines all of experience, suffering, struggle, isn't that a justification of having lived? What are mergers, profits, schemes, aspirations, triumphs in the face of the profound and quiet joy that comes from entering into and becoming a part of a single aspect of truth?

He sat with his eyes closed for so long that the window became dark, then slowly brightened as the moon rose and fingered it. He was not asleep, but he was certainly not aware of his physical surroundings, until the sound of the telephone brought him back from wherever his spirit had been wandering. Then he opened his eyes, saw the moonlight outside, the darkness in the room, and leaned over and snapped on the desk lamp.

The telephone rang loudly in the quiet, empty house and Hugh, still lost in his thoughts, let it ring several times before he got up and went into the hall to answer it. He was thinking, It's probably for Emily, anyway, one of her innumerable girl friends who like to get her on the phone and chat for three quarters of an hour about nothing. But it might be Tomlinson ringing me up about the merger. He took up the receiver and answered abruptly. A heavy male voice with a slight foreign accent said:

"Meester Deming? This is Nick."

"Nick who?"

"Nick that runs the speak down on Yesler Avenue. You remember? You been to my place."

"Oh yes, I remember. What can I do for you?"

"It's Annie. She's been shot. The police raid our place tonight and somebody start shootin'. Annie come in from kitchen and get hit. I think she's gonna die."

"Annie—oh, God," he whispered, an icy hand on his heart. *Love's not Time's fool.*

"She said to call you. The priest's been with the Sacrament."

"I'll come right away. Where is she?"

"At her place. You know where she live?"

"Yes. Yes, I know." He slammed down the receiver, struggled into his coat, grabbed his hat. Damn it, Emily had the car and it would take as long to get a taxi as to go on the streetcar. A hot, unreasonable fury possessed him—anger at Emily for taking the car, anger at God, at fate, at the bullet that had found Annie. But she can't die. I need her. I won't let her die. I'll put her in a hospital, get the best doctors in town. Annie dying? It wasn't possible. Annie was too strong, too real, to die. Little people like Emily and him died, but not Annie. He rushed out of the house and met his wife just coming up the steps to the porch.

"Emily, where is the car? Give me the keys," he cried.

She stared at him in surprise. "Where are you going? The car's in the garage, of course."

"Give me the keys. I've got to get down to Yesler Avenue as fast as possible." He grabbed her purse from her, fumbled in it for the keys.

"Well, for pity's sake, you needn't be so rude, Hugh. Why do you have to go dashing down to Yesler Avenue of all places at this time of night—Hugh!" She stared, frowning, after him as he tore down the steps with the car keys.

He drove like a demon along the dark streets, taking the corners on two wheels. It seemed to take him hours to get across town through the traffic. Policemen whistled after him, but he didn't even hear them. Once he narrowly missed hitting a truck as he dashed through a red light.

He parked the car in the alley off Yesler Avenue. There were a police car and a big gray sedan with a doctor's caduceus on the license plate already there. The café was dark, but above, in Annie's apartment, lights shone steadily out upon the night. An officer sitting in the police car snapped on his lights and spoke to Hugh as he went by.

"My name's Deming," cried Hugh, impatient at being stopped. "I was sent for. I'm a friend of Annie Jordan's."

"Okay," said the officer, and nodded. "You can go up."

Hugh pounded up the stairs, opened the door to the apartment without knocking. Nick, the big dark Greek, disheveled and white-faced, got up from the leather armchair where he'd been sitting with his head in his hands.

"It's good you come," he said hoarsely. "Annie's in there, with the doctor." He jerked his head toward the bedroom. The door was shut and when Hugh rapped on it a tired-looking bald man in shirt sleeves opened it.

"I'm Dr. Miller. You must be Mr. Deming. Nick said he'd called you."

Hugh nodded, went quickly to the bed, the high, white, spotless bed where Annie had held him in her strong arms and given him peace and comfort and courage. She lay with her eyes closed, her hair still in braids around her head, the coverlet drawn up to her chin. Her face was pale and it seemed much thinner and more haggard than when he'd seen her last. He drew a chair closer to the bedside.

"Annie," he murmured. "Annie, my darling."

Her eyes fluttered open, she turned her head slowly as if with great effort, and looked at him. "Hugh," she breathed, and smiled, and a sudden radiance was on her face. Very slowly the coverlet moved and she brought her hand out, laid it, palm up, on the bed. He bent and pressed his lips to the hot, dry palm. It had a strange, sweetish smell and he thought, That is the smell of Death. In spite of her smile, her radiance, the warmth and aliveness of her dark eyes, Death was in the room and they both felt it. It kept them from being quite natural together, as if there were a formal guest present who wouldn't understand their relationship, so they couldn't talk freely. But they could gaze at each other and Annie could smile and he could hold the hot, dry hand tightly in his, as if by clasping it securely he could keep her from slipping away with the unwelcome guest.

Annie knew who was in the room too. Her old enemy that had taken away her children, her husband, Rolfe Linden, her first love, Mae, her mother—whose face she had first seen when she bent over Lorna, the Variety girl, when she was a child, had come at last for her. But now she was not afraid of him. He had come for her but she could hold him off until she had seen Hugh again. When the bullet went searing through her breast she'd cried out in terror, but after the doctor had done what he could for her and she lay in her own bed, feeling the life ebbing out of her strong body, she'd said, "Doctor, I'm going to die." He nodded, his eyes pitying. "How much time do I have?"

"A few hours, perhaps. Not much more."

She was not afraid then, only grateful that there was a little time left.

Before the earnest, thin-faced young priest, successor to Father Donegan's successor, had heard her confession, shriven her, given her the Sacrament, she'd motioned to Nick, who came quickly across the room, his broad, swarthy face contorted by emotion. "There's someone I want to say good-by to, Nick. His name—his name is Hugh Deming. He lives out in Laurelhurst. Will you call him now?"

So now he was here, beside her, holding her hand so tightly, gazing at her with all the love and tenderness of his whole life in his eyes. There were no gold flecks in them now, there was no irony, only the darkness of his pain.

"Dear Hugh," she whispered. "You came. I knew you would. I had to see you once more, to say good-by."

"Don't leave me, Annie. I need you. I love you so," he cried desolately.

"I'll never leave you, Hugh. I've not been a good woman, but

I've always loved you. Maybe that makes up for everything else." She smiled and her eyes were tender and brave. He thought she had never been so beautiful. "I'm not afraid, Hugh. I'll take what's coming to me."

He wanted to stay; he wanted to be the last one she looked at or spoke to, but presently she fell asleep and the doctor told him, "Better go now. She'd want you to. It's not pleasant to remember someone you've loved as dead, or to watch them die. If you go now, you can remember her as sleeping."

He went out and got into his car, but he didn't go home right away. The moon was gone and it had been raining a little. The streets under the lights looked smooth and dark. He drove slowly down to the docks, parked the car, rolled down the window, and sat staring at the blackness of the bay, lifting his face to the cool, damp night wind. The waterfront was empty of life; there were no lights anywhere and no sound but the faint wash of water about the piles. It was about one o'clock in the morning, and though it wasn't cold, he was shivering.

He didn't know why he had come down here, what he expected to find, what comfort or help, or answer to his pain. The dark, empty waterfront was desolate and bleak. There was no comfort here, no answer, nothing but the memory of a bright-haired child and a warm-lipped girl, both of whom were gone. The faded but still beautiful and tender woman they had become was gone now too. Annie was dying. Perhaps, even as he sat with the smell of the bay in his nostrils and the touch of the fog on his cheek, she was dead. Perhaps the long, mournful blast of a foghorn on Alki Point, muffled and ghostly, was marking her passing. Child, girl, woman, all gone—and he had had so little of her. Yet even as he clenched his fists at the grief in his breast, he knew that he had had the most and the best.

Emily was in bed, with cold cream shiny on her face, her hair in a net, but she was not asleep. She got up on one arm and stared at him as he came into the room, angry words trembling on her lips. But at the sight of his haggard face, she kept them back. "What's the matter, Hugh?" was all she said.

He looked at her without seeing her. He was seeing still the white face and the shining eyes of the woman he had said good-by to for the last time. "Annie Jordan died tonight,

Emily," he answered in a flat, tired voice. He turned away and began to take off his clothes.

There's nothing the living can do for the dead but go on living. Sometimes that's not so easy as it sounds. Sometimes you wish with all your soul that you could lie down in a quiet grave and be done with the whole noisy, complicated business. But if you're worth your salt, if you're worth the love of a woman like Annie Jordan, you don't lie down, however sweet to aching bones and weary soul the oblivion of the dust would be. You stumble on, because at the end you hope with all that's left of faith or illusion or fantasy that she'll be waiting for you with her warm smile and her tender arms, and you've got to make her proud to have waited.

The Hugh Demings were having a party. It was the first one they'd had in several years, the first one since the North Star had pulled itself out of the hole and started to make money again. It was really a housewarming, Emily said, and she had a right to be excited and proud about showing how completely she'd done over their old house. It had got so run down when Hugh's business was bad that she'd practically torn it down and made a new house out of it.

"We've spent more than we planned on it," cried Emily gaily, so happy to be able to take the light, casual tone about money again, "but then it'll last us the rest of our lives and we hope Marcia will want it after we're gone."

"All the improvements are Emily's ideas," said Hugh with a charming gesture of admiration toward his pretty, vivacious wife who, though her blond hair was quite white now, really looked years younger than her handsome, aristocratic husband. "She's the interior decorator in the family."

"You've done wonders with it, Emily," said Marguerite Brookes, a stately, iron-gray woman in her late forties, with that indefinable air of intellect, irony, and tolerance that sometimes comes to a woman after suffering, loneliness, and the necessity for making her own way in a man's world without recourse to her sexual charms. Emily was proud that Marguerite was still her friend after all these years, after her trips abroad, her career as a newspaper woman, and the best-selling novel that had just come out.

"Emily always did have a flair for doing houses," said Essie Keating in her schoolgirlish enthusiasm.

"And Hugh always had a flair for living," smiled Erica Crawford, still handsome at sixty-odd.

Hugh kissed her hand, remembering, as he would remember to the last, how she had let him down when he went to her for help in starting the North Star, and all because he'd taken the Carltons' hired girl, Annie Jordan, to the Nesika Club Ball. How long ago and far away that all seemed, in the days when they were young, when Seattle, now a sophisticated world port, was young and eager and struggling for her life. And yet the picture of the tall, noble, titian-haired girl in the green satin ball gown with her wide violet eyes dancing, her warm red lips curved in an eager smile, was as clear to him—no, clearer than the faces of these old friends at his housewarming party.

They were all there, all the old crowd, and they were celebrating not only the redecorated house but the merger of the North Star and the smaller, but very sound, Pacific Line. So Ben Tomlinson, president of the Pacific and now Hugh's partner, was there as well, fluttering Emily with compliments and beaming at Hugh. It was all very gay, very optimistic. Emily was once more in her element. She wished Marcia had been able to come up from San Francisco, where she was studying art, but then young people these days were bored by social gatherings of their elders.

There had been several years when she was really worried about Hugh and his business. Once she'd had the awful thought that, with the strikes and all, he might lose the North Star. He'd even tried to get her to sell this house and put the money into the business. But something had made her hang onto it and how glad she was that she hadn't given in to him. Somehow he'd been able to raise the money he needed and now the North Star was in better shape than it had ever been. It just went to show that there was no use in worrying, things always worked out—if you were smart, of course, and, with a proud glance at her husband, she had to admit Hugh was smart.

He seemed quite happy now, too, though for several months after Annie Jordan died he'd looked dreadful. She hadn't even dared to talk to him about it, to ask how he'd known, if he'd been with her when it happened, if that had been the mysteri-

ous call he'd made that night when he dashed off in the car
to Yesler Avenue.

She knew perfectly well that there had been something between Hugh and Annie, but if Annie had tried to take him away
from her, she hadn't succeeded. Now after all the years she
didn't hold any grudge against her, poor thing. No, she rather
pitied her, dying as she'd been born, on the waterfront, in
spite of all her good looks and money. Emily felt that she hadn't
a thing to reproach herself for as far as Annie was concerned.
Heaven knew she'd been good to her in the days when Annie
hadn't a thing. She'd never let on to Hugh that she was jealous,
she'd done her best to help her. As a matter of fact, hadn't she
launched Annie into First Hill society and introduced her to
her own friends, when everyone knew she'd been her mother's
hired girl?

They were drinking champagne in the drawing room,
Emily's charming baroque drawing room, and everyone had
proposed a toast, to their lovely hostess, their host, the house,
the partnership, even to Auld Lang Syne. It had come Hugh's
turn and he went about with the iced bottle in a napkin, deftly
filling their glasses, finally his own. The glasses were new ones,
delicate, long-stemmed, expensive, and Emily was admiring
them as the wine sparkled against the light.

"How about a toast from you, old man?" asked Rolly Collins
a bit tipsily.

Hugh smiled at him and there were gold flecks in his ironic
gray eyes. He looked very handsome and confident in his
dinner jacket, holding the bubbling glass of champagne aloft
in his thin fingers. Tomlinson eyed him with approval; he'd
done well to go in with a man like Deming: he had class as well
as brains.

"Yes," said Hugh quietly, and something in his voice made
everyone stop talking and look at him, "a toast. I'll give you
one, ladies and gentlemen of Seattle. I ask you to drink to the
woman who started out life on the waterfront, made the First
Hill accept her and, of her own free will, finished out her life
on the waterfront again. To Annie Jordan, my friends, a
woman of courage, honesty, and beauty, such as we will not
see again. To Annie, as fine a lady as Seattle ever bred. God
rest her gallant and immortal soul!"

He drained his glass in one gulp and there was not a sound in the room as everyone else did likewise. And then, with a smile at himself for the sentimental and melodramatic gesture, but knowing it would have thrilled Annie to the core, Hugh hurled his glass against the fireplace, shattering it to bits. As if carried away by his passion, all of the guests threw their glasses on the hearth, too, and only Emily was left, clutching hers and staring in consternation at the wreckage.